THE
VALIANT

THE
VALIANT

Lesley Livingston

HarperCollinsPublishersLtd

Published by HarperCollins Publishers Ltd

First Canadian edition

HarperCollins books may be purchased for educational, business,
or sales promotional use through our Special Markets Department.

HarperCollins Publishers Ltd
2 Bloor Street East, 20th Floor
Toronto, Ontario, Canada
M4W 1A8

www.harpercollins.ca

Library and Archives Canada Cataloguing in Publication information
is available upon request.

ISBN 978-1-44344-628-0

Printed and bound in the United States of America
LSC/H 10 9 8 7 6 5 4 3 2 1

For John

I

THE STEAM RISING off the backs of the cantering horses faded into the morning fog. Our chariot raced toward the far end of the Forgotten Vale, and Maelgwyn Ironhand— my charioteer, constant companion, and frequent adversary—pulled back on the reins.

"No!" I shouted. "Faster! Make them run faster!"

Mael didn't bother to spare a glance over his shoulder at me. He knew any argument would be futile. Instead, he gave the ponies their head and let them run. We flew over the ground like ravens diving over a battlefield. The horses snorted and strained, hooves drumming the grassy track and sending mist billowing in our wake.

I stood behind Mael with a spear gripped tight in my right fist and my feet braced against the swaying motion of the chariot's suspended deck. The wind screeched in my ears, and the ground was a blur beneath our wheels. We'd never gone so fast before, and my heart hammered in my chest. I shifted and moved past Mael, stepping out in front of the chariot's platform to balance on the square-sided draft pole that ran between the two horses.

"Fallon—be *careful*!" Mael called as one of my feet slipped on the wood.

I hissed through clenched teeth as I almost fell and nearly lost my hold on my spear. Switching up my grip on the weapon, I regained my balance and peered ahead at the far end of the vale, where the ground sloped sharply upward into the grave barrow of a long-forgotten occupant. A single, rough-hewn stone crowned the round summit, and at the base of the hill, we'd set up a man-high target—a tree stump padded with hay, wrapped in canvas, and painted with the image of a grimacing, snaggle-toothed Roman soldier.

I grinned, exhilaration prickling my skin. The wind whipped my hair back out of my eyes, and I saw everything with crystal clarity. It was as if time had stopped and was waiting just for me.

Carefully, one foot in front of the other, I made my way forward on the draft pole as the horses thundered on. I held my breath until I could feel the rhythm of their matched strides in my bones. Then I hitched the spear up onto my shoulder and ran the length of the chariot pole until I stood perched between the shoulders of the galloping horses, my feet braced wide on the wooden yoke harnessing them to the chariot.

My goal that morning was as simple as it was impossible: successfully execute a chariot maneuver called the

Morrigan's Flight, named after the fearsome winged war goddess who flew over battlefields collecting the souls of the worthy dead. I'd watched my older sister, Sorcha, attempt it time after time. The idea was to run out along the narrow pole between the horses of a careening chariot, throw a spear, hit a target, balance for as long as it took for the spear to stay lodged, and then run back to the safety of the chariot deck. It was dangerous. It was thrilling.

It was the supreme act of a true Cantii warrior.

And I'd never seen anyone do it. Not even Sorcha.

The last time Mael and I had attempted it, I'd lost my footing completely and dropped between the horses, barely managing to catch onto the pole with one arm and my knees. If I'd fallen, there was a good chance I would have been killed—trampled by hooves or run over by the chariot's wheels. But the goddess had not seen fit to take me that day, and Mael had managed to pull the horses to a stop before I lost my grip. The bruises had taken weeks to fade, and Mael had shouted at me for almost half an hour, his face flushed crimson, and swore we would never, *ever* try such a thing again.

He should have known I wouldn't leave him in peace until we did.

So here we were, racing at breakneck speed across the floor of the Forgotten Vale. Because at the break of dawn that morning, I, Fallon, youngest daughter of Virico the king, chief of the Cantii tribe of Prydain, would turn seventeen years old. Old enough to be made a member of my father's war band, just like my sister before me. And I was determined that before that moment came, I would master the Morrigan's Flight.

And Mael, with his clever, steady hands on the reins, would see me do it.

From somewhere in the Otherworld, I imagined Sorcha watched as well.

"On the field of battle, you're either a warrior or you're in the way," my sister had scolded me one afternoon as my wooden practice sword missed its mark by a wide margin. She'd already proved herself to be one of the finest warriors of the Cantii tribe, and it was a lesson she had drilled into me over and over again until the day she died—killed in a skirmish defending the Island of the Mighty from Caesar's invading legions.

"Are you a weapon or target?" Sorcha had asked. "*Choose*, Fallon!"

So I chose—that day and every day after.

The weight of the spear on my shoulder and the sword at my hip were as familiar to me now as my tunic and boots or my favorite cloak. As comforting as my father's rough laugh or the roaring fire in his great hall. As heady as one of Mael's slow smiles that, more and more often, seemed meant just for me . . .

The thrumming of the chariot ponies' hooves raced through my limbs like the pulsing of my blood. In another moment, Mael would have to steer the chariot into a sharp turn to avoid running up against the steep sides of the Forgotten Vale's barrow.

Now or never . . .

My fingers tightened on the spear shaft, and the target loomed large in front of me. I leaned forward over my bent knee, felt the spear tilt into a moment of perfect balance . . . and *threw*. The slender missile arced through the air like a deadly bird of prey, black against the dawn-pink sky.

I held my breath.

"A hit!"

Not perfect—the spear struck the target a handsbreadth to the left of where a flesh-and-blood man's heart would have beat—but still, it was a good, clean blow. Mael's elated shout confirmed that. I punched my fists skyward in victory before sweeping my arms out to either side, stretched wide as wings. I felt for that fleeting instant as if I really *were* the goddess Morrigan in flight, swooping low over a battlefield to collect the souls of the glorious dead.

Then, as Mael eased the chariot into the turn, one of the ponies stumbled.

The animal scrambled to regain its stride, and the yoke I was balancing on bobbled with it. My gesture of triumph turned into a frantic flailing as I lost my balance and grabbed at the air to try to right myself. I heard Mael's jubilant shout distort into a cry of warning as I pitched sideways over the shoulder of the horse and cartwheeled helplessly through the air. My head hit something hard, and the world spiraled into darkness.

Dull silence muffled the first strains of a lark's song.

• • •

"Fallon!"

The warmth on my cheek was either the kiss of the sun or the spill of my tears. Or was it blood? That was probably it, I thought dimly. I'd hit my head and split my skull open, and now I was going to die. On the morning of my seventeenth year.

"Fallon!" Mael cried again.

His voice sounded very near and very far away at the same time.

"I must be dead," I murmured. "Or else I'm dreaming . . ."

If this was a dream, it was a vivid one. One as clear as the dream that often haunted my nights, when the Morrigan, goddess of death and battle, would appear, terrible and magnificent in a cloak of raven feathers. In a voice like smoke and ashes, she would call me "daughter."

My eyes fluttered open, and I found myself staring up into Mael's face, his nose only inches from mine. I realized that the warmth I'd felt on my cheek had been his breath.

"You're not dreaming, Fallon," Mael said, his eyes wide with worry.

I grinned up at him.

Who cares for merely dreaming about the Morrigan, I thought, *when you can fly like her?*

Like I just had. The thrill of that moment still tingled in my blood.

"Well, if I'm not dreaming," I teased, "then I suppose I must be dead."

The dread vanished from Mael's face, chased away by a look of hot fury. "You're not dead either," he snapped, the anger in his voice barely leashed. "Though damned well not for lack of trying."

"Why are you so angry?" I asked irritably, grunting with the effort of raising myself up on one elbow. In the near distance, I could see my spear where it still quivered in the practice dummy's torso. "Look!" I pointed over his shoulder. "We did it—"

"*You* did it," Mael said. "And then *I* almost killed you!"

"That wasn't your faul—"

"It was!" He glared down at me fiercely. "And if you ever make me do something as stupid and reckless as that again, I just might kill you, and it won't be by accident!"

"Mael—"

"Are you trying to fulfill Olun's prophecy?" he asked. "Is that what you're trying to do?"

I rolled my eyes. It was true my father's chief druid, Olun, had divined that I would one day follow in my sister Sorcha's footsteps. But she had been killed on the field of battle. The Forgotten Vale was nothing more than a placid meadow.

"I was a fool to let you talk me into this." Mael shook his head. "You seem determined to test the will of the Morrigan."

I opened my mouth, but for once no sharp-tongued retort was forthcoming. It wasn't as if I weren't used to him scolding me—we'd grown up together, since I was five and he was six, and we had spent most of those years enthusias-tically arguing. Mael was the youngest son of Mannuetios, king of the Trinovantes to the north, and as young boys, he and his brother, Aeddan, had been sent to foster with our tribe—to grow to manhood as one of us, ensuring peace between the two kingdoms. One of the first things Mael had done upon meeting me was break my baby finger with a wooden practice sword in a play fight.

Ever since that moment, he'd harbored an annoying streak of overprotectiveness that was at constant odds with his natural inclination to fight with me at every opportunity. It drove me mad. The two of us together were like flint and iron, forever sparking off each other. Most of the time I was hard-pressed to decide if I couldn't stand Mael . . . or if I'd be lost without him. But as I looked up at him, I saw genuine worry in his eyes. I realized he really had thought I was hurt.

"Mael," I said, reaching up to brush back the strands of dark hair that fell in his face. "I'm sorry. I—"

His lips on mine silenced my apology, muffling my words with his sudden, hungry kiss. My eyes went wide . . . then drifted shut, plunging me into a red-lit darkness. My heart was a glowing ember bursting into flame, and all I could think was that this was what joy felt like. Fierce and demanding. My eyelids fluttered open again, and I gazed up at Mael, at the flecks of dark silver in his eyes. They glinted like the raw iron our blacksmith melted down to forge swords and daggers and all manner of dangerous and beautiful things. Suddenly, I knew the answer.

Lost.

I would be completely lost without Mael.

My pulse surged loudly in my ears, and my fingers tangled in his long hair as I drew him down to me again. Mael's full weight pressed me back into the damp grass, and his broad hands slipped beneath me, fingertips slowly sliding from my shoulders all the way down to the small of my back. My spine arched as he lifted me up off the mossy ground, wrapping his arms around my torso and pulling me close to his chest. His mouth traveled from my lips to the side of my throat, beneath my ear—and then I heard myself gasp, first with surprise and then in protest, as he suddenly tore himself away from me.

The breeze that now flowed between us prickled my skin as Mael threw himself onto his back with a sigh. He lay there for a moment, chest heaving and face flushed, and I wondered if we'd done something horribly wrong. It was the first time I'd ever kissed anyone like that.

But then he rolled his head toward me. His gray eyes flashed dangerously.

"Today," he said in a ragged voice.

"Mael?" My head spun dizzily.

"This morning." He sat up and rolled back onto his knees in front of me, grasping me by the shoulders and pulling me toward him. "This *very* morning, Fallon."

I gazed at him in wary confusion. "What about it?"

"I'm going to go to Virico, and I'm going to ask him for your hand." The words tumbled from him in a rush. "*Now.* So that he can announce it tonight at the feast of the Four Tribes. In front of everyone and—"

"No!"

"What?" Mael said, faltering. "Fallon—"

I shook my head a little wildly. "My heart . . . it's already yours, Mael," I said. "You don't need to ask for my hand—"

"Yes," he said, adamant. "I do."

"You can't have it!" I felt a tiny shiver of panic in my chest. "Not yet."

"I thought . . ." He groped for words as his cheeks reddened. "I thought you—"

"I *do*."

How could I explain it to him? It wasn't that I didn't want him. I did, even if I'd only just begun to realize how much. But there was something I wanted . . . *needed* first.

I needed the chance to earn my own name.

I bit my lip. "It's just that tonight my father is going to make me a member of his royal war band. I know he is."

I watched as Mael's face clouded over. The feverish moment of our kiss was slipping away.

"Please, Mael." I reached up a hand and pressed it to his cheek. "You have to wait for me. I can't let anything stand in the way of this. I've worked too hard. I don't want to give Virico any reason not to give me that honor."

Mael pulled away from my touch. "Sometimes I wonder if you care more for your sword than for me," he said.

"How can you even say that?" I snapped, ignoring the small voice in my head that hissed the very same thing. "You're already a member of the war band! You would deny me the honor and glory of fighting at your side?"

That stung. I could see it in his eyes. "No," he said. "I would never deny you that, Fallon."

I reached for his hands. "Just wait a little while, Mael, until I'm a true warrior. We can go to my father then, and we can have everything we ever wanted—together."

"All right," Mael said finally, his familiar grin returning. "I'll wait, Fallon, as long as it takes. But maybe we can make the wait feel shorter."

Then he kissed me again, and for once, I forgot all about arguing with him.

II

THE DAY'S AFTERNOON was bright and brilliant and all the more beautiful for my having spent its morning kissing Mael in the Forgotten Vale. But inside my house in Durovernum—the house that I once shared with Sorcha—it was dark. I let the heavy leather door curtain fall closed behind me and moved through the room lighting the lamps.

Over the years, Sorcha had collected more than a dozen of the things—shining, delicately wrought metal or carved alabaster or clay painted with jewel-bright glazes—and hung them from the ceiling poles in our cozy little house on chains of different lengths. My favorite was the one shaped like a bird, with bits of blue and green glass set into the wings that made it glow with a fey light. The lamps had mostly come from far away, as had most of my sister's precious things, brought over in ships by traders from places across the sea. Places like Gaul and Greece and Aegypt. And Rome.

As much as Sorcha had taken delight in professing her hatred for Caesar at any opportunity, that hate hadn't influenced her fondness for fine and decorative things from the lands his legions had conquered. Just another one of my sister's many contradictions, I suppose. I once saw a mosaic in a trader's stall, and *that* was what imagining Sorcha was like—a multitude of sharp, shining pieces that, taken together, made up a whole image. Told a whole story.

As I lit the last of the lamps, I thought about the day they'd told me my sister was dead, killed by the Romans. The women of the tribes of Prydain—Cantii and Catuvellauni, Trinovantes and Iceni—could choose to fight alongside the men or not. Many did and with such skill that they were feared as much as the men—more so, even. The legions thought that the women warriors of the Island of the Mighty were demons, aberrations whose corpses they burned in heaps after battles so that their black souls could never escape to inhabit another body. Of course, I knew just how ridiculous that was. A primitive superstition. The fighting women of the tribes of Prydain were as good as they were because they worked at it. I worked at it—hard.

It was as simple—and as complicated—as that.

Cast in the ethereal glow of flickering lamplight, I stood staring at the wavering apparition reflected back at me from the polished bronze mirror hanging on the wall— another of Sorcha's exotic treasures. I raised an eyebrow at the ragged creature. Even in that uncertain light, I saw a smudge of dirt on my left cheek, partially obscuring the smattering of freckles there. The long tunic I wore over my shift of thin wool had once been a bright red-and-purple check but was now worn to faded shades of rust, stained from climbing hills and fording brooks and fighting Mael day after day in the vale. A tangled, unruly crown of fox-brown strands had escaped from the plait to which I'd hastily consigned my hair in the dark hours before dawn. At the age of seventeen, I might have the lean muscles and the long, strong legs that a warrior ought to have, but I would have to make myself presentable for when my father honored me with my full warrior status.

Just like he had my sister before me.

Sorcha was older by nine full years, and she'd never let me forget it. There were two baby brothers born between us, but they had both been lost to marsh fever before the age of three, and our mother had followed them to the Otherworld herself only days after I was born, leaving Sorcha to raise me—and keep me out of trouble—when our father the king was too busy ruling a sprawling tribe of brawling Celts to pay me much heed. The fact that she probably got me *into* more trouble than she ever kept me out of never bothered me a bit. She was everything I wanted to be when I grew up. Strong and sharp and dangerous as the sword she carried on her hip, Sorcha was my goddess even more than the Morrigan we both worshipped. I followed her everywhere, stumbling along on baby legs behind her as she ran, deer-swift, through the forests of our home, always looking for an adventure—or, better yet, a fight to pick.

And then, one day it all changed.

Caesar and his legions landed on our shores—not once but twice. And the second time, they took my father, King Virico, prisoner in a hard-fought battle. When the gathered tribes rode out in their chariots to free him, Virico's royal war band led the charge. Three days later, Father came home. Sorcha didn't. My fierce, bright, beautiful sister was gone. Dead.

Just like that.

It had been almost seven years since the legions left our shores, having declared the Island of the Mighty sufficiently conquered. In all that time, the Romans had not returned to Prydain, the island they called Britannia in their strident native tongue. Of course, the traders had never left—they'd been here before Caesar had set foot on our shore, and they'd stayed when he'd departed, "triumphant." Since that time, we'd been left in peace.

But one day, the legions would return to finish what they'd started. Prydain was too rich a resource for gold and tin and timber—and "barbarian" slaves. Caesar and his kind wouldn't be able to resist. The armies of Rome would return and we would be ready to fight them when they did. *I* would be ready to fight, just as my sister had.

Only I wouldn't fall to the thrust of a Roman sword.

The night Sorcha had ridden out in her chariot for the last time, I'd sat on the end of the bed watching her in the mirror as she buckled the straps of her breastplate and adjusted the hang of her sword on her hip. Angry at being left behind yet again, I complained loudly to Sorcha's reflection about how I wanted to go out to fight Caesar's legions with her.

She ignored me as long as she could.

"Enough!" Sorcha said finally, rounding on me. "Have you *really* thought about what it means to be a warrior, Fallon?"

I blinked at her, noticing for the first time the turbulence in her gaze.

"Have you?" She sighed. "Because I have. It means you kill. You kill men. You kill women. All while they are trying very hard to kill *you*. And if one of them is better at it than you, then you die. Are you so eager to dance with death, little sister?"

I was ten years old. I didn't know what to say.

What I should have said was "Don't go."

But instead, I just pouted and stayed silent. Sorcha left our house and never returned to hear my answer to her question. That was the first night that the Morrigan visited me in my sleep and named me—*me*, not Sorcha—her daughter. It was a sacred thing, fearsome and awesome all at once, and I'd never told anyone. But I'd always kept the memory of her voice locked away in my heart.

I shook myself free from the clutches of those memories. Never mind that night. After this night, the Cantii would see me as the newest member of my father's royal war band, not just as the legendary Sorcha's little sister.

Facing the mirror, I picked up the carved bone comb that lay among a pile of bracelets and ear hoops on top of a wicker trunk. The occasion demanded that I should at least put a little effort into my appearance. Normally, I would have called for the bondswomen who attended me to deal with such things. But today seemed somehow as if it was meant to be mine alone, and I wanted to savor it—what had already happened and what was to come—without the drone of gossipy slaves in my ears. The merry chaos of this evening's feast would come soon enough. Even with the distractions of choosing a tunic and shift, setting out jewelry, and taming my hair into submission—things I had little patience or skill with—all I could think of was what my father would say at the feast.

As the sun sank over the far purple hills, I imagined how he would welcome me into his war band with silver words praising my prowess with sword and spear. Indeed, the great hall would be crowded with Prydain royalty, including Aeddan, Mael's older brother by two years. After the passing of their father, Mannuetios, he was now king of the Trinovantes.

The thought of seeing him made me smile. We'd all grown up together when Aeddan was still a fosterling in our tribe, but Mael and I hadn't seen him in a good long while. Not since their father's great betrayal. But after our morning spent in the vale, Mael had gotten word that Aeddan and his train of Trinovante chiefs had arrived in Durovernum. I had sent him off to greet his brother while I untangled the brambles from my hair.

Every two years on the Eve of Lughnasa—which also happened to be my birthday—the kings of the Four Tribes came together to feast and toast each other with wide smiles and enough thick, foamy beer to strengthen the bonds of friendship forged in the alliances of years past. This would be Aeddan's first time there as king, newly returned from a long period of exile in Rome after his father was killed, executed for selling vital information to the Romans. Mael never spoke of his father's betrayal, but he'd remained with the Cantii since that time, past the usual age of fostering, because of it.

As for his feelings toward his brother, Mael had always known that when he returned from Rome, Aeddan would be king, not him, and so he bore him no ill will. The three of us—four, if you counted the times Sorcha indulged in our mischief—had grown up together, and I'd feared that Mael might come to resent his brother. But he never did, which was a great relief to me. We were like family, and I would have hated for anything to come between us.

I finished dressing with care, adjusting the delicate silver torc around my neck with nervous fingers. I could hear laughter and shouting outside my door.

The festival atmosphere that had slowly grown throughout Durovernum over the preceding weeks had finally burst into full bloom. Beyond the town's wooden palisades, in the fields leading down to the docks on the River Dwr, there were games and contests and stalls selling bolts of brightly colored cloth, arm rings and furs, food and drink, and songs that could be bought from the bards to woo a lover from afar or shame a rival without bloodshed. Charioteers raced their pony-drawn carts up and down the winding tracks (none with *quite* the skill or daring of Mael and me), and the very air crackled with anticipation of the feast that would begin after sundown.

At last, the sky shaded to indigo in the east, and the rich smells that had seasoned the breezes all day—spit-roasting boar and venison stewed in great cauldrons—drew the nobles of the Four Tribes and their freemen and freewomen to gather in the great hall.

I took a last nervous glance at myself in the mirror. I'd brushed the thick waves of my hair until they shimmered down my back, and I'd dressed them off my face with a circlet of red gold that twined about my brow. I had to admit, the look suited me. A gown of leaf-green wool under a russet-and-purple mantle draped the lines of my body. The torc around my neck gleamed, and the stacked bronze and silver bangles on my wrists jangled as I pushed aside my door curtain and headed up the winding path to my father's great hall.

Once inside, I was enveloped by the smells of roasting meat and peat smoke and had to snake through the crush of bodies to find my seat by the hearth.

"You're dressed like a proper queen this night," Clota, my father's chief bondswoman, said, chuckling as she leaned over to fill my cup with mead. "And more than one lad here tonight seems to have noticed finally that you are a *girl*."

I rolled my eyes and reached for a platter of honeyed oatcakes and apples, too nervous to eat much. I shifted on the low bench seat near my father's left hand and wondered where Mael had gotten to. Clota might have been joking, but in truth, I could almost feel the looks from all about the hall—glances that traced the lines of my limbs, the planes of my face. But when I sought them out, there was only one person who was bold enough to return my gaze.

And it was not Maelgwyn Ironhand but his brother, Aeddan. I grinned and raised my hand in greeting, but Aeddan did not smile back. Instead, he just raised his cup to me.

He knows, I thought, my stomach knotting a bit. *Mael told him.*

Aeddan was two years older than his brother, but they were unmistakably related. Both had dark hair, worn long, and almost identical slate-gray eyes. Like his younger brother, Aeddan was handsome and clever and good with a sword. But—to me, at least—his had always seemed more of a brooding presence, sitting in the shadows just beyond the circle of firelight. Where Mael's eyes could shine bright with passion or burn dark with anger, Aeddan's gaze always seemed to me a bit cool. Sharp. Like the blade of a fine iron knife waiting to be used. The veneer of Roman culture that he'd adopted from his time in that place—he drank wine and draped his cloak over one arm like a toga—only emphasized the contrast between the brothers. But as different as they were, I had always loved them both: Aeddan like a brother, Mael . . . as something more. Much more, it seemed. I turned away from Aeddan's gaze before he noticed the blush creeping up my cheeks.

Clota passed by in that moment, and I lunged for her

tray, snatching up another mug of spiced mead. I'd gulped the first one down far too fast in an attempt to steady my nerves. I glanced around the room again, suddenly desperate to find Mael's face. I thought I saw him pass through the archway of the great oak doors and half rose from my seat to go to him. But then a drift of conversation between a grizzled old bear of a Catuvellauni warrior and a pair of young men—freemen of a visiting chief from Gaul, by the strange look of them—caught my attention.

"How goes the resistance, then?" the old bear asked. "Do the Arverni and the Carnutes still harry the Romans in Gaul and set fire to their forts?"

One of the freeman with tattoos on his cheeks and red-rimmed eyes spat. "There *is* no resistance since Arviragus surrendered. The coward."

I was pretending not to listen but could barely hide my shock. *Arviragus? A coward?* Impossible. I had met the Gaulish warrior king when I was young and he was but a prince, but I'd been awed by his bravery and skill with a sword. He would never surrender to the Romans.

"He was no coward," his companion said loudly, chewing his words through a mouthful of meat. "But he was a fool. Letting himself be taken by the Roman. I'd have fallen on my own sword first."

"Be careful how you speak!" the older man snapped, his eyes flicking to where my father, Virico, sat, gazing out over the gathered crowd.

"Why?" Dark beer sloshed over the rim of the young warrior's mug. "I simply speak the truth."

I realized in that moment that he either didn't know or didn't care that, like Arviragus, my father himself had once been captured by Caesar. Or that his beloved daughter Sorcha had led an army to free him and in doing so had been lost herself.

His tattooed companion began to guffaw. "Maybe he's right, Biron. Perhaps these Prydain tribes have the way of it. Why even fight the Romans? Easier to let them think they've had their way with you, and in the morning, they'll just hitch up their skirts and leave you in peace."

Drunkards, I seethed, my hand tightening on my dagger.

I was close enough to my father to see that he'd heard the exchange. For a moment, I wondered if he'd silence the fools with his blade, but his only reaction was to toss back the rest of his own drink and stand.

Virico Lugotorix rising to his feet was a sure way to draw the attention of even the drunkest of revelers. Two of the hearth slaves heaved a heavy log onto the great fire at the same time. As firefly sparks bloomed around him, my father looked like the king of some fiery underground realm. His chestnut hair and beard gleamed, and his handsome face glowed crimson.

"*Tuatha!*" he bellowed. "Welcome. The voices of the Four Tribes sing you peace. The Island of the Mighty carries you on her green shoulders. Fill your bellies and your hearts this night in my hall, and we shall be as one people. One tribe. More so for the good tidings I tell you now."

The men and women in the hall fell silent and leaned forward, straining to catch the next words of Virico's grand

pronouncement. I leaned forward too, my fingertips biting into the edge of my seat as I waited, breathless, for my
father's call to me to join his elite warrior band. Finally, I
would have my chance to make him proud—as proud as
Sorcha ever did.

"My daughter Fallon is the jewel of my house," he continued, gesturing toward me. "She is of age now, as of this
very night. Her heart is golden, and her sword is a spark in
the darkness. And I would have her take her place among
my war chiefs, as both her mother and her sister did before
her . . ."

My cheeks flushed, and I felt elated as the blood rushed
from my head to my feet and back again, leaving me hot
and cold in waves.

". . . but for this."

Virico's voice lapsed into echoing silence.

This? I looked up at him.

He refused to meet my gaze, and when he spoke again,
it was like the sound of a blade's edge dragging over a whet-
stone. He lifted his head and called out a name: "Aeddan
ap Mannuetios!"

Aeddan? I stood up and tried to speak, but my voice fled
from me in that moment.

"Come forth!" Virico bellowed. "Come and claim my
daughter's hand before our gathered friends here in my
hall."

No, I thought. *He's made a mistake.*

"Aeddan!" Virico shouted again. He beckoned with
one hand, fingers winking with gold rings. "Chief among

our dear friends the Trinovante, my soon-to-be son, come forth!"

A roar went up from the gathered crowd, but I was shocked into silence. The smoke-dark air seemed to thicken, pressing against my skin.

I glanced wildly around the room, searching until I finally spotted Mael's ashen face. He stood frozen near the stacked barrels of beer and mead, surrounded by a group of laughing Trinovante chiefs and freemen—young men from Mael's own tribe, all friends of Aeddan's. His dazed expression turned to fury in a moment. I saw him shout his brother's name, but I couldn't hear him over the noise. At the same time, Aeddan worked his way through the press of bodies packing the hall, accepting hearty, undeserved congratulations with a grin tugging at his lips. Only I saw how the bashful expression never reached Aeddan's dark eyes.

This is all a terrible mistake. Father is drunk. He's not thinking clearly . . .

"Mael!" I shouted above the raucous din. "Do something!"

Mael could stop Aeddan. Talk reason to him or, at the very least, challenge his absurd claim! We could still stop this. We just had to get to my father.

Mael shouted back, but I couldn't make out the words. He was too far away. And Aeddan was too close, moving nimbly through the crowd of gathered tribesmen and tribeswomen toward where I stood.

"Father!" I reached out a hand, grabbing at Virico's

sleeve, but the cries of the chiefs and their freemen shook the very air of the great roundhouse and drowned out my protests.

Virico's head swung around, his eyes fever-bright in the firelight. "I knew you would be upset," he said in a low, urgent voice. "But I *cannot* make you a war chief, Fallon. I lost your sister to the sword. I will not have you suffer the same fate as Sorcha. I cannot lose you both."

"No!" I shook my head desperately. "Father, you can't do this to me."

But just then Aeddan reached me. An even more thunderous shout erupted from the gathering as he spun me around and kissed me hard on the lips.

It was the second time that day that a son of Mannuetios had kissed me.

Only this time, it felt like poison pouring into my mouth.

I struggled to push Aeddan away, but there was nowhere to push him to. The throng was crushing. The women of the Cantii converged upon me with fierce embraces and well-wishing. Some of them burst into song, and others whirled and threw their arms in the air. If there was one thing every good Celt loved, it was love itself. They sang of it, fought for it, wept bitter tears into mugs of mead over the loss of it, and—if the slightest hint of a joyous union so much as wafted past on a breeze—seized the opportunity to celebrate it ferociously.

Over near the mead vats, there was a commotion as Mael struggled against the crowd toward Aeddan and me. I thought I might have actually seen him throw a punch. But then Aeddan blocked my view and forced me back a step. That close, I could see his face was flushed—with drink or desire or both—and his dark eyes shone. The crush of bodies, the brightly woven cloaks and jangling jewelry, the braided hair and painted eyes, lips, mouths, tangled tattoos and torcs and shouting, the stench of beer and bodies and meat . . . for the first time in my life, I thought that I might actually faint.

When the scuffle by the vats upended a large, foaming tub of mead, the crowd suddenly ebbed in that direction with cries of outrage and shouts of drunken laughter cheering on the combatants. In the ensuing chaos, I ducked beneath Aeddan's arm and ran for the great hall doors.

III

LIGHTNING LASHED THE NIGHT SKY over Durover-
num. In the time I'd been inside the great hall, black storm
clouds had rolled in and the sky was pouring rain. I could
barely see to make it back to my house.

Once inside, I stirred the banked coals of the brazier
to sullen life. It did nothing to ease the chill that gripped
my bones. Not only had my father as good as severed the
sword-hand from my arm, he'd cut the heart out of my
body. And then given it to the brother of the boy I loved.
My father had betrayed me not once but twice.

I spat out a string of curses wrapped around Virico's
name and dropped to my knees in front of the fire. And
then I began to slowly, methodically, remove all the ornaments I had so carefully chosen just hours before. The
rings and the bracelets and earrings that marked me as
a woman . . . the torc around my neck that marked me
as a princess . . . even the dagger in the sheath at my hip

that marked me as a warrior. Suddenly, I wanted none of it. One by one, I stripped them all off and dropped them onto the fire, watching as the pale flames licked the shining, precious metal black.

I wished, in that moment, that my father had never come home from Caesar's camp. It was his fault Sorcha was dead. She'd gone to save him and died a hero. The kind of hero my father had just denied me every right and opportunity to ever be.

And I hated him for that.

For that, and for taking Mael from me. That morning, I'd turned down Mael's marriage pledge, and for what? For the chance to seize a destiny that had never been mine to take in the first place. The brazier flames blurred before my eyes as I fought back furious tears.

"Drink with me?"

I spun around on my knees, blinking away the wetness, to see Aeddan leaning on my doorframe. He pushed the hood of his rain-soaked cloak back from his face and dangled a small amphora of Roman wine and two mugs with his other hand.

"Well, wife?"

"I'm not your wife."

"Not yet."

"Not ever," I said. "And if you call me by that word again, it will be the last sound that ever worms its way between your teeth."

He laughed.

"Come on," he said through a grin. "Fallon, think of your father."

I stood to face Aeddan, wary. My gown was soaked through from the storm and clung to my body, but I refused to hide behind crossed arms. Instead, I dropped my right hand to rest on the hilt of the dagger at my belt—except the sheath was empty. I had tossed the dagger into the fire. Aeddan's glance flicked from my hand to the fire in the brazier, and he frowned faintly. He stepped inside, and the curtain fell closed behind him, shutting out the hiss of the rain.

"Think how much Virico wants—*needs*—alliances like this one," he said.

"Surely he could have given me to your brother and still had his alliance with the Trinovante."

"True." Aeddan shrugged as he stepped further into the room. "Indeed, I think it was Virico's first thought. But fortunately, I convinced my uncle to counsel him otherwise."

The packed-earth floor of the little roundhouse felt as though it were dropping out from beneath my feet. I was so angry that I couldn't even find words to hurl at Aeddan. My rage had me dumbstruck.

"Virico knows how close you and Maelgwyn have always been," Aeddan continued. He moved across the room to a low couch and sat, placing the wine cups on a small table. "Close as brother and sister . . ." The shadow of a sneer curled his lip. "Your father—after a deal of convincing, to be sure—came to realize it. He came to see that it wouldn't be fair to give you away in a match that was nothing more than sibling affection and no real love."

But I do love Mael.

And I'd had the chance to tell him—to be with him—in the vale that morning. I loved Maelgwyn Ironhand, and Aeddan knew it. He'd known it all along, even before I did. I saw it in his gray eyes, and I saw that he hated his brother because of it. Because of me.

"Count yourself lucky that your father has a care for your heart, Fallon," Aeddan said, working the stopper from the wine jug. "As do I. You should be glad."

"Forgive me if I don't rejoice," I spat.

Aeddan stood, and the amphora slipped from his fingers and smashed on the floor. Wine leaked out of the broken vessel like blood from a wound.

"There has always been something between us, Fallon," he said urgently. "Hasn't there? If I hadn't gone away—if it had been Maelgwyn and not me who had been forced to flee to Rome . . ."

In two paces he was across the room, gripping me hard by the shoulders. A flush crawled up Aeddan's sharp features, and a vein pulsed at the side of his neck.

"I never forgot about you," he said. "I always knew that one day I'd come back for you. I can take you places, Fallon. I *will* take you places. It's all set in motion already. And you'll be happy—I promise you! Rome is a place of wonder. They build palaces of gleaming stone, and the air is like perfume. But there's more, Fallon. They're fierce. They have fighters, warriors like you've never known."

"Like the Roman legions your father sold our people out to?" I snapped.

Aeddan barely flinched at my outrage. "I'll show you things you could never have imagined, Fallon. Not even in your dreams. And we'll finally be together."

I stared at him in disbelief. I had never—not once in my life—thought of Aeddan that way. The very idea that he had woven some kind of fantasy in his mind and wrapped me up in it was beyond me. He leaned in to kiss me again, but this time instinct took over as Aeddan's fingers dug into my flesh. I dropped back into a defensive stance, knees bent and head down. I went again for my knife—which, of course, wasn't there—and instead gritted my teeth and jammed my knee into his groin, shoving him away as he gasped in pain and staggered back.

From behind a sweep of dark hair, Aeddan's eyes glinted dangerously in the darkness. His fists knotted at his sides. "That wasn't nice, wife." The breath rasped in his throat. "A Roman woman would know how to better control herself. But there'll be plenty of time for me to teach you—"

"*Aeddan.*" Mael's voice cut through the air like a knife.

"Hello, brother." Aeddan straightened up and turned around slowly. "Come to share in my soon-to-be-wedded joy?"

Two swords flashed in the darkness, and Aeddan suddenly found himself collared by Mael's twin blades, crossed in front of his throat. They bit into the flesh just above the king's torc he wore. Mael pressed his brother back toward the door, relentless.

"Get out," he said. "Before I stain my swords with your worthless blood."

"And here I thought that you'd be happy for me, little brother." Aeddan lifted his chin and glared at Mael above the blades, but he backed up a step nonetheless. "For her, at least. I bring Fallon a chance to escape. I will take her to a place where she'll live like the warrior queen she's meant to be. You? You'd just wind up getting her killed in a tribal raid one day."

"I said get *out*!" Mael roared and drew back his blades to strike.

But Aeddan was already gone, slipping out and disappearing into the black rain. Mael stood there for a long time, his back to me, shoulders heaving. Then he sheathed his swords and turned, anguish twisting his face.

"Where *were* you tonight?" I asked.

"Aeddan," he spat. "His chieftains kept me from you."

His gray eyes were full of anger and hurt. There was blood at the corner of his mouth and the shadow of a new bruise blooming along his jaw. I remembered the uproar near the beer vats in the hall.

"Did you know this was going to happen?" he demanded. "Is that why you refused me this morning? To be with Aeddan?"

"What?" I stared at him, incredulous. "How could you even think such a thing? I meant what I said, Mael. You alone have my heart."

Mael's anger vanished almost instantly, but the hurt remained deep and dark in his eyes. "Fallon, I'm sorry. I just . . ." He swallowed thickly. "You are all that has been in *my* heart since the day we met. When I sleep, I see your face. When I wake, I long to. You are as fierce and as beautiful and as deadly to me as your sword is. And so I promised to wait, but then . . ."

"Then what?"

"Then Aeddan was there." His mouth twisted in disgust. "And he was kissing you."

"I wasn't kissing him."

"I know!" He angrily clawed back the wet hair from his face. "I know that now. I'll go to him. Virico. I'll tell him that we've already laid claim to each other's hearts."

"You can't. It's too late."

I knew my father. Had Mael fought his way through to me in the hall . . . if he had stood before Aeddan and challenged him there and then, Virico might have considered such a claim. But it was a lifetime too late for that now. My father would not go back on a pledge—one made in front of the whole of the Four Tribes—and he would not change his mind. He would not suffer his chiefs to call him weak. Or cowardly. He had suffered enough of that in the days after the Romans had returned him from capture. How, his freemen had asked, had the king not taken his own life rather than suffer the shame of Roman captivity? How had he come back to Durovernum alive when his own daughter had died in battle?

It had taken Virico Lugotorix years to regain the respect of the chiefs.

He would not risk it now. Not on my account.

"And I'll never be a warrior now," I said slowly, feeling the weight of each word.

Mael shot me a sharp glance.

"Don't." I held up a warning hand. "If my father had made me choose, if he'd even bothered to give me a choice, know this: I would have given up my sword for you, Maelgwyn Ironhand. *You.* Not your brother."

"Well, it's too late for that now, isn't it?" The bitterness returned to his voice. "If we had gone to your father this morning, none of this would have happened."

"How could I have known, Mael?" I almost shouted. "I am the one left with nothing, and *you're* jealous of cold steel!"

A wave of misery swept over us both, and we stood there, staring at each other with helpless regret and longing. How had everything gone so wrong so quickly? It should have been a night of celebration for me. But my proud moment lay shattered and strewn at my feet.

"We'll go," I said. "We'll leave tonight and go west. There are tribes who would be happy to have us, and we can be together."

"No." Mael's fists clenched, white-knuckled, at his sides. "I'm not running like a coward. This is my home, your tribe, and Aeddan has no right to take that away from us." He strode to the door, slapping aside the leather curtain to let in a gust of dark rain.

"Mael!" I ran after him, grabbing him by the arm. "Where are you going?"

"To find him. He *will* set this right." Mael shook free of

my grip. He hitched up his swords and tugged his cloak hood over his head. "And if he doesn't, I'll kill him."

"I'd have killed him myself if it would have solved anything! Mael!" I called. *"Mael!"*

But he was already gone, vanished like a shadow into the stormbound night. What he left behind was a hollow space in my chest that began to fill with a hot, heavy anger. I would be the master of my own fate. Me and the goddess Morrigan. No one else—and certainly no man. Mael and Aeddan could fight over me until they were both bloody. My father could deny me my blade. But they couldn't force me from my warrior's path unless I let them. Sorcha never would have let anyone choose her fate for her.

"Go then," I said, my voice loud in the emptiness of the room. "I won't be here when you get back."

IV

WHEN MY FATHER WAS A BOY, he'd traveled far to foster with a fierce warrior tribe across the narrow Eirish Sea in the west. That was where he'd met my mother, herself no older than I was when I first met Mael. Years later, when Virico was a man grown, he'd returned to woo her.

She'd waited, knowing he would.

I wasn't about to wait around for Maelgwyn to return for me.

Not in Durovernum.

I couldn't possibly stay the night somewhere Aeddan or my father could find me. Instead, I picked up my sword in its doe-skin scabbard and stuffed it inside the bedroll I slung over my shoulder. There was one place I could spend the night—the one place Mael alone knew to look for me, whenever his foolish pride and rage left him.

He should have said something, I thought bitterly.

You didn't.

The thought stopped me in my tracks. No. I didn't. I hadn't.

When the moment came for me to stand up to my father, I'd just stood there dumbly.

Target practice.

Well. No more. Now I would be a moving target.

I threw on my cloak and slung the strap of the bedroll across my torso. With one last glance over my shoulder at my house—a place I suspected I might never see again— I pushed through the doorway and out into the night. I could hear the distant sounds of the revelers gathered in my father's great hall, still celebrating my vile betrothal, but beyond that, the bustling town of Durovernum was a place of shadows and fog. The rain had abated, and a silvery mist began collecting in the ditches. The gates of the town would be shut and locked, the walls guarded for the night, but that didn't matter to me. I slipped between the chieftains' roundhouses, past the smithy and the stables, to the place where I knew the earthworks were piled up close enough to the top of the town wall that I could climb over. I'd taken that route so many times with Mael that I could probably have followed it blindfolded.

Mael.

I tugged the hood of my cloak around my face. I would go to the Forgotten Vale, and I would wait there to see if Mael would follow. A day—two at the most—and then I would leave.

He'll come. He has to.

And then we would run. Go west. Travel through the

mountains of Cymru where the Dobunni tribe lived and on through the territory of the mysterious Silures. I would sail across the Eirish Sea to the land of my mother. A place where it's said that if the land ever felt the tread of legion sandals, the very earth itself would rise up like a wakening green giant and shrug them off like fleas.

I can make a life for myself there, I thought as I ran. *We can.*

My mother's kin would welcome me as a warrior, and Mael and I could fight side by side the way we were supposed to. That thought kindled the first tiny spark of hope since Virico had stood in his hall and pronounced my doom.

"She's not yours, damn your eyes!"

I froze.

The damp air distorted the cry, turning it ghostly, but it was Mael's voice—followed by a grunt of pain and the muted clashing of blades. My heart hammered in my chest as I eased around the corner of a goat shed, peering in the direction of where the noise came from. The fog had grown thick, and I saw ghost-dancers whirling in the heart of that silver pall.

Mael and Aeddan.

Their shadowy forms grasped and grappled with each other, pulling apart and lurching together. The fog suddenly cleared enough for me to see Mael's face as he charged toward Aeddan, the circling blurs of his two swords clearing the air before him. The blades rang as they met with Aeddan's, locking up in the space between the two brothers as they tried to overpower each other. Suddenly,

Aeddan reared back and head-butted his brother sharply. Mael reeled away in pain, blood running down his face. The fog swirled, hiding them from my sight again.

When it parted once more, I saw Mael, blades held high above his head, charging at Aeddan. My heart hammered, and I heard myself whisper, "Mael."

There was no earthly way he could have heard me.

They were too far. It was only a whisper.

And yet, his swords—slashing downward to block his brother's attack—faltered. For just an instant. It was enough. Aeddan was right there. Charging forward, his blade thrusting for Mael's heart—

NO!

My scream echoed silently inside my own head, but Mael's shocked cry alerted Durovernum's wall sentries. I heard a shout and the sound of running feet.

I couldn't breathe. Couldn't move.

I clung to the wall of the goat shed as Mael's eyes locked with mine. He opened his mouth, and a dark gout of blood bubbled up and spilled down his chin. Aeddan wrenched the dagger out of his brother's flesh, and Mael collapsed. He fell on his face in the mud, horribly still. Aeddan's teeth were bared in a grimace, and he looked half-mad.

"Brother," he croaked. "Maelgwyn . . ."

Then he turned, searching to see what it was that had fatally distracted his brother. His eyes found my face in the darkness.

"Fallon?"

The shouts of the sentries were closer now. Aeddan

glanced wildly over his shoulder and then back at me. For a moment, he hesitated. Then he bolted into the fog, running in the direction of Durovernum's wall. In an instant he'd disappeared, swallowed whole by the night.

The world around me turned red.

If Aeddan managed to escape Durovernum that night, he would vanish into the forest and run all the way back to his own halls deep in the heart of the Trinovante lands, where he would be safe. A murderer . . . but safe. I angrily wiped the tears from my eyes as I began to run, heading in the direction Aeddan had gone. That wasn't going to happen, not while I drew breath. When I reached the town wall, I scrambled up the mud-slick earthworks and tumbled gracelessly down the other side. Crouching, I peered at the ground. Aeddan had left a clear trail of footprints in the muddy earth. As I stood, a thick drift of clouds swept over the full moon, like snuffing out a flame. It didn't matter—I knew which way to go. The forest in front of me was hung with shadows, but I plunged into the trees, following the path of freshly broken branches that marked Aeddan's way. He was headed toward the cart path that would lead him to the main road.

He was running like a coward. A murderer.

The sword I'd stuffed inside my bedroll rattled in its sheath as I ran, the sound keeping time with the single thought that repeated over and over in my head.

Mael's dead . . . Mael's dead . . . Mael's dead . . .

I stumbled blindly on, deep into the forest, with one singular purpose: vengeance. It was only after I had run far longer than it should have taken to pick up the cart path that I realized I was lost. I stopped and listened. Over the plashing of rainwater dripping from the forest leaves and the rasp of my own breathing, I could hear another sound.

The sound of rushing water.

No.

I was near the river. I had gone in the exact opposite direction from where I'd meant to go. I cursed loudly, then clamped my hand over my mouth. Aeddan could be somewhere nearby. I'd be a fool to alert him to my presence. The only way I wanted him to know I was there was when he looked down to see my sword in his guts.

Cautiously, I pushed through a screen of saplings and found myself at the broad bank of the River Dwr. A break in the clouds spilled down moongleam, and I looked down to see my reflection staring back at me from the dark water, green eyes glowing like the eyes of the cats we kept to kill rats.

And I will kill a rat this night, I thought.

I wrapped my heart in fury to keep the despair at bay as I knelt on the sodden grass of the riverbank to retrieve my sword from my bedroll. Before I could reach it, the moon disappeared behind the clouds again. As the river turned back to blackness, I caught the glimpse of a shadow looming up behind me in the reflection. I spun around, thinking Aeddan had found me first. My hand went instead for my dagger, only to remember I'd left it lying in the embers of my home fire.

It wasn't Aeddan.

A broad-shouldered man swung his fist like a mallet at my head. I fell, consumed by a dark red tide.

When I awoke, I knew from the motion of the wet planks beneath me that I was on a boat, gliding silently down what I guessed was the Dwr.

Out of the cauldron and straight into the flames, I thought as a cold dread pierced the nausea that already knotted my guts. This was the second time I'd been hit on the head in less than a day. I groaned and opened my eyes.

The man from the riverbank was sitting on a bench in the middle of the little skiff, staring at me. Seeing that I was awake, he crouched down in front of me and grabbed my chin, forcing me to look up into his face. His eyes were two different colors—one watery blue, the other muddy brown. I opened my mouth in anger, but he put a finger, rough and calloused, to my lips.

"Shh . . ." He grinned, an ugly twisting of his mouth behind a matted beard. "Cry out and that'll be the last sound you make. You understand?"

His other hand pressed a knife blade up under my left ear. The scream building in my throat died instantly. I couldn't escape if I was dead.

"There's a good little Cantii bitch." His mismatched gaze roamed over me. "She's not too ugly," he called quietly over his shoulder to the skiff's other occupant, a dark-haired man who pulled easily at the oars. Then he turned back to me and rolled the dagger blade over my cheek. "If you behave, I won't have to ruin your face. You might even fetch a decent price."

A slave trader, I thought, numb with disbelief. The lowest kind of creature—cunning peddlers always looking to capture and barter the lives of anyone unfortunate enough to cross their path unawares. My tribe came by most of our bond-slaves through war and raids. Traders were reviled as parasites, a blight that had accompanied Rome to our shores.

This one wore no torc. No arm-ring. No ornamentation of any kind to mark him as a freeman or anything other than lowborn. Of course, I realized, neither did I in that moment. I wore none of the embellishments that would have marked me as the daughter of a king. I had disavowed that status. My arms and neck were bare. No gold dangled from my ears. My boots and tunic were muddied and torn from my mad dash through the forest. They probably thought I was just a lowly thrall, easy picking. They were wrong. And I'd show them that—as soon as I could get to my sword.

"Were you running from someone, little slave?" asked the man at the oars. He spoke Latin like all the traders did, so I could understand him well enough, but his voice had a rolling lilt that I couldn't place.

I ground my teeth together and said nothing. They laughed quietly at my silence. Over his shoulder, I could just make out the shape of a galley riding low in the water.

"No matter," he said, guiding the skiff toward the ship. "Whoever it is, you'll be far enough away from them once we get to Rome."

Rome.

The word stunned me like another blow to the head. Over the sound of the waves lapping the sides of the skiff, I could hear muffled voices drifting down from the galley deck—male, gruff, hissing hard-edged words into the night, and a smaller, forlorn noise. Weeping. A girl. Maybe a young boy. Silenced with the sharp ring of a slap. It seemed I wasn't the only prey the slavers had hunted that night. But I was probably the only one foolish enough to have run right into their arms.

The skiff bumped against the side of the ship that loomed above us like a sea beast from a child's bedtime tale. Someone threw down a rope ladder, and Odd Eyes motioned me toward it with his knife. The boat rocked as I clumsily rose to my feet, almost pitching me into the black water. For an instant, I thought I might just do that—fling myself overboard and swim for all I was worth.

Almost as if he heard my thoughts, Odd Eyes grabbed me by the hair and forced my head up, pointing with his knife. Standing at the railing, I saw a stocky form holding a bow, an arrow already nocked and the bowstring half-pulled.

"You even think of taking a bath and my mate there will put a hole in you before you hit the water," he hissed in my ear.

I had no choice but to climb the ladder, Odd Eyes and the dark-haired man following close behind. I'd never been on a seagoing vessel before, and my knees buckled as the deck of the ship tilted beneath my feet. I took a deep breath and tried to imagine that the rolling motion was the swaying of my racing chariot. This was just another challenge, I told myself. Just another adversary to beat.

I looked around for any possible escape, but Odd Eyes was right there, shoving me roughly toward a hatch in the middle of the deck that yawned like a gaping black maw. I heard the scrape of iron on wood as the anchor was dragged slowly on board, and I felt the ship lurching forward in the river current. As the forested riverbank slid away behind us, I bolted toward the ship railing. I made it three or four steps before Odd Eyes grabbed me and dealt a lazy backhand to my jaw that sent me reeling.

"Take her below," Odd Eyes growled, pushing me toward a heavily muscled man. "She's got an urge to run. Convince her otherwise."

V

EARLIER THAT NIGHT, I had knelt on the floor of my house and slid the slender silver torc from around my neck. The torc had been a symbol of my status within the Cantii tribe. The daughter of a king. I had cast it onto the flames of the brazier and thought I'd never feel the cool, heavy caress of metal around my throat again. I was wrong.

This new ring of metal was colder. Heavier.

And it marked me in just the same way—only now my status was "slave."

The collar was made of coarsely wrought iron. Dull and chafing, hammered on with a bolt and tethered to a stout post in the hold by a chain through a ring. It was loose enough that it sat on my collarbones, but I still felt like I was choking. My people were fiercely protective of our freedom. To be a freeman or freewoman was to have status in the tribe. Respect.

I crouched in the darkness of the hold, the mingled

stench of fish-rot, mildew, sweat, and fear clogging my
nostrils. My boots were soaked through with river water,
and my feet had gone numb because of it. I slid the boots
off and put them aside, rubbing my cramped toes between
my palms. By the light of a single, swinging lantern that
guttered and smoked, I could make out a handful of others
chained, like I was, to posts. Men and women, most of them
young or at least not old, all of them able-bodied. The dark-
haired man was clearly a discerning trader. And a thief.
The people in the hold of that ship—myself included—
hadn't been bartered for or bought in Durovernum. We'd
just been taken, like cattle in a raid. But by the time the sun
rose and any of their masters noticed they were missing,
the slave galley would be safely down the river and sailing
out to sea, on its way to make the channel crossing to Gaul.

And taking me along with it.

I stared at the swinging lantern and thought of the ones
hanging in my house. Just like one of Sorcha's lamps, I
was about to travel across the world, to a place where I
would be sold for a handful of coins. Something brushed
against my ankle, and I jumped, shuddering, as the eyes of
a rat flashed up at me, red and gleaming in the dimness.
I tucked my cloak tighter around my legs and feet. Time
passed with the rocking of the ship and the stink of rank
seawater sloshing. I heard the hard snap of canvas sails in a
freshening wind, and a leaden weight of despair made my
heart sink. I knew we must have reached the mouth of the
river where it emptied into the sea.

I thought of Maelgwyn, dead in the fog.

I'm never going to see him again, I thought, and the realization hit me like a killing blow. I'd only just begun to see Mael as something more than a brother or friend, and suddenly he was gone. Gone from me forever—and not just him. My father, my tribe . . . they were all as good as dead to me. I squeezed my eyes shut, but everyone and everything I was leaving behind were there, floating like ghosts in my mind. I didn't know what else to do, so I whispered a prayer to the Morrigan, the triple goddess of blood and battles. Maybe not the most appropriate deity, under the circumstances, but the one to whom I most often prayed. My throat was parched, and my voice, when I tried to say the first of the three names of the Raven Goddess, came out as a crow's rasp.

"Macha . . ." I licked my lips and tried again. "Macha. Red Nemain. Badb Catha . . . hear me. Wind, carry my words. Shadows and darkness, see my plight. Let the Morrigan hear my plea. Give me strength to vanquish my enemies and wreak my vengeance . . ."

I whispered the prayer over and over again until finally I slipped into a deep, exhausted sleep.

Thin beams of sunlight crept through the cracks between the deck planks and pierced the gloom. I blinked blearily in confusion for a moment before I was able to figure out where I was and what had woken me. Odd Eyes crouched on his haunches in front of me, grinning. His mismatched gaze raked my face and limbs.

"Not too ugly," he said again, as he had on the skiff. But

he spoke not in Latin this time but in the language of my own people. His accent told me he was Catuvellauni, and the sound of it turned my fear to anger. The slaver was a Celt. But from a tribe notorious for their sly, thieving ways. I decided once I escaped—and I *would* escape—I would cut his throat in vengeance for this affront to the Cantii and the house of my father.

He must have seen the defiance flare in my eyes.

"Prickly Cantii bitch. Think you're better'n me?"

"I know I am," I said.

"Ha!" he barked. "I'm not the one with the collar around my neck."

"No," I said. "I suspect your thieving kind wouldn't know the feel of metal around *your* neck."

He grabbed a handful of my hair and forced my head back, thrusting his face so close that I could feel his hot, sour breath in my ear. "Don't insult my honor, little thrall," he growled. "You stink of the swamps and the muck of that bloody island same as I once did."

"At least I don't stink of Rome," I said through gritted teeth.

The blow came almost before the hated word had left my tongue—a short, sharp jab to my stomach. Gasping for breath, I couldn't cry out as I felt Odd Eyes grasp at me, his thick fingers fumbling at the lacing of my tunic. I kicked and swore at him, but I was chained, and he was much stronger. I didn't know if I could fight him off. I heard the sound of my tunic ripping—

And then he was gone.

I fell forward into empty air, and my eyes flew open. Dust motes danced crazily in the slivers of sunlight through the deck planks, swirling around a silhouetted figure. It was the dark-haired slave master from the skiff. He stood above Odd Eyes—who was suddenly flat on his back—and he held a long knife in one fist. There was a moment of still-ness that stretched out between the two men, broken only by the hitching sounds in my throat as I tried to catch my breath.

"Get up, Hafgan," the slave master said calmly.

"I was only—"

"I said, get *up*."

Odd Eyes lurched to his feet. "Wasn't doing anything with the little slave that hasn't been done a hundred times, I'd wager."

"Enough, Hafgan." The slave master turned to me and said, "Did he hurt you, girl?"

I shook my head, tugging my tunic down where it was ruched halfway up my thigh.

"Good." He sighed and resheathed the dagger at his belt. "Means I don't have to hurt him." He turned back to Odd Eyes—Hafgan—and said, "Bring her up on deck. Unscathed."

He pushed past Hafgan and stalked toward the ladder. "Now, Hafgan."

I scrambled in the semi-darkness for my boots, but they were gone. Stolen while I slept. None of the other slaves would look at me as Hafgan muttered darkly, unfastening the chain attached to my collar and yanking me roughly to my feet. Up on deck and blinking in the watery sunlight, I could see off in the distance the white chalk cliffs—sacred to the goddess, guardians of the Isle of the Mighty—soaring above the breaking surf. I had never seen the shores of my home from so far out on the sea before. The sight of the cliffs diminishing as the sails billowed in the wind and the ship gathered speed made me want to weep.

Hafgan prodded me forward across the deck toward the canvas tent near the stern. He reached out in front of me and slapped aside the flap. I squared my shoulders and cast a black glare at him before I ducked my head and stepped into the interior. The slave master sat in a low backless chair in the middle of the tent, watching me with a frown. He was younger than I'd thought, perhaps only in his mid-to-late twenties. But his full, neatly trimmed beard and rich garments—and the cool look in his eyes—made him seem older. He carried himself with an air of authority and must have been utterly ruthless to have achieved an elevated station among his gang of brutes at such a young age.

He had my sheepskin travel roll resting across his knees, and I swallowed against the knot of fear in my throat as he dismissed Hafgan with a cursory wave. The silence that followed stretched out between us as he regarded me wordlessly. Eventually, he seemed to come to some kind of decision about me. His lip twitched, and he looked down at his loosely clasped hands.

"They call me Charon," he said finally. "I'm from Macedonia. I don't expect you would know—or care—where that is."

I shrugged. He was right. I didn't know where Macedonia was, but it sounded very far away.

"And who are you?" he asked.

I hesitated, surprised. Were slave traders always so curious about their property?

Charon's eyes flicked back up to my face. "What's your name?"

Perhaps, I thought, if I told him who I really was he would ransom me back to my father. But the stirring of hope in my heart was extinguished with my next thought.

Why would he believe you?

There was absolutely nothing I could do to prove my identity short of demanding they turn the ship around and go knocking at the doorpost of my father's great hall to ask if he'd been missing any wayward daughters of late. And if—say, by the capricious will of the goddess—that actually happened?

In running away, I had no doubt humiliated Virico, and I was certain Aeddan's snake-tongue had already poured poison lies into his ears. My father would probably just give me back to Aeddan and be done with it. He'd made it plain in his feast hall last night that he didn't really care what happened to me. I watched Charon warily as he reached for my sleeping roll and unfurled it with a sharp tug. My few possessions spilled out across the deck between us, and my sword dropped to the planking with a dull clank. I stared at its decorated bronze and doe-skin sheath, a twist of longing tightening in my chest.

"Where did you get that?" Charon waved a hand at the blade. "Did you steal it?"

"I didn't steal it!" I glared at him. "I'm not a thief like you."

He raised an eyebrow at me. "And what is it I've stolen, exactly?" he asked.

"Me." I jerked my chin in the direction of the ship's hold, where the other slaves were chained. "Them. We don't belong to you."

"And who do you belong to, little slave?" His dark eyes glinted.

Again, I closed my mouth, still unsure of whether or not to reveal my identity. The sword rested inches from my toes, and my fingers itched to reach for the weapon, but I knew that would only get me killed.

Charon stood and crossed the space between us, reaching for the blade himself. He pulled it free of the scabbard, and his thumb swept back and forth over the markings engraved on the blade, just below the hilt. The beauty of its clean, lethal lines still took my breath away. That sword, and the destiny it represented, meant more to me than anything. The design was a knotted triple raven—the mark of the Morrigan—and I remembered with stark clarity the day Sorcha had taken me to the blacksmith. I had perched on a high stool in the firelit forge and witnessed, for the first time, the birthing of a blade.

Sorcha had left the sword behind, hanging on the wall of our house, when she had ridden into battle. When she didn't return, I had claimed it for my own, promising to honor her legacy as a warrior.

"Whose sword is this?" Charon asked again.

I felt suddenly as if my fate hung, suspended, on the cusp of tipping one way or another. The shadow of a seabird flew across the tent wall. Or maybe it was one of the Morrigan's ravens.

"It's mine," I said in a dry whisper.

"Who gave it to you?"

I bit my lip and stayed silent.

"Tell me," he said. And then, after a long pause, "Please."

There was something about the way he said it that compelled me to speak the truth. Maybe it was just the unexpected "please," but it seemed as though it went deeper than mere curiosity.

"It was my sister's," I said.

Charon's eyes narrowed. "Your sister must be a fine warrior to handle a blade like this."

"She's dead." The words sounded flat and ugly in my ears. "When I was young, she left one day to fight the Romans. She never came home. Now the sword is mine."

I watched Charon's jaw work as he chewed the inside of his cheek, lost in thought. Then he blinked rapidly and turned away, and it was as if a veil had fallen behind his eyes, his expression unreadable once more.

"It's a fine blade," he said, hefting the slender weapon and testing its balance. "I wonder that she didn't take it with her into the field."

"My sister could kill a man with a dull fish knife," I said fiercely. "*She* was the weapon. The blade she used was of no consequence."

It was true. Sorcha had owned many swords, many daggers—all of them marked with the same triple-raven knot—and yet this one was special. She'd said as much on the day we'd gone to the forge. It was a twin to the sword she carried, but *this* sword would be mine one day, she told me. And when that happened—when the day came that I was old enough and worthy enough and the sword passed into my hands—I was to guard it with my life. Because, Sorcha told me, it would mean my life. I hadn't known exactly what she'd meant, but my sister had often said things like that. Sorcha, when she was alive, had made it a custom to spend long hours in close, secret conversation with Olun, my father's chief druid. The druiddyn were the sages and mystics of our tribe. They dealt in portents and prophecies, and I'd often wondered if Sorcha had known something in the days before she left to fight Caesar's men. Something she didn't—wouldn't—tell me.

I wondered if that was why she'd left the blade behind, as a legacy for her little sister. Maybe Sorcha had known she was going to die and leave me to grow up without her.

Even if she had, she still would have gone, I thought. *Just like I would have. That is the warrior's way.*

"Such ferocity you have," Charon said. "Following in your sister's footsteps, perhaps?"

I felt a shiver across my shoulders at his words, like the brush of dark wings on my skin. Following in Sorcha's footsteps was exactly what the druiddyn had foreseen as my destiny. The Morrigan, it seemed, had willed it otherwise. I could only hope that the path she'd set my feet upon would lead me to a fate as honorable as my sister's.

"Can you fight?" he asked.

"I can fight," I said, lifting my chin. "Better than you. Better than all of your men."

Charon raised an eyebrow at me. "Really."

"Give me back my sword and find out for yourself."

"No . . ." He laughed and slid the blade back into its sheath. "No, I believe you. And so I'll keep this out of your reach. For now."

He stepped out through the tent flap, and I heard him speak to Hafgan. "Take her back down to the hold," he said. "Let the rest of the men know that she is not to be mistreated."

"You keeping her for yourself?" Hafgan leered.

I froze. It was something I hadn't considered.

"Just do it," Charon said. "Tell them I'll chop off the hand of the first man who touches her and feed it to the fishes."

I silently thanked the Morrigan as I descended back down into the darkness of the slave ship's hold, grateful for the smallest of mercies. Still, I knew that the journey ahead of me would be long and terrible . . . and Charon's continued kindness was the very last thing I could count on.

VI

SCALP TO SOLE, I was one long mile of misery. I had lost track of how many days it had been since the Lughnasa feast in my father's great hall. How many nights would it have been since they'd laid Maelgwyn's body on the funeral pyre? If I closed my eyes, I could imagine it. His swords crossed on his chest, the flames climbing upward to lick at his face, hungrily consuming him.

Did Aeddan run all the way home, I wondered, *or did he skulk back to watch from a distance as the smoke and sparks rose into the sky to carry his brother's spirit to the Otherworld?* I swore to myself—every day of that whole horrible journey I swore—that I would find a way to return and make him pay for Mael's death. They would have to remove my chains at some point—either to sell me or to put me to work after I'd been sold—and when they did, I would run. Hide. Make my way home and have my revenge. I swore it on my soul.

Mine and Maelgwyn's. I owed him that.

But as the weeks wore on, my oaths began to sound hollow in my ears.

As it did every day on that infinite stretch since we'd landed on the northern shore of Gaul and began our trek overland, the caravan rumbled to a stop around midday, as the sun reached its apex. The air around the cage carts would grow hot, rank with the stench of unwashed bodies and sickness and fear, and full of dust and flies beneath a glaring sun. My once-pale, freckled skin was burnt and tender. My eyes and nostrils were full of road grit, and my throat was parched and raw. I'd lost count of the towns and villages we'd passed through, where the townsfolk stared and the children dared each other to throw rocks at the cages.

But that morning, instead of the usual midday break, our caravan joined up on the road with another wagon train coming from the east bearing more slaves and trade goods. The two groups blended together, and I was moved into a larger cage cart. This one was populated entirely with girls—an even dozen of us altogether—around my age.

The girls in the cart all wore slave collars the same as mine, with a single long chain running through the rings attached to their collars, linking them together, and then through more rings that were bolted to the cage bars. I was prodded up into the enclosure and my collar attached to the end of that same chain.

Strung together, I thought, *like twelve broken beads on a tarnished necklace.*

We were also each chained to a partner, linked in pairs to the girl that sat opposite us by manacles around our ankles. I never had recovered my stolen boots, and without them for protection, the iron shackle chafed horribly and the skin on my ankle and across the top of my left foot quickly became blistered and raw. Over the next two and a half days, the agony grew so that I couldn't take it anymore. When Charon himself passed near my cage, I loudly asked why the leg chain was necessary.

"Raiders." He nodded at the encroaching hills, cloaked in heavy forests. It was the first time Charon had spoken directly to me since we'd been on board the ship. "When Caesar broke Arviragus's resistance and thrashed the Arverni tribe and their allies almost out of existence," he continued, "the few survivors fled into these hills. They've nowhere to go and no other way to live. This is lawless country now, and I'd be a fool to make it easy for a raiding party to come and steal my property now, wouldn't I?"

"Your already stolen property," I said.

Charon laughed. "And how pathetic would you be if you were twice pilfered, little slave? You should be grateful I take such precautions. The raiders would not be so gentle." He paused before moving on. "We'll be traveling through the night," he said. "It will be dangerous, but less dangerous than making camp. Perhaps you'd be good enough to offer up a prayer to your fearsome raven goddess that we don't draw any unwanted attention down upon us."

For a moment I didn't understand how he would even

know what goddess I prayed to. But then I remembered
he still had my sword, etched with the Morrigan's triple-
raven knot. Charon had recognized it. And remembered.

The slave master grinned at me wryly. He unstoppered
his leather water bag and sloshed a generous measure into
the dust-dry cup that rested on the floor beside me. I was
too thirsty to be astonished. I greedily sucked down the
few mouthfuls of water, letting the cup fall to rest again
on the wagon floor between my feet. My raw, raging thirst
slaked for a moment, I leaned my head back against the
cage bars and closed my eyes. After a long, silent moment,
I could feel the other girls watching me with envy or dull
curiosity. Or outright animosity.

I did my best to ignore them as darkness descended on
the winding road and the shadows of the forest swallowed
the caravan whole.

Hours passed, and a full moon rose high overhead in a
star-spattered sky. I groaned and rolled my head on my
stiff neck. The girl on the far side of the cage—the one I
was chained to by my left ankle—was staring at me with
bleak hostility. She had been ever since Charon had poured
the water in my cup.

Beneath a high forehead made even higher by the
white-blonde hair braided tightly back from her face in
rows, her eyes were blue, but so pale in the moonlight that
they almost seemed silver. And they were just as cold and
hard. In the three days we'd been shackled together, I'd
never heard her utter a sound. Until now.

Her voice, when she spoke, was deep and strong. Her words, harsh: "You think you're precious, little vixen?"

The corner of her lips—as chapped and peeling as mine—lifted in a sneer. She spoke in Latin, probably learned from traders, the same way I had. Only hers was thickly seasoned with her native barbaric accent. I had heard one of the slavers say that some of the other girls were of the Varini tribe, a warlike people from cold northern lands. She certainly fit the description herself.

"Think you're special," she said. *"Ja?"*

Then she leaned forward and, heedless of wasting precious moisture, hawked and spat on the floor of the cart between my feet. The other captives were now awake and watching us with darting, anxious glances. I took a deep breath to cool the sudden burn of anger in my chest.

Then I frowned, tilting my head as I regarded the other girl.

"Forgive me if I've misunderstood you," I said in the best trader-learned Latin I could muster. "Your accent, after all, is terribly ugly . . . but did you just call me a dog?"

Her sneer hardened into a mocking smile. "Fox." She waved dismissively. "Small, pointy, wild dog. Cowardly things. Very noisy when they . . ." Her Latin failed her then, but the obscene gesture she made with her fingers more than conveyed her meaning.

I felt my shoulders go tight, and one of the other girls snickered.

"Scavengers." The Varini girl shrugged. "But, *ja.* That's all you seem to me. Not so very special."

But I had been special, I thought. Once I had been special to a boy with steel-gray eyes who had loved me, and I had thrown all of it away. My hands clenched into fists at my sides. She noticed and raised an eyebrow.

"Not so very tough."

As we glared at each other across the cramped space, the other occupants of the cage wagon shifted away from the two of us, rattling the chains.

The Varini girl shrugged again and nudged my empty water cup with the toe of her sandal. "Or maybe he doesn't think you're special. Maybe he just thinks you're in heat, little fox—"

My vision blurred, and I heard myself snarl in rage as I launched myself across the cage. I was brought up short and sharp by the iron ring around my neck which, of course, was still attached to the chain that ran through the rings on all the other girls' collars. Still, the force of my lunge was such that a girl on the other end of the cage cart was yanked hard over into the girl beside her, cheek mashing up against the other girl's shoulder, who then fell against the girl on her other side.

They squealed in startled outrage, and the other girls began to scream and shout too as the Varini girl threw herself out of my range, dragging along the girls on her side of the cage. A chaotic tangle of limbs and chains writhed and thrashed as the endless days of fear and frustration boiled over into violence. The Varini was tall and lanky, and when she lashed out at me with one long leg, the leather sole of her sandal slapped painfully against my thigh. I grunted in pain and half rolled over. The girl next to me flailed at me with balled fists but didn't really know how to fight.

I knew how to fight.

In the confined space, hemmed in by bars, it was easy enough to land blows—but it was just as easy to have them land on me. I took two glancing hits from the Varini girl's long-reaching fists before I felt my own connect solidly with her ribs. She yelped and twisted to avoid a follow-up punch, dragging the chain-linked girls in her wake. The cage cart tilted perilously as it raced along the dirt track.

The driver, sitting in front of the cage on a wooden seat, swore loudly as our frenzied thrashing rocked the cart, and he banged on the bars of the cage with the stout oak club he carried. He shouted at us to settle down or he would stop the wagon and give us all a beating.

I barely noticed. I was too busy reeling from a punch to the face.

Pain exploded from my left cheek, and a red mist descended in front of my eyes. After all the days and nights of dull despair and helplessness, the fierce urge to fight something, anything—any*one*—welled in my chest. I howled in fury and swung my clenched fists in a double blow that caught the Varini on the temple and sent her reeling.

"You're both mad!" a girl with long black curls shouted above the chaos. "Stop! You'll get us all killed!"

In the darkness, the skinny wheels of the wagon bearing our prison cage weaved crazily in the rutted tracks of the road. The driver, had he been thinking, could have immediately dealt with us at a standstill. But Charon had warned his men not to stop, and there was no wagon behind us to notice the commotion. Ours was the last vehicle in the caravan that night, except for a heavy, guarded ox-pulled provisions wagon that was even slower. Slow enough to have fallen far behind and out of sight.

Which meant that there was nothing to stop me from trying to shove the Varini girl's ugly insinuations back down her throat. I only had to reach her first. I wedged my left hand beneath the metal ring that circled my neck so I wouldn't choke, and then I hauled on the slave chain with all my strength. I managed to gather just enough slack to connect to the side of the Varini girl's head with the full force of my right fist. Her head snapped back. She fell heavily against her side of the cage with enough force to send the whole cart careening sideways.

The slave driver shouted in alarm as the wagon rocked wildly on the uneven road. As the cage suddenly tipped over and began rolling down a steep embankment, girls screamed and grappled for anything to hold on to. My shoulder hit the roof of the cage with enough force to send blinding pain shooting through my whole body, and the girl chained on my right landed on top of me, driving the wind from my lungs. When the cage came to a halt at the bottom of a ditch, there was a moment of utter stillness, broken only by the spinning creak of the two wheels churning away uselessly above our heads. The other girls began to groan and whimper, pushing themselves to their hands and knees, tangled in their chains and each other's limbs.

The cage had split apart like a rotten fruit, and I staggered to my feet and stepped free of the broken bars. The two cart horses, their shattered yokes hanging from their necks, scrambled to their feet and bolted back up the embankment. I sucked in my breath at the sight of the slave driver, who'd been pinned beneath one of the animals. His head was bent at an unnatural angle, and his mouth was frozen open in a silent cry of shock. A slick of dark blood painted the side of his face, and his eyes were empty and staring.

I stumbled back a step, and the chain that had held me tethered to the other girls by the ring around my neck slid free and fell to the ground in pieces, broken links chiming tuneless music as they hit the stony ground beneath my feet.

I'm free! I thought as elation surged through me.

No. Not exactly.

I cursed as I saw that the shackle that circled my left ankle was woefully intact. I was still bound by the short length of stout iron links to the Varini girl, who was clambering unsteadily to her feet. She seemed to realize—at the very same moment that I did—the irony of our situation. In the trees high above our heads, I heard the throaty chuckle of a raven and imagined it was the wry laughter of the Morrigan, amused at my predicament. My goddess was capricious in her affections. I'd always known that. But I was beginning to think that when she'd called me daughter, it was only to mock my efforts to live up to that honor.

I glanced around at the faces of the other girls, pale moons in the darkness, and said, "This is our chance."

Not one of them moved. The Varini girl said nothing, but I saw the muscles of her jaw clench. When I locked eyes with her, she gave me a curt nod. So be it. Together we stepped carefully, away from the twisted mess of bars and planks. I hesitated briefly when the dark-haired girl—the one who had shouted for us to stop fighting—put a hand on my arm.

"This isn't a chance. This is madness," she said in a low, frantic voice. "Listen to me—I was born into my lot. I've been a slave my whole life, with never the chance to be anything but. And I'll still gladly take that fate over running wild through this countryside, waiting to be caught and killed by lawless men. Killed if you're *lucky*. You heard what Charon said."

I looked over her shoulder, out at the deep, dark, utterly still forest.

"I heard him," I said. "I don't believe him. These hills are deserted. There is nothing here but the spirits of the Arverni murdered by Caesar's legions." I said it in a voice loud enough to almost make myself believe it. "Stay here if that's what you want." I lifted her hand from my shoulder. "But I'll take my chances with dead men, lawless or not."

"Wait." She bent down and yanked off her worn leather slippers and held them out. When I hesitated, she thrust them at me. "Take them," she urged, nodding at my own bare feet. "Take the shoes and my prayers to the goddess for you. You'll need them both."

The girl's gaze was strangely compassionate. She knew just by looking at me that I wasn't like her. I wasn't a slave—I never had been. I'd only ever been a princess and a warrior. The irony, I realized, was that she was stronger than me because of it. This was a girl who would choose to stay chained if it meant that her odds of survival were even so much as a hairsbreadth better. And there was strength in that choice—the sheer, bloody-minded will to survive no matter how dreadful the circumstance. Maybe honor wasn't always something won by a blade, I thought. And maybe it couldn't be so easily stripped away, even in servitude.

I ducked my head and snatched the shoes from the girl's fingers, shame heating my cheeks. "Thank you," I murmured as I stuffed my feet into them.

The soles of the leather slippers were almost worn through in places, but they fit snugly. As I straightened up from tying the lacings, my Varini shackle-mate reached down and grasped a fistful of the iron links that tethered us together.

"If you slow me down," she growled, "I'll hack your foot off with a sharp stone."

"I won't slow you down," I said. "So long as you keep your big, flat feet out of my way."

Pale blue eyes blinked at me for a moment. Then the Varini grinned—an expression utterly devoid of mirth—and said, "Run."

VII

IT WAS AWKWARD AT FIRST—the Varini girl's legs were longer than mine—but once we settled into a rhythm, we made surprisingly good speed through the forest, navigating an increasingly steep incline by moonlight.

But then my foot hit something hard and angular, and I stumbled and fell forward onto my hands and knees. The tall blonde stumbled to a stop, cursing in her own tongue before spinning on her heel to tower over me, one fist clenched.

"Clumsy idiot!" she snarled, her voice a raw scrape of sound in the darkness. "I told you if you slowed me down I'd—"

"Hack my foot off," I snapped. "I remember."

I looked down at the thing that had tripped me and tugged on it. With one good heave, I stood to face the Varini, lifting a short, broad-bladed sword streaked with dirt. I smiled as she froze, staring at the weapon in my hand.

"Perhaps I should just remove yours instead," I suggested sweetly, "and save us both the burden of each other's continued company."

In the silver wash of a moonbeam, I could see the dints and burrs of battle damage along the edge of the sword's blade. Beneath a generous layer of rust, it didn't even so much as glimmer in the pale light. But it was still a weapon. A useful one.

One of a pair, it seemed.

My moment of superiority vanished as the Varini's eyes suddenly narrowed and she lunged for the pile of leaves at my feet. When she stood, her fist was wrapped around the hilt of her own found weapon—another sword, almost identical to the one I held. We had stumbled upon a weapons cache left over from the great battle of Alesia.

I knew the stories. I'd heard them told around the fire of my father's great hall. Four year earlier, word had reached our tribe that, across the sea, the king named Arviragus—the mighty Arverni chieftain, the brave rebel the Romans had come to know by his war title, Vercingetorix—had been defeated by Julius Caesar in his wars against a confederation of Gallic tribes. And not just defeated. Shamed. Shackled and dragged off to Rome in chains like an animal. I shuddered at the thought. I couldn't imagine a worse fate for such a man.

Alesia had been the battle that had ended the war. Caesar had surrounded the fortified town with not one but two rings of earthworks and hunkered down for a devastating siege. The defenders had eventually sent their women and children out into the no-man's-land between the fortifications, hoping that Caesar would allow them to go free. He hadn't. Instead, he'd let them starve.

Desperate, the Gauls had eventually been forced out of the town and into pitched battle with the legions, to no avail. And Arviragus had ultimately surrendered—but not before tens of thousands of Gaulish Celts had died. Tens of thousands more had been taken as slaves. And the once-bustling town of Alesia—what remained of it—had been left to rot, surrounded by crumbling fortifications and ditches filled with bones and brackish water. And, it appeared, ancient rusting weapons.

The Varini girl and I stared at each other for a long, tense moment. Then I let out my breath and lowered my battered blade.

"Come on," I said. "I'm in no mood to kill you, and if Charon and his slavers come after us, rusty swords aren't going to be much help if we're still tethered together like a pair of oxen."

She thought about it for a moment, then shoved her own rusted weapon through the rope belt tied around her waist and gestured me forward. When we finally reached the ruins of the hilltop town, the night's cloud cover had grown heavier. By the little moonlight that managed to break through, we could barely make out the ragged breaches in the high stone wall. We clambered through one of the gaps, the chain between us hissing over the tumbled stones like a warning whisper.

Once inside, I could see the peak of a large thatch-roofed

building rising up out of the center of the town, higher than all the rest. It reminded me with a sharp pang of homesickness of my father's great hall, only much larger, and the outline of the roof was irregular, as if half of it had fallen in. Most of the buildings were nothing more than skeletal remains. Here and there, darkened windows set in the shells of mud and wicker walls stared vacantly at us like the eye sockets of empty skulls. In places, torn door curtains and scraps of leather awnings flapped listlessly in the chill breeze.

The place was utterly deserted.

"There." The Varini pointed with her blade. "There's a well."

Dragging the slave chain between us, we stumbled toward the low, round wall that surrounded the well. But as we approached, the small hairs on the back of my neck rose. I saw the remains of a smashed water bucket that lay next to a frayed coil of rope. When we were close enough to peer over the low wall, the Varini girl gasped and covered her mouth.

The well was filled more than halfway to the top with pale, tangled bones. Skulls and long bones, cages made of ribs, the smaller bones of arms and legs. Bodies once, thrown into the well until they stacked up, one on top of the other, now bleached and arid where they piled higher than the water level. A lingering waft of decay hung in the air over the well.

That's your imagination, I chided myself, even as I felt the bile rising in my throat. *Those people have been dead for years.*

"They fouled the well," the Varini girl said, her voice gone guttural, as if she was also on the verge of retching. "Stuffed it full of corpses to make the water undrinkable."

"The Romans must have done it." I shook my head in disgust, unable to keep my feet from carrying me backward. "After they broke the siege. So the Arverni wouldn't come back here."

"Or the Arverni did it," my companion said. "So the Romans couldn't use the town for themselves after they won."

"That's horrible," I said. "They wouldn't do that to their own dead. It's a dishonor."

"It's *smart*," she countered. "It's war. Don't leave anything behind for your enemy to use. Scorch the earth, kill the cattle, foul the water."

I looked at her. "And what do you know of war?"

She shrugged. "My people have been at war with each other since Askr and Almr first grew out of the ground as trees," she said, "and the gods uprooted them and made of them the first man and woman. Real war. Not your island cattle raids, but war. The kind of war where you can stand on a hillside and look down on a valley and not see the grass for all the men fighting."

I tried to imagine just what that would look like.

"Then?" the Varini girl continued. "There is no thing called dishonor. No thing called honor. There is only winning. Only losing. And if you lose, you don't leave a freshly made bed behind for your enemy to sleep in."

"Your people sound particularly unforgiving."

"*Ja.* Only we call it practical. Where I come from, when one tribe wants to move—to live somewhere else, somewhere better—they burn their houses before they leave."

"What?" I frowned at her. "That's not practical. It's ridiculous. Why would they do that?"

"So they can't change their minds." She pointed straight out into the darkness ahead of her with her sword. "There is only forward. Only tomorrow. No yesterday, no going back. And nothing of value is left behind, so nothing is truly lost."

I thought about the idea of feeding the past to the flames.

Wasn't that what I had done? And had I left anything behind of value?

Father . . .

. . . who was willing to give me to a husband I didn't want and couldn't love.

Maelgwyn . . .

I blinked back the tears that suddenly rimmed my eyes and saw, in my mind, the flames of my own hearth. The fire that I'd fed with my torc and my dagger. I might as well have burned my house down. I'd certainly set fire to my yesterdays. And I'd left, intending never to return.

"What happens when you come upon another tribe that doesn't feel like moving on?" I asked.

She grinned wolfishly. "Then . . . you fight."

"Is that what happened to you?"

"*Ja.* I was born in a place that should have been called Hel, because that is what it was. The land was harsh, the winds bitter, the herds scarce, and the food scarcer. Why anyone would live there in the first place is, to me, a"—she struggled for the Latin word—"a mystery." Her expression grew rueful. "Our thane must have grown more brains than his fathers before him, though, because he decided that we would go to other lands. Warmer, more plentiful, but already taken by another tribe. Still, we went. And then, when we got there . . . the Suevi had more swords and better food. So, stronger fighters."

"What happened?"

"The Varini—my people—sold as many of us as they could to the Suevi, so there would be fewer mouths to feed, and then they moved on. To a place where the Suevi weren't."

Something about the way she told the bald truth of her tale made me look at her twice. Her face was impassive, but I thought I saw a shadow flit behind her gaze.

"Who sold you?" I asked.

"My mother."

"*What?*"

"She got a good price," she said flatly, then turned her head and spat. "May she rot in filth in Hel's icy wasteland until the end of days."

I was staring at her, openmouthed, I knew. And as I stared, I saw her mask slip just enough for me to recognize it. Pain. "I'm sorry."

She laughed harshly. "I don't need pity from the likes of you, little island fox. Pity is for the weak."

Silence spun out into the darkness all around us. I didn't know what to say. I didn't like her. At all. And I suppose I could have felt a kind of grim satisfaction about the hardships this rude, brutish, irritating girl had endured. But I didn't. I couldn't imagine how that had felt—to have your own kin treat you like a possession. A cow or a cloak or a sword to be sold or bartered away. But then again, wasn't that what my own father had been willing to do to me? Give me away like some kind of prize to Aeddan? Maybe the Varini girl and I weren't all that different.

"What's your name?" I asked her finally.

"Why?"

"I don't pity you," I lied. "But I would like to mourn you if the time comes when I have to kill you. And I can't do that if I don't know your name."

The blonde girl's winter-cold eyes narrowed slightly. Then she uttered a sharp laugh and slapped me—hard—on the back. "I am Elka," she said.

"That's it?" I coughed, catching my breath after the blow. "Just Elka?"

"You don't like my name?"

"No." I shook my head. "No, it's a good name." I stood up taller and dipped my head in what I hoped she would interpret as a gesture of respect. "I am Fallon. I mean, I *was* Fallon ferch Virico, daughter of a king. Before all this. But I guess I'm just Fallon now."

Elka considered that for a moment and then nodded. "*Ja*," she said. "It's better that way. We belong to no one, you and me." She looked down at the chain that stretched between us. "Only to each other, until we can find a hammer or a good heavy axe."

The remnants of the town's shattered edges had begun to smudge and fade with a mist that rose as Elka and I searched from ruined house to ruined house to find some kind of useful implement with which to free ourselves from our shackles. I wondered silently what would happen when we did. Would my reluctant companion leave me to my fate and disappear into the forest as fast as those long legs could take her? Would I do the same to her?

"Tell me something," Elka said, poking at a drift of leaves and refuse with her rusted sword. "What did you do to gain his favor? The slave master."

"What do you mean?"

"I mean the water." She tilted her head. "And how you always got porridge in your bowl before any of us. And the way Charon talked to you almost as if you were a person."

I straightened up from searching. "I don't know."

"Really."

"I don't!" Although I knew, of course, what she was thinking. "I wouldn't. All I know is that Charon told his men they weren't allowed to touch me."

Elka raised an eyebrow at me.

"On the ship, Hafgan—the ugly one with the mismatched eyes," I muttered, feeling my face grow red, "he . . . he tried to . . . ."

Elka's expression darkened as she realized what had

happened, what I couldn't put into words. I tried to shake off the surge of revulsion and fear from those moments in the slave ship's hold. "Nothing came of it," I said in a rush. "Charon found us and stopped him before he could do much more than tear the hem of my tunic. He told Hafgan in plain terms that he'd cut the hand off the next man who so much as laid a finger on me."

Elka's angry frown turned contemplative. "But he never told you why?"

I shook my head.

"Maybe he wanted you for himself."

"Pfft." I rolled my eyes. "That must be why he never laid a finger on me either."

"You're lucky."

"Did they . . ." I didn't know how to ask the question. Or even if I should.

"No." She shook her head. "One of them tried. The brute with the long orange beard. You know the one?"

I nodded.

"I bit off half his ear and kicked him in the balls so hard he still limps. You might have noticed."

I had noticed, actually. He not only limped, he scowled. A lot.

Elka grinned fiercely. "If we hadn't run away, Charon would've had to pay that bastard blood money, taken out of whatever price I fetched once we got to Rome," she said. "But I also heard him say that whoever bought me would wind up paying far more than the price of bruised balls and half an ear. He seemed pretty sure of it, so I guess he decided I was worth keeping alive. Anyway, none of the other slavers felt much like trying their luck after that."

We'd both been lucky, it seemed. I whispered a prayer to the Morrigan that our luck would hold just a little longer.

"Do you think he'll come after us?" I asked. "Charon?"

Elka opened her mouth to answer, but suddenly the hairs on the back of my neck rose, and I grabbed her wrist, pulling her down behind rubble that used to be a wall. I hissed at her to be quiet. Shadows at the edge of the weedy town square stirred and grew long, and I feared that my very words had conjured Charon and his men out of the night. Beside me, Elka held her breath.

But I was wrong. It wasn't the slavers.

It was worse.

VIII

A PAIR OF MEN stepped out from between two burned-out houses and moved silently through drifts of gathered mist on the worn soles of their leather boots. They were long-haired with thick beards and dirt-smudged tunics. For a brief instant, I thought that they might be ghosts— shades of the Arverni dead—but they stepped into the clearing, and the moonlight didn't shine through them. And the mist moved where they walked.

Elka shifted closer to me so that we were crouching shoulder to shoulder.

"You said the Varini are a warlike tribe?" I murmured, nodding at the sword in her hand. "I hope they taught you how to fight with something more than your knuckles before they bartered you away."

She spat a quiet curse as the taller of the two gestured in our direction. They knew we were there. They were coming for us. And they were not alone. Other shadows detached themselves from the darkness, and suddenly another pair of men was moving across the town square toward us too. I hissed at Elka and nodded in the direction of the new threat, and I could almost hear her pulse start to race. With nowhere to run, Elka and I stepped into the middle of a wide, clear space where we had unobstructed views on all sides.

"Back to back," I said tensely.

She shifted her body so that her shoulder blades jammed up against mine.

The slave chain hissed along the ground as the men closed in around us. I kicked at it to keep it out from underneath my slippers, and one of the men—the taller of the first pair—swung a short-hafted pike at Elka's head in an artless, horizontal slash. She ducked without blocking and shifted to the side, bending around my left flank so that I could move with her. I saw what she was doing and dropped into a crouch as she twisted. The man reared back again, and while his attention was focused on Elka, I sprang forward with a low, darting thrust that tagged him solidly on the upper thigh. He howled in pain, flinching as the point of my sword pierced his worn breeches and sank into the muscle there. I pulled my sword out and blood spilled down the front of his leg. It was the first time I'd ever wounded a man, and I felt a savage rush of excitement.

"Not such easy meat as he thought." Elka's voice was in my ear, panting with fear or exertion—I couldn't tell which. "That was nice, little fox."

"Thanks," I said. "For all the good it—"

"Hai!" Elka exclaimed and threw herself against my spine, hard enough to knock me forward. Blades clashed beside my ear as Elka fended off her attacker, but I was too occupied in that moment to help. The partner of the man I had wounded had learned from his companion's misfortune and came at me with a feinting attack instead of a direct swing. I saw beneath the matted tangle of his overgrown beard that he wore an iron collar. Just like me.

Only not like me at all. Because if the slaves of the Gaulish tribes were anything like the ones owned by my own tribe in Prydain, they weren't allowed to be schooled in the arts of war. And I, most certainly, was.

"They're *slaves*!" I shouted at Elka. "They're not trained!"

"Tell *them* that!" Elka shouted back as she dropped to one knee and threw herself to the side to evade another clumsy blow that—training or no—would have broken her head open.

As she dodged, I covered her, scything through the air with my sword and screaming curses that startled the man so much he actually backed off a few paces. Elka scrambled to her feet, and together we faced them, shoulder to shoulder.

"They're just girls!" the brigand with the leg wound shouted. "Cut them down!"

In all my life, I'd never actually been in a *real* fight. Never gone on a raid, or warred over territory, and—in spite of all my declarations of warrior prowess—I think I'd always secretly wondered if I'd be able to handle myself in an actual battle when the time came. Now, one look at the men backing off, one of them clutching a wound made by my blade, told me that I would. I had. The first taste of real battle was sweet on my tongue, and I felt a surge of hope. We could do this. We could *win* this fight.

Maybe.

"Just girls my ragged arse!" one of the other brigands spat. "Demons is more like!"

They were afraid of us. A spark somewhere deep inside of me flared to life. The tiniest blue flame, with nothing of tinder to catch onto except the delusional hope that I could somehow fight my way back to freedom. The spark snuffed out the moment the brigand attacked again . . . and the rusted blade in my hand shattered into shards.

I gripped the hilt of the broken old weapon and desperately wished it were my own gleaming sword, the one Charon had taken from me.

The brigand in front of me lifted his weapon high. And then—

"Enough!" Charon's distinctive accent roared through the ruins, echoing off broken stone walls. As if my very thoughts had conjured him out of the thin night air—summoned his shade like an Otherworld demon—the slave master stepped out of the darkness and into the moonlight. And suddenly, there was nothing but empty space in front of me.

The brigand was just . . . gone.

In that moment, I completely understood why, young

as he was, Charon's men respected—or, perhaps, feared—him. With one swift motion, Charon had grabbed the brigand by the shoulder and yanked him around. Two more moves and the man lost first his sword hand . . . and then his head.

His blade, hilt still clasped in dead fingers, spun through the air. The man's head toppled from his neck and bounced away into the undergrowth, the whites of his eyes glinting in the moonlight. The headless torso slumped to the ground, and Charon wiped his blade on the dead man's sleeve. The relief I felt was followed swiftly by a stab of fear. Elka and I had been rescued only to find ourselves once more in the hands of our captor.

And he wasn't very happy with us.

Charon stepped over the corpse at his feet and grabbed me by the slave collar, hauling me close so that I was almost nose to nose with him. I could smell wine on his breath. He'd probably been traveling in ease, riding in his private covered wagon, when the cage cart had overturned. Although my pulse thrummed in my throat, beating wildly against the knuckles of Charon's fist, I forced my eyes to meet his. If I was going to die, I was going to stare into the face of my death when it happened.

I held my breath. But after another long moment, I saw the white fury fade from behind the slave master's eyes.

"You cost me a man, and you cost me a wagon, and yet here I am, rescuing you from the ravages of your own stupidity," he hissed. "I must be mad."

"Leave me here among these ruins, then," I said, half-defiant, half-afraid he would do just that, "and I'll trouble you no more."

"Don't tempt me," he said. "Listen to me. You're a fool, and you know nothing. You don't even know what you're worth. But I do."

My eyes snapped back up to his face.

"And that's the only reason you're still alive," he said. "But understand this: If you try and pull a stunt like this again, if you even so much as *think* about running, I swear by all the gods, I will stake you to the ground myself and leave you for the wolves."

He let go of my slave collar, and I stumbled back a step, knocking into Elka. She put out a hand to steady me. Charon jabbed a finger at the tall Varini girl. "And you," he said. "You've already cost me blood money. I should kill you right now just for the trouble you've caused."

I felt Elka's fingers close tightly on my arm, but she said nothing.

"I can't sell you dead," he growled. "But if you don't fetch a price that'll make it worth my trouble, I'll sell you instead to some fat Roman bastard senator who'll make you wish you *were* dead."

He turned and gestured to his men to collect us and our surviving attackers, who now knelt in the dust at the feet of the slavers. "Get them back down to the road. And get a chain on these other animals. Might as well glean all the profit we can from this misbegotten night."

"What of Clodhar?" Hafgan asked, nodding toward the road.

"What of him?" Charon said. "He's dead. His incompetence cost me a cart and a night's rest. He can lie in that ditch till the scavengers scatter his bones."

He turned and stalked off into the night, leaving his men to deal with us. I turned to Elka, who kicked at the iron links that bound us together.

"I guess we're stuck with each other then," she said. "For the time being."

"There are worse fates," I said.

She rolled an eye at me.

"Not many, but some."

A grin flickered across Elka's face as Charon's men barked at us to get moving. The slave chain hissed sullenly along the ground, but I realized that I really was grateful that the tall, fierce Varini girl was tethered to the other end.

IX

FROM THAT POINT ON, the journey south became a drudgery of crushing sameness. The days crawled past the bars of my cage, the landscape veiled in a pall of dull yellow road dust: hills, then forests, then fields rolled by; waving golden crops ripe for harvest replaced by fields of stubbly, shorn stalks; pale blue skies and high pink clouds giving way to the vaulting darkness above me as I lay sleepless, shivering and aching.

And then, one day, our caravan crested a high hill, and there, laid out like a dream before us, was a place I never, in my wildest flights of fancy, could have imagined: the port of Massilia, sprawled on the coast of a vast sea the Romans called Mare Nostrum. From the time when I was barely old enough to run like a wild creature out beyond the walls of Durovernum, Sorcha and I would go down to the market stalls to barter with the traders for bolts of fine, bright cloth and pink salt and spices from lands where the sun was so hot, they said, you could die of its kiss.

One of the traders, a thick-bodied man with skin like boiled leather, would dock his ship at Durovernum twice a year and spin tales of the cities he'd seen and the people he'd traded with. I would perch on the bales of merchandise stacked on the docks and listen to his stories of far-off lands. That was where I had first heard of the great middle sea, whose waves washed the shores of many different lands, lands like Greece and Rome and Aegypt. The trader had told me that Mare Nostrum meant "Our Sea" in Latin, and I had marveled at the arrogance of Rome, which would dare to lay claim to the very elements of the earth. The goddess must have laughed at them, I'd thought. I certainly had.

But I wasn't laughing now as I finally saw with my own eyes the things the trader had spoken of. The stone walls of Massilia gleamed so brightly in the sun that I had to squint to look at them, rising up against the backdrop of a sea the color of the deepest sapphires and nestled among green and brown hills cloaked with olive trees. The road we were on had widened steadily over the last day's traveling until it was broad enough to let four ox carts go side by side down toward the great north gate. Our own caravan joined the multitude of foot and cart traffic that streamed toward the bustling city that, as far as I could tell, held more people within its walls than I had thought were alive in the whole world.

My mouth kept dropping open, and I would choke on road dust as the city loomed ever closer. When I glanced over at Elka, she was in the same state—wide-eyed and torn between fear and wonderment. Everything seemed like something out of legend. In the shadow of the soaring walls, the city became less of an imposing majestic place and more a heaped, jumbled gathering of wealth and squalor existing side by side. Heady perfumes and the stink of offal wrapped around each other, woven into an overwhelming tapestry by the ocean breeze. Wicker cages full of fowl and small game swung from carts, squawking and chittering excitedly, filling the air with a haze of fur and feathers. Tens and tens of incomprehensible languages rang in my ears. Houses and temples and other buildings made of stone—structures that made my father's great hall seem like a sheepherder's hut—rose above the street, level upon level.

All of it—the sights and sounds and smells—tangled together into an assault on my senses that made me want to clap my hands over my ears and hide my head. But there was no escaping the chaos as our cart plunged on, heading right toward the very heart of Massilia. With only the bars of my cage between me and the pushing, shoving, singing, shouting crowd, I'd never felt so vulnerable.

But the people on the road paid us little heed—we were, after all, just one more load of trade goods to be sold in the marketplace in Rome—and by the time we'd passed beneath the massive arch of the city gate, my panic had mostly given way to curiosity as Charon's drivers shouted and cursed, bullying their way toward Massilia's famed docks. Eventually, we came to a stop beside a ship with the same maroon-and-blue-striped sail as the slave galley that had taken me away from my home.

Charon appeared, swinging himself down from the back of his covered wagon, and hailed the ship's master. I watched the two men clasp wrists in greeting, and I could tell that the ship captain was agitated. He gestured with impatient swipes back toward the ship. I glanced over and saw that the ship's rails were lined with Roman legionnaires. Dozens of them. They bristled with weapons and armor, and beneath the brims of their helmets, their faces looked like statues carved by the same sculptor, equally stern, hard, uncaring.

The sight of them made my blood run cold.

These men, I thought, *are not warriors. They are soldiers.*

I tried to imagine what it must have been like for the tribes of Prydain—for the men and women of the Cantii and the Catuvellauni—to face those soldiers. How had it been for Virico or Sorcha? How had it been for Arviragus and his doomed coalition of tribes in Alesia? These were stone-cold men trained to kill—not with heart and fire and fury, not with the joy of glorious battle, but as a single, unthinking whole, like drones in a beehive.

Eventually, one of the soldiers—one of some sort of rank, I guessed, judging from the helmet plume and his immaculate cloak—strode forward to speak to Charon, and the slave master waved away the captain.

"Caius Antonius Varro!" Charon held out his hand and greeted the legionnaire with cheer. "Well met, Decurion."

The two men clasped wrists in greeting.

"What are you doing in Massilia?" Charon continued. "Official business?"

"The port authorites made a request of Caesar to lend the services of my detachment," the legionnaire replied. "So that we may escort cargo ships safely to Rome. I'll be traveling with you on the last leg of your journey."

Charon raised an eyebrow. "This would be in regards to the 'pirates' my captain tells me of? He thinks the authorities are imagining things, Decurion. Or exaggerating."

The Decurion shrugged. "They can think whatever they like. My father's trading partners lost three ships to bandits in the last month alone," he said.

"Three?" Charon frowned. "Senator Varro must be beside himself."

"The merchants' guild has been trying to keep the matter quiet in order to avoid a panic, but you can be assured that what I tell you is truth," the Decurion said. "And I'm sure you wouldn't want to jeopardize the safety of your current inventory. I can tell you that, with Caesar's Triumphs looming near, there is fierce competition in the capital right now for the kind of slaves you always seem to have on offer."

Charon grinned, leading the Decurion back up onto the deck. "Come see for yourself," he said.

As the slave master and the Decurion talked, Hafgan and his men had unlocked our chains, herding us from the caravan cages toward the galley. A miserable clot of human livestock, we shuffled up the sea-slick gangplank to huddle on the deck of the ship. The Decurion began pacing through our ranks, and I secretly examined him as he examined us. Even though most of his face was obscured by the cheek-plates of his helmet, I'd already got the impression—by the timbre of his speech and the way he carried himself—that he was fairly young.

Probably the brat son of some minor official given a plush ceremonial appointment in the legions as an officer, I thought. *What a charming escort.*

"I must lack a discerning eye," he said eventually. "I see nothing at all remarkable here."

Charon didn't rise to the slight. He just leaned against a stack of barrels, arms crossed. "Travel takes its toll," he said. "They'll clean up all right, this lot. Trust me."

The young Decurion's gaze landed on me, and I could see that in his estimation, I was less than a filthy runt in a kennel. I swallowed the biting words that only would have earned me a slap as he swept past, heading toward the captain's tent near the stern of the ship, where there would no doubt be wine and refreshments laid out for him.

As Hafgan appeared to herd us all down into the darkness of the ship's hold, the smoldering disdain I had carried most of my life for the legionnaire's kind—for the soldiers that had killed my sister and dishonored my father—flared to a bright-burning flame of hatred. And my soul fanned that fire wholly in the direction of the young decurion named Caius Antonius Varro.

X

IN THE HOLD OF THE SHIP, the darkness was absolute, the air close and damp, overwhelming with the reek of seawater. We'd been sailing for hours, and it must have been close to midnight. Most of the slave captives dozed, lulled by the groan of wood and creak of rope and the rhythmic slap of the waves on the hull. I sat huddled with my knees drawn up, staring wide-eyed into the gloom, when suddenly the galley heaved over, shuddering terribly, as something slammed into her broadside.

At first I thought it must have been wild waves born of the storm. I could hear the crack and rumble of close, heavy thunder. But then the hull planks next to my head groaned and splintered inward. We'd been hit by something far more solid than seawater.

A flash of lightning—sliced into squares by the iron grate covering the hold hatch above—illuminated a chaos of gushing sea and screaming slaves plunged into night-marish terror.

I clambered to my feet, screaming for Elka.

"Here, Fallon! By the hatch!" she shouted and I saw her wave her arms over her head in the aftergleam of the light-ning before everything faded back to black. "Ten paces to your left!"

"Where's the ladder?" I called, reaching blindly out in front of me and staggering through knee-deep foaming water. I felt Elka's strong fingers grasping at my wrists, and I clutched at her, stepping over the flailing bodies that tumbled through the water toward the hole in the ship's hull.

"What's happening?" Elka gasped, placing my hands on the steep ladder that led up out of the ship's hold. I grabbed the rungs and held on fiercely as other hands in the darkness grappled onto me. Someone clutched at my ankle and was threatening to drag me under the water. I heard a man's frantic scream as his fingers lost their grip. The scream turned to a gargled choke, but I couldn't help him. If I let go, I would be lost. I squeezed my eyes shut and hung on.

More water—rain or waves, I couldn't tell—poured down into the hold from the hatch grate above our heads, and Elka and I clung to each other and the ladder, hunched against the deluge. From up on deck, we could hear frantic shouts and barked commands, the thunder of running feet. And then the clashing of iron—blade upon blade.

We hadn't run aground. We hadn't been swamped by

a rogue wave or drawn the wrath of some god of the deep. The galley had been rammed, and we were being boarded by pirates. Not so imaginary after all. The wound in the galley's flank from the pirate ship's ram was a mortal one. The vessel groaned like a great beast in its death throes as water rushed in through the shattered timbers. From above, an angry orange glow and the acrid tang of oily smoke filtered down into the hold. Fire. The ship's coal braziers must have been knocked over. If they had set any of the oil stores alight, the wooden deck would burn, no matter the rain.

"We have to get out of here," Elka shouted, gesturing up toward the deck. I turned and scurried up the ladder to the top. But, of course, the hatch grate was securely latched from the other side. I thrust upward with all the strength of my legs, jamming my shoulders against the iron bars. The grate didn't give so much as a hairsbreadth. I squeezed my fingers together and thrust my hand through one of the square gaps in the grate, but I couldn't get the leverage I needed to budge the latch. I slumped back down onto the top rung of the ladder, panting, blood from scrapes on my knuckles and wrist bones running down my arm. Above us, the deck planking thrummed with the impact of feet and bodies.

"It's no use!" I called down to Elka. "Is there any other way to—"

Suddenly there was a crashing thud, and the body of a man fell across the grate. His mouth and eyes were frozen open in a horrible death grimace. Wine-dark blood flowed from a gaping wound to his chest, but I saw that he was still clutching a dagger. I stuck my hand through the grate again and held my breath as I carefully worked the weapon free from the dead man's fingers. If it fell, if I dropped it, I'd never find it again in the darkness and the rising water. Slowly, I coaxed the hilt into the cup of my palm until I could get a firm grip. Then I worked at the grate latch with the blade. Sweat, rainwater, and the dead man's blood poured down my face and arm and made my fingers slick and clumsy, but agonizing bit by creaking bit, the latch moved . . . and slid free.

I shoved my body against the grate, and it swung up on oiled hinges. The dead man rolled off to one side, and I scrambled upward out of the hold, groping wildly for the dagger as it skittered across the deck and disappeared over the side into the waves. Elka surged up the ladder after me, followed close behind by the rest of Charon's captives. We poured up out of the hatch opening like ants from an anthill, hoping for a chance at survival. But as nightmarish as it was belowdecks, it was arguably worse above. Under a fearsome sky, the deck of the galley was a maelstrom of bloodthirsty pirates, ruthless legionnaires, and angry slave traders.

The pirate vessel was painted black, with black sails and a high curving bow with a stout ironclad battering ram fixed beneath wicked-looking painted eyes. The ram was buried in the side of our ship like the goring tusk of a wild boar. On the other side of the galley, a smaller vessel with sleek lines—the Decurion's ship, I guessed—was moored to ours with ropes. The legion soldiers were firing arrows into the throng of pirates hurtling over the galley's opposite rail and leaping from their own vessel onto the deck of the galley to fight hand to hand. In the light of the fire, I looked up to see Decurion Varro balanced like a cat upon the galley rail, the flames reflecting off the blade of the sword in his hand. Lit by the fire against the flashing thunderclouds, he looked magnificent. Like a god. No, like a conqueror.

Something snapped in my mind.

The noise all around me receded in a wave until all I heard was a distant, throbbing pulse like a muffled heartbeat. A legionnaire gutted one of the pirates not three strides in front of me, and the man twisted in a horrid dance as his guts spilled. He dropped his weapons—a pair of short, curved swords—and one of them landed at my feet.

I picked it up.

Through the red mist that drifted down before my eyes, I no longer saw a ship, or pirates. I could see only soldiers. Legionnaires in their uniforms, hacking and slashing and killing. Where the young, arrogant Decurion stood, I saw only a nameless, faceless commander of Caesar's legions.

I saw only the man who'd murdered my sister.

In that moment, Caius Varro was Rome. And I . . . I was Vengeance.

I ran at him, howling. If I was going to die on a cursed ship in the middle of a cursed ocean, I was going to die a proper Cantii warrior and take a soldier of Rome down with me to our watery graves.

"Are you insane?" the Decurion shouted, desperately defending himself. "I'm not your enemy! I'm trying to save your worthless hides!"

I answered with an incoherent snarl as I slashed at his head. Our blades locked up, and we stood there nose to nose, straining against each other, my strength fueled by battle madness. He shoved me away, and I stumbled backward. I collided with one of the pirates, who responded by yanking his dagger out of the guts of a slave and thrusting the blade at my exposed neck.

Before I could react, the Decurion lunged forward and tackled the pirate, knocking him off the side of the ship . . . and saving me from a dagger through the throat. Without another word, he wheeled around and grabbed me by the shoulders, shaking me so hard my teeth rattled. The red fury cleared from my sight, and Decurion Varro thrust his face close to mine, his chest heaving beneath his armored breastplate.

"If you're going to kill a man tonight," he rasped, "I suggest picking one who's trying to kill *you!*" He spun me around and pointed with his sword in the direction of the marauders rushing toward us.

I felt my eyes go wide as I switched up my grip on the sword in my hand and shifted my feet into a defensive stance. The motion of the ship reminded me of my chariot back home, and I bent my knees and rode the next surge, letting the momentum propel me forward as a pirate covered in elaborate tattoos lunged at me. There was no art to his attack—no elegance, certainly—and he wouldn't have needed any if I had been just a slave. As it was, my blade slashed across his ribs, and I'd already moved on to fight the next man before he even realized he was wounded.

The rest of the fight was a blur until suddenly the Decurion had me by the arm and dragged me toward where the other captives were being hoisted over onto the escort ship. I saw Elka among them, as well as the dark-haired slave girl whose name I still didn't know. I threw one leg over the rail as the captain shouted orders to cast off the grappling lines.

We're safe, I thought.

Then I looked back over my shoulder and saw that Charon the slave master was still aboard the doomed galley. I watched as he struggled against the increasingly steep pitch of the deck, scrambling for a rope with one hand while hauling along a small wooden trunk with the other.

Mad, greed-eaten fool! I thought. *He'll die before he gives up a box full of meaningless possessions.* But my next thought was: *And what will happen to me if he does?*

Charon was my captor. The man who'd hammered an iron collar around my neck and the source of all my recent misery. But he was also the only thing that had come between Hafgan's brutality and me on that first ship. He'd rescued Elka and me from the Alesians. And as terrified as I was of my fate once I got to Rome with Charon, it was far more terrifying to think of getting there without him. I hesitated another moment. Then I swore angrily and, questioning my own sanity, threw my leg back over the rail. Barely holding on by my fingertips, I stretched out my other hand toward the struggling slave master.

"What do you think you're doing?" Elka shrieked.

I didn't have a good answer, so I ignored her and

concentrated on not falling into the sea. When Charon saw me reaching for him, his face split into a strange, wild grin, the whiteness of his teeth startling in the gloom.

"Here!" he shouted, heaving the trunk up toward me.

"Leave the damned trunk behind and climb!" I shouted back.

"No!" He shook his head wildly, panting. "I need this."

"You're mad!"

The galley shuddered beneath my slipping, sliding feet. But it was obvious that whatever was in that box, Charon wasn't going to leave it to sink. I grasped at the bronze handle of the trunk and pulled with all my might. The effort gave Charon just enough leverage to scramble up the rest of the way, and together we lifted the thing over onto the other ship, tumbling along behind it an instant before the two vessels drifted free of each other.

I shouted at him, furious. "How little you must think of human life that you'd risk your own—and mine!—for a box of trinkets."

"Thank you," Charon gasped, chest heaving from his exertion. "And trust me when I tell you, Fallon, this trunk holds the key to *both* our fortunes."

He sat down heavily on top of it and wrung the water from his sleeves. I could only stand there, blinking at him dumbly as the firelight from the sinking galley was extinguished in the cold black waves.

I couldn't, in that moment, remember ever having told him my name.

XI

I WAS ALIVE. I could feel the rising sun on my face and the salt breeze in my hair, and it was only because a Roman had saved my life. *A Roman soldier.* The very thought clattered around in my head like a loose spoke on a spinning chariot wheel.

The decks of the legion troop ship provided cramped quarters as we sailed east across the Mare Nostrum toward Rome. The smaller of the two vessels, it hadn't been equipped with anything like a proper complement of slave chains or manacles, and the hold was now full of cargo and soldiers. So we captives were essentially not quite so captive for the duration of the journey, free to wander the decks largely unfettered, so long as we didn't get in the way or make any moves to escape—which, in the middle of that vast sea, would have been suicide. And having made it as far as we had, none of us were really inclined to throw our lives away, even when we weren't sure of our fates.

When the second morning broke, clear and golden, the green ribbon of an island appeared on the horizon. The wind had died to a gentle breeze, and anyone who wasn't performing some sort of nautical duty was slumbering— the sailors down in the hold, the soldiers in tents pitched on the deck, the slaves curled in bundles of snores tucked in between stacks of cargo.

Only I was maddeningly wide-awake.

The island in the distance seemed to float upon the waves, unreachable and dreaming, like one of the Blessed Isles in the stories of my people. I don't know how long I stood there, leaning on my elbows, before I realized that there was someone else awake and up on deck: Decurion Varro.

He stood at the railing less than ten paces away from me, staring out over the same green-and-blue vista. I almost didn't recognize him without his helmet and armor. Dressed in a simple tunic under an undyed woolen cloak to stave off the morning chill, he could have been a merchant or a peasant, except for the corded muscles of his arms and the air of military swagger in his posture, even at rest. His hair was chestnut brown and cut legionnaire short, and his cheeks and chin were bare of even the hint of stubble. Shorn and shaved, he seemed at first glance almost vulnerable, and I was surprised to see that he was barely a man at all, only a few years older than me.

He's almost still a boy, I thought, then checked myself. It was a dangerous illusion. He wasn't a boy, and he certainly wasn't vulnerable.

I'd never seen anyone quite like him before. The young men of the tribes were a colorful lot, fond of rich patterns and hues in their clothing, and many of the men wore their hair long and adorned themselves with torcs and wrist cuffs wrought from gold and silver and bronze. There was a wildness to them—a passionate individuality—that made them dangerous and beautiful all at once.

The Decurion was their antithesis. Sharp-featured and starkly handsome, with every angle of him like a honed blade edge. A walking weapon, without adornment or decoration. When he turned to meet my gaze, I became acutely aware of my own appearance. Of the state of my tattered dress, the skirt scratchy and stiff with dirt. My hair hung in filthy ropes, and the dirt was so thick on my skin I was sure I looked like I'd been rolling in a swine wallow. Not so long ago—when I'd been the daughter of a king—men's eyes had lingered upon me at the Lughnasa feast. Gold at my throat, a circlet on my brow, a jeweled dagger on my hip. But that was another world, another life. And, more to the point, another girl.

But in the eyes of this arrogant young man, I thought, I certainly wasn't royalty. In his eyes, I was probably less than human—closer in dignity to a pack animal, no doubt. I turned to glare at the passing scenery, seething inwardly. But then the deck planks creaked, and I glanced back in surprise to find him standing right beside me.

After a long moment, he said, "Is there something wrong with my face?"

With a start, I realized I must have been staring.

His mouth twitched into a mocking grin. "Or are you just trying to decide whether or not to attack me again?"

"I . . . No."

I reached for something to say that wouldn't make me sound half-witted. He'd caught me off guard with the lightness of his tone. I'd expected nothing beyond disdain from someone like him. But then, I thought, perhaps this was his way of proving his superiority—by showing me he didn't need to act superior. I wasn't about to let that happen. I decided I would match his casual manner.

"No," I continued. "I'm just surprised to see you without your helmet on, that's all. I was beginning to think you slept in it."

"Only when I bed down in hostile territory." His eyes, clear, bright hazel, flicked at me. "Perhaps I'll wear it tonight."

"The bravest warriors of my tribe have been known to charge into battle naked," I said. "You seem to have things backward, legionnaire."

He laughed and said, "I'm a decurion—an *officer* in the legion. And *you* don't act like a slave."

"Don't I?"

"No. You don't." He reached out suddenly and took me by the wrist, lifting my hand so that he could examine my upturned palm. "But you have the hands of one." He ran a fingertip over the places where my skin had toughened like rawhide from hour upon hour of holding swords and spears and the reins of a chariot. "That is how you got those calluses, isn't it?"

I pulled my hand sharply from his grasp.

The Decurion shrugged and then pointed toward the horizon.

"That is the island of Corsica," he said.

I didn't know why he thought I cared. I squinted against the sunlight sparkling off the water, straining to make out details of the shoreline. I could see hills and, farther to the south, cliffs. Beaches. No houses or docks.

"Who lives there?" I asked finally, when it became clear that he wasn't leaving.

"No one, really." He grinned. "Sheep. Bees. A few ill-tempered natives too intractable even to be useful as slaves."

"It sounds ideal."

"For you, I imagine it would be."

I couldn't quite untangle the meaning of his words. Was he disdainful? Amused? I felt my temper flaring. Why was he even speaking to me? Was it just a perverse desire to remind me of my place, among the ill-tempered natives?

I smiled acidly as I tilted my head and regarded him. "And here you've only known me for such a short time to form such strong opinions of my character. How very wise and insightful you are, Decurion."

"I know nothing of your character," he said, deftly ignoring my sarcasm. "Not even if you have one. All I know about you—*really* know—is that you've got a bit of skill with a sword. Maybe even some training, judging from those calluses. But you drop your leading shoulder too much when you stand in a defensive posture." He adjusted the leather bracer on his forearm, tightening the buckle. "And your wrist is weak. You'll need to work on that."

"Because I'm sure Charon will sell me to a master eager to enhance my skill with a sword," I said bitterly. "You and I both know I'll be sold to a brothel or a fishmonger or a salt mine. But I thank you for that flight of fancy, Decurion. It'll sustain me in my miserable servitude, I'm sure."

He looked taken aback, but I didn't care if I'd offended him. I was about to be sold. And if it amused this pampered son of a senator to tease a slave in her last moments of relative freedom, well, it didn't amuse me.

It angered me.

"I did not think to offend you," he said slowly.

"Why would you even think of me at all?" I said. "What does it matter to you if you offend me or wound my pride? I'm a slave."

"So it seems."

"What do you mean by that?"

He paused before answering me. "What I think . . . is that appearance and reality don't always agree with one another. And I think Charon got more than he bargained for when he plucked you by the roots from your native soil." He pushed back from the rail. "But I also know that even a weed, cultivated with care, might eventually yield a wildflower."

"A wildflower in a garden is still considered a weed, Decurion," I said quietly, then turned to leave. I felt him watch me as I walked away.

• • •

Rome.

And I had thought Massilia was a place of wonder.

We sailed inland, up a wide river called Tiber from the bustling port of Ostia on the coast. As we approached the capital itself—the so-called beating heart of the civilized world—the river traffic increased until it was almost impossible to see the water for all the boats, and the galley captain steered toward what looked to be a private wharf on the west bank of the river just inside the city walls. Looking east, I could see hundreds and hundreds of thin gray plumes—smoke from multitudes of cooking fires— rising up into the still evening air like ghost souls. The sun reflected off the hills and many-tiered terraces of the city, clothing her in a soft, blushing glow. Temples and public buildings stood adorned with marble figures and sculpted scenes floating atop colonnades carved of white marble veined with gold and pink and silver.

From a distance, Rome was serenely majestic.

Close up, it was a starkly different story.

Once off the ship, we were herded through a tangle of narrow streets hemmed in by looming structures that blocked out the blaze of the sunset. I could feel eyes on us as our gang of fresh fodder for the auction block was shuffled along.

The voice of the city was a cacophony of noise pressing against my skin. Men whistled and called out obscenities as we passed. Even with my coarse trader-learned Latin— in some cases, especially with it—I could understand what they said, and it made my flesh crawl. There were women too out in the streets. Some carted baskets and bales of goods and went about their business. Some stood in doorways with eyes and lips painted garishly, wearing filmy garments that did less than nothing to conceal their skinny bodies. One greasy-looking creature wore nothing at all and instead sat chanting before a cobbled-together altar, her limbs draped in writhing, brightly patterned snakes.

I shuddered and stumbled quickly past her, now anxious to catch up with Charon's personal wagon, which rumbled along at the head of our ragged train. It turned sharply and disappeared beneath an archway. The slavers prodded us to follow. Once we were through the gate and standing huddled in a sandy courtyard, the madness of the city streets receded to a dull throb, the noise kept at bay by high, thick walls, plastered smooth and topped with jagged points of broken stone. A pair of iron-bound oak doors swung shut behind us, and the sudden, complete silence was deafening. And terrifying.

Then the slavers were among us, dividing us up and leading us off in groups of men, older women, boys, girls . . . and then Elka and me. The two of us were the last to be led away, through a stone archway and down a long colonnade. I wondered if we were being singled out. Perhaps Charon had changed his mind and decided to punish us for our ruinous escape attempt.

To my relief, the place we were led wasn't a cell or a dungeon. It was a bath. A proper Roman bath, mist-wreathed, sweet-scented, and blissfully warm. I'd heard stories of them back home from the traders, and I'd tried without success to imagine what one would be like. I'd only ever bathed in the River Dwr or in the big copper tub that stood in the corner of my little house, filled with water heated in a cauldron over the hearth fire.

I gazed around, openmouthed.

Elegant fluted columns held up a vaulted ceiling painted with scenes of gods and goddess and strange creatures emerging from waves, horses with fish tails and white bulls wreathed in sea foam. In the center of the ceiling were set panes of colored glass that cast blue and green wavering light onto the surface of the still, steaming pools below.

Elka let out her breath in a low whistle.

I had to grudgingly admit to myself that I was glad the Varini girl was still with me. In a way, she almost reminded me of my sister. Sharp-tongued and haughty, but good in a fight, at least.

As we stood there, a matronly woman strode briskly in through one of the archways, followed by a bent-backed old crone swathed in a drab black robe. The first woman introduced herself as Maia and ordered Elka to unwind the braids that bound her long pale hair close to her head. Then she told us to disrobe. With fingers grown weak and clumsy, I plucked at the knotted lacings of my ragged tunic and handed it over. Maia took the garment and held it with two fingers, her nose twitching. When she took Elka's, her nostrils actually pinched shut in protest.

She handed them off at arm's length to the crone, who gagged and rolled her rheumy eyes. "We'll just be burning these, then," she grumbled as she shuffled out a side archway.

"Right." Maia clapped her hands. "Into the plunge with you both."

She pointed at the nearest pool and then at the tray of sea sponges and cakes of lye soap and pumice stones that sat off to one side. When she turned to see Elka and me both staring at her, unsure of what to do, her mouth quirked into a wry grin.

"Couldn't sell you to pig farmers in your present state," she said. "Now. Into the cold pool and scrub off as much of that travel muck as you can. Gruoch will be back to assist you once she's disposed of those rags. You've probably both got fleas, so use the soap—it's got rosemary and lavender to kill the little buggers—and lather it through your hair. Thoroughly. More than once. And don't dawdle."

I couldn't have dawdled if I'd wanted to. The water was almost too cold to step foot in, let alone sink to my chin. But every time Elka or I tried to leave the pool before we'd sufficiently lathered and rinsed our hair, Gruoch, the old crone, would bring a willow switch down on our knuckles or shoulders in a painful, precisely aimed slap. I'd never heard Elka curse so colorfully, not even in Alesia.

Finally, once we'd achieved a level of cleanliness that Gruoch determined entitled us to leave the *frigidarium*—for that, I learned, was what that torturous ice bath was called—we ran, scurrying and hugging ourselves, arms and legs covered in gooseflesh—to a different pool called the *tepidarium*. We flopped like landed fish down the shallow submerged steps, splashing and sinking into the warm, scented waters beneath the fantastical glass and mural ceiling.

And it was the closest I'd been to happiness in months. *The closest since Mael.*

I closed my eyes and sank into the soothing warmth, feeling my muscles melt like they had when he'd kissed me that morning in the vale. I'd almost forgotten what that had felt like. The steam rose off the surface of the water until I couldn't see old Gruoch where she sat on her bench. Even Elka, drifting motionless on the other side of the pool, was just a shadow. I could have stayed there forever, my hair floating out all around me, wrapped in mist and dreaming and the scent of flowers.

I barely felt the tears sliding down my cheeks.

XII

"DON'T TART THEM UP *TOO* MUCH." Maia briskly ordered her women about the room she called the "tiring room," where Elka and I were being prepared for sale. "But for Juno's sake, do something about the sunburn and freckles. Put this one in something green, nothing sheer, but make it short. She's got the legs. And leave her shoulders and arms bare. The blonde one wears braids well, but do something with that forehead of hers. It's far too high. And give her one of the leather cinchers. She's got a good small waist for all she's big-boned. No *pallas* for either of them. We can't have them too covered up. The auction is scheduled for the ninth hour this morning, and Charon wants them ready well before then."

She ordered us both to sit on the stools and forbade us to move, speak, or fidget.

One elegant woman with hair dyed an unnatural shade of deep purplish red attacked my snarled locks, brandishing brushes and hairpins made of polished bone and silver.

I didn't twitch a muscle for fear of losing an eye to the flurry of implements. She brushed out my long brown hair until it gleamed. But where I would have simply dressed it off my face with combs or a circlet, this woman began to twist and fasten, pulling strands up from the sides of my head and weaving them together at the crown. Her fingers moved in a swift, intricate pattern. I could feel my hair piling up on my head, bit by bit, and felt dizzy from the scent of perfumes.

When I muttered something under my breath questioning the necessity of such effort to sell a few slaves, the woman laughed quietly and leaned down to whisper in my ear: "What do you think *we* are, my dear?"

My confusion must have shown on my face.

"Let me give you a piece of advice," she murmured. "Rome only exists because of slaves. That's how it functions. We are its muscles, its brains, and most of all its secrets. You are now a part of that world. You are what you are, no matter what you once were. But there is power in such a position. Understand that. And learn to use it."

Her breath in my ear was warm, but her words sent a chill down my spine. I hadn't even guessed that this refined woman was a slave. But of course she was. Trained, specialized, highly skilled, but not free.

Power? I wondered. I'd never felt so powerless in my life. I wasn't even allowed to scratch an itch.

I stayed still and silent while another woman took over, powdering and painting my face so that I resembled one of the figures adorning the walls of the room. After my hair and my face were done, a plump, smiling dressing woman prodded me over to stand near the shelves. She began pulling down basket after basket of carefully folded garments in an array of colors I'd never even seen before.

She bustled back and forth between me and Elka, who now looked entirely unlike the girl I'd come to know. Her fine, pale hair was back in braids, but far more elaborately woven this time. And she wore a wide band of silver around her forehead that narrowed to a peak between her brows. It made her look both regal and predatory at the same time— like a hunting owl—and it emphasized her ice-blue eyes, which were lined with dark kohl.

"Slaves are usually sold naked in the marketplace, you know," Maia said. "But Charon plays a different game than the average trader. A smarter one. He instructs us to make you appear not as you are but as you could be. He sells *potential* to the good people of the Eternal City. Prestige. Fantasy. And they pay him handsomely for it."

Potential for what? I felt as though I might be sick.

The dressing woman draped Elka in shades of blue and mauve, and then she rummaged around in a basket and brought out a length of shimmering green-gold fabric. The woman held it up in front of me and almost chirped in delight.

"Oh! This makes your eyes shine," she said. "Perfect! Arms up now!"

She slid the sheath of material down over my torso, pinning it at my shoulders and gathering it in flattering drapes at my waist and hips. Then she ruched up the hem to show as much of my legs as possible. She clad my feet in laced-up boots and slid thick bronze bracelets onto my wrists. Lastly, she fastened a belt of polished bronze discs set with purple stones around my waist. The cosmetics woman dusted some kind of powder over my arms and legs, and then finally I was led in front of a long, polished bronze mirror.

I gasped at the sight.

"It's all in the presentation, dear," the dressing woman trilled with a grin.

A creature made of living molten gold stared back at me.

The dust on my limbs and face shimmered in the sunlight that spilled in from the courtyard, making it seem as though I was lit from within. My hair was twisted into dozens of plaits that the dresser had woven into a subtle crest that lifted high over the crown of my head and flowed down my back. The effect somehow reminded me of the crested plume on a Roman warrior's helm.

Then Elka stepped up beside me. Our transformation from two filthy castoffs was staggering.

She was carved out of glittering ice.

And I was golden, forged in flames.

The only discordant thing about our reflection was the dull iron rings we still wore around our necks. I reached up and traced a fingertip over the rough surface. The skin beneath was rough too. Calloused. Even if the collar were removed, I would bear the marks for a long time to come.

"It's a pity, that," the woman who'd fashioned my hair said, leaning against the mirror and regarding the collar. "It clashes with the rest of the look."

I glanced back at her, noticing that her long neck was smooth and white and bore no collar. "You don't wear one."

"*I* would never try to escape." She smiled wryly.

"You think I would?"

She snorted softly. "Given even the hint of a chance. I can see it in your eyes like it was written there in fire. I, on the other hand, have no need. I've made my own freedom, and that is something I'll never give up. Especially not for some hollow ideal of that word."

Hollow? I thought. How could she even think such a thing? Freedom to my people was like air or water or love. It was essential to life. What kind of freedom could she possibly have made for herself without liberty? I wondered how I would survive in this new world I'd found myself in. I wondered if I'd ever understand it. I swore to myself that I would never be like her, so imprisoned that I didn't even need a collar to obey my masters.

I curled my fingers into fists at my sides to keep from clawing at the iron circle. She might have been content to live life as a slave, but I was the daughter of a king. And I *would* find that warrior girl inside me again and find a way to set her free.

"We could try to find a scarf to cover it."

"No!" I shook my head. "No. I would prefer whoever buys me to know exactly what it is they're getting."

I saw a glimmer of respect in the woman's gaze as she reached out and patted a stray lock of my hair into place. "Then you're ready to go."

XIII

THE FORUM. The marketplace of Rome. Except it wasn't so much a place as it was a violent assault on the senses. The crush of people and animals was terrifying—so loud, I thought my eardrums would burst—and that was while I was still hidden away in one of the covered wagons Charon transported his slaves to market in.

The men and women I'd traveled with for weeks, while not all given the same kind of elaborately costumed treatment as Elka and me, had at least been polished up to some degree. One or two of the handsomer lads wore only loincloths with wide, ornamented belts, and they had been oiled so that their muscles gleamed. I saw that the girl with dark hair who had given me her slippers was wrapped in a sheath so sheer that the sunlight shone through it. I was happy to see that she also had new leather sandals that laced up her calves.

As the wagon rattled along, the wheels clattering over

the paving stones of Roman streets, I could hear the wagon drivers shouting at the buyers and sellers crowding the Forum to make way. The tumbled strains of many different kinds of music floated over the general chaos—bells and drums and flutes, voices raised in song—and, again, I was torn between fear and curiosity. I peeked out between the curtains and saw what awaited us.

Market day.

The wagon rumbled to a stop, and I could see that a raised wooden stage and temporary wooden seating had been built along one side of the plaza. The stands were already full to capacity. In the back row, people were shaded from the morning sun beneath colorful fabric awnings suspended on long poles held by slaves. The whole scene boasted a kind of festival air that reminded me of Lughnasa and made me long for home. I could feel waves of anticipation surging off the crowd, as if they waited for a troupe of performers.

Gruoch shouldered me aside so she could also peer through the gap in the curtains. She made a little noise in the back of her throat and muttered, "Huh. The Collector is here. That should make for an interesting bit of bidding."

"The Collector?" I asked. "What's that?"

"Not what. Who. His name is Pontius Aquila." She pointed with one gnarled finger at a man with sharp features and silvering hair seated in the second row of the stands. He sat beneath a fringed shade, tended to by an oiled, muscular slave. Aquila's robes were also fringed and banded with a purple stripe. He glared above the heads of the audience as if their presence were not worth acknowledging.

"He's a politician with a fancy title, the so-called Tribune of the Plebs, but he's as base as they come." She snorted. "No manners, and rich off other people's money. But he knows a valuable piece of flesh when he sees it. And he'll stop at nothing to add to his collection once he does. I've seen his bullyboys start brawls at the auctions if he's outbid."

I only understood half of what she was saying and couldn't tell if it was truth or just gossip. But my stomach turned queasy at the thought of a man like that haggling over the price of my life. Not that there was anything I could do about it in that moment. As the audience settled themselves, a portly man wearing an outlandish wig of bright orange curls and a voluminous robe stepped forward onto the stage.

"Citizens!" he boomed. "Gather and feast your eyes on this banquet of flesh and fancies! Premium lads and lasses from all corners of the known world."

He prattled on and on, his speech flowery and rapid-fire as he luridly described his wares—us. Eventually, I tuned out the auctioneer and concentrated instead on watching the parade of slaves and the crowd of wealthy Romans who sought to buy them.

The orange-wigged auctioneer skillfully badgered and cajoled the crowd into bidding higher and higher sums for each new slave as Charon himself wandered among the patrons, chatting amiably, extolling the virtues of his wares alongside the whistles and bids from buyers and cat-calls from onlookers standing at the fringes of the crowd. If Gruoch's satisfied muttering was to be believed, they all sold for more than the asking price. Charon had clearly seen something in each one of us that I hadn't.

I wondered what he'd seen in me.

The dark-haired girl—the one who'd told me she'd been a slave all her life and preferred it to a life of uncertainty—surprised me most of all. She'd been kind to me, and I don't know why, but that made it a shock to discover that, according to the auctioneer's leering patter, she'd actually been raised in a preeminent whorehouse in western Gaul.

The Cantii, like most of the tribes of Prydain, had always kept slaves. We bought and sold them the same way as we did our cattle. Slaves had meant swept floors and lit fires and clean water carried in heavy clay pots. I was ashamed to admit I had never given them much thought. They just . . . were. I had been so very blind. And stupid. And now I was learning what it was like to have someone else decide my fate.

I'd been right that night in ruined Alesia. The dark-haired girl was stronger than me. I watched as she took control of her own auction, posing for the crowd and driving the bids ever higher. After fetching a very good sum, she was led away to a cart where an ample-bosomed brothel owner waited, dripping with gold. She held her head high as she went.

The crowd whistled and cheered.

But the show wasn't quite over yet. The ranks of Charon's stock were thinning, and there weren't more than a handful of us left. Then suddenly Gruoch was prodding me in the ribs with her willow switch, and Elka had gone pale as frost on a winter pond. They were sending us out together.

But first, Hafgan stepped forward and, with grim amusement glinting in his mismatched eyes, knelt down in front of us. Before we knew what he was doing, he had clamped a short chain around our ankles, tethering us together just like before. Elka and I exchanged a confused glance. None of the others had been treated like this so far.

With a grunt, Hafgan pushed us out onto the stage. Once we'd shuffled out onto the platform, I was paralyzed with fear. I couldn't see faces. I could only see shapes. Colors. The sheen of the gold dust that painted my limbs sparked fire at the edges of my vision, and I thought I might pass out.

"Behold these marvelous daughters of Minerva!" the auctioneer bellowed.

I closed my eyes and waited for the bids to start coming in, wondering bitterly what paltry sum I would fetch. I was no healer nor body servant. I had no exceptional skills in this strange world.

The auctioneer didn't start the bid-asking. Not immediately. And when I opened my eyes, I realized that the crowd was staring at us, wide-eyed and silent. In the bright sunlight, Elka and I glittered and sparkled, dazzling. I saw the brothel mistress lean forward, a gleam of interest in her sharp gaze.

She wasn't the only one. Pontius Aquila, the man Gruoch had pointed out to me as "the Collector," shifted in his seat, one gold-ringed fist clenched tight and resting on his thigh. He focused his attention wholly on Elka and me, and where the Collector's gaze fell upon me, it seemed to burn my skin with its intensity. I flinched and looked away as Charon stalked onstage, draped in a richly bordered tunic dyed a deep sapphire blue. In his hands, he carried two short broadbladed swords. Charon turned and dropped the swords on the stage between us, the blades ringing like bells.

Elka and I stared in confusion at the swords. Were we to fight each other?

And then the two brigands from Alesia climbed the steps up to the stage.

Oh goddess . . .

One carried a wicked-looking pike, the other—his thigh still bandaged from where I had wounded him that night—bore a long sword. He radiated a long-simmering anger, and I knew just by looking at him that the Alesian meant to settle a score on that stage.

"These men," Charon cried, "survived the sieges of the mighty Caesar only to be brought low by two fierce, beguiling young women—Furies who appeared in their midst one dark night, bound by chains, bearing swords, fighting like she-wolves."

The slave master spoke in a musical cadence, weaving a tale of a night in the wilderness, atop a hill, in a ruined Gaulish town—a gripping story of runaway slaves, of brigands and danger, and now . . . a chance for revenge.

"He's laying it on a bit thick," Elka muttered.

"Here! Now!" the slave master boasted with a flourish. "For the enrichment and entertainment of you fine citizens of Rome, I present the chance for these noble barbarians to seek redemption! To decide their ultimate destiny in mortal combat with these two deadly beauties, as skilled with swords as the Amazons of legend! Aaaand," Charon drawled, drawing out the tension of the moment, "if either of these Gauls can defeat these girls—daughters of the goddess Minerva herself, I *swear*, and on sale exclusively as a pair today—I will grant them their freedom."

I gaped at him. Why was he doing this?

But as I looked around at the gathered crowd, buzzing with excitement—some of them even trading wagers—I began to understand. I'd heard that male slaves who could fight were often bought and trained for combat in arenas. For the crass entertainment of the mob, which was mad for blood sport. I'd always considered the notion repugnant. And I knew what contempt the legions held for the women warriors of my tribe, so it had never even occurred to me that the Roman masses would consider my sex capable of that kind of fighting.

But it was clear to me that Charon saw that as my fate. He had all along.

Not a brothel. Not a salt mine. An arena.

There are your exceptional skills for you.

The Alesian accepted Charon's challenge with gusto. With a roar, he stepped forward and swung his sword, the blade whistling past my ear.

It's a good thing I injured his leading leg that night, I thought as I dove frantically out of the way. He staggered between Elka and me, stumbling over the chain that leashed our ankles and pulling my feet out from under me. I scrambled on hands and knees to get to the swords Charon had left on the stage. My fingers closed on a hilt, and I clambered to my feet as the second brigand—far more wary and perhaps less vengeful than his partner—circled around us.

"Fallon!" Elka's voice held a warning note.

"I see him," I said.

Together, we shifted away as the man approached. He was lanky, with long, ropey arms, and his blade whistled as he swiped it menacingly side to side through the air in front of him.

"This one's got reach on me," I said in a low, tense voice to Elka.

"Not on me," she said. "But I think he learned that lesson in Alesia. He won't make the same mistake as his friends did."

Elka stepped out to try and goad him into an attack. Instead, he made as if to lunge toward my blade but, at the last moment, spun and hewed at Elka's weapon in a wide arc that sheared a handsbreadth of iron off the end of her cheap sword.

Elka drew back sharply, her weapon suddenly useless, and the chain pulled taut between us. My leg went out from under me again and I fell to the ground, only to see the first man—the one I'd wounded in Alesia—looming above me. He raised his pike high over his head in both hands and let out a cry of vengeance. I gasped the Morrigan's name—the only supplication I had time for—and threw my arms up in front of me, knowing the blow would cleave through me like an axe through kindling.

It never came.

Instead, with a powerful thrust of her long legs, Elka had launched herself toward us, howling with battle madness. The point of her sword blade disappeared up under the man's helmet chinstrap. There was a frozen moment of silence from the crowd. And then the man's chest bloomed suddenly with a dark crimson that flooded down over his painted skin. Through the grate of his helmet, I saw his eyes roll back in his head, and he dropped the pike behind him. As he sank to the ground, grasping weakly at the sword lodged in his throat, Elka freed her blade with a grunt. I scrambled to my feet, kicking away his body.

Standing shoulder to shoulder with Elka, I could feel her shaking violently. For all her talk of war, I wondered if that was the first man she'd ever killed. I wondered if I'd survive long enough to find out.

With that kill, the watching crowd realized this wasn't just a show designed to inflate auction prices, and they howled for more blood. The brigand's, Elka's, mine, it didn't matter. It made my stomach turn. This was what the Romans thought of as entertainment?

And they called *us* barbarians.

Charon came forward and held a long painted stick horizontal between us and the remaining Alesian, keeping us separated as two other men leaped up onto the stage to drag the body off to a waiting cart.

Elka watched them go, her face pale beneath the makeup.

In the lull in the action, I looked out at the crowd and saw the sharp-featured Pontius Aquila flick his card up, as if to do no more than whisk away a fly. The first bid was his, the Collector's. As one of Charon's men ran forward with a bucket of sawdust to spread on the bloodstained stage, a flurry of cards fluttered up into the air, held up by patrons scattered throughout the stands. Each one was followed by another card flick from Aquila to outbid them, and the orange-wigged auctioneer called them out rapidly, gleefully pitting the bidders against each other.

My mouth went dry at the thought of the Collector owning me—or Elka, for that matter—and I scanned the other bidders in the crowd, torn between feeling helpless and hopeful. It was then that a flash of crimson caught my eye, and I recognized the figure of Decurion Varro moving through the crowd. He was carrying what looked like Charon's trunk—the one I'd helped the slave master rescue from the sinking galley—up to the back row of the stands. I saw him stoop to speak to one of the patrons sitting beneath the shade of a yellow-and-white awning. After a moment, the Decurion left the box with the patron and climbed back down the wooden steps to disappear back into the crowd without so much as a glance toward the stage.

Charon lifted the wooden staff out of the way and

stepped back, indicating with a flourish that the fighting should continue. Bolstered by the roaring crowd, the betting, and the bidding, the remaining Alesian snarled in rage and charged at me. Suddenly, time seemed to stop. The sound of all those voices clamoring for violence faded to nothing. It was as if I were a young girl again, fighting my first real match with an iron blade instead of wood. For an instant, it seemed I stood not in the blinding-bright sunshine of Rome but in the cool green light of the fields outside Durovernum, sparring with Sorcha while Mael cheered me on.

The Alesian tried a feint and shifted his aim midstrike, but my training and instincts—all the memories stored in my muscles and blood—took over. My blade swung up at a sharp angle and met my attacker's weapon, screeching up its length in a flash of sparks. My momentum carried me a step further, and I brought the sword back around and down in a vicious slash across the man's extended forearm. Blood spurted, crimson and sparkling in the sunlight, and with a cry of pain he drew back, clutching his wrist.

My sister had laid the foundations upon which I'd built my skills as a warrior. And even if I'd never been made a member of the royal war band like she had, I'd be damned if I'd dishonor Sorcha's memory in front of that crowd of braying Romans.

A crouch, lunge, and another slash, and the Alesian was down on one knee with a gaping wound in the meat of his calf muscle. The tip of my blade was bright with blood, and I was almost surprised at how easy it had been.

But then he heaved himself back to standing and, heedless of the injury, lashed out with a swift kick to my ribs. I let out a grunt of pain and collapsed on all fours, gasping for breath. A second kick from him flipped me over onto my back. Through watering eyes, I could see blood dripping from his leg as he drew back his foot to deliver another kick.

I braced for the blow.

"Stop!"

The command, shouted in a husky female voice, rang through the air. Almost before the sound of it had died on the still air, Charon's men leaped up on the stage to seize the snarling Alesian. They hauled him away from me as they relieved him of his weapon. I rose to my feet and stood swaying as a tall woman, dressed in a sleeveless leather tunic and close-fitting trousers, stalked down the stairs from the back row of the stands.

"Ah, Thalestris." Charon turned slowly toward the trousered woman. "Always a pleasure to see you here at our humble displays of talent. Does your *Lanista* wish to make a bid that will curtail the action so soon?" He gestured to the stands, where another woman sat, a richly embroidered shawl draped over her head so that her face was in shadow. "But things were just getting entertaining."

"If by 'things' you mean these girls, we would prefer that they remain capable of entertaining," the woman called Thalestris said in stridently accented Latin. "My mistress, the Lady Achillea, is willing to offer a generous bid well over and above what you have already received in order to end these proceedings, before your wares become damaged beyond all salability."

Charon frowned. "Your bid would have to be—"

"Twenty thousand denarii."

Charon's jaw drifted open a bit. "Twent—"

"Each."

"No!" A voice of pure outrage shouted from the audience.

Charon turned toward the disruption and cupped his ear. "Do we have a higher bid? Ah, the noble Tribune of the Plebs."

The muscles in Pontius's throat jumped as he swallowed, and I could see him grinding his teeth even from the stage. "I'll pay twenty-five for just the one in green," he said. "You can charge whatever you want for the other."

A chill like ice water ran through my veins. Could one slave owner really prove better than the other? I didn't know. All I knew was that I did not want to go with Pontius Aquila. No matter how much he wanted to pay for me.

Charon graciously inclined his head, deep regret lining his face. "So sorry, noble Tribune. The girls are to be sold as a pair. The terms of sale, as you know, are set before the bidding begins. To change the rules now would be unfair."

Pontius Aquila's mouth disappeared in a hard line, and his face flushed to almost purple. Beside him, his bare-chested slave hunched his shoulders and glowered.

"Do you wish to improve upon the Lady Achillea's bid for both girls?" Charon asked.

Aquila clenched his fists and threw his bid card to the ground. He had been outbid.

Charon nodded at his auctioneer. "Sold." His dark eyes shone with triumph.

Thalestris waved dismissively at the Alesian as Charon turned back to her. "You can keep your Gaulish thug," she said. "The Lady Achillea, of course, has no use for him. Perhaps Tribune Aquila would appreciate his rugged charms."

The onlookers cheered and jeered as Pontius Aquila stood, his gaze full of a startling, palpable wrath. Without another word, he turned and stalked down the steps of the stands, disappearing into the Forum crowd. I felt relief at watching him go.

"Perhaps not," Charon said mildly as the crowd roared with amusement in the wake of the man's departure. Then he turned back to Thalestris with a grin. "In that case, I accept your gracious offer on behalf of the Lady Achillea for these two spirited lasses and grant this fine Alesian fellow his full freedom," he said.

That delighted the crowd even more. The Alesian seemed overwhelmed as Charon waved for him to depart the stage so that the smith could remove his collar. Even I had to admit that the gesture was surprisingly decent. Doubtless it was coldly calculated and purely for effect, but still.

"My paymaster will settle the account and arrange for payment." Thalestris beckoned forward a broad-shouldered bald man. Then, in a low voice meant only for Charon's ears, she said, "You have my compliments, Charon. That was cleverly done. But be careful, slave master. Achillea doesn't like being played. And neither does *he*."

I wondered fleetingly who "he" was, but then Thalestris spun on her heel and stalked off after the Lady Achillea, who was already making a swift exit from the marketplace, along with a train of attendants. Elka and I stood there, blinking in astonishment.

Who had we just been sold to?

Charon concluded the auction and, as the crowd began to disperse, sauntered over to us. He put a hand on each of our shoulders. "I knew I could count on you both to fetch a princely sum," he said, his white teeth showing through his neatly trimmed beard. "The most I've ever made in a single sale. Thanks be to Artemis, I listen to my hunches!"

"And who, exactly, did your hunch say would pay so much for a pair of girl barbarians?" Elka asked.

"Congratulations, ladies." His smile faded, and his next words were like a dagger of ice down my spine. "You are now the property of the Ludus Achillea, foremost training academy for female gladiators in all of the Republic. Owned and operated by the honorable consul of Rome, Gaius Julius Caesar himself."

XIV

"IT'S NOT A BROTHEL."

"I know. I heard. I just . . ."

"You *like* to fight."

"Yes, but . . ."

"Well then, what's the problem?"

"It's not honorable!"

"Oh." Elka snorted. "Is that all?"

"All?" I gaped at her. "It's everything!"

She rolled her eyes and settled back on the padded bench of the cart we rode in. "You're a slave, little fox," she said. "You don't have honor anymore."

But she was wrong. I knew there had to be more to honor than just one's station in life. That was what Sorcha had taught me: that actions meant more than accolades. That honor was something worth fighting for—and dying for—no matter what house you were born into. Still, I wondered. After all, had I ever considered any of the slaves of my father's house honorable?

I turned away from Elka and stared sullenly instead at the shaved, oiled head of the paymaster who sat in the front of the cart, driving the black horses with a sure hand.

"Remember," Elka continued, "our life now is simple: Fight, kill, die, and look good doing it."

I shook my head. "Did Charon really say that?"

Elka nodded. "Right after he said we'd been sold to a murdering tyrant. Yes."

Julius Caesar. The tyrant.

I could barely believe I'd been sold to the man who'd invaded my homeland. This, I thought, was injustice on a mythic scale. All I'd ever wanted was to fight—but *against* the man who'd dishonored my father and killed my sister. Not *for* him! And not in an arena. Never that.

The Morrigan was having a great laugh at my expense.

"I don't know what you're complaining about." Elka sighed. "Like I said, there are worse fates for a slave than ending up a gladiatrix."

I gave her a sidelong glance. "It's blood sport, plain and simple. Something to amuse the mob—you saw how they reacted to our fight with the Alesians. You *heard* them. It was disgusting!"

"I heard they feed you well at a ludus."

I opened my mouth to protest that I didn't care one bit about the victuals, but then my stomach growled so loudly that Elka heard it over the rumbling of the carriage wheels and burst out laughing. Even with my troubled heart, it was hard to stay indignant in the face of her mirth. And, I grudgingly admitted, for the first time in months we were traveling in a carriage that had no bars. There was no chain around my ankle. I was clothed in something other than rags.

But I was still a slave.

I reached up to ease the press of the iron ring resting on my collarbones. Sometimes I forgot it was there. And sometimes it seemed to weigh heavier than gold. But I also knew that Elka was right. I was a slave, but before long I'd be a slave with a sword and a full belly. And, I vowed, soon I would gain the strength to free myself.

As we followed the westering sun into the countryside, Elka turned contemplative. "I wonder who will have to work harder to earn their keep," she mused. "You and me, or Kassandra."

"Who?"

She rolled her eyes. "Are you joking? You took the girl's shoes and you never bothered to learn her name?"

The image of the dark-haired girl, striking an evocative pose for the appreciative crowd, flashed in my mind. "How do you know that's her name?"

"You're hopeless." Elka shook her head at me. "I asked her."

Our wagon crested the rise of a long hill, and Elka whistled low.

We'd been traveling north, and the land stretched out on both sides in rolling waves dotted with stands of tall trees. The road we were on—the Via Clodia—was wide, arrow-straight, and like no road I'd ever traveled upon.

Our wagon flew over large, flat paving stones, the ride smoother than anything I'd known in my war chariot back home. In the distance, the graceful stone arches of an aqueduct traversed the land like some great stone serpent. Even I had to admit that the accomplishments of Roman ingenuity were marvels to behold.

Now, directly ahead of us, a broad expanse of water stretched into the distance, reflecting the purple and scarlet of the setting sun—Lake Sabatinus, as I soon learned it was called. A broad path lined with tall cypress trees led to a sprawling stone compound nestled on the shores of the lake. We had reached the Ludus Achillea.

The tiled roofs of the buildings were elegant and ordered, the main villa surrounded by a profusion of outbuildings—stables and kitchens and, I surmised, some sort of barracks for the different ranks of "students." It looked a little like a palace, but I felt my stomach clench at the sight of the high, smooth wall that surrounded the ludus, topped with iron spikes. This place was no palace. It was a well-appointed cage.

As the curtained carriage in front of ours, transporting the Lady Achillea and her attendants, rumbled through the gate, Thalestris leapt out while it was still in motion. She walked back to the carriage Elka and I rode in and signaled for the driver to halt so she could swing herself up to stand between us. Every move she made was precise and purposeful. Feet braced wide, she rested one hand on her hip as if she wore a sword there. I suspected that most of the time, she did.

"Welcome to the Ludus Achillea," she said, her eyes

flicking back and forth between us, appraising, calculating. "Your new home until such time as you earn your freedom or you die. The latter is more likely. But work hard, work well, and you will be treated fairly and with dignity."

Fairness and dignity? I seriously doubted that.

"Wherever you have come from," she continued, "whatever you did, whoever you were . . . forget. Kill your past and bury it deep in the earth of your heart. It will not help you here. It will only shackle you. This place is a sisterhood. These girls are your family. The Lady Achillea, the lanista of this place, is your goddess. And *I* am your new mother."

"Couldn't be any worse than my old mother," Elka shrugged.

Thalestris shot her a look that plainly said, *Don't be too sure of that.*

"There will be an oath swearing at the rising of the next full moon," she said, "for you and for some of the other girls who are recently arrived. It is a sacred time. And this is a sacred vocation. Do not ever dare to think otherwise. Be proud, and be thankful to the Fates that they have brought you here to become a gladiatrix. Bring honor on this house. Bring honor on yourselves. Win. Be valiant. Now go."

Honor.

I'd always thought I'd known what that word meant to me. That night, I took my first steps toward learning what the word "honor" meant to a gladiatrix. And I took those steps in a graveyard.

It had been well after the supper hour when we'd

arrived, so Thalestris escorted us to the kitchens to gather plates of leftovers from the evening's meal that we could eat in our quarters. Coming and going, we saw only a few of the other girls in residence. We spoke to none of them. I was glad of it, mostly because I was beginning to feel a bit ridiculous in the wilted, travel-stained remains of my auction costume. They'd stripped us of most of the finer accessories before loading us into the wagon, leaving me with not much more than the tunica and boots. Elka, for her part, didn't really seem to care—she was far too concerned with balancing the towering heap of meat and cheese and fruit she carried as she walked to really even notice.

Our quarters were small, narrow rooms, barely big enough to hold the straw pallet that served as a bed. There was an open, empty trunk at the foot of it for personal belongings. I had none. No torc, no sword, not even a decent set of breeches or a good warm shift made of well-spun wool . . . nothing that identified me as Fallon. No tokens or mementos of the life I'd led. The loss of my sister's blade felt like I was missing a limb. And the only thing I had left of Mael was the memory of his kiss . . . and the look on his face in the moment he died.

I kicked the lid of the trunk shut and turned my back on it.

A single candle on the high windowsill cast dancing shadows on the walls as I finished eating. I was sitting on my bed, too exhausted to even undress and lie down for sleep, when there was a knock on my door. It swung open before I could respond, and I looked over to see a tall, slender girl standing in the doorway. She had short, dense hair cropped close to her skull and dark skin. I tried not to stare, but I'd never seen anyone like her before. She ignored my rudeness and simply gestured to the candle.

"Get your boots," she said. "Bring the light. Come with me."

Outside in the hallway, I saw that the girl carried a cloak.

"I am Ajani," she said, holding it out to me. "Put this on."

I took it with a grateful nod, for the night air held a damp chill. "Fallon," I said and slipped the heavy wool over my shoulders, pulling the hood up around my face. "Where are we going?"

The whites of her eyes shone in the darkness. "To say goodbye."

She turned on silent feet and padded down the corridor. I followed, the candle flame sputtering in the breezes that slipped between the pillars. Ajani led me out into the courtyard at the heart of the ludus compound, where a gathering of girls and women stood in a cluster, some of them holding torches, all of them cloaked and hooded. If Elka was there, I couldn't tell which of the cloaked figures she was. No one spoke. At the center of the crowd there was a funeral bier draped in a gauzy white cloth.

And from the shape of it, a body beneath the shroud.

Six figures stepped apart from the crowd and approached the bier, lifting it up onto their shoulders as if it weighed no more than a sack of feathers. A procession formed behind them as they moved with stately dignity toward the gates of the ludus—which was, on that night, open to the world. I fell in behind Ajani and followed. Once outside the ludus compound, the sky seemed enormous to me. Growing up, I'd been so used to being hemmed in by the trees and forests of the Island of the Mighty. But now I felt small beneath the vast canopy of stars.

Mouse small . . . too small to notice . . .

I slowed my pace, dropping back in the ranks of the gladiatrices until I trailed behind them. If I could lose myself in a hollow and wait until they were far enough away, perhaps I could make a dash for freedom.

And the collar around your neck? How will you outrun that?

The cold metal twinged against my skin.

I might be just a wee mouse outside those walls, but the slave iron marked me as easy prey for an eagle. Runaway slaves were criminals, punished by flogging or branding—or outright death. I was in the middle of a foreign land, friendless and forsaken. Running—at least, running without a plan—would only get me killed. Somewhere over one of the distant hills, a wolf howled, and I quickened my pace to catch up with the others.

We walked for a while in silence. In the distance, I could see the dark shapes of other villas, and everywhere we passed, there were lamps burning brightly in all the windows. I was reminded of all the sleepless Samhain Nights I'd spent growing up in Durovernum, nights when the shades of the unquiet dead walked the earth and the lamps in all the houses burned until dawn to ward them away. Now, I felt as though I were one of those hungry, roaming shades—torn away from the world, but still tethered to it.

We kept walking until a low stone wall with an arched portal appeared in front of us. We passed through, and at first, I didn't understand what the place was. On the Island of the Mighty, we burned our dead or buried them beneath mounds of earth. We did not lock them away in cold little houses made of stone where their spirits would be trapped forever, barred from ever reaching the peace and plenty of the Otherworld.

But our procession wound past all those marble tombs, toward an isolated spot beyond. There I saw another kind of grave, with a log pyre stacked above it. We formed a circle, and those bearing the bier lifted it up and placed it on top of the pyre. In the place where I stood, I was close enough to see that the pit dug in the earth beneath it was filled with shallow baskets bearing all kinds of food—meat and bread, jugs of wine, a wheel of cheese—and other baskets that held personal belongings. A mirror and an ivory comb. Neatly folded clothing. Weapons—a lot of weapons. I counted three swords, a pair of spears, a small round shield, and a belt adorned with throwing knives. An impressive collection.

But there was one last item to be added to the grave hoard, it seemed.

The woman who'd led the procession—the Lady Achillea, I assumed—stood at the head of the grave pit, her face hidden in the depths of her deep hood. She reached beneath the folds of her cloak and brought forth a lamp, a delicate thing hanging on a slender chain.

"To light your way in the darkness," I heard her murmur. She let the chain slide through her fingers, and the lantern dropped gently into the pit on top of the other things. Then she raised her voice and said, "Her name was Ismene. Let it be known. She was a sister of our *familia*. A gladiatrix of House Achillea. She fought as we fight, with bravery and with skill. Five days ago, she fought to win honor in a match with a warrior maid of the House Amazona. She won, but Ismene was grievously wounded in that fight. Our surgeons did what they could for her. Last night the goddess Nemesis, she of the midnight brow, in her great wisdom called Ismene to the realm of heroes and sent forth Mercury to guide her there. She feasts now in the halls of Dis, she spars with Minerva, and she waits for all of us to join her there, and we mourn her absence even as others have this very day joined our ranks here."

I swallowed the knot in my throat. She was talking about Elka and me. But I swore in that moment that I would never wind up in this graveyard like this girl, burned and buried in soil far away from home.

"So it goes," the Lanista continued, and something about the way she spoke teased half-forgotten memories from the back of my mind. "The circle of glory, the river of blood. Mourn her, gladiatrices. Celebrate her. Make her proud."

There were sounds of weeping coming from some of the hoods that hid the faces of the girls, and even the Lanista's voice quavered with emotion. But I thought I heard one girl to my left scoff in quiet derision. Had there been a rivalry within the sacred sisterhood of the ludus? Perhaps "sisterhood" at the ludus, as in life, could be a double-edged sword.

One of the gladiatrices stepped forward with a torch and thrust it in between the logs of the pyre. The white shroud caught fire instantly, and the sudden updraft of heat sent it fluttering into the sky above our heads like the spirit of the dead girl released from her body. It hovered there, fluttering for a moment, then burst into a ball of brief flame before raining back down as ash upon us. I thought of how we'd never had the chance to burn Sorcha's body. The Romans had never given her back to us. Then I thought of Mael. I didn't even know where they had buried him. If I had been there, I would have made my father raise a barrow for him in the Forgotten Vale and crown it with a standing stone. Then I would have lain down and wept until the grass upon it grew long, watered with my tears.

Through the shimmering air, I looked on the face of the girl who had been called Ismene. She looked like she was sleeping. I searched my heart for a prayer to offer, but I did not know the gods the Lanista had spoken of. I only knew my own. So I formed a silent prayer for the dead girl I'd never known but in that moment felt a strange kinship with.

"May the Morrigan keep your soul," I whispered in my mind.

Yours and Sorcha's and Mael's.

As I hoped, one day, she would keep mine.

XV

"BY THE MORRIGAN'S BLOODY TEETH!" I spat as I stumbled forward, dropping painfully to one knee in the sand of the ludus practice yard. The wooden sword in my hand was wrenched from my grip, tangled in the hemp net that my opponent wielded. "This isn't fair!"

The other girl heard me—and laughed.

Of course it was unfair. After the long journey through Gaul, my muscles had gone soft from lack of decent food and exercise. I had all the strength of a runty kitten. With clumsy fingers and, *yes*—damn Caius Varro's eyes—weak wrists. And none of that seemed to matter to the girl who stood waiting for me to stand up so she could knock me down again. Her name was Meriel, and she fought, so I'd been told, in the style of a *retiarius*-class gladiator, wielding strange weapons—a three-pronged spear called a trident, and a woven rope net—like she was dancing with them.

She was my first sparring partner of the day.

I was beginning to think she might be my last.

Meriel's pale skin was freckled where it wasn't covered in the thin blue lines of tattoos, and her dark red hair was tied up on top of her head in an unruly rat's nest of twists and plaits. Her eyes looked upon me with the leaden gleam of cold gray rain. I knew her look. She was from Prydain. *Home.* Only she was from the far northern reaches, where the tribes were brutal and barbaric. And, as a rule, very good at killing things.

So am I.

Never mind that the only things I'd ever actually killed, up to that point, had ended up in the cauldron for supper. With a grunt of effort, I pushed myself back up to my feet.

"Well, come on then, *gladiolus*," Meriel sneered in barely understandable Latin buried beneath a guttural accent.

"Gladiolus," I'd learned, was a nickname bestowed on all the new recruits—a pun meant to diminish us by calling us flowers. Pretty to look at but easily trampled.

"Come on!" Meriel barked at me again. "Show us why you are worth all the monies!"

She rubbed the fingers and thumb of one hand together. "So many *sestersii*. And for what? Falling down?"

Word of the price paid for Elka and me had obviously gotten around. It wasn't my fault someone paid that much for me, I thought bitterly. Behind Meriel, I saw that a group of the other ludus girls had gathered and were watching us. They were all laughing, except for the one with long black braids, who just watched. Her name was Nyx. I'd seen her sparring on several occasions, and she'd impressed me with her technique. I, on the other hand, was clearly impressing no one.

I'd figured out fairly quickly that you could tell how well and how often some of the girls had fought by how they were kitted out. The ones who'd earned a purse or two or more wore bronze or leather wrist bracers or belts, or they had better weapons beyond the ludus-supplied gear. Nyx, by the look of her, was one of the better fighters. She wore tooled-leather shin greaves and wrist bracers and a belt around her waist that was decorated with bronze medallions and coral studs.

I was dressed in a simple tunic provided by the ludus. An ugly, shapeless thing stitched of undyed linen and belted with a plain leather belt. It was indistinguishable from the ones Elka and the other new arrivals wore. And distinguishing oneself, I soon learned, was at least as important in the arena as winning.

Meriel made an exaggerated show of waiting patiently as I retrieved my weapon and held it at the ready again. The wooden blade trembled only a little in my hand, but the small round wicker practice shield strapped to my left wrist felt heavy as iron as I lifted it into position. Meriel circled to my left, threatening with her trident, the net held down by her side. I'd never fought against such weapons before, and I thought they were ridiculous—more suited to a fishing skiff than an arena. I didn't know how to defend against them.

Maybe I didn't have to. Why defend when all I had to do was attack?

My sister Sorcha's voice echoed in my mind: *"Weapon or target . . . Choose, Fallon!"*

Weapon.

With a snarl, I ducked low beneath the whistling swipe of Meriel's trident and, with a distinctly *un*-defensive move, batted it from her fist with the edge of my shield. The tactic would have left me wide open for a thrust, except that her spear was tumbling through the air and landed far from her reach.

Now I have a weapon, and she doesn't—

Wrong. The net in her other hand whipped forward like a living extension of her arm. The lead weights at its corners stung painfully as the thing tangled around my legs and I went down in a heap for a second time. I was angry enough to beat Meriel. I just wasn't strong enough.

She snorted. "You'll never win a bout the way you fight."

I bit back a retort and kicked at the hemp snare.

"At least you bruise pretty colors, gladiolus," Meriel said, snapping the net out from under me with a flick of her wrist, leaving stripes of angry purple welts on my legs. *"That* ought to get the crowd's attention. Assuming you ever make it to a real arena."

She grinned and bent down to pick up her trident and, slinging it over her shoulder, walked away. Whistling.

The crowd of other girls broke up and went back to their own practice, all except Nyx. In the short time I'd been at the Ludus Achillea, I'd noticed that she seemed to be the nominal leader among a group of the academy's "veteran" students. Veterans like Meriel. We were of a similar age, I reckoned, and from what I'd heard in passing, I knew Nyx had been virtually raised at the academy from the time she was nine years old, an orphan of Greek peasants killed in a tribal raid.

As one of the senior gladiatrices, she often acted as a kind of lieutenant to Thalestris, drawing up sparring-partner lists and scheduling drills, and so far, on her watch, I'd faced off against most of the academy's toughest fighters—even in my less than optimal condition. By comparison, the other girls who'd arrived only a few weeks earlier than me hadn't even really started sparring yet. They were still doing basic strength and agility drills, facing off mostly against practice dummies. It was either a testament to my obvious if rusty skills . . . or an attempt to cull the weakest member of the herd.

Nyx leaned against a practice post, arms crossed, watching me as I climbed wearily to my feet. Her expression was unreadable. I couldn't tell if she was mocking me or not, but I decided to find out. I took a step toward her, but Thalestris appeared in that moment, stalking back and forth across the yard with her wooden staff in hand, and I wasn't about to bring *that* kind of trouble down on my head. Nyx had an ally in Thalestris, and one of the first things I'd developed on arrival at the Ludus Achillea was a healthy respect for its chief fight mistress.

The girls of the Ludus Achillea had paired off again and returned to sparring. I watched them for a moment, all so different and yet each one the same—each one striving to be the shining star in the arena—and I knew I'd been right when I'd first suspected that the ludus "sisterhood" might be a treacherous sea to navigate. Meriel, with her sea god's trident, was a painful reminder of that. Back in Durovernum, I'd had the luxury of choosing whom I fought against, but that was clearly no longer an option. I headed toward the weapons storage building so that I could maybe find a throwing spear or a bow to practice solo with.

But I knew that eventually I was either going to have to face my fellow ludus-mates head-on or curl up like a hedgehog and let them kick me around the pitch.

Weapon or target, my sister always said.

I felt the small hairs at the nape of my neck prickle, and I suddenly remembered something else Sorcha often said. *Never let down your guard until you're off the field of battle.*

Whether it was instinct, luck, or the Morrigan whispering a warning, I twisted sharply to one side just as the throwing knife spun past my ear. The point of the blade stuck in the scarred face of the wooden target ten paces in front of me. I didn't turn to see who'd thrown it. I just kept walking and, as I passed the target, reached out and yanked the still-quivering dagger from the wood. A thin line of crimson marred its edge, and I felt the sear from where it had kissed the side of my neck. I wiped the blood off on the hem of my tunic and thrust the knife into my belt.

I had just acquired my first new possession.

That evening, I decided a good long soak was in order to soothe the bruises and muscle knots, and I shuffled wearily over to the bathhouse. The lateness of the hour meant that the only other occupants were Elka, whom I met in the dressing foyer, and Ajani, lounging on a bench in the steam of the *calderium*. I'd found myself watching the Nubian girl practice her archery in between my own training bouts, impressed by her sharp-eyed aim and dexterity. And her quiet confidence. Ajani was no show-off, even if she had every right to be.

I hung up my tunic on a hook and padded over to the hot pool, sinking up to my chin with a sigh that was almost a groan.

"You missed all the fun today, little fox," Elka said as she sank down beside me and tipped her head back into the steaming water.

"Fun?" I shook my head to get the water out of one ear. "When did this so-called fun happen?"

"Just after you were finished getting pummeled all over the practice pitch by Meriel." Elka grinned. "You left, and Nyx had a few unkind things to say about your abilities in your absence."

I shrugged. "She probably had a point. I was terrible today."

"The only point she has," Elka said, "is the thorn she's had stuck up her arse about you ever since we first got here. The gods alone know why—it's not as if we're the only new recruits. Anyway, I guess I just got sick of her casting an evil eye at you everywhere you went."

I sat up, blinking away the spangles left by the steam on my eyelashes. "What did you do?" I demanded.

Her eyes widened with mock innocence. "I simply

asked when Nyx was going to call off Meriel and her other attack dogs and muster up enough guts to fight you herself." Elka stretched her arms above her head and knit her fingers together with a sigh of satisfaction.

"Oh, dear goddess," I groaned. "You didn't."

"She did."

The surface of the water rippled, and I turned, peering through the steam to see that Ajani had slipped into the pool to join us, an amused gleam in her wide, dark eyes.

"She also said that once you had finished fighting all of Nyx's lackeys, you'd be more than happy to explain to her personally all the ways she holds a blade wrong."

"Elka!" I gaped at her.

"Well, she does." Elka rolled her eyes. "She hooks her thumb over the crossguard—which we both know is the best way to lose a thumb—and she's all white knuckles. Brutish grip. No finesse."

"Nyx didn't take the criticism very well." Ajani's lilting accent gave her precise Latin a musical quality. "Started screaming in Greek about clawing Elka's eyes out and feeding them to the stable dogs."

"Was *that* what she said?" Elka asked. "I'm not up on my Greek."

"You didn't have to do that," I said. "I can fight my own battles."

"I know." She grinned. "Only, you didn't even seem to know you had one brewing. Besides," she continued, "someone had to liven things up around here. All we do is eat, sleep, and whack-whack-whack with wooden swords on wooden posts. At least now we've got something to keep us on our toes!"

"That much is for certain." Ajani propped her elbows up on the mosaic-tiled edge of the pool and grew serious for a moment. "Elka may have actually done you a favor, Fallon. I've seen this kind of thing happen here before. Better to lance the boil before the infection grows too deep. Still, you should be careful. Both of you."

I swam over to the edge of the pool and hoisted myself out of the water.

"I'm going to bed," I said, plucking a towel from a cubbyhole in the wall. "Please try not to win me any more mortal enemies before tomorrow?"

Elka saluted me with a grin and sank beneath the surface of the lavender-scented pool. I dried off and dressed, and walked out into the darkness. The ludus guards were somewhere making their rounds, but I didn't run across any of them. Instead, it seemed as though the academy grounds were utterly deserted. And yet, all the way back to the barracks wing, I could not ignore the feeling that I was being watched.

The sensation set my nerves jangling.

I crossed the courtyard where the moonlight-limned figure of the goddess Minerva gazed dispassionately down at me. In the darkness, I almost didn't notice the dead crow lying at the statue's feet. But when I got to my room, I definitely noticed the single black feather resting on my pillow.

It was stained with blood.

XVI

"GLADIOLUS!"

The mocking epithet rang out across the practice ground, and I groaned, knowing it was most likely directed at me. Again. I glanced up from stretching out my calf muscles to see Nyx crossing the sand, her long dark braids swinging behind her and Thalestris's wooden staff slung carelessly over her shoulder.

My guts knotted in apprehension. That morning, Elka had scoffed when I told her of the crow and the feather and said I shouldn't worry about a silly attempt to spook me. But I could tell that she was amused by the prospect of stirring up a little trouble among the other gladiatrices, whose ranks we would soon officially join. If we survived the training.

"Gladiolus!" Nyx shouted again. "You! The skinny Celt."

I gritted my teeth. Decent food, a bed that wasn't the floor of a cage, and an overabundance of exercise had begun to restore my body after the rigors of the slave train. But I still had a long way to go before my strength and reflexes were back to where they should have been.

"Today you'll spar with . . ." Nyx's gaze roamed over the ranks of the other students. "Gratia."

I swore under my breath. Here, I thought, was my payment for Elka's mischief. Gratia was an ox-necked thing who didn't speak so much as she just grunted, and she handled her wooden *gladius*—the practice weapon meant to approximate a Roman short sword—like a stone mallet. Nyx grinned coldly at my reaction and gave me a sharp nudge with the end of her staff.

"Get going, gladiolus," she said. "The day's wasting away."

I endured a round of thoroughly crushing sparring with Gratia and, after all the other girls had retired to either the dining hall or the baths, slunk off to a corner of the stable yards to sit under the noon sun and massage my aching shoulders. I sat there, staring dully at the ground and watching my shadow creep out along the ground past the edges of my toes. Gratia fought in the style of the *murmillo* gladiators, with sword and heavy shield. It suited her physique—and her penchant for thoughtless brutality—and made her something of a force to be reckoned with in the arena. It also compensated for her utter lack of personality.

And *that* was something that the masters of the *ludi*, the gladiatorial games, coveted above all else.

Flair.

The ludus fight instructors drilled that into us almost as

much as weapons technique. Winning a fight was one thing. Winning the crowd was another. But I had yet to even settle on a particular style. Most of the new girls had already begun to discover their natural inclinations toward one style of fighting over another. Me? The sword and round shield were as familiar to me as walking, but the majority of the other gladiatrices fought that way. I'd never distinguish myself with such common methods. I could shoot a bow and drive a chariot, and I certainly threw a spear well enough . . . and I sincerely doubted whether any of the girls at the ludus could even come close to executing the Morrigan's Flight, even Nyx. The fleeting remembrance of that morning back in the vale triggered a wave of emotions that swept over me.

I had done it. And Mael had seen me do it.

Maelgwyn Ironhand.

Lethal and beautiful, every move—every cut and thrust, slash and block and feint—had been, for him, like dancing, as if Mael had heard music no one else could. Sometimes, when I'd watched him practice with his blades, I almost thought that I could hear it too.

That music had been silent since the night he died.

On a bench near the stables, there was a stack of short wooden staves that had been roughly carved to uniform lengths and now sat waiting to be turned into practice weapons. I walked over and picked up two that looked to be of equal balance. They needed shaping, sanding, and polishing, and leather wrapped around their hilts. But, for my purposes, they'd do nicely.

I looked around to see if there was anyone to watch

me. There wasn't. The only other creature in sight was the swaybacked donkey that stood placidly munching at a hay manger. I gave him a sideways look and vowed in that moment I would learn—and not only learn, but *master*—the gladiatorial style of the *dimachaerus*: the double-sword-wielding warrior who fought with a blade in each hand.

Mael had been the Cantii equivalent of a dimachaerus, an absolute genius with two blades. Growing up, he had developed a series of drills for himself. For two years he'd tried to get me to fight two-handed with him, but I'd been happy with my sword and shield and spear. And the other young Cantii warriors soon tired of getting themselves beaten black and blue fighting against him. So, mostly, he fought the weathered stump of an ancient, lightning-blasted oak. Mael used it as a practice post, and the old forest guardian bore the scars of its encounters with his blades graciously. I thought about all the times I'd sat in the grass watching him practice, and wondered if I could reproduce those patterns from memory.

There was only one way to find out.

I walked over to the stable post and took up a ready stance in front of it. I closed my eyes for a moment and remembered the rhythms, the sounds of the patterns of Mael's drills. Then slowly, tentatively, I began to emulate them. At first, I was clumsy. Awkward. And then, gradually less so.

I could feel the heat of the sun moving across my back, shifting from one shoulder to the other before the clack-clack-clack of my swords against the stable post began to sound like something other than a demented woodpecker. I don't know how much longer it was before I fell so deeply into the patterns that I closed my eyes and the rhythm didn't break, or even slow down.

Left high-left side, right low-right side, left low-right side, right high-right side, sweep and switch . . .

The patterns changed and became more complex as I practiced. I felt, for the first time since the morning of the Lughnasa feast, as if Mael were right there, close enough for me to reach out and touch. I almost felt as if his spirit guided my blades for real. But when the heat of the sun on my left shoulder went cold—blotted out by a shadow—my eyes snapped open. I saw the silhouette of a crested helmet on the barn wall in front of me. Without thinking, I spun around, both wooden blades slashing horizontally through the air.

"Aiy!" Decurion Caius Varro yelped, leaping back to avoid the blows.

My momentum carried me forward, and suddenly, as if released from a spell that had kept me mesmerized as I'd practiced, I felt the full weight of exhaustion hit me. I staggered a few steps toward the Decurion, who put out a hand to stop me from falling on my face.

"Tell me," he said after a moment, "are you going to get tired of attacking me anytime soon?"

I glared at him, silent except for the breath heaving in and out of my lungs.

"Working on that wrist strength, I see."

"What are you doing here?" I panted.

His lip twitched with amusement. "I was watching you," he said. "It was quite entertaining. And enlightening. I'm not sure what grudge you bear that poor stable post, but it's obvious you have some real talent and some training."

"Some," I agreed dryly.

He nodded. "But you're clutching your weapons too tightly. You're sacrificing accuracy and fluidity for brute force."

I rolled my eyes and brushed past him so I could return the wooden blanks I'd been using to the pile for finishing. But when I looked down at them, I saw that they were ruined, with the unpolished edges dented and hewed to splinters. I threw them into the basket of scrap wood beneath the table. It was possible the Decurion had a point, but I certainly wasn't going to tell him that.

I sat down on the bench beside the table and kneaded at the burning in my neck muscles with tingling fingers. After a moment, I realized that the Decurion was still standing there watching me. There was a look of curiosity—or maybe it was uncertainty—on his face.

"What are you *really* doing here, Decurion?" I asked.

He sat down on the other end of the bench and clawed at the chinstrap of his helmet, lifting it off his head. His hair was damp with sweat from the day's hot sun and plastered to his scalp until he scrubbed his palm briskly over his head to make it bristle.

"Officially?" He shrugged. "I'm running errands on behalf of Caesar to his Lanista."

"And unofficially?"

"Satisfying my curiosity. Or trying to . . ." He glanced over at me and paused for a moment, as if trying to decide whether or not to continue. Then he asked, "What does a mark in the shape of a knotted triple raven mean to you?"

My breath stopped in my throat, and everything around me seemed to get very quiet. Even the singing of the birds in the trees died to silence. And in that stillness, I could hear the Morrigan's throaty dream-voice whisper my name. Was she telling me to trust him? Or was she trying to warn me?

"Why do you ask?"

"Why don't you tell me?" he countered. "If your expression is any indication, it clearly means something."

Of course it meant something. It was the symbol of my goddess and the brand that had marked my blade. I had no idea why he was asking, but even the way he posed the question made me cautious. I didn't know how to answer, and so instead, I just stared at the donkey, which stared back, no help at all.

"All right." The Decurion sighed. "Let me tell you a little story."

I eyed him warily and stayed silent, listening.

"The slave auctions are almost always an entertaining bit of distraction for the good citizens of Rome," he continued. "And never more so than when Charon comes to town to market his wares. He's theatrical, certainly. Shows every piece of—" He bit off his words abruptly. "That is, he shows every, uh, *person* off to their best potential. Costumes, cosmetics, wigs . . . the works. As I'm sure you noticed. But your mock duel? That was extravagant, even for him."

"It was hardly a mock duel," I said. "A man died. I don't think Charon was expecting that."

"No, but he also thought it worth the risk. The high price he got for you bore that out. And *that's* what was so surprising about the whole affair." The corner of the Decurion's mouth lifted. "Truthfully, sparkling costumes and a dead Alesian notwithstanding, there was nothing particularly extraordinary about your performance that day."

I sputtered in outrage, but he was right. Even that day's kill had belonged to Elka, not me.

"Pontius Aquila started off with a high enough bid," he continued, "but then, in the interval while they cleared away the corpse, Charon sends me into the crowd with a message for the Lady Achillea."

"What message?"

"A trunk." He watched for my reaction. "With a sword in it. A sword with a triple raven etched upon the blade."

My mind flashed back to the chaos of the slave galley sinking beneath me as I helped Charon heave his trunk over onto the other ship. Was that what had been so vitally important to him? My sword?

"Achillea offers a sky-high price, well beyond the means of the other bidders, and that seals the deal right there. For a pair of unknown, unqualified, *potential* gladiatrixes." The Decurion's clear hazel gaze bored into me, unblinking. "So tell me: What am I missing?"

"I'm flattered you think so very highly of me."

He ignored my sarcasm. "It's your sword, isn't it?" he asked. "How did a lowly thrall come by a blade like that?"

I shot to my feet. "How dare you assume I was always a lowly thrall!"

He grinned—a wily expression—and said, "So I was right." He leaned forward on the bench, as if to get a closer look at me. "I guessed as much after we spoke at Massilia and I said you didn't talk like a slave. You're freeborn, aren't you?"

"Of course I'm freeborn," I snapped. "I'm the daughter of a king!"

My words hung in the air between us. For a moment, I thought he might scoff at me for making such an unbelievable claim. But instead, his gaze darkened and his grin disappeared.

"Surely you're joking?" he asked.

"What if I am? What do you care if I'm a queen in my own land or a cowherd?"

"Because you're not *in* your own land anymore," he said. "This is Rome. Treachery and opportunism and back-stabbing run in her veins like lifeblood, and if you've never had to live your life constantly looking over your shoulder, then you have no idea how dangerous it can be. The Lady Achillea is a close friend of Caesar's. And when Caesar isn't off in other lands making war, he's here in Rome making enemies. It's my job to make sure those enemies can't use the few friends he has against him."

"What has any of this to do with me?"

"I don't know. Yet. But the mark on that blade clearly

meant something to the Lanista, and Charon knew it would. I'd like to know what that something is."

"Then you'll have to ask them," I said. "All I know is that it's the symbol of my goddess—sacred to the warriors of my tribe. There is power in the mark. Perhaps the Lanista recognized that."

"I suppose that's true," he said, frowning in thought. "Your people aren't the only ones who think of ravens as omens. Although most Romans would consider them bad ones."

I thought about the dead bird and the bloody feather someone had left in my room. I'd thought it was just a prank at the time, but now I wondered if I shouldn't tell the Decurion about it. I knew more than he did just how powerful a symbol the raven was—and how dangerous. But no—how could there possibly be a connection between my sword and the feather?

And, at any rate, the crimson plume of the Decurion's very Roman helmet stirred in the breeze and reminded me that he belonged to the legions that had invaded my home. He was the enemy of my people. He was not my friend.

"If the Lanista thinks you're worth keeping out of Pontius Aquila's collection, then you're worth keeping safe," the Decurion continued. "The Ludus Achillea is *Caesar's*, remember? He owns it—and everything and everyone in it—and it's worth a lot of money. And, as much as some people might think the gladiatoral games are nothing more than a decadent indulgence to keep the mob distracted and mollified, there's more to it than that. There are rivalries that run generations old, and deep divides both politically and philosophically among the Republic's elite. There are those in the senate who whisper of Caesar's increasing power. Of his superior airs. They say he's been tainted by the Aegyptian queen, Cleopatra. That she's convinced him he should be treated as a god, not a man. An emperor rather than Rome's chief consul."

"So? I still don't understand what any of this has to do with me."

"Caesar's perceived arrogance has caused a great deal of resentment among his peers in the senate. But the plebs—the common people—adore him." He looked at me. "They love him for just such things as, well, *you*. Or, rather, what you might become in time. Caesar's games are the best. His fighters, the best. His upcoming Quadruple Triumphs are his gift to the people of Rome, a massive celebration such as this city has never seen. They are meant to cement his popularity in such a way that the senate will never be able to cast him down—not without risking the wrath of the mob. *That's* how important Caesar's gladiators are to him. Now do you understand?"

I did. Or, at least, I thought I did.

Someone called Caius's name, and he glanced over his shoulder to where another legionnaire approached, leading a pair of horses. "I have to go," he said.

"Before you do," I said, "tell me this: You could have

just asked Charon about the sword mark the next time you saw him. Why did you seek me out instead?"

He was silent for a long moment, staring at me, and I wondered if he would give me an answer. Then he said, "I was curious about you."

"Why?"

"On the ship, I saw something in you."

I raised an eyebrow at him. "And that was?"

"The absolute need to fight. To be free. That's something I can understand."

I wasn't so sure he could.

"Some years ago," he continued, "there was a revolt. A gang of slaves—gladiators, in fact—rose up and challenged the might of the Republic. They fought the legions for a very long time, and they very nearly won. But it took one man—a man named Spartacus—to ignite the spark that turned to flame. I've always admired him, even though he went against everything I'm supposed to fight for as a soldier of Rome. I thought, on the ship, that I saw that same kind of ember glowing in your eyes. I suppose I wanted to see if it was still there."

I felt a sudden prickling behind my eyes. How could I even hope to keep such a spark alive when it seemed my life was destined to play out behind the high walls of an arena?

I blinked the tears away quickly, but not before the Decurion saw. His expression softened.

"A gladiatrix, if she's good enough, may one day earn enough in the arena to buy her freedom, you know." He reached into the basket and pulled out one of the wooden blanks I'd hewed to kindling. He tossed it to me and grinned. "Just be good enough."

My mind reeled with the implications of actually, one day, being able to make enough money to buy my freedom back. No one at the ludus had told us that yet. Then I remembered just how very much money I'd been sold for. Good enough would have to be very good indeed.

The Decurion laughed at my stunned expression. "I'll be back soon, on Caesar's business," he said. "Perhaps I might look in on your progress."

"If it pleases you, Decurion," I said, distracted.

"It would." He hitched his cloak higher on his shoulder. "My curious mind and all. Also . . . another thing that would please me is if—when it's just the two of us together—I'd like it very much if you would call me Caius instead of Decurion. Or better yet, Cai."

I thought about how very unlikely it was that we'd find ourselves in such circumstances again. "As you wish . . . Cai."

A moment of silence stretched between us, and then he sighed heavily.

"What?" I blinked at him.

"That's the part where you're supposed to say: 'And *you* can call *me* . . .'"

I hesitated for a moment.

"Fallon."

Cai smiled. A slow, inward-turning smile, like he'd just learned a secret. "Be well, Fallon," he said. "Be careful. And

tomorrow . . . try tucking in your chin and imagine breathing all the way down your arms, right out the ends of your
fingertips and into your swords. Let go. Relax *into* the work
instead of fighting *through* it."

Shaking my head, I watched him mount his horse and
ride off in a haze of dust. Sound advice, maybe, but it
seemed to me that there was far too much fighting ahead
for me to ever think about letting go.

XVII

THE DAY OF our gladiatorial oath swearing approached with the swiftness of a late summer tempest and just as much foreboding. For weeks it had seemed nothing more than a distant threat, an occasional rumble like thunder on the horizon. But now, the very air of the ludus training grounds seemed to bristle with the furious, pent-up energy of a storm cloud ready to burst.

Thalestris and the other fight masters—two hard-bitten ex-legion soldiers named Kronos and Titus—had been observing our progress with eagle-keen eyes, and the tension among the girls was palpable. I know I felt like a walking bundle of flayed nerves, both on the pitch and off. Just because the ludus had bought us as slaves didn't mean they couldn't sell us again if we didn't measure up as potential gladiatrices. As much as I loathed the idea of living under the yoke of the ludus, performing like a trained animal for the delight of bloodlusting crowds, the prospect of getting dragged back to the auction block to be sold as a failed fighter was far more odious—and, truthfully, terrifying.

At the same time, what Cai had told me that day by the stables had kindled in me a tiny spark of hope. If I could become a gladiatrix, there was a chance—a faint hope, maybe, but still—that I could one day earn my freedom with my sword. *"Just be good enough,"* he'd said.

So I fought with the Meriels and the Gratias of the academy, and I even sparred with Nyx—at Thalestris's cruel behest—one miserable raining afternoon in a bout that lasted forever and saw us both end up covered in mud and bruises. I bit down on the urge to whimper every morning from the ache in my muscles, and I spent every spare second I had hacking away at the stable post with my two practice swords under the disinterested gaze of the donkey.

I worked on my presentation—on flourishes and salutes to the (as yet imaginary) crowds of onlookers—and on my style. Some of the girls who'd fought in the arenas already had patrons who sponsored them, wealthy patricians who flaunted their riches by equipping their favorite fighters in the games with better weapons and fancier armor.

Me, I spent the hours I wasn't practicing or sleeping digging through the baskets of scrap leather in the weapons-makers' shops, fashioning wrist bracers and a pair of shin guards for myself. I incised the spiral patterns of the Cantii on them with the point of my dagger. They weren't anywhere near as fancy as some of the bronze ones the other girls wore, but they were something. A start. They'd have to suffice until I could attract a patron of my own.

By barely measurable increments, the days became less grueling. And through it all, Elka was there to lift my spirits with her blunt humor and fierce friendship. As much as I hoped that I would make it all the way to the oath ceremony, I hoped just as fervently that she would too.

"You're getting good, little fox," Elka said as she ambled over, wiping the sweat from her tall brow with the back of one arm. "You could almost pass for a Varini, the way you fight."

I grinned at her. "And you could almost pass for a Cantii." I nodded at the spear she held in one fist. She'd been practicing her throwing all morning, and she had a sharp eye. "Only *we* throw our spears from the decks of racing chariots."

"Chariots are for girls." She laughed and nodded toward the gate in the compound wall that opened out toward the shores of Lake Sabatinus. That day the gate stood wide, and we could see a pair of the swift, light war carts racing along the strand. Mounted ludus guards rode nearby, keeping the charioteers under watchful eyes, but I envied them even that illusion of freedom.

The drivers were Nyx and another girl whose name I didn't know. Nyx lashed furiously at her ponies and pulled ahead of the other chariot with a triumphant shout. The wing of black hair flowing out behind her reminded me of the crow feather that had been left in my room.

I'd cleaned the dried blood off the thing and put it under my pillow. I slept with it there as a kind of secret act of defiance. Crows and ravens were sacred to the Morrigan, and

I didn't think she'd take kindly to one of her own being gutted for the purposes of a prank. Every now and then I wondered if I'd been foolish not to report the incident to Thalestris or one of the other masters, but I didn't want anyone to think I couldn't fight my own battles. Not before the oath swearing. And if the dead bird and bloody feather had been meant to frighten me, they'd failed to do so. If anything, they spurred me on. The goddess was on *my* side. At least, that's what I kept telling myself.

I didn't know who'd left the thing—or why. I might have suspected Nyx, but that's all it was: a suspicion. And she hadn't followed up with any similar threats. Still, I frowned as I watched her race down the lakeshore, urging her horses on with the crack of her whip. A shadow of unease crept across what had been my good mood.

Elka nudged me with her elbow. "Come on," she said. "I was joking. Here. Help me practice."

She led me over to the far side of the yard, where there was an assortment of targets set up. One of them was made from an old round shield pinned to a post through its center. It had been painted like the spokes of a wheel, divided into numbered sections, one to twelve. Kronos the trainer had explained to me what the number markings meant and how to read them, but I still got confused sometimes and mixed them up. So we made a joke out of it every time Elka asked me to spin the shield wheel and pick a number.

"Thirteen!" I would call out and spin the wheel so that the markings blurred.

Elka's spear invariably pierced the twelve: XII.

"Only off by one!" she would say. For some reason the joke had yet to grow stale. And her aim had yet to falter. As a prospective gladiatrix, she was good. And she actually seemed content—happy, even—that her fate had led her to the Ludus Achillea and the chance to live and die as one.

Which makes her either stronger than me . . . or weaker.

I didn't know which.

The evening before the ritual, I was beyond restless. I felt as though I would jump out of my skin if I stayed another moment in my cell, pacing a groove in the dirt floor and wondering if I would still be sleeping on that same narrow cot after the oath swearing.

Even after a full day of hard practice, I wasn't the least bit tired. The blood hummed through my veins like trails of busy insects, and my fingers opened and closed on the air as if searching for lost weapons. But my mind and heart were torn in opposite directions. If I was chosen to take the oath, then my fate would be inextricably tied to the Ludus Achillea. If not . . . I didn't know. The very idea of being set adrift in the middle of a foreign land—maybe sold, maybe just turned out into the streets of Rome—set my heart pounding with the possibilities of escape . . . even as it turned my mind to the probability of death or dishonor in those same streets.

When I finally couldn't take the closeness of my four walls any longer, I plucked my cloak off the hook on my door and slipped out into the barracks corridor. The sun had dropped below the horizon, and the sky was darkening swiftly. I could smell the lake, cool and fragrant on the air, and longed to run along the shore, outside the gates of the compound. I would have to content myself with a run on the paths meandering through the gardens.

I heard the muffled sounds of blades clashing, distorted by the evening mist, but I knew that all the other students had retired for the night. My mind suddenly tumbled back to the night Mael and Aeddan had fought in the fog. It had sounded just like that, like the sound of the Morrigan laughing.

Without thinking, I followed the ringing echoes toward a small torchlit courtyard. There I saw Thalestris, dressed in her usual breeches and sleeveless tunic, fighting with another woman. Both of them were helmed and lightly armored, fighting with short swords and shields. And both of them were staggeringly good.

I guessed at the other fighter's identity: the Lady Achillea herself.

Your new goddess, Thalestris had said on that first day at the ludus.

I spat in the dirt at the very thought.

I already had a goddess, and no matter what trials she saw fit to put me through, I would not forsake her for someone who thought fighting for the sport of the masses was the least bit honorable. Achillea was no true warrior.

And yet, even as I watched, I had to admit that she certainly fought like one. There was something *thrilling* about the way the Lanista fought, something unique and undeniably compelling to watch in the way she angled her body in defense, the way her head craned sharply to one side when she attacked. It was like nothing I'd ever seen. I wondered where she'd learned her technique, but it could have been anywhere, from anyone. Since the day we'd arrived in Massilia, I'd heard more indecipherable tongues and seen more shades of flesh and hair and eyes than I'd ever imagined possible. As far as I could tell, the slave traders catering to their Roman patrons were more than happy to sell all the tribes of mankind.

I knew that this sparring session was a private one and that I probably wasn't supposed to be there, but I still stood there, peering around the column with fierce curiosity. I'd only ever seen the woman who owned me at a distance. The Lanista had a terrace that overlooked the practice grounds, and that was where she watched us from, a shadowy shape beneath an awning. Her palla was always pulled up over her head like the hood of a cloak, even on hot days.

I'd heard from Ajani that the Lady Achillea had once, not too long ago, been celebrated far and wide, the toast of Rome's arenas. She'd built a reputation in only a few short years as the best gladiatrix the world had ever seen. But then there'd been an accident, a terrible crash during what had been a particularly wild chariot race in the Circus Maximus, and she hadn't been seen in the arena since. Morbid curiosity made me wonder if she'd been deformed by her injuries. Simmering resentment made me hope she had. It was childish of me, I knew—after all, it wasn't her fault I'd gotten myself taken by slave traders in the first place—but I couldn't help it.

I realized, suddenly, that the sounds of dueling had died away, and I glanced over to see that the two women had ended their match. And they were both staring at me standing dumbly in the breezeway. I could feel their gazes on me even though I couldn't see their eyes behind the metal grates of their visors. I jumped and would have scurried away if the Lady Achillea hadn't said something to Thalestris, who gestured for me to stay where I was.

I waited as the Lanista, still in her helmet, gathered her gear and left through a far archway without a backward glance. Thalestris sheathed her sword on her hip and lifted off her own helmet, tucking it under her arm, and walked toward me. I expected some kind of punishment, or at least a thorough tongue-lashing, for having intruded, but she just smiled at me coolly.

"Perhaps one day you will fight like that, yes?" she said.

"Like you? Or the Lanista?"

She laughed, a throaty chuckle that sounded almost like a warning growl, and shook her head. "You should have seen her back in her arena days," she said. "After her accident she retrained herself to fight in a way that turns injuries into assets, weakness into strength. But you should have seen her then. She was the original, and she was the best."

"What do you mean, she was the original?" I asked, suppressing the urge to boast that one day *I* would be best. *Better than both of them.*

"The original gladiatrix."

"She was?"

Thalestris nodded. "Caesar sent her into the arena as

the first woman ever to compete in the ludi—well, the first of two—and the mob in the stands went wild with excitement."

"Who did she fight against?" I asked.

"She fought against a Scythian captive like myself—the Greeks and the Romans call us Amazons—and she won the day brilliantly."

"Did you know the other warrior?"

"She was my own sister."

"What happened to her?"

Thalestris looked at me. "She lost the day," she said. "Not quite so brilliantly. I honor her memory."

I stared at her. "Achillea killed your sister and now you work for her?"

The very idea was abhorrent to me. I could barely stand living in a place owned by Caesar, the man whose soldiers my own sister had died fighting. The thought of working closely, day after day, with someone who had my kin's blood on their hands was unthinkable. Amazons were either heartless or spineless.

But even though I knew my disgust must have shown in my expression, Thalestris's eyes never wavered from my face, and her gaze remained placid as she said, "When Caesar eventually gave her this ludus to run on his behalf, the Lady Achillea came to me and asked for me to be her *Primus Pilus*—her First Spear—the head trainer of the glad-iatrices. She respected my skills as I respect her." She lifted her head proudly. "Of course I accepted. I am descended from an eternal line of warrior women. I cannot *not* fight."

I thought of all the times I'd said almost those exact same words—to Mael, to Sorcha . . .

"I came to Rome a captive just like you," Thalestris said. "And I am still a slave. But now, thanks to this place, I am also a teacher. I'm proud to have been given the opportunity to pass along the skills and knowledge of my ancestresses. And the gladiatrix in the arena, thanks to us, is no longer a freakish curiosity as it was in the early days of Achillea's first fights. Even the men, the gladiators of the Ludus Maximus, respect us now."

Maybe so, I thought. But even from my limited interactions with the Romans, I also knew perfectly well that those same gladiators were still considered *infamia* by the patrician class and the plebs alike. Dishonorable. On a level with the whores and the gravediggers, those who fought and died in the arena were considered tainted. So what did it matter if they respected us or not?

"Go." Thalestris put a hand on my shoulder and nodded toward the barracks. "Sleep. Wake. Eat. Fight. That's all you need to do until tomorrow night."

She left me there in the darkness, thinking about what she'd just said.

I don't know how long I stood there, but when I turned to go back to my quarters, there were shadows in the alcoves of the courtyard that hadn't been there before. One of the shadows stepped forward, and I felt a warning flutter trace up my spine. My thoughts spiraled back to that night in Alesia.

Only these were no brigands.

These were my "sisters." Or, at least, they would be if I was chosen to take the oath.

Behind me, I heard the sharp crack of a chariot whip, and I understood instantly that Thalestris and the Lanista weren't the only ones I had to prove myself to. My hand dropped automatically to my hip, but I wasn't wearing a weapon. I didn't even have my dagger stuck in my belt. I cursed silently and took up a ready stance, wondering where the first attack would come from.

I didn't have to wonder long.

Another crack of the whip, and a line of fire licked across the backs of my legs. I fell to my hands and knees with a grunt. A ring of laughter echoed around me, and I blinked away sudden tears of pain trying to see who, exactly, my attackers were. There were four or five of them—it was hard to tell in the darkness as they circled me—and they all wore visored helmets. But I was fairly certain I knew who at least two of them were just by the weapons they wielded.

Nyx and Meriel.

I clambered back up to one knee and staggered forward to avoid the next sting of Nyx's whip, only to trip over the web of a retiarius net as it slapped viciously against my shins and sent me tumbling back to the ground.

Where I was defenseless.

The girls kicked and punched at me in the darkness, and I curled into a ball to try to avoid the worst of it. I could tell by the way they avoided my head and stomach that the blows they rained on me were designed to bruise, not brutalize. But that didn't make them hurt any less as I clenched my teeth to keep from crying out. I suspected that what they really wanted was to leave me battered and sore enough so that my performance the next day at practice—my last chance to impress the Lanista—would suffer.

Lady Achillea would see me fighting lame and would judge me on my diminished performance—enough, maybe, that I would be sent from the ludus. And I decided, in that moment, I wasn't going to let that happen. Stay or go, it would be on my merit or the lack of it, not because of some petty ambush by girls who thought they were better than me.

They weren't.

Beneath the laughter and taunts, I heard a guttural, animal howl of protest. It was me. My voice. As it rose in volume, I pushed myself up off the sandy ground and shook off my attackers. Their circle fractured, and I sprinted past two of them toward a pair of torches set in a sconce on the courtyard wall. I grasped the flaming brands and spun back around, wielding the things as if they were my dimachaerus blades.

"Get away from me!" I snarled as I spun circles of flames in the dark air, batting the whip away from me and almost setting the retiarius net aflame. "Stay back or burn, you jackals!"

One girl screamed in alarm as my torch set her tunic hem smoldering, and she quickly fell back, slapping at the cloth. The firebrands flared and flamed in my hands, trailing smoke and embers in the dimachaerus patterns I'd practiced, as my attackers backed off. When I lunged straight at the girl with the whip, she turned and ran, melting back into the night, the other girls following close on her heels. I shouted after them to come back and face me.

In truth, I was just as glad they were gone.

My arms and legs throbbed as I let the torches drop to my sides.

I squeezed my eyes shut to clear the afterglare of fire blindness. When I opened them again and lifted my head to the cool night breeze, I saw a figure, cloaked and hooded, standing on the balcony above the courtyard, watching me. The Lanista. I couldn't see her face, but I knew it was her. I could feel her gaze on me, sharp and appraising. I straightened up, standing as tall as I could, and met her gaze. She stood there for a long moment. Then she turned without a word and disappeared into the darkness.

I ground the torches in the sand, snuffing out their light.

The next day, I hobbled out to the practice yard, where the throbbing, livid bruises on my legs and arms went glaringly unremarked upon. Except, of course, by Elka when she saw me in the armor shed. I could only guess the meaning of maybe half the stream of Varini invective that spilled from her mouth, but I still got the general idea. And I agreed wholeheartedly.

"At least Meriel was right," I said through gritted teeth as I sat on the bench, carefully buckling up my shin greaves. "I do bruise pretty colors."

"You hold her down and I'll be happy to see if she does the same!" Elka spat.

"I don't even know for certain if it was her last night—I know, I know"—I held up a hand—"of course it was. And Nyx, and probably Lydia and Gratia. I know. But I'm not going to give them the satisfaction of seeing me so much as wince today."

"Like you're doing right now?"

"Hand me my helmet." I settled it on my head and lowered the visor. "There. Now no one can tell."

Elka snorted and shook her head, then held out a hand to help me stand.

It was the longest day I'd ever had at the ludus.

I was terrible. My routines were stiff and clumsy, and every blow I landed hurt me far more than my partners. And when I finally returned to my quarters that evening, bone-sore and heartsick, I was certain I would find my trunk packed and waiting outside the door of my cell. They would send me off, back to the auction block, and I would be sold off in disgrace. Or maybe I would be turned over to the kitchen steward, to spend my days scrubbing trenchers and making meals for the girls who fought in the arenas.

By the time I got back to my room, I had thoroughly envisioned every wretched scenario imaginable . . . only to find a new, neatly folded tunic lying on the lid of my trunk. Beside the tunic, there was a broad crimson leather belt that cinched tight with fine bronze buckles, and a pair of red-dyed leather sandals that laced all the way up to the knee. There was also a lamp—a fine new oil lamp to replace the dim little lump of tallow candle that sat in a clay dish on my windowsill.

I remembered the lamp the Lanista had lowered into the grave of the gladiatrix Ismene, and a shiver ran up my spine. I had been chosen to swear the oath. The lamp would light my cell until the day I won my freedom.

Or died.

I lit the wick, setting it carefully up in the window as the light from the setting sun faded. There was a burning tightness in my throat, but just then Elka burst through my door, and I swallowed my tears. She glanced from me to the lamp in my window to the tunic on the trunk.

"Ha!" she exclaimed. "I knew it! I *knew* we'd both be chosen to take the oath. That cow Nyx can choke on it! And so can her little gang of thugs."

She'd brought her own lamp from her room and thrust it at me. "*Look* at this!"

It was made of polished, translucent stone that looked as though it had been carved from a block of winter ice. The flickering flame within glowed gently, blue and gold. Like Elka herself. I wondered if the lamps were chosen to suit each girl.

"Alabaster," Elka murmured, mesmerized. "I've heard of this, but I never expected to *own* something made of such magic."

Her blue eyes were wide with wonder, and maybe something a little like joy, as she cradled the delicate lamp in both hands. I felt a surge of happiness for her. Whatever else the Ludus Achillea was, it seemed that it might one day prove to be a place Elka could call home.

But I also felt a pang of envy hiding beneath my

happiness for my friend. The lamp that had been chosen for me was shaped like a bird, with delicate glass pieces— bright greens and blues and yellows—set into the wings, and it reminded me of summer days spent running wild through the Forgotten Vale. It also reminded me of one of the many lamps that had hung from the rafters of my house—the one that had been my favorite when I was a little girl. For a moment, as I stared at the bright-shining flame within, I was back there, in that place, listening to Sorcha tell me stories about the spirits that lived in those lamps.

Home for me, it seemed, was still Durovernum.

I suspected, in my heart, it always would be.

"We are going to put the Ludus Achillea on the map, you and I," Elka proclaimed with airy disregard for the academy's already stellar reputation. "The arena crowds aren't going to know what hit them!"

Then she hugged me and hurried off to get ready for the oath swearing, her breathless excitement carrying away some of my own anxiousness. As I stripped off my plain-spun tunic and shrugged the fine linen sheath over my head, I tried to speculate not on what was to come in the future but just on this one night. I'd been told that the male gladiators took their oaths in daylight. With the harsh eye of the sun looking down on them, the men stood in sand circles and said the words that would bind them to that life, until either death or their hard-earned winnings set them free.

But the women of the Ludus Achillea swore their oaths at night.

Under the light of the Huntress Moon.

When I got to the practice yard, I saw it had been decorated for the occasion. Garlands of green leaves and sheaves of lavender and lemon verbena hung between the pillars of the courtyard colonnades, perfuming the night air with heady scents that mingled with the smoke from the braziers. There were torches on poles set in a wide circle, and the sand of the yard had been raked smooth.

Elka and I and the five other new recruits entered through the archway, dressed in identical white linen tunics and belts and sandals. We wore our hair unbound and our faces unpainted. All the other girls—full-fledged gladiatrices—waited for us, dressed in the same white tunics, but the resemblances ended there. Over the course of innumerable bouts in arenas large and small, scattered throughout Rome and the surrounding countryside, each of the girls had accumulated trophies and keepsakes and ornaments. Not surprisingly, there was an abundance of weapons and armor. The gladiatrices of the Ludus Achillea wore them proudly that night, as badges of well-deserved honor.

I looked around at all the swords, daggers, tooled-leather wrist bracers and greaves, and armored girdles and breastplates decorated with symbols and scenes. Some of the girls wore torcs about their necks, like the one I'd left in the embers of my hearth fire back home, and some wore no jewelry at all but had painted the skin of their bodies with swirling designs or had woven feathers and beads into their hair.

There were seven of us being formally inducted into the ludus that night, and we wore nothing to distinguish us.

We hadn't earned that yet.

The intoxicating scent of stone pine incense drifted through the indigo night as we walked out into the circle of torches. I recalled the same scent from the gladiatrix graveyard, and I remembered the anonymous, snickering disdain I'd heard mixed in with the sounds of weeping that night. I wondered fleetingly if Ismene had made more friends here than enemies before she'd died.

Will I?

I stopped myself from reaching up to touch the raven feather I'd tied into my hair before leaving my cell. The thing had become almost a talisman to me. In the darkness a war horn sounded, like the Morrigan herself blowing her bronze carnyx, and I felt the cold finger of fate trace up my spine. As the shrill, shimmering notes died to silence, we stood, shoulder to shoulder, facing the ranks of gladiatrixes we would soon join.

Beneath the training-ground portico, I could see a group of men sitting in carved wooden chairs, speaking in low tones, aristocratic heads bent together. Dignitaries and lanistas from other ludi invited for the occasion, they would be entertained with a lavish feast in the ludus guest residences afterward. I recognized one of the men who stood there, the one with the silver hair and hawkish features that they had called the Collector. He'd tried to purchase Elka and me at the auction, and had stormed off after being outbid by the Lanista. He looked even more unhappy now than he did then, and he seemed to be actively trying to avoid another man in the gathering.

I'd seen enough of his stone likenesses scattered around Rome to guess his identity from his torchlit profile, but even if I hadn't, I would have known him instantly. Here was a man who wore power like a cloak, effortlessly, comfortably. The thrill I felt at having been chosen to swear the oath conflicted with the raw dread of knowing just who, exactly, I was swearing my oath to. Gaius Julius Caesar, proconsul of Rome, the great dictator himself, had come to the ludus to attend the oath swearing of his newest crop of thorny wildflowers.

At his side sat a woman, Caesar's mistress—although none dared call her so out loud—the Aegyptian queen, Cleopatra. Her slender frame was draped in the soft folds of a snowy-white cloak, the hood pulled up so that I couldn't see much of her face. But when she laughed at something Caesar said, it sounded like the chiming of silver bells. I found myself craning my neck to try and catch a better glimpse of her, wondering what kind of woman could so enthrall the most powerful man in the world.

Standing off to one side of the aristocratic gathering were several soldiers, Caesar's praetorian guard, and Caius Antonius Varro, dressed in full ceremonial armor. Our eyes locked for a moment, and the ghost of a smile curved the Decurion's lips, softening his angular face. For a moment, I found myself frozen in his gaze. What did he see when he looked at me standing there, surrounded by my fellow gladiatrices? Did he still see the wild-eyed slave girl from the ship? Or did he now see me as the warrior I'd always known myself to be?

But then my attention was ripped away from him as, with another blast of the war horn, *she* appeared: the Lady Achillea, lit by the red-gold flames of the torches, driving a war chariot through one of the far archways.

No.

Not the Lady Achillea.

Sorcha of the Cantii.

My sister. Returned from the Morrigan's halls.

XVIII

THE FLAMES OF THE TORCHES flared wildly in a gust of night wind, turning the dark air crimson. There was a tremendous roaring in my ears as all the blood rushed from my head, and I thought I might faint. Sorcha of the Cantii stood tall in the war cart, holding the reins steady in her hands. My sister was alive.

The practice arena spun in dizzying circles all around me as Sorcha drew the horses to a stop in front of us and stepped down from the chariot platform. Gone was the Roman garb of Lady Achillea—the *stola* and *palla*, the crested helmet. She was dressed instead in the traditional garb of a Cantii war chief, wearing a forest-green cloak fastened with a massive silver brooch at her right shoulder. I wondered giddily if the statue of the goddess in the courtyard didn't look upon her with raw envy.

She was magnificent.

It was almost exactly how I remembered her from the

night she rode out of Durovernum for the last time—to face
the Roman legion on our very own soil. She was still as
beautiful as I remembered, slender and lean-muscled, with
her bronze-gold hair spilling over her shoulders to tumble
in loose waves down her back. Something I *didn't* remember was the pale streak of silver that ran through her hair
above her left eye, which seemed darker than her right.
Thin blue lines, painted in woad—the bright blue paste we
used to mark the warriors of my tribe—swirled across her
cheeks and forehead. A sword, carved with a triple raven,
was sheathed on her hip. It was identical to the one Charon
had taken from me that first night after my capture. I bit
the inside of my cheek hard enough to taste blood, if only
to drive away the memory of the morning I learned she
was dead.

My sister wasn't dead. My sister would *never* die. My
sister was a goddess.

Sorcha guided the horses with an expert hand as they
drew her war cart in a slow circle around the oath takers,
who all stood together with heads held high, shoulders
back, and eyes fixed fiercely forward as if searching out the
next adversary, the next challenge, the next target.

"Target or weapon, Fallon . . . Choose."

Her voice echoed in my head.

And what did you *choose, Sorcha? How did you come to this?*

With a sudden shock, I remembered Olun the druid's
prophecy: that I would share the same fate as my sister.
And here I was, having followed her footsteps all the way
to Rome to accomplish just that. In that moment, I would

have whispered a prayer to the Morrigan to ask for her guidance, but I suspected she was too busy laughing at me to have heard.

I glanced at the ranks of the gladiatrices and saw that more than one of them wore an expression that was almost worshipful. Over the years I'd grown up mourning her, my sister had clearly inspired these girls. I swallowed hard against the tightness in my throat.

Sorcha stepped down and reached into the chariot, drawing forth a bow and quiver. Wordlessly, she presented them to the student named Tanis at the end of the row. The girl dipped her head in respect and took them, her eyes shining. I'd seen Tanis practicing with Ajani and suspected that, in time, she had the potential to become just as good.

The next girl was a Phoenician—I gathered that was a place somewhere on the other side of the Mare Nostrum—named Damya who frequently proclaimed herself "descended from a proud warrior race." I was inclined to believe her. When her turn came, Sorcha reached back into her chariot and brought forth a heavy rectangular shield and a bronze arm guard, fashioned of jointed metal plates like the scales of a fearsome dragon. And the fearsome Damya burst into tears of joy at the sight.

I knew that in the weeks since we'd arrived at the ludus, Lady Achillea—no, Sorcha—had been watching us. I'd seen her up on her terrace, observing, analyzing how we fought and what we fought with. I'd never realized just how closely she'd watched us. But that night she presented us with our first earned weapons, matched perfectly to each girl's talents. It was cleverly done, I thought, as I watched each new recruit's eyes brighten and their spines straighten with pride. I wondered just what weapon she had chosen to bestow upon me.

The next three girls, I suspected, had only just made the cut to take the gladiatrix oath. They all showed promise and fierce enthusiasm but had yet to move beyond the basic combat drilling stage to distinguish themselves with a particular weapon. Accordingly, each was presented with the same oath gift of a gladius and small round shield—the standard weapons every gladiatrix learned to master before moving on to other disciplines—but that didn't mean that Sorcha hadn't put just as much thought into personalizing them. Each sword was made to fit the hand of the girl, and each shield was decorated with a different animal that was clearly chosen to match their personalities. Wolf, Lion, and Serpent were all delighted.

Elka was next. She had, of course, distinguished herself over the long days of practice when it came to throwing a spear. And when it came to *not* throwing it, those long arms of hers, together with the reach of an even longer weapon, made Elka virtually invincible as she wore her opponents down from afar. Accordingly, her oath gift was a small round shield and a slender spear with a polished, pointed iron blade that gleamed in the moonlight. I could tell without even hefting it that the weapon was perfectly balanced. Elka marveled at the craftsmanship when Sorcha laid it across her calloused palms.

And then it was my turn.

I stood there, shoulders back, head high, eyes focused somewhere over Sorcha's left shoulder as, wordlessly, she stalked back from retrieving my oath gift from the chariot. And what she gave me . . . was already mine.

My sword.

The only thing other than me that had survived the long journey from Durovernum. The thing that had convinced Charon that I had value and had prompted my sister to buy my life for a ridiculous amount of money.

It seemed that she had commissioned a new leather sheath for it, dyed black and embossed with the intricate, tortuously beautiful artwork of our people. Sorcha belted the sword around my waist and, as its comforting weight settled against my left hip, my hand dropped reflexively to rest on the hilt. It felt as though a severed limb had suddenly been sewn back onto my body.

But then I noticed that on my right hip there hung a second—empty—sheath. I frowned in confusion, then glanced up into my sister's face. With a start, I saw that there was the thin line of a scar, beneath the blue-painted designs on her forehead, running from the shock of silver in her hair down to her over-dark eye. She stared down at me, her expression fierce and hard, as her right hand crossed her body to her own left hip, and she drew the sword she wore.

It was a twin to my blade.

The sword she had carried into battle the last time I'd seen her.

With a swift, brief-as-lightning flourish, she resheathed

the blade in the empty scabbard on *my* hip. A murmur rippled through the watchers beneath the portico. The dimachaerus technique—fighting with two swords—was a rare choice among gladiatrices, and so the second sword was a rare gift. Of course, no one there watching would come close to understanding the true significance of Sorcha's gift to me.

I wasn't even sure if I understood it.

But when I looked up into my sister's face, for a moment I saw something dark and shining moving in her gaze. Then the moment was gone, and Sorcha spun away from me to thrust her arms skyward, fingers splayed, rings and bracelets glittering, and her voice rang into the night air in the ancient war cry of the Cantii. For a fleeting instant, I wondered just what Caesar thought of that. But when he neglected to instruct Caius to step forward and run my sister through with his sword, I decided that he must not care.

She must make him a lot *of money,* I thought bitterly.

Thalestris stepped forward to join my sister, her deep voice ringing out with the words that we, as initiates, were compelled to echo back.

"Uri . . . vinciri . . . verberari . . . ferroque necari."

I will endure to be burned . . . to be bound . . . to be beaten . . . and to be killed by the sword. It was the sacred gladiatorial oath, sworn by men and women alike when they joined the ranks—willingly or no—of the gladiatoria.

"I don't really care to endure any of that," Elka muttered, "given a choice."

But there was no choice. That was the whole point.

"Simple words. Simple promises," Sorcha said as Thalestris's voice echoed to silence. "This oath is the oath we all swear. Not to a god, or a master, or even to the Ludus Achillea . . . but to our sisters who stand here with us. Our sisters. This is the oath that binds us all, one to one, all to all, so that we are no longer free. We belong to each other. We are bound *to each other*. In swearing to each other, we free ourselves from the outside world, from the world of men, from those who would seek to bind us to Fate and that which would make us slaves. We sacrifice our liberty so that, ultimately, we can be *truly* free."

I swallowed the hard knot of fear and uncertainty that stopped up my throat and joined my voice with the others that rang out like chimes in the darkness. And once I did, I felt as though someone had unearthed a box buried deep inside of me. There was a lock on the box, rusted shut, but I could almost feel the turn of a key. I had not come to this place of my own accord, and I had not come looking for my long-dead sister. But the Morrigan had nonetheless led me to find her again. And now, within the confines of these walls, in this place of women warriors, with my sword back at my side, maybe I could begin to look for myself.

But that would come later, on the training grounds.

First, there were the formalities of the rest of the evening to endure. As our voices died away into the darkness, Caesar stepped down from the dais and approached his newly sworn-in gladiatrices, the other ludus masters following in his wake for what seemed to be an informal inspection of our ranks, which meant we were obliged to stand there while Caesar and his guests paced back and forth across the torchlit yard, discussing our various physical attributes as if we were a flock of new lambs and they were a gathering of discerning butchers.

It was unbearable. My sister was there—right *there*, not twenty paces from where I stood—and I couldn't go to her. Even if I could, I didn't know what I would have done. Scream at her? Throw my arms around her? I honestly didn't know.

With the Aegyptian queen on his arm, Caesar beckoned my sister over. I watched Sorcha approach him and was struck by what seemed like a flutter of hesitancy in her step. My sister, who was afraid of nothing and no one. At least . . . she hadn't been. It had been a long time since I had known her.

"It was careless of you to lose Ismene," he said quietly. "She was one of our best."

Ismene. That was the name of the dead girl at the funeral my first night at the ludus. A pained expression flashed across Sorcha's face, but Cleopatra and I were probably the only ones close enough to see it.

"I don't like to lose, Achillea."

The silent implication hung in the air. Caesar let it.

And then, a moment later, he shifted his shoulders beneath the heavy drape of his toga and continued to move down the line of girls. Mighty Caesar had made his point. Sorcha followed him without once glancing in my direction.

"These new initiates hold great promise," Caesar said, raising his voice so the other guests could hear. "I've no doubt you'll train them to take their place as champions in the arena. You always do. Don't you agree, Aquila?"

Caesar made a show of searching Aquila out in the crowd. Of all those gathered dignitaries, only one man had remained seated when Caesar stood. The man known as the Collector seemed vastly unimpressed by Caesar's newest additions to *his* collection.

Caesar glanced back at his other fellows and spread his hands. "Pontius Aquila does not seem to agree," he said.

Up on the dais, Aquila stiffened in his seat.

"You don't approve of my new acquisitions?" Caesar's mocking tone acquired a note of warning. "Or perhaps you don't approve of me. Of my winning ways."

It was clear to me that there was more to the animosity between the two men than a simple rivalry between their ludi. I remembered what Cai had said to me about how the games were almost an extension of the power struggles between the Roman political elite. I glanced over to see that Cai's gaze was fixed on Aquila, his expression stony.

"Since your fighters cannot beat mine in the arena, perhaps you'd best find another pastime," Caesar continued. "Politics, perhaps. Come then, Aquila, take back the Republic from me, Tribune."

Aquila stood—slowly—and turned to Caesar.

"Your pardon, Caesar," Aquila said through gritted teeth. "I find myself indisposed from the heat of the day."

It hadn't been an unusually hot day, and the chill of the

evening had turned almost biting. Caesar turned back to
the others, rolling a sardonic eye.

"Someone fetch the Tribune a cup of wine then, to cool
his fever," he said. "And so that he may toast my noble
warriors who have taken their oaths this night."

Then the matter was dismissed, among guffaws and
mockery of Aquila, and Caesar turned to converse with
his other guests about his upcoming Quadruple Triumphs.
The event would celebrate his victorious military campaign, including his conquest—such as it had been—of my
own home.

"Will they run for an entire month, as I've heard?"
asked one portly man wearing rings on each of his fingers
and both thumbs.

"How else do I properly honor the legions and their con-
quests these past years?" Caesar answered. He tilted back
his head to look up into the dark sky, but his gaze turned
inward. "And I will dedicate them to the memory of my dear
daughter, Julia, the brightest light of my life, too soon gone."

I leaned forward, listening to the men talk. I had heard
that Caesar's only daughter had died in childbirth while
he was away, busy ending the lives of so many others on
my island. A part of me wanted to gloat—to think that he
deserved to lose his beloved kin—but the pain of losing
Sorcha was too raw in my own heart.

The pain of *thinking* I'd lost her.

I stole a glance at her where she now stood at Caesar's
elbow, but Sorcha's expression betrayed nothing of her
thoughts.

"I'm thinking of reenacting my conquering of Britannia as one of the major performances in the Triumphs," Caesar mused, turning to her. "I remember only too well how fiercely you and your women fought against my legions, Achillea. Only this time, I thought I'd turn it around and have your girls fight one of the other ludi, dressed as the shining spirit of *my* legions."

The suggestion was met with much nodding and exclamations over Caesar's brilliance. I gritted my teeth. I'd sooner die than reenact my people's loss, let alone playing the role of a hated Roman soldier.

"And we'll throw in a few of the showier gladiators dressed up as Briton princes, just for the excitement. With the bounty of talent I've seen in your stables, and even at Pontius Aquila's House Amazona, I think a large-scale gladiatrix battle would go over well, don't you?"

"Of course, my lord." Sorcha nodded. "I'll have the drill instructors intensify the girls' practice so that they will be ready."

"Thank you, Achillea, I knew I could count on you." He turned and gestured for the others to follow in the direction of the guesthouse, while Sorcha led Cleopatra in the opposite direction.

Thalestris stepped forward to round up all the girls and send us back to the barracks for sleep. My feet followed the others, but my mind stayed with Sorcha.

My dearly departed sister had some explaining to do.

XIX

I LAY ON MY PALLET in my cell, staring up at the full moon as it crossed the deep black square of sky framed by my tiny window. It felt as though it were the unblinking eye of the Morrigan staring down at me, silently admonishing me for doing nothing about the fact that she had brought me to my sister, who was alive and well and currently enjoying her robust health within shouting distance.

What, the goddess seemed to be asking, was I going to do about it?

After the oath ritual had been completed, Caesar and the men had retired to the guest quarters to drink wine and, I imagined, brag to each other. Cleopatra, I'd heard two of the kitchen slaves say, kept a pleasure barge—gifted to her by Caesar and reserved for her personal use—moored at a villa on the far side of Lake Sabatinus. Her entourage had rowed it across the water for her visit to the ludus, and that was where the Lanista would privately entertain the Aegyptian queen with wine and delicacies late into the night.

Unsurprisingly, sleep eluded me utterly.

Instead, I lay on my cot tossing restlessly and contemplating the sharp turn my life had just taken. As outlandish as it seemed, as bizarrely coincidental, my long-dead sister not only lived, she lived in a palatial house not more than a stone's throw from my cold, cramped cell. After seven long years.

I sat up with a start.

Caius Varro's mystery, at least, was solved: my sword.

Charon had kept my sword, the blade that bore my sister's triple-raven mark, and I suddenly understood he'd kept it because he'd recognized it—and me. That was what the slave master had meant when he'd said the trunk was the key to *both* our fortunes: his fortune, my fate. He must have known who the "Lady Achillea" really was, which meant he'd known that he could likely sell me to her for a royal ransom.

My thoughts turned then to Virico, my royal father. After our mother had died birthing me, Sorcha had become the shining light in his world. And when she'd died—no, when she'd *disappeared*—that flame had been snuffed out forever. My brave, handsome father had lived as a broken man ever since. I could only wonder what my abduction had done to him.

And it was all her fault.

The anger toward Virico that I'd kept alive in my heart, like a glowing ember, flared brightly. Only now, its heat was directed toward Sorcha. Seething, I threw off my blanket, swinging my bare feet to the cold stone floor. The back of my neck was damp with sweat, and I felt like there was a fire burning deep inside my skull. I dressed and threw on my long woolen cloak, pulling the hood up over my hair. Then I quietly opened the door to my cell and slipped out into the corridor, padding swiftly toward the archway that led out into the practice yard, where the flower garlands still swayed between the extinguished torches.

Unlike what I'd been told about most men's ludi, especially the ones that had a high ratio of criminals-turned-gladiators, we had guards at the Ludus Achillea but no locks on the cell doors—not in the barracks, at least. I knew that there were other cells, down near the stables, that did have bars and locks, for the rare occasion that a student merited extreme punishment, but I'd not known any of the girls to spend even a single night in them in the time I had been there. My sister ran a well-mannered academy.

Still, that didn't exactly mean that wandering the academy grounds in the deep of the night was encouraged. But I wasn't on any midnight kitchen raid, and I didn't plan on getting caught by the guards. Cold anger washed over me like winter rain as I padded swiftly down the deserted corridor and out onto the grounds of the compound. As I neared the guesthouse, I could hear men's voices, but I turned down a different path.

A fist of apprehension closed around my heart as I set off across the practice arena and slipped through a breezeway, into the outer yard, heading toward the massive wooden

gates that opened out onto Lake Sabatinus, where the charioteers would race their carts. The gates were carved with
scenes of women fighting in various settings—against each
other, against wild beasts, on horseback and in chariots,
throwing spears and shooting arrows—and they stood open.

Out on the lake, the Aegyptian queen's barge was
moored to the ludus pier. The bow and stern of the elegant
watercraft were carved like bundles of reeds tied together
and painted in red and gold and blue. I could hear women's
laughter drifting from the large tent pitched in the middle
of the broad deck. I started down the beach toward where
the dock jutted out past the gleaming line of white foam of
the water's edge.

For a brief, fanciful moment, I imagined that Nyx
would suddenly appear in her chariot to chase me down
the strand and crush me under hooves and iron-rimmed
wheels.

Of course, she didn't. But there was someone else
there, standing on the landward side of the pier. I squinted
and saw it was Thalestris, and I saw that she was armed.
I didn't think there was any way the grim fight mistress
would let me near my sister tonight. But when she saw
me approaching, Thalestris seemed to hesitate a moment.
Then she loped up the gangplank and ducked into the tent.
I waited on the beach, wondering. Guards armed with
short, powerful-looking bows stood on the deck, fore and
aft of the tent, watching me with stern gazes.

After a few moments, Thalestris reappeared and beckoned me with a curt wave of her hand. The mist lay heavy

on the dark mirror of the Sabatinus, and the only sound was the lapping of wavelets on the barge as I stepped aboard. The white-and-gold fabric of the tent pavilion billowed gently in a bare hint of breeze off the shrouded waters of the lake.

Silently, Thalestris ushered me into the tent and left me there.

Inside, as my eyes adjusted to the dim light of hanging oil lamps and a gently glowing brazier, I could make out two figures reclining opposite each other on Roman couches. My sister and Cleopatra, queen of Aegypt. Up close, I saw that she bore little resemblance to any of the people I'd already met who claimed descent from that fabled land. Of course, I remembered hearing that it was because she was actually more Greek than anything. I'd also heard her called ugly and awkward, but I thought she was beautiful in a strange, compelling way. An overlong nose and eyes that were huge beneath strong, arching brows gave her a feline quality, and her face was framed by a helmet of thick-twisted braids held in place with gold and turquoise beads. Her dress was made of layers of sheer, pleated linen that floated out around her exquisitely.

She gazed at me with a frank, open curiosity, and I wasn't sure how to react in that moment. When I'd been the daughter of Virico, king of the Cantii, I'd occasionally been called upon to play gracious hostess to a gang of unruly Celt chieftains, but this? I almost forgot about Sorcha for a moment. I was intently aware, suddenly, of my unbrushed hair and the creases in the tunic I wore.

And the iron collar around my neck.

Nervously, I looked over to the woman whose features were as familiar to me as my own. My sister had barely aged.

"You've grown," she said by way of greeting.

"It's been a long time since you left us." My voice sounded weirdly strangled to my ears. "I was just a little girl."

"You were hardly that." Her gazed roamed over me, but her face remained impassive.

I felt my heart thudding in my chest and was overwhelmed with the urge to run to her and throw my arms around her, weeping with the joy of having found her again. My brave, beautiful sister. I quashed the impulse mercilessly.

"I'm surprised you remember what I looked like at all," I said instead. "Do you even remember my name?"

"Don't act the wounded child," she said. She turned back to Cleopatra. "Majesty, I am sorry for this one's intrusion—and her behavior."

"Oh no." Cleopatra held up a hand. "No need to apologize, believe me. I'm well acquainted with the . . . frictions, shall we say, that can arise between siblings. Especially sisters."

"Your majesty is too gracious."

"Not at all." She waved her hand. "I am honored to bear witness to a family reunion. Please, forget I'm even here." She grinned, a slightly feral expression, and winked at me.

I remembered having heard gossip among the ludus girls that Cleopatra's sister, Arsinoe, had tried—unsuccessfully—to wrest control of the Aegyptian throne from her.

Cleopatra had wanted her killed, but Caesar had other, perhaps crueler ideas. He spared Arsinoe so that he could trot her out like a trained animal in a victory parade of his captive enemies during his upcoming Triumphs.

Clearly, Sorcha had told the queen who I was and how I'd come to be at the ludus. And yet she hadn't seen fit to reveal herself to me before the ceremony. "Why?"

The word tore from my lips. Sorcha frowned at me.

"Why didn't you *tell* me before now?" I tried to keep my voice steady. "Before just . . . just appearing in front of me—in front of everyone—like that! I've been living here in a cell all this time, and it never even occurred to you to let me know that you were still alive? That you owned me?"

At this, my sister had the good manners to grow flushed and look away. "You know nothing of the *why* of things, Fallon," she muttered.

"You're right," I spat. "I only know I've grown up thinking my beloved sister was dead."

"She is. I am not the girl you knew."

"No. I suspect not. I'm sure Father would agree."

I saw the fingers of Sorcha's right hand clench. "He is well?"

"He lives."

"I'm glad—"

"Broken and heartsick, as he's been for years."

The clenched hand again. Sorcha and my father had been so close. I knew it was cruel of me to say such things, but I was hurt. And angry.

"I never wanted that," Sorcha said quietly. "And I certainly never wanted *this*."

"What?"

"You." Her eyes flicked back to my face, and her gaze was searing. "Here."

The words felt like a slap in the face—hard and sharp and stinging. "Then why did you buy me?" I asked, furious with myself at the way my voice broke. "Why bring me here?"

"Well, it certainly wasn't because of how you fought at the auction!" she said sharply. "I thought I taught you better than that. That Alesian would have cut you in two in another moment if it hadn't been for Elka stepping in to save your hide!"

We glared across the tent at each other. The whole argument suddenly felt like a moment plucked from my childhood when I'd once again done something dangerous or foolish. Or simply not good enough.

"I brought you here to keep you safe," she said. "Because you were somehow foolish enough to be taken by slavers and *lucky* enough that one of them was Charon. I had to keep you from being sold into a situation a hundred times more dangerous. But to do that, I put the fate of every other girl in this ludus at risk."

"I don't have the faintest idea what you mean."

"I don't expect you to." With a huff, she pushed herself up off her couch and strode over to a side table that held a wine jug and goblets. She sloshed a generous measure of dark red wine into one of the goblets and took a long drink before turning back to me. "You're not in Durovernum anymore, Fallon. You're here. And there's not a damned thing either of us can do about it. You belong to this ludus now, and that means you belong to Caesar, and if any of the other lanistas knew who you were, they wouldn't hesitate to hurt you to get to me. I can't be your sister here."

"Or anywhere, it seems."

She glanced at me sharply.

"Does *he* know who I am?" I asked sullenly. "Your lord and master, the mighty Caesar?"

Sorcha glanced sideways at Cleopatra, who'd remained silent throughout our entire exchange. I belatedly remembered that the foreign queen was Caesar's consort, but she remained unruffled by my rudeness. She plucked a grape from the bunch on the plate in front of her and popped it into her mouth, her grin never wavering. She seemed to be enjoying herself.

"He does *not* know who you are or why I bought you." Sorcha put her goblet down hard enough to rattle the other dishes on the low table. "No one does beyond the three of us here and Charon, whose silence on the matter I paid for handsomely. Here, you're just another gladiatrix, and if the goddess is good, no one will ever know the difference."

"Surely Caesar must wonder at the price you paid for me," I said.

"I manage this academy on his behalf, and I've yet to give him cause for complaint. And even though your contract is made out in his name, it wasn't his money."

I blinked at her. "What?"

"I didn't spend Caesar's money." She looked at me, her gaze unnerving in the growing light. "It was mine."

"Well, obviously this life had been very good to you. I can see why you never came home—"

"I fought for every sestersii tooth and claw. I saved everything I won, and I was going to *buy* the Ludus Achillea outright. I would still operate it under Caesar's name, but any girl who fought for me would do so as a free person. No more slaves. I had already pleaded my case to Caesar, and he was agreeable, so long as I had the money."

I stared at her. "I didn't think a woman in Rome could take that kind of control over her own fate," I said.

Cleopatra leaned in. "That's exactly what your sister said when I first suggested she buy the ludus years ago. And truthfully, there are those who would tell you it is so. Crusty old power-mad patricians who balk at giving any kind of power to the 'weaker' sex. But Caesar, for all he is called tyrant, is a man who will listen to reason if it's to his ultimate advantage. Even—sometimes *especially*—when it comes from the lips of a woman. It's why some of the senators fear him—and hate me."

"Her Majesty has been a great friend to me during my time in Rome," Sorcha said, nodding at the queen.

Cleopatra shrugged. "A woman ought to be able to chart her own course in life."

"Which is exactly what I was doing"—Sorcha turned to glower at me—"before I had to open my coffers to spill such an exorbitant amount of money on you, little sister." She sighed. "I was almost there. Now it will take me years, if ever, to gather that sum again. I can no longer fight in the games. Not with a dim eye and a weak arm."

"What happened?" I silently cursed myself for asking the question. I didn't want to care, but she was still my sister.

She paused, her expression unreadable, and for a moment I thought she wouldn't answer. But eventually she said, "I attempted the Morrigan's Flight during a pageant."

I sucked in a breath, imagining the moment vividly.

"I fell, of course," she continued. "It's an impossible feat. The chariot wheel clipped my shoulder and ran over my helmet, leaving me with this." She waved a hand at the scar on the left side of her face.

I fought an absurd urge to tell Sorcha about my own successful—*mostly* successful—attempt at the same maneuver, as if I were still a little girl trying to impress her older sister.

"It ended my days in the arena. And there's not one girl in the ranks who could draw the kind of purses I did in my day." Her frustration was palpable, like the close, crackling feeling on your skin before a storm. "I even had the papers drawn up so that if I died, the ludus would pass unencumbered to Thalestris so that she could continue my legacy and keep the gladiatrices safe. And free."

"Papers?" I frowned.

"A contract. Signed and witnessed and legally binding."

I'd heard of such things, but it seemed a very silly way to do things. Vellum could burn, papyrus could tear. What in the world was wrong with a good solid blood oath?

"Romans and their contracts." I shook my head, angry

and confused that Sorcha had stooped to such nonsense. "Bits of parchment and scribbling—"

"*Yes.*" Sorcha was adamant. "And *every* bit as binding to them as a blood oath is to you and me. Don't you see? Freedom, Fallon. That's the only thing that's ever mattered. It's why we fought the Romans on our own soil. It's why Arviragus laid waste to his own lands. And if I have to fight now with silver coins and ink and paper instead of a sword to win freedom for me and mine, I will still do it with a warrior's heart."

"Why didn't you come to me when I first got here?" I asked quietly. "Was it because you didn't think I was worthy?"

"No. I stayed away because . . ." She turned her face from me, and the light from the glowing brazier washed her profile in fire. "Because I feared you wouldn't think *I* was."

I didn't know what to say to that. Sorcha had never been anything but worthy in my mind, up until that night.

"I know you think that what we do here is somehow less honorable than the kind of fighting our clans do back home," she continued. "But it's not, Fallon. The world is a great deal wider than the fields and forests around Durovernum. You think the royal war band was more honorable than the men and women who fight and die on the sands of the arena? Back there we fought over stolen cattle and slighted pride. Here, I'm fighting for family. For a sisterhood. For *you.*"

Suddenly her eyes narrowed, and she shot to her feet.

Before I could react, she reached out and snatched the black feather that I'd forgotten was still tied in my hair.

"Where did this come from?" she asked, holding it up between us.

"A bird, I should think."

"Where did you *get* it?"

"I found it on my pillow one night when I returned to my cell from the baths," I said. "The same night I saw a dead crow at the feet of the Minerva statue."

I watched, astonished, as all the blood drained from my sister's face. She tore the ebony quill from my braid and snapped it in two, throwing it into the flames of her brazier. A thread of black smoke rose from it, and a faint acrid stink wafted through the tent.

"Fallon, all these years, you've thought me dead. It would be for the best if you continued to think of me that way. You cannot—you *must* not—tell anyone who you are."

For a moment, it seemed to me as if my sister was abandoning me all over again. But then I saw the look in her eyes and saw that wasn't what this was about. An uneasy shiver ran up my spine at the look in her eyes. It reminded me of when one of the chariot horses would spook at something only their animal senses could perceive. I remembered the conversation I'd had with Cai—about ravens and omens—and I wondered if the feather curling to ash in the brazier hadn't been some kind of portent. A warning, maybe, or a threat.

"Promise me, Fallon," she demanded.

Either living in this treacherous place had unhinged her, I thought, or there was something she wasn't telling me. Either way, it seemed as if my brave sister had been reduced to jumping at shadows.

"All right," I said. "Fine. I promise."

My gaze drifted over to Cleopatra. Sorcha didn't seem to mind the Aegyptian queen knowing who I was. But Cleopatra smiled at me, gently this time.

"The Lanista and I are old friends," she said. "And dear. I keep her secrets as she keeps mine. Do not fear me, Fallon."

I nodded. For some reason, I trusted her.

"Understand this," Sorcha said. "You'll get no special treatment from me either. You will train, and you will fight. You will be rewarded or punished commensurate with your actions. Eventually, you will enter the arena, and, the goddess willing, you will not die there."

"The will of the goddess won't be the one keeping me alive," I said. "I'm not target practice anymore, Sorcha."

Something flitted through her gaze then—a fleeting emotion that I imagined might have been a touch of pride. She blinked and turned away.

"Tomorrow," she continued, "you will go with the other new girls to the blacksmith down at the stables. He will remove your slave collars. You'll still be the property of Caesar, but at least you won't have to look like it."

The very thought of ridding myself of the horrible thing made my heart lurch. But then it sank again. I wasn't free. I was still a slave in this place, and I wasn't about to forget that.

I wasn't about to let Sorcha—my sister, my owner—forget it either.

XX

IF THALESTRIS, with her spear, hadn't been watching me like a hawk as I headed back toward the ludus gates, I might have made a break for freedom. In the wake of the oath taking, and coming face to face with Sorcha, I was a roil of emotions. The lake's beach, stretching out in a gentle curve to the north, beckoned. I could run. I could even swim. But to what? To where? And to whom?

Even if I could forgive my father—and as the days and days had taken me ever farther away from him, I started to think that maybe I already had—I wasn't foolish enough to think that I could make it all the way back to the Island of the Mighty on my own, without even the swords my sister had gifted me.

And then there was my sister herself.

Try as I might, I couldn't just leave this place that Sorcha seemed to have made her own. Not before I truly understood what had made her choose this life over the one she'd once shared with me. Now it seemed I shared *my* life with her—and with the other girls and women of the Ludus Achillea.

I'd spoken an oath to it.

And, if Sorcha was to be believed, I was the reason their freedom was in jeopardy.

I turned and retraced my steps back up the strand and through the gates into the compound. Halfway back to my cell, I was surprised to discover that I wasn't the only one wandering the ludus grounds that night.

"Good evening, Decurion Varro."

Cai didn't exactly jump out of his skin at the sound of my voice, but he spun around smartly. I thought for a moment that I might have heard the rattle of his sword in its sheath—a soldier's training—but then he saw it was only me. Unarmed, for once.

"I'm sorry," I said. "I didn't mean to startle you."

His shadow merged with mine on the path as he said, "It's Cai, remember?"

Cai. I tested it out in my head. For the first time, it seemed to suit him. Probably because there was nothing of the Decurion about him in that moment. He'd shed the dress armor he'd worn for the ceremony and was dressed simply in a tunic and toga. His head was bare of helmet, and there were matching silver cuffs circling his wrists instead of bronze arm guards. The legionnaire's upright-ness was gone from his stance, and he moved with a kind of easy grace. But, I noticed with a smile, he still wore a sword strapped to his waist.

"What are you doing out in the darkness alone?" he asked.

"I couldn't sleep," I answered truthfully.

He studied my face for a moment. Then he offered me an elbow. "In that case, will you honor me with your company, fair gladiatrix?" he asked, a hint of amusement in his voice.

I hesitated. That's really what I was now: a gladiatrix. For a moment, it felt as if the collar around my neck were growing tighter, choking me.

"Fallon?" Cai looked at me. "Are you all right?"

"I'm fine," I said.

I took a deep breath as I slipped my hand into the crook of his arm. If the world insisted that I was now a gladiatrix, worthy of Roman attention that went beyond mere curiosity, then I would play the part.

Cai wrapped his hand over mine, and his fingers were warm and strong as we walked in the gardens that stretched between the ludus compound and the high, thick walls that surrounded it. I would catch proper hell if any of the guards found me alone in the night with a man. But right now, I didn't care. I could feel the tension leave my shoulders and arms the longer we walked in silence. Cai's presence was a steady, calming one.

"I didn't think to see you tonight at the oath swearing," I said finally.

He shrugged. "I was simply here in my official capacity."

"And that is?"

He smiled tightly. "As Caesar's errand boy, of course."

"You're hardly an errand boy."

"Oh, yes I am," he said. "My father saw to it that I would find myself in a position that was both useful to him and, to his way of thinking, useful to me."

"And have you found it useful?" I asked.

"I serve." He shrugged again. "As far as useful . . . well, occasions such as this afford me the opportunity to brush elbows with my patrician betters, even if it means I have to stomach the company of the likes of Pontius Aquila for the evening."

"The Tribune of the Plebs?" I asked. "The one people call the Collector?"

"Not to his face." Cai grimaced.

"He and Caesar don't seem overly fond of each other."

Cai laughed softly. "You have a gift for understatement, Fallon. The Tribune is here tonight at Caesar's invitation—an invitation he could hardly refuse—and it's positively killing him to have to stand there making polite conversation all night. Which, I think, was Caesar's intention. That and to flaunt his newest acquisitions."

"Like Elka and me. Aquila tried to buy us," I said, remembering. "That day in the Forum."

Cai nodded, thoughtful. "Until the Lady Achillea swooped in with her sizable purse, yes. He has an insatiable thirst for the games, and his stables of fighters are almost as impressive as Caesar's. Aquila is far from rich, but politically, at least, he's a power to be reckoned with. Personally,

I find the man—and his appetite for death in the arena—repugnant. But I'm required to be cordial because my father is an investor in several of Aquila's ludi. One of which is the House Amazona."

"The other gladiatrix school?"

"The same."

"Our rival, then. But that means your father holds interests in direct competition with Caesar's." I looked up at him. "Isn't that a conflict of loyalties for you?"

"I'm an officer in the Roman legion, Fallon," he snorted. "And the son of a senator. It makes me impervious to moral conundrums."

I couldn't tell if he was serious or not. It was irritating, the way the Roman mind seemed to work. And the Roman mouth. Cai, as far as I could tell, could say one thing and mean another entirely, and he didn't seem to find anything inherently confusing in that.

"But I will say this," Cai continued, oblivious to my frustration. "If it hadn't been for Pontius Aquila, I might never have met you. It was at his request that I was in Massilia to escort Charon's galley. And barring that one moment when you tried to stab me, I found the experience . . . gratifying."

I raised an eyebrow at him. "Gratifying?"

He smiled. "Extremely."

I'd found that Latin could sometimes be tricky when it came to the exact meanings of words. But there was no mistaking the tone of Cai's voice, nor the look in his eyes.

I felt heat rising in my face. He found me attractive—that much was plain—but something had changed in his gaze since the first time he'd looked at me on the legion ship after the pirate attack.

"I've found myself wondering about the place you come from," he continued. "About your tribe. I wonder, do they all fight like you do? Are the men as fierce as the women?"

"Is that a polite way of asking if the women of my tribe fight naked?" I asked.

I'd meant only to tease him, but his eyes went a bit wide, and I wondered if I had been far too bold. I had forgotten myself and spoken not like a slave but like his equal. Like the daughter of a king. Remembering Sorcha's warning not to reveal my real station, I bit my tongue to keep from mentioning it again.

Cai didn't seem to notice. "Why don't we just leave my thirst for knowledge unslaked for the time being?" He grinned at last. "The air tonight is too cold for such a contest anyway."

For a moment, we just stood there, looking at each other. It was the first time we'd shared a joke that wasn't bitter or barbed. Cai's grin widened to a smile and he gestured to a stone garden bench that stood just off the path. I followed and Cai sat down beside me, drifting into silence again. The smile faded on his lips as something else clearly occupied his thoughts.

"Fallon, I've been thinking," he said finally, turning to meet my gaze. "I've watched dozens of men and women speak the oath you swore tonight. And I've seen just as many fulfill that oath on the arena sands. I never thought anything of it, but tonight it was different."

"Why?" I asked.

"Because it was you."

"I must have said the words wrong." I laughed, suddenly feeling a little nervous.

Instead of laughing with me, Cai leaned forward, his face pale and earnest in the moonlight. "No," he said. "In fact, the way you said it, it was the truest I ever heard those words ring. And I realized that I don't want to see you burned or bound or beaten . . . or killed by the sword."

I laughed again. This was definitely not the turn I'd expected the conversation to take. Surely we were still joking? I was surprised to see that his expression remained serious.

"Listen," he said. "My father is one of the wealthiest men in Rome. I can go to Caesar—he owes me at least one favor for my years of service to him—and I can offer to buy your contract. I could—"

"*What?* No!"

I sprang to my feet and stared down at him.

"You would dishonor me?" I said angrily.

"Dishonor you?" He blinked at me. "Fallon—"

"I will not be bought and sold like livestock, Caius Varro! Not again. Certainly not by you."

Cai's mouth dropped open, then closed and slowly hardened into a line. "You know the life you have committed yourself to often ends in death," he said.

"All life does."

"I would not have you die at all if I could help it, Fallon."
He stood and moved to take my hand, but I crossed my
arms tightly in front of me and took a step back. "But since
I don't have the powers of the gods, I would beg this favor
of them: I would not have you die any day *soon*."

"Your faith in my abilities as a warrior is nothing short
of staggering," I snapped.

"You're not the only girl in the arena who can swing a
blade!" he snapped back.

I'd almost begun to think that Cai was different—that
there was even a chance that he believed in me. But suddenly, it felt just like being a little girl again, listening to
Sorcha tell me that I would be target practice for every
warrior I met on the battlefield. It felt like when my father
denied me a place in his royal war band because he feared
that he might lose me, that I couldn't hold my own on the
battlefield. Sometimes I wondered if even Mael had simply
thought me more reckless than brave.

"I thought you said you admired my spirit," I said. "I
thought I reminded you of Spartacus."

"I did." His voice softened as he took me gently by the
shoulders. "You do. Fallon, Spartacus is dead because he
decided he wanted to live free, and he had to rebel against
the might of the whole empire to do it. And yes, he has my
admiration, but it does him precious little good in his present state. I only want to keep you away from the arena so
that you can avoid a similar fate."

I shook my head. "You just heard me swear an oath,

and with my next breath, you would have me break it. I am a daughter of the house of Cantii."

"And what does that mean?"

"It means I don't break promises—even ones I wouldn't have made, given a choice—and I will not break this one. Not even for you, Caius Varro."

Cai's eyes flashed.

"Not *even* for me?" he asked, tilting his head. "Does that mean I'm something to be taken into consideration in your decision making, Fallon?"

I wished I could take the words back. I wasn't even sure what I had meant.

"Do not flatter yourself, Decurion," I muttered, turning away from his gaze and shrugging free of his grasp.

Silence stretched out between us, and it became increasingly difficult to hang on to my indignation. Especially when I heard him let out a low, throaty chuckle. I looked back to see him grinning at me.

"You think about me," he said.

He took me again by the shoulders, drawing me toward him. I could feel the heat coming off his skin. In the cool night, I wanted to take that warmth and wrap it around me like a blanket. I wanted *him* wrapped around me. I knew I shouldn't. If anyone caught us together, I would most likely be flogged, and Cai would be shamed. But he didn't seem to care in that moment. He moved closer to me, and the cloak I wore fell back away from my shoulders, as Cai's hands lightly moved up my arms, over my shoulders and down my back to my waist, tracing my body through the thin material of my tunic. I shivered, and he looked down at me.

"You're freezing," he said, stepping back to tug the edges of the heavy wool cloak back over my shoulders.

But I wasn't freezing. I burned. Everywhere his hands had touched me, the skin was seared as surely as if I had been branded there.

He lifted a hand to my cheek, and I felt the rough calluses there, left behind by the countless hours his fingers had spent wrapped around the hilt of a sword. But when he bent his head beside mine, his breath teasing my neck just below my ear, and he murmured my name . . . I froze. I couldn't see Cai's face. Instead, all I could hear in my mind was another whispering voice.

Mael's.

"What's wrong?" Cai whispered, sensing my sudden reluctance.

I shook my head and squeezed my eyes shut.

"You're a senator's son, and I . . ."

"What?"

"I am *infamia*." I opened my eyes and looked up into his face. I might as well embrace the cold truth of the night. "Even if the ludus wouldn't punish me for being here, with you, if they found us together . . . the oath I swore tonight marks me as sure as a brand on my skin."

His gaze darkened. "You think I care about that?"

"You should."

"Fallon—"

"I should return to my quarters now, Decurion. You'll excuse me."

I turned and walked—ran, really—away from him before I betrayed myself any further. My heart pounded in my chest, and my throat ached with unshed tears. Even though I'd heard Mael's voice, plain as day, in my head, I'd also realized, for the first time, that I could no longer picture his face.

I couldn't remember what he looked like.

The image of him had been slowly fading over time, and I'd let it slip away. To be replaced by the face of another—of our *enemy*. What kind of a monster was I? Tears seeped through my lashes and ran down my cheeks, burning with shame.

As I made my way back to the barracks, taking a shortcut between the baths and the cooks' quarters, I heard sounds—voices coming from around the corner of the grain shed. It seemed that Cai and I weren't the only ones indulging in midnight strolls. I stopped and held my breath, wiping the wetness from my cheeks. The ludus guards may not have caught me in an embrace with a legion officer, but I still didn't exactly want to have to explain any weepy midnight wanderings to them. All I wanted was to get back to my cell and collapse on my pallet.

But the voices continued.

"Does he know she's here?" asked a female voice. "Within barely a half-day's ride of him?"

A man laughed in reply, an ugly sound.

"You mean Mandobracius?" he said. I recognized the voice and froze—it was Pontius Aquila. The Collector.

"Is that what he's calling himself now?" the woman asked.

"One of his fellow barbarians coined that gem after he won his last bout—they all speak Latin like they're chewing on shoe leather—and it seems to have stuck."

Mandobracius? I puzzled through the mangled Latin to arrive at something like "Devouring Arms." A gladiator, I gathered, from the mention of a bout. I wondered if those gathered elites ever talked of anything else.

"No," Aquila continued. "No, I haven't told him yet. That sort of information could prove priceless when it comes time to bending that wretched barbarian to my will. He's damned lucky things turned out the way they did—no thanks to his incompetence."

"It's uncanny," the woman said.

"It's fate. That girl *will* be mine. The gods have willed it so." His voice turned suddenly low and threatening. "In the meantime, you'll not breathe a word of it to Mandobracius—or to anyone else. Do I make myself clear?"

The woman made a choking noise of assent. It sounded as if he was physically threatening her. I thought to make a noise—a cough or a shoe scrape on the gravel, as if I'd just now come walking up the path—but then I heard the woman bid Aquila good night, albeit a little hoarsely. I pressed myself against the side of the grain shed, fearing that they would find me eavesdropping. I feared for the girl they spoke of, the one Pontius believed was his.

I wondered if it might be me . . .

Don't be ridiculous. I gave my head a stern shake.

What Cai had said to me earlier was certainly true—I wasn't the only girl who could swing a sword. And so far, in my brief time at the Ludus Achillea, I hadn't done anything to distinguish myself. I was nothing more than a green little gladiolus in the eyes of Sorcha's dignified guests.

Girls like Nyx and Meriel were the ones who caught the wealthy patrons' eyes, not me. Not yet. Still, it was good to know that Sorcha and Cai hadn't exactly been exaggerating the Roman propensity for secrets and double-dealing. I heard the voices moving on, growing faint in the distance, and I let out a slow breath.

Let the ludus owners and their lanistas backstab and bargain. I cared only for bed and sleep and maybe a dream or two. I smiled wearily as I loped down the path back to the barracks. I hoped my dreams would be good ones, because in the morning, it was back to the basics of sand and sweat and the sword.

But this time, it would be as a gladiatrix in my own right.

Not just a maybe, a someday.

A *would be*, I vowed.

XXI

MY FIRST DAY as a gladiatrix began with the stench of blood.

"What happened?" I asked fight master Kronos as he elbowed his way through the girls gathered at the edge of the practice pitch. The smell curdled the honeyed porridge in my stomach that I'd only just wolfed down.

"Accident" was his brusque response in passing. "Need a stretcher."

I turned on my heel and ran after him to help. Just inside the equipment shed, there were several canvas stretchers hanging on the wall.

"Take an end," Kronos grunted at me, lifting one off the storage hooks.

We sprinted back out into the yard, Kronos bellowing for the girls to make way. As we neared the arena, I saw the crumpled body of a girl lying in a pool of blood, shockingly red against the white-gold sand. She was the one Sorcha had gifted with the sword and shield with the lion motif at the oath swearing. Her sparring partner, the girl with the serpent shield, stood nearby with a blank look of shock and a bloodied sword.

Lion's hand still held her sword too. Only it lay in the sand a little distance away from her, the slender fingers still curled around the hilt of the weapon. The sight of it was jarringly wrong.

Thalestris was on her knees, tearing linen into strips and wrapping Lion's arm as tightly as she could while crimson spurted in time with the beating of the girl's heart. Her eyes had rolled back in her head, and her mouth was open, a low animal-sounding moan coming from it.

"What happened?" Kronos asked the fight mistress as he and I set the stretcher down beside the injured girl. The other gladiatrices stood helplessly in a ring.

"Fools," she grunted through clenched teeth. "Thought they'd do a bit of sparring with their oath gifts. Neither of them has ever held a real blade."

Especially not one as sharp as a blade chosen by my sister. Lion and Serpent should have known better. But I'd also seen how very excited they'd been, and I could hardly blame them for wanting to play like giddy children with their new toys. Now Lion would never fight again—if she even survived the injury—and I shuddered to think what Sorcha would do to Serpent.

I glanced at Lion's severed hand and choked back the bile that rose in my throat at the sight of the gleaming white bone sticking out of the end. I looked away to see Sorcha running from the main house, her face contorted and her hair and robes spread wide in her wake. The avenging Fury.

Serpent went even paler as the Lanista approached.

When my sister stopped in front of her, Serpent burst into tears.

She could have her flogged, I thought, *or turned out of the ludus.* But then, to my complete surprise, Sorcha stepped forward and gathered her into a fierce embrace. I knelt there in the sand, staring as Sorcha rocked the girl like a frightened child.

Thalestris finished doing what she could for the injured gladiatrix, and then the ludus physician—a quiet, broad-shouldered man named Heron—helped Kronos get the girl onto the stretcher. They rushed her toward the infirmary as I stood there, not knowing what to do.

I felt a sudden spattering of fat raindrops, and then the clouds opened up, pouring down rain in hissing gray sheets. Lightning split the sky, and Thalestris shouted for everyone to get inside, that the day's practice was cancelled. The arena was deserted in moments. And still I stood there. The rain was almost blinding, reducing the world around me to a circle in the sand—just me, and Lion's sword, and her hand. In the confusion, the trainers had forgotten it. Not that it mattered, really.

And yet, I couldn't just leave it lying there. I stripped off my cloak and knelt down in front of the sword and hand. The rain had washed away the blood, leaving the fingers pale and cool. Spreading my cloak out on the sand, I picked up the hand and blade and shifted them gently onto the wool. I wrapped them up as carefully as I could—exceedingly mindful of the sharp edge of the blade—and cradled them like a bairn as I put my head down and slogged through the now muddy pitch toward the infirmary.

As I entered, I could smell the sharp tang of the vinegar antiseptic they used to clean wounds, and my stomach turned over. Lion was lying on a cot, and the neat white bed linens were stained with red. Sorcha sat beside her bed, smoothing the hair back from her pale face, while Heron and his assistant worked to stanch the flow of blood. As I watched, the surgeon wiped his hands on his apron, leaving more red there, and disappeared behind a curtained wall. He returned with a bronze brazier full of angry red coals and a metal bell-shaped tool that had been heated until it glowed.

My stomach didn't so much turn over at the sight as threaten to hurl its contents back up again. I knew what would come next. My gasp alerted Sorcha to my presence, and she rose from the girl's bedside and hurried over to me.

"What are you doing here, Fallon?" she murmured urgently. "You shouldn't be—"

"I brought this." I pulled back the corner of my cloak to reveal Lion's hand and held the bundle out toward my sister. "I didn't want to leave it in the rain," I said. "I didn't know what else to do . . ."

Sorcha looked down and then, after a long moment, back up at me. She blinked rapidly and reached out, gently drawing the cloth back over the hand and the sword it still clutched.

"That was honorably done, Fallon," she said. "I'll take care of it."

She took the bundle from me and then wrapped an arm around my shoulders, leading me out of the infirmary. "Come on," she said. "You shouldn't be here right now."

The screams of agony and the stench of seared flesh drifted down the corridor behind us. Sorcha walked me all the way back to the barracks in silence.

"You won't send her away, will you?" I asked, fearing that Lion—whose true name I still didn't even know— would be turned out of the ludus to wind up a beggar in Rome's filthy back alleys.

"Weren't you listening during the oath ritual?" she asked. "We don't abandon our sisters."

For a moment, I thought the irony would escape Sorcha. But then a faint flush crept up her face, and she glanced away from me. I decided to let the moment pass. Some things were more important.

"But she can't ever make back the money you've lost in buying her slave contract," I said. "She's useless to the ludus now."

"You have such a low opinion of this place. Of me."

She looked at me, and I saw actual hurt in her eyes. Her gaze drifted down to the iron ring that was still around my neck. I had refused to go with Elka when she'd gone to have hers removed. She'd told me I was an idiot, and perhaps she was right.

Sorcha shook her head. "I suppose I've earned that. But I do wish you would at least give the ludus a chance before condemning it as a place as cruel and cold-hearted as its mistress. I have to go prepare Antonia's hand for a proper burial. Thank you for bringing it to me. The Morrigan watch over you, Fallon."

And then she was gone.

I watched her walk away like a queen or a priestess toward the tiny, elegant building that served as a kind of multifaith temple for all the girls of the ludus. I could no longer hear the screams of the handless Antonia with my ears.

But they echoed in my mind for a long time after.

Practice resumed the next day, under a dismal gray sky that threatened more rain but refused to pour. None of the girls talked about what had happened the day before, but all of them—even the veteran gladiatrices, I noticed—fought their bouts and drills with wooden blades. Within a few days, though, everything was more or less back to normal. With the exception of Neferet (the Aegyptian girl with the serpent shield), who vehemently refused to continue practice. Instead she spent most of her waking hours in the infirmary helping Heron tend Antonia in the struggle to keep her wound from succumbing to infection.

Six days after the oath swearing, Caius Varro returned to the Ludus Achillea with missives from Rome for the Lanista. But instead of leaving after his correspondence was delivered, he accompanied Thalestris out to the yard, where the girls were all hard at work. I had to stop myself from greeting him as he passed by. I knew he was on Caesar's business, likely reporting back to him on our progress.

Who do you think you are now? I reminded myself bitterly. *In the eyes of any Roman, Caius Varro is a legion officer, and you're nothing more than a diversion for the howling plebs— a vulgar bit of sweaty, bloody entertainment.*

As much as Sorcha proclaimed the honorable nature of my new occupation, I still didn't believe her. I wanted to . . . I just couldn't. Especially when Cai strode right past me, deep in conversation with Thalestris. He didn't even so much as glance in my direction. I hated that I had been looking in his.

But then I heard whispering and giggling and realized I wasn't the only one watching Cai. Thalestris shouted at us all to stop gawking and get back to practice. She pounded the butt of her staff on the arena sand, and her fight masters moved in, whips snapping through the air in case any of us needed extra motivation. I ducked my head and went back to my practice routine. In recent days, I had focused my concentration—ironically enough, just as Cai had suggested—on relaxing into the work. On letting the memories stored in my muscles and blood take over. On breathing all the way down into my swords. The less I thought about the next move, the easier it came, until it felt like I was dancing with a blade in each hand—

"Gladiatrix Fallon!" Thalestris's voice rang out. I finished the sequence—my last two hits landing solidly on the practice post with loud cracks—and turned, wiping

the sweat from my brow. I jogged across the sand to stand
before her.

"Mistress?"

"The Decurion wishes to spar with you."

I could feel the eyes of the other gladiatrices on me. I
glanced back and forth between Cai and Thalestris. For a
fleeting moment, I thought she was joking. But the look on
Cai's face was anything but amused.

"Do you have a problem with that, gladiatrix?" Thalestris asked.

"No." I straightened to attention. "No, of course not." I
nodded a brief bow at him. "Decurion. As you wish." The
only man I'd spared with since arriving at the ludus was
Kronos, the trainer. I felt an anxious flutter at the thought
of facing off against a legion-trained soldier.

Don't be ridiculous, I thought, steeling myself for the
bout. When I trained as a warrior back in the Vale, I would
have longed for a fight like this. An opponent like Caius
Varro.

"Gladiatrix." Cai inclined his head, giving no indication
whatsoever that he and I had almost kissed only a handful
of days earlier. Or had we? Suddenly I wasn't so sure.

In the bright light of day, Cai seemed a very different
creature than the one I'd strolled through a moonlit garden
with. Even dressed in a simple soldier's tunic and leather
sandals and not in a decurion's armor, there was an air of
command about him. And something else—something I
couldn't put my finger on. It almost seemed for a moment
as if he was angry.

Focus, I chastised myself. *You're imagining things.*

"I'm afraid I don't know how satisfying a seasoned soldier like yourself will find such a bout, my lord." I grinned as I tightened the leather thong on the bracer wrapped around my forearm, trying to lighten his mood. "I am, after all, only a woman. With weak wrists."

He didn't smile. Instead, he stalked past me and plucked two wooden practice blades off the weapons rack and tossed me one.

"There's only one shield left." He gestured to the *parma,* one of the small round shields favored by many of the gladiatrices.

I considered it briefly. But it was just a practice spar. Neither of us wore any armor. There was no real danger in the exercise, and so I declined.

"I'll do without," I said. "Thank you. I wouldn't want an unfair advantage."

Cai shrugged and strapped the shield onto his own arm. I blinked at him in surprise, but he ignored my reaction and picked up his wooden gladius, sinking into a ready stance. I remembered the first time I'd encountered him, how arrogant he'd seemed. And I wondered if the other night I hadn't been imagining things, and if this was the true Decurion.

I bent my knees and rocked forward on the balls of my feet, waiting for him to come at me. Cai didn't even blink as he stared me down. There was no indication of where his attack would come from . . .

And suddenly, I was ducking for my life!

Cai's blade—even blunted and wooden as it was—would have made a pretty dent in the side of my head if my instinct to move—*now!*—had come a fraction of an instant later. But, before I was even aware of it, I was now crouched in front of the Decurion, having narrowly avoided his blow.

He followed up with a second diagonal slash, and I went from a crouch to a diving roll to evade it. When I sprang back up to my feet, I swept my sword in a vertical block over my right shoulder and prayed to the Morrigan I'd anticipated his next move correctly. I had—for all the good it did me. The force of his next slash knocked the wooden blade from my suddenly numb fingers and sent it tumbling across the yard. I glanced up at his face, startled. I was even more surprised by what I saw there.

Cai wasn't Cai anymore. Not in that moment.

He was Caius Antonius Varro, soldier of the legions of Rome.

He was my enemy.

Wordlessly, he stepped back and pointed to my sword with his, indicating that I should go pick it up so that we could continue. I flexed my hand and shook it out, wincing as the blood flowed back into my prickling fingers.

I felt anger flare in my chest as I picked up my sword and turned to face him again, circling warily to my left this time as Cai advanced. Facing him as warrior to warrior, with the harsh sun carving the angles of his face into sharp relief, I saw nothing of the young man who'd seemed so very concerned for my well-being only a few nights earlier.

If it was, indeed, Cai's intent to demonstrate to the ludus at large that I was no more than . . . well, no more than target practice to him, he was certainly going about it enthusiastically. And with an intensity that left my sword-side shoulder and arm burning as blow after blow from his blade rained down on mine. Meanwhile, my own blows fell harmlessly on his shield.

"Don't *think*, gladiatrix!" he admonished me. "Don't hesitate. There is breath and there is movement, and that is all. Now, fight! *Move!*"

He was relentless, he was humorless. And while I didn't think he was trying to hurt me, he was definitely trying to beat me. After a quarter hour or so, I no longer cared that I'd almost kissed him. Furious, I realized that a part of me had been holding back, and I gave myself over to the fight. I was a warrior. I was a gladiatrix. And if Caius Varro had come to me that day looking for a fight, by the goddess, he was going to get exactly that.

"Are you so sure you don't want that shield now?" he asked through gritted teeth. Our blades had locked up and we were nose to nose, grunting and thrusting, trying to outbalance each other.

"I don't like hiding behind things," I grunted back. "It feels like cheating."

Except I was about to do just that. Cheat. As we strained against one another, leaning heavily on our swords, I let my focus drift off to one side of the courtyard . . . and let out a little gasp.

I was shocked when that oldest of ruses actually worked.

Cai's gaze flicked over, following mine, and the pressure eased off my sword for the briefest of instants. I assumed he'd seen right through my little trick and was mocking me, ready to dance away from my blade. With a cry, I wound up with all the strength I could muster and delivered a slashing blow to his exposed flank.

I heard his rib crack like the slap of a hard-shot arrow.

Cai dropped to one knee in the sand with a cry of pain.

The fight masters were on us in a flash. Thalestris shoved me out of the way, warning me with her *rudis* staff to stay back. I was stunned that my laughably obvious attempt at misdirection had worked. I glanced up and realized it was because there actually *was* something unexpected in the shadows at the edge of the pitch.

For the first time since the accident, Antonia was out of the infirmary. She sat ghastly pale in a chair well back from the edge of the practice enclosure. Her right arm lay cradled in her lap, heavily bandaged, the strips of linen dark and discolored from the stubborn seepage of blood and from Heron's salves.

I felt my face redden with shame. If I'd known she was sitting there watching, I never would have tried to trick Cai like *that*. I would have to apologize, I thought. And try to explain.

"You *really* don't like that boy, do you?" Elka said, strolling over to stand beside me as Kronos helped Cai stand. Elka had her practice spear slung over one shoulder and a satisfied grin on her face as she watched the Decurion stagger painfully to his feet. "Wonder how it feels for the legion to be on the receiving end for once?"

I didn't answer her. Once, not so long ago, I would have laughed right along with my Varini friend—two girls from two tribes that had both felt the hobnailed tread of the legion's sandaled foot. But in that moment, all I could feel was the shock of my blade slamming into Cai's ribs. If we'd been using real swords, he'd be dead.

And I would have killed him.

"Have you really thought about what it means to be a warrior, Fallon?" Sorcha had once asked me. *"It means you kill. You kill men. You kill women. All while* they *are trying very hard to kill* you. *And if one of them is better at it than you, then you die."*

Conflicting emotions of savage triumph and regret tore at my heart. I wondered what Aeddan had felt in the instant when his blade sank into his brother's flesh. Elation? Satisfaction? I shuddered and pushed the memory away.

"That was well done, *gladiolus*."

I turned to see Nyx standing there, looking in the direction Cai had gone.

"That Decurion is an arrogant arse," she said. "Maybe now he'll understand that even the lowliest gladiatrix is worth being wary of."

She slapped me on the back—a blow that fell somewhere between hearty and pummeling—and shouldered past Elka to join the rest of the veteran students gathered at the far end of the pitch. I watched as Cai moved stiffly toward the infirmary with the help of a trainer. I looked down at the wooden sword still clutched in my hand. It felt heavier than lead.

I handed it to Elka, who took it with an amused shake of her head. It was time for the midday meal break, but I found myself without an appetite. Instead, I headed to the baths and immersed myself in the cold pool, scrubbing savagely at the dust and sweat caked on my skin. My stomach was churning with emotions as I dressed and combed my fingers through my damp hair, pulling it back into a loose plait.

Then, for the second time in only a handful of days, I found myself standing inside the door of the infirmary. Heron was just on his way out, and he paused to offer me a wan smile and a pat on the shoulder.

"In the arena," he murmured, "that blow would have won you the adoration of the crowd, you know."

I nodded my thanks. He was right. What I'd done in practice was the very thing I'd been trained to do in a bout. Why, then, did I feel so bad for having done it? Heron pulled the door shut behind him, leaving only me and his most recent patient alone in the room. Cai was sitting on the end of one of the cots, his clothes stripped away except for a length of linen wrapped around his hips like a kilt and more linen—strips of it—wrapped tightly around his torso. As I approached, I tried not to notice the lean, defined muscles of his chest and arms. He didn't look at me as I sat down on the low stool in front of him.

"Broken?" I asked.

He shifted, wincing.

"I'm sorry," I said. "I didn't mean for that trick to really work. I didn't think it had—"

He shook his head. "Cracked. It'll heal. And it was well-deserved anyhow, even if you'd broken my rib in half. My behavior was inexcusable, and I beg your pardon, gladiatrix."

His apology confirmed what I'd begun to suspect.

"You mean your attempt to teach me a lesson?" I asked quietly.

He didn't answer.

"This is about Antonia, isn't it?" I pressed. "The injured girl. You wanted to show me how easy it would be for me to wind up like her. How easy it would be for another fighter to beat me."

He raised his head, his gaze boring into me. His eyes were red-rimmed, and his face, even clouded with hurt, was devastatingly handsome. "Yes."

His admission should have filled me with anger, but it didn't. Maybe it was because in that moment he reminded me so much of how Mael, with his ridiculous overprotectiveness, used to treat me sometimes. It wasn't that Cai didn't think I could handle myself, but he worried about me all the same. I hadn't been imagining things the night of the oath taking. Cai cared about me.

He shifted again on the bed, clearly uncomfortable, and stifled a groan. I poured him a cup of cool water. He gulped it down thirstily, and when I reached for the empty cup to take it back, he circled my forearm with his long fingers.

"I was wrong, you know," he said. "Your wrists aren't weak. Nothing about you is."

"Decurion—"

"Cai."

"Cai—"

His hand ran up the length of my arm, then drifted upward to rest against the side of my face. His palm was warm, and I found myself leaning into his touch before I could stop myself.

"I've never known anyone like you," he whispered. "Ever. Since that moment on the ship."

"The moment when I tried to kill you?"

"No. The one when you put yourself at risk to help Charon, the man who'd put you in slave irons, in the middle of all that chaos and death. You are uncommon in your bravery, Fallon. You are stronger than any woman I've ever known." He smiled ruefully. "And you seem determined to haunt my dreams."

I stood abruptly, feeling my heart pounding in my throat. If Cai had been a slave, even if he'd been a simple merchant or tradesman, it would have been different. How laughable for a once-princess of the Cantii to even think such things. There was a time when he wouldn't have been near good enough for me. Now he was so far above my station as to be in the stars. To even allow myself to be swept away on the tides of my imagination was madness . . .

"Fallon." Cai pushed himself stiffly to his feet and took a step toward me. "Look at me."

I did. I shouldn't have. Embers of desire flared in his

hazel eyes, and suddenly all of my reasoned arguments as to why this should never—*could* never—happen fell silent. A roaring silence muffled the voices in my head telling me to turn around, leave, don't look back . . .

He was close enough to take me in his arms, if he wanted to.

But he didn't.

"This can go no further," I said in a choked whisper. "We both know—"

Cai pulled me tightly to his bandaged chest and held me there, even though I knew it must have hurt him to do it. I looked up at him, and he kissed me with a hungry desperation that tore the breath from my lungs. His hands tangled in my hair, and my arms tightened around him. He hissed in pain—or pleasure, I couldn't tell which—but he didn't stop kissing me.

Not for a long, dizzying while.

No one had ever kissed me like that before, not even Mael. I didn't know anyone *could* kiss me like that. It seemed as if time stopped in that moment and everything I'd gone through—every hardship and horror that had led me to where I was—had been worth it for this. For him.

But then I felt his hands brush the iron slave collar I still wore around my neck. I heard the whisper-scrape of his soldier's calluses on the raw metal and pulled away from his kiss. Cai's eyes were shut, his chest heaving.

"Cai," I breathed. My lips tingled from his kiss.

He opened his eyes and cradled my face, holding me so

that I couldn't look away. "I ask you again—I'm begging you—*will* you let me buy your contract, Fallon?" he asked in a fierce whisper.

I swallowed hard again and shook my head. "No, Decurion. I will not."

Cai dropped his hands and stepped away from me. Then he turned, bending to retrieve his tunic from where it lay on the cot. He stood with his back to me for a long, aching moment. And his expression, when he turned back, was once more remote. It was as if he'd closed a heavy door and shut himself away from me.

"So be it," he said. "Then you should know that one of my missives from Caesar to your Lanista was this: You and the other seasoned girls are to go on the circuit starting in three days' time."

"The circuit?"

"A tour of the regional arenas outside of Rome." He looked at me, the flaring passion in his gaze buried beneath an ashen layer of pain. "Caesar and some of the other senators are sponsoring a circuit of gladiatorial bouts leading up to his Quadruple Triumph. He wants the gladiatrices to create names for themselves before they appear in his Triumph events. At the end of the circuit, Caesar will choose one gladiatrix to perform in the role of Victory in a reenactment of his conquest of Britannia."

I thought of Nyx and how there must be others like her at the other ludi. Girls who were just as competitive, willing to do almost anything to win a role like that. The competition would be fierce and dangerous. Perhaps even deadly.

"So," Cai continued, "as a gladiatrix of the Ludus Achillea, you will go and you will fight. You'll probably survive. Perhaps you'll even survive unscathed. Maybe you'll make a name for yourself."

He looked over to the rumpled cot where Antonia had been convalescing. From where I stood, I could see that there were rust-colored stains on the edges of the sheet.

"Or maybe you'll wind up like her."

"You tell me I'm so strong, and yet you don't really believe it." I shook my head. "You don't believe in me."

"Of course I do. But there's strength and then there's stubbornness. Recklessness. You think you need to prove something? To whom, Fallon?" His gaze burned my skin. "To me, to the Lanista, to Caesar himself, maybe? Do you really care what a bloody-minded tyrant thinks of you?"

"I'm not going to fight for Caesar, Cai," I said, adamant. "If I'm going to fight, I'm going to fight for *me*. No one else. Because that's the only honorable thing left for me to do."

"Honor is nothing but a dangerous lie, Fallon," he said. "In battle, there is no honor, not really. Caesar never won because he was honorable. He isn't. He won because he was clever and tenacious and used whatever means necessary, just like you did today."

"I didn't—"

"You cheated. And you won. And here's a piece of advice." He gripped me by the shoulders hard, and his next words sounded more like a warning than advice. "The next time someone offers you an advantage in a fight—a shield, a better sword, an opening for a cheat, or a moment of weakness in your opponent—do yourself a favor: Stuff your high-minded sensibilities and take it. Your adversary might not be so noble as you. And your honor will only wind up getting you killed."

XXII

MY SMALL ACT OF REBELLION—the refusal to have my slave collar removed—did not go unnoticed. One sweltering afternoon, Sorcha tracked me down after the other girls had drifted off to the baths or dining hall, finding me alone in the weapons shed as I filed the burrs from my practice blade with a metal rasp.

"We have body servants here at the ludus, you know," she snapped by way of greeting. "Baths, barbers, clean tunics in the quartermaster's stores. A blacksmith—several, in fact—all perfectly capable of cutting that collar off your neck."

"I shouldn't think you'd want to get rid of it," I said as she stalked circles around me. "After all, wasn't it part of my outrageous purchase price?"

"Don't be a brat. I could force you."

"Of course you could." I shrugged and returned to the task at hand. "You own me."

"That's not how I treat my girls, and that's not how they treat themselves—not if they want to win."

She stopped pacing and picked up an oilcloth, holding out her hand for my sword. I gave it to her, and she wiped the filings carefully from the blade, checked the smoothness of the edge with her thumb, and placed the sword back on the rack with the others.

"You are as much the weapon as the blade you wield, Fallon," she said. "And you need to start taking care of yourself the same way you take care of your equipment, or you'll be of no use in a fight when that day finally comes."

I glared up at her, but I had to admit that Sorcha had a point. I'd been pushing myself hard on the training ground. Too hard. By the end of each day, I was often so exhausted that I would forgo the bathhouse so that I could simply collapse on the pallet in my cell. I think part of me reasoned that if my body was tired enough, I would fall asleep regardless of the thoughts that galloped like runaway horses inside my head. Thoughts of Caius Varro and Maelgwyn Ironhand. Thoughts of my father and of home and how I'd never see those green shores again.

I blinked back the tears I refused to shed in front of my sister.

"When was the last time you had your hair trimmed?" Sorcha asked me in a gentler tone.

I glanced up at her. "What does it matter?"

"Come with me."

She turned on her sandal heel and stalked out of the shed, leaving me no choice but to follow her across the practice yard and through the breezeways that led to her private accommodations. Once inside her chambers, Sorcha sat me at a bench in front of a cosmetics vanity.

A floor-to-ceiling tapestry hung on the wall of the room. It depicted the moment when the Greek hero Achilles defeated and killed the Amazon queen Penthesilea, her blood woven from bright crimson threads. I guessed that was how they'd come to name the first two gladiatrix ludi—after that epic struggle between heroes.

Sorcha fetched a comb and a pair of silver shears and worked through the tangled mess of my hair with ungentle tugs of the comb. I sat there glowering, arms crossed. After she was through torturing my scalp, she picked up the shears.

"You've become such a shaggy thing, like one of those ponies you used to drive to exhaustion," Sorcha muttered as she snipped away at my neglected tresses. "It's an absolute wonder Caius Varro has taken such a shine to you."

My jaw dropped open.

"Don't deny it," she said. "I've never seen him ask to spar with any of the other girls at the ludus."

"Perhaps the Decurion respects my skills in the arena," I said stiffly.

"The arena had best be the only place he's encountered your skills," she said, and her reflection raised an eyebrow at me. "I mean it, Fallon. It's one of the strictest rules we have here at the ludus. I have no use for a gladiatrix who's lost her wits to lovesickness."

"I haven't!"

"Good." She nodded, then paused. "Why ever not?"

"Sorcha!"

"I only mean that he's kind, rich, from a powerful family, and not unhandsome. I wouldn't ever allow it, of course, but I'd at least understand." She stopped snipping and regarded me seriously for a long moment. "You're not pining for a boy from home, are you? Maelgwyn Ironhand? I know you two were close, but—"

"Mael's dead."

Sorcha fell silent. She'd grown up with Mael and Aeddan too. "I'm sorry to hear that. What happened?"

I closed my eyes and could picture the fog-bound lane from that night . . . but not Mael's face. "Virico gave me away to . . . to someone else." My next words dropped, leaden, from my lips: "They fought. Mael lost."

"Did you love this other boy?"

"No." I couldn't bring myself to tell her that the other boy had been Aeddan.

"Then why would Father do such a thing?" Sorcha frowned.

"Because I wanted to join his war band, and he didn't want me to fight and die like you." I glowered at her reflection. "Like he *thought* you had."

She laid down the scissors and lifted my hair off my shoulders, smoothing it down my back. "I'm sorry to hear it, Fallon. Truly. And I wouldn't have allowed it if I'd been there."

"Well, you weren't," I said.

Her reflection gazed at me for a long moment, cool and

appraising. Finally, she seemed to come to a decision about something.

"I'm going in to the capital tomorrow morning to take possession of six new chariot ponies," she said. "Thalestris is too busy with the younger girls' training, and Kronos and I will need an extra hand. I was going to take Nyx, but I want you to come with me instead. And while we're there, I want to show you something that might help you understand. Now go. Meet us at the stables at daybreak. Don't be late."

Help me understand what? I wondered.

The next morning, Sorcha turned a corner off a bustling street near where we had left our wagon at a stable close to the Circus Maximus. She led me down a narrow lane, Kronos following close behind us, until it dead-ended in front of a small, squat residence, an unassuming structure with only a single heavy door and no windows. Sorcha tugged on a rope hanging by the door, sounding a bell on the other side of the featureless wall. After a long moment, a small square opened behind a metal grate, and a man peered out. When he saw my sister, he closed the door again without a word, and I heard the sounds of lock and key and of a heavy slide bar grating as it was hauled aside.

The heavy oak door swung inward, and Sorcha nodded for me to precede her inside. The man who'd opened it was armored like a legionnaire, but he was older and battle-scarred.

"Lady," he said to my sister in a voice like a boot heel crunching gravel. "He's not expecting you—"

"I know. Is he well?"

The man shrugged bulky shoulders. "Is he ever?"

Kronos waited by the gate as the man gestured us across a tiny courtyard open to the sky to where he unlocked another heavy iron-bound door and let us through into the dim vestibule of the interior building. The only source of light came from a few torches set in wall sconces. Unlike most of the Roman houses I'd been in up to that point, there were no windows here, no airy colonnades, no natural light.

The room was long and narrow. In the far corner, at the opposite end from where we stood, I could see a brazier glowing, but it did little to illuminate the figure that sat hunched and wrapped in a cloak on a low couch. I glanced at Sorcha, who put a firm hand on my shoulder and walked me forward.

"My lord?" she called out softly as we approached.

The figure didn't move.

"My lord?" she called out again, louder this time. "Arviragus?"

Arviragus? I thought. *No. No—that* can't *be him!*

But it was.

The man the Romans had called Vercingetorix—the godlike chieftain of the Arverni—who'd come within a handsbreadth of beating Julius Caesar himself, sat with his arms resting on his knees, long hands hanging limply in front of him. He stared into the fire, and there wasn't even a flicker in his eyes to indicate he knew we were there.

"They used to keep him in the Tullianum," Sorcha said in a low murmur. "It's a prison here in Rome, a dreadful subterranean place. But when it started to look as though he might actually die there, they moved him to this place. A cage with some comforts, but still a cage."

"Why keep him alive all these years?" I whispered.

"Because there hasn't been a proper Triumph since Alesia."

"But why didn't Caesar just kill him there? On the battlefield?"

"Because Caesar is a shrewd conquering hero," she said. "And Alesia is very far away from Rome. Remember what your fight masters have told you, Fallon—it's what you've been training for all these weeks. The mob loves spectacle above all else. And Caesar plans to give them exactly that. He's kept his greatest adversary alive so that, when the time came for his Triumphs, he could parade Arviragus in front of the plebs to show the people how fearsome the Arverni chief was. To remind them why they need Caesar to lead and protect them."

I glanced back toward the corner. "He doesn't look very fearsome."

"He will. They will dress Arviragus up and chain him to a stake. They'll probably get him good and roaring drunk, and then they'll trot him through the town on a cart decked with the spoils of war and the shields of the fallen."

"And then?"

"Then they'll take him to the prison and strangle him, out of sight, where no one needs to see him die like an animal."

Those words struck me like a physical blow. I had grown up worshipping the handsome, fiery Arviragus. He'd been my hero almost as much as Sorcha, and to see him as he was now, with the fire leeched from his soul . . .

"Caesar asked me to come here to visit him," Sorcha murmured to me. "As a comfort—someone who knew him as he was, someone to talk to—and so I've come every few months for the last four years," she said. "Sometimes we talk. Mostly he sits there silently and drinks."

"Why would Caesar ask you to do that?" I asked.

"To remind me that he could have done the same to me—or to Father—if he'd so desired. That he still could."

I glanced at her, but her eyes were fixed on the figure by the fire.

"But I also think he grew to admire Arviragus," she said. "Even as he sought to destroy him. My visits are a small mercy, though. Sometimes I wonder if my presence makes it better for him or worse." She tightened her grip on my shoulder. "Come now. Greet the king."

The closer we got, the heavier the stink of stale wine. Sorcha crouched down in front of Arviragus and took his hands gently in her own.

"I've brought someone to see you, lord," she said softly. "You knew her when she was a little girl. You taught her swordplay, like you taught me."

He blinked, just a little, and his gaze searched the

darkness in front of him until it found my sister's face. "Did I?" he muttered, half to himself. "Did I?"

I nodded. "In Durovernum, when I was small."

His eyes shifted, blinking and bleary, to focus on me.

"Bright little thing," he murmured.

He beckoned me closer with a clumsy wave, and I knelt before him. His breath was foul, but I could still see—in the angles of his face beneath the tangle of overgrown beard— the hero I'd worshipped as a child.

He squinted at me. *"Fallon . . . ?"*

I tried to smile at him. "That's right."

"She is a gladiatrix now," Sorcha said.

"Gladiatrix . . ." Arviragus murmured again. He lifted a shaking hand to my cheek. "I'm so sorry, bright little thing."

"For what, lord?" I asked, my voice small and lost in the dim air.

His words caught in his throat as he answered. "For not making the world a place where you could choose to fight for yourself."

I glanced at Sorcha, who bit her lip and looked away.

"But you did," I said, turning back to the Arverni king and remembering when he was a prince—and my hero. "When I was little, you didn't just teach me how to hold a sword. You taught me that the fight is in *here*." I put a hand on my heart, my voice growing stronger. "And that it was up to me to decide how and when to use it. I saw what was left of Alesia. When you surrendered to Caesar, it was because there was nothing left to fight for. But the fight itself was more important than the loss. You will be remembered as a hero, my lord. And that is at least as important as being one."

Tears spilled from his eyes, and before I could say anything else, he pulled me to his chest, wrapping me in a fierce embrace. When he pushed me away, finally, it seemed as though the tears had washed away some of the fog from his gaze.

"Talk to me, Fallon," he said. "It has been so long. Tell me of yourself."

Sorcha retreated to the far end of the room with the guard, leaving us alone for a little while. Arviragus was lucid for most of our conversation—which surprised me, considering the amount of wine he imbibed even in that short time. He asked me how I had come to be in Rome. His eyes flicked over to Sorcha when I told him I was now owned by the Ludus Achillea, but he didn't say anything. I didn't belabor the point. Sorcha was the only friend he'd had in his captivity, and I wasn't about to air my resentment in front of him.

When he asked me about the upcoming circuit, I felt the heat of shame creep into my cheeks. The girls of the Ludus Achillea would be competing for a lead role in the Triumphs—the very same celebrations that would see Arviragus paraded through the streets of Rome to be put to death. But the Arverni king was a strategist first and foremost, and he brushed aside talk of his own impending fate to counsel me on mine.

"A role like that'll carry a hefty purse if you win," he grunted thoughtfully, scratching at his beard.

"I don't care about the money!" I scoffed.

"Eh?" Arviragus peered at me through bloodshot eyes. "Why not? Everybody else in the Republic does."

"I have my honor." I lifted my chin. "I won't dress up as some silly spirit of Victory and fight for Caesar like a trained ape."

"I would."

I gaped at him.

"I've learned a few things over the years, Fallon," he said. "I told you I was sorry about the world I left behind when I surrendered to Caesar, and I am. You say there was nothing more for me to fight for, and you were right. But you can't change the ways of the world if you're no longer a part of it."

I frowned.

"In your case, *money* makes you a part of it," he explained with a grin. "The favor of Caesar makes you a bigger part of it. The ability to one day rid yourself of that collar and all it stands for makes you a force to be reckoned with. Think about that, Fallon. Be an idealist, by all means, but be a pragmatic one."

"You think I should fight for Caesar?"

"I think you should fight for yourself," he said. "But those things needn't be exclusive. Temper passion with control, conviction with cunning. *Win*, Fallon, the way I didn't."

His fingers fumbled as he reached for the wine jug, almost spilling it. I took it from him and poured another measure into his cup. He nodded his thanks and drank deeply.

"In the arena," he continued, "it won't be enough just to fight your best. It's never enough to simply win the battle. What you have to win is their hearts. Caesar's heart. Charm them, beguile them, seduce the mob. That will make *him* fall in love with you. Because unless Caesar loves you, you cannot truly claim Victory."

I heard the sound of someone discreetly clearing her throat, and I looked up to see that Sorcha had returned. She nodded toward the door. Arviragus grunted, tossing the rest of the wine down his throat in one gulp, and waved for me to go with her. My heart hurt at the thought of never seeing him alive again. As I turned to leave, he called out to me one last time.

"Be brave, gladiatrix," he said. "And be wary. Bright things beget treachery. Beautiful things breed envy. Once you win Caesar's love, you'll earn his enemies' hate."

"The Morrigan keep you, Arviragus," I said.

He laughed at that. "She won't have much choice, soon."

As Kronos drove me and Sorcha back to the Ludus Achillea, I watched the six new chariot horses trotting behind us down the road, tethered on a line. They seemed to me to be creatures that embodied the perfect balance between spirited and obedient. Passion and control, like Arviragus had said.

I turned to Sorcha. "Why did you take me to see him?"

"To show you why I did what I did," she said. "To help you understand why I came here to Rome and fought for Caesar and never went home again."

"You did it because of Arviragus?"

"No." She shook her head. "I did it because of Father. And you."

"I don't understand—"

"I wasn't *captured*, Fallon!" Sorcha exclaimed.

Of course she was captured. My sister wouldn't have surrendered. Ever.

She sighed.

"When I left Durovernum for the last time," she continued, "I knew I wouldn't ever go back. I had Olun cast the auguries for my fortune, and they told me so, unequivocally. I thought it was because I would die in battle, but that wasn't it. There was a battle, to be sure. It began that evening and carried on into the night, and Caesar saw me fighting in the field. He discovered who I was and understood why I was there: to free Father."

"I always thought *I* would one day die on a battlefield because Olun told me that I would share the same fate as you!" I said. "I thought you lost the fight, Sorcha. We all did. We thought you were dead and that Caesar only decided to release Virico after the other Prydain kings sued for peace."

"That's what he wanted you to believe." A thin, crooked grin bent her mouth. "But the truth was that Caesar had already agreed to release Virico long before."

"Why would he ever do that?" I scoffed.

"Caesar had sent a message to me secretly," she said. "He is a brilliant commander in the field, but he's also a shrewd opportunist in his civilian life. He already owned massive stables of gladiators and made rich sums of money off them. That night, when he saw me, a woman of the Cantii fighting on the battlefield as fiercely as any man, he saw the opportunity to birth a new phenomenon: female gladiators."

I didn't know why my sister ever would have agreed to such a thing.

"We made a *deal*, Fallon," Sorcha said, sensing my unasked question. "My life for Virico's. My servitude for his freedom. Virico would live—and live free—and you would grow up with our father there for you." She nodded down the lane toward Arviragus's prison. "You see what captivity does to the soul of a man like that. I couldn't let that happen to Father, so I made a deal with a demon. I'd do it again."

She lapsed into silence. For the rest of the journey back to the ludus, I thought about Arviragus and Virico and the sacrifices my sister had made—and continued to make—for me. Was it possible I had been so wrong about my own sister? I needed to find a way to make amends.

On my way to my barracks cell, I cut across the deserted practice yard of the place that had somehow become my home. As I reached the center of the sand circle, I felt a strange, dizzying sensation and heard the sound of wings beating overhead.

I looked up, and the sky was clear. Empty.

But in my mind, a throaty voice whispered, *"Daughter"* and *"Victory."*

I felt my cheeks flush.

"Freedom." I'd begun to worry that the Morrigan had turned her favor from me. But her voice in my head told me she was still with me, and it seemed she had a message—one that I finally understood.

Arviragus had been right: The role of Victory carried with it the promise of a substantial purse, but it had never even occurred to me that I would find a pure use for filthy Roman sestersii.

Sorcha had taken me to see the Arverni king so that she could show me one truth. But the Morrigan, I suspected, had sent me there so that Arviragus could teach me another. The hazy fog of an idea began to take solid shape in my mind. There was a chance, however slim, that I could redeem myself in the eyes of the goddess and my sister and make something worthwhile out of the whole great mess I had made for myself.

I remembered how Sorcha had bargained with Julius Caesar, and I thought that maybe—just maybe—there was more than one way to deal with a demon.

XXIII

THE DAY BEFORE we were due to begin the journey that would take us to our first destination on the circuit tour, Kronos knocked on the door of my quarters and told me that I had a visitor waiting for me in the small garden courtyard. Before I could ask him who it was, he'd gone. But I could think of only one person it might be.

Caius.

As much as my heart skipped a beat at the mere thought, I wasn't sure I was up to another argument with him, and so I almost didn't go. But I did, and when I stepped into the cool tree-shaded yard, I was surprised to see that my visitor wasn't Cai but Charon the slave trader.

To say I was surprised would have been an understatement.

My former captor, the man who'd stolen me from my home and then sold me into slavery, sat on a marble bench beneath the branches of a fig tree, carving one of the ripe purple fruits into slices. He popped a slice into his mouth and stood when I approached, a smile lighting his face. He cut another slice of fig and wordlessly offered it to me on the blade of the knife.

I took it and sat on the bench facing him.

"Gladiatrix," he said. "It's good to see you again."

I regarded the slave master coolly. "Is it?"

He laughed softly. "You are her very mirror, Fallon."

"Whose?"

"Your sister. Sorcha." He reached for another fig from a low-hanging bough. "She was extraordinary in her arena days, and I understand you're following closely in her footsteps."

"Who told you that?"

"Caius Varro. Your sparring partner." Charon grinned at me. "His father, the senator, entertained me at his *domus* in the capital two nights ago. I politely inquired as to why the lad was wincing with every breath."

"I see." I bit into the sweet flesh of the fig and tried to keep my expression neutral.

"He seems to believe that you're not very happy with him at the moment," he said. "Pity, seeing as how Caius just received orders that he's to escort Caesar's gladiatrix corps on the circuit tour. You're going to be seeing a lot of each other."

There was that skip of my heartbeat again.

"I have something for you, gladiatrix." Charon reached under the bench and hauled out a large wooden box. "I know the Lady Achillea gifted you with dimachaeri swords—"

I rolled my eyes at him. "One of which she got from *you*, yes."

"But I also know that you haven't the means to equip yourself with anything else." He glanced at me as he lifted the box onto the bench between us, and his dark eyes glittered. "On the circuit, you'll be fighting against other gladiatrices who've already won purses—enough in some cases to kit themselves out head to toe with the best weapons and armor money can buy."

I frowned. It was true. In my time training for the games at the ludus, it had been made abundantly clear to me that skill was one thing. Showmanship was another. I could fight like the goddess Minerva and perform with all the flourish of the bull-vaulting acrobats I'd heard tales of, but if I didn't look the part, I wouldn't win the crowd. And winning the crowd had become a fierce motivator for me, ever since my visit with Arviragus. I remembered the king's words. It wasn't enough to simply win the fight; I had to win their hearts.

I glanced down at the crude leather wrist bracers I'd crafted for myself.

"I don't need charity," I muttered.

"Not charity, patronage." Charon lifted the lid from the box. "My patronage."

He smiled and handed me a set of greaves—bronze shin guards—that were beautiful and made for someone just my size. But that wasn't all. The greaves were matched with a pair of bronze wrist bracers, again sized for my wrists. But the real surprise came when Charon drew forth a magnificent breastplate, embossed with subtle patterns that echoed the knotted, swirling designs of my own tribe. It was studded with bronze fittings in the same style as the greaves and bracers.

I couldn't contain the gasp of delight that escaped my lips as I reached out and took the breastplate from his hands. My pride warred with my gratitude—and my relief—but only for a moment. Wearing such a thing, I would rival not just Minerva but the Morrigan herself! I held it up in front of me and was surprised to find that it looked as though it would fit me like a second skin.

I looked up at Charon from under raised eyebrows.

"How did you manage to get the proportions so accurate?" I asked.

"Ah, yes, well, I asked Cai for his help." The slave master cleared his throat. "He made a best guess, I suppose."

I remembered the sensation of Cai's hands traveling over the lines of my body and felt my face flush with heat.

Charon was good enough to pretend not to notice. He turned back to the box and withdrew a battle kilt made of bronze-studded leather straps. "Here. It goes with this."

I hesitated, regarding him suspiciously.

"Why are you doing this?"

Charon took the armor back from me and laid it gently in the box. He closed the lid and, after a long moment of silence, slid the box toward me with a sigh. "I traveled with Caesar's legions when he invaded Britannia," Charon said quietly. "To assess the slave prospects."

I felt myself grow very still as he spoke.

"Sorcha. I saw her for the first time in Caesar's camp, in his tent. And I loved her the moment my eyes met hers. I still do." He held up a hand. "And nothing ever came of it. Nothing ever will. I came to terms with that a long time ago, Fallon."

"She never even tried to come home," I blurted out, the old hurt surfacing like a toothache. "She could have at least sent word."

"To what end?" Charon said gently. "Your sister Sorcha is no more. And Achillea belongs to Caesar, who will never let her go. She's far too valuable to him. How would the torment of knowing that his daughter was alive be any kinder to you and your father than letting you both think she was dead?"

My head spun. All I could picture in my mind was my heartbroken father sitting night after night in front of the banked embers of the fire in his hearth, drinking slowly from a great mug of ale late into the night, his gaze roaming the shadows of his hall as if seeking her out. All I could think of was that he'd made the decision to marry me off to Aeddan because he didn't want to lose me like he'd lost her.

I looked at Charon and saw that his dark gaze was also clouded with memory.

"My love for Sorcha is an old, scarred-over wound on my heart, the ache dulled by the passage of time. Finding you ripped that wound open again. I *knew* there was something about you from the first moment." He shook his head. "Then I found your sword, and seeing Sorcha's mark on the blade confirmed it. By then it was too late to let you go, so I decided that the best thing I could do was bring you here, to her."

"And sell me to my own sister for enormous sums of money."

"I might be a romantic." Charon grinned wryly. "But I'm also a businessman."

"Does Sorcha know how you feel?" I asked. "Does she know you're in love with her?"

"She didn't. Not at first." He looked at me, and his gaze sharpened noticeably. "Not until I tried to buy her slave contract from Caesar."

"You don't know my sister very well," I said. "She could never love someone who owned her like livestock."

"No, and that's why I love her. But you misunderstand me, Fallon. I could never own Sorcha," Charon said. "The moment her contract was in my hands, I would have torn it to pieces."

"You would have?" I frowned at the slave master in confusion.

"Of course I would have." He snorted. "And so would Caius Varro."

Up until that very moment, the legalities of Roman contracts had been a bit lost on me. I suppose I'd never even considered that a contract, once it was written into existence, could simply be torn and made worthless by whoever held the paper.

Charon shook his head. "I'm assuming Caius made an offer to buy your contract? Don't tell me you actually think Caius wanted to *own* you."

"I . . ."

But that was *exactly* what I had thought.

Cai . . .

I blinked hard, remembering the anguish in Cai's face as he'd begged me to let him buy my contract. I hadn't understood what he intended to do with it. And *he* hadn't understood why I wouldn't let him grant my freedom. Instead, we had let our tempers get the best of us, never bothering to figure out the true meaning of our words.

I rose to my feet. I needed to find Cai and explain.

Charon stopped me before I could leave.

"One more thing . . ."

He reached into the leather scrip that hung from his belt and handed me a small vellum scroll, sealed with a blob of black wax.

The wax seal was imprinted with a sigil of some kind. I glanced at it and then back up at him.

"I can't read this," I said.

"I know." He smiled and pressed the scroll back toward me. "That's not for you to read."

"Then what is it?"

"It's for you to keep. As payment for a kindness done." Charon chuckled at the expression on my face. "You've made me a lot of money, Fallon, and not just on your own sale. The price your sister paid for you will serve to goad others on to pay similarly for my wares in the future. It's all in the perception of things. You've guaranteed me money I wouldn't have made had you not helped me rescue the trunk that bore your own sword. That was the proof of your identity and the only reason I made that kind of profit on your sale. I'm not blind to the irony of the situation."

He ran his hand over the lid of the box of armor.

"Once outside the walls of the ludus, you won't be safe. Cai will do his best to look after you, but the ways of Rome—and Romans—are still foreign to you. And you, Fallon, being you, will draw attention—not all of it benign. You'll need to be careful, and you'll need to curb your— what should I call it—your *impulsive* nature.

"That scroll," he continued, "is for you to use only if you happen to find yourself in a bad situation with no avenue of escape."

I plucked at the edge of the scroll's black wax blob with a fingernail.

"Leave it sealed," Charon said, reaching to cover my hand with his.

"What is it?" I asked, frowning. "Some kind of magic?"

He laughed a little. "Of a sort, I suppose. It's a promise."

"Of what?"

"Money."

I felt my mouth twist in a sour grimace. "Does it always have to come back to that?" I asked.

"It's the kind of magic that appeals to most Romans." He squeezed my hand once and let go. "Keep this safe and hidden, and keep it with you at all times when you leave the grounds of the ludus. And if you ever find yourself in need—*dire* need, mind—give that scroll to whoever it is that threatens you. Unless they hold the wealth of Caesar himself in their hands, I promise this will save you from almost any peril. It guarantees substantial payment upon the safe delivery of your person to my house."

I sat there, stunned by the generosity of his gifts. Charon was a man who bought and sold souls. And yet his own soul was a slave to the love he had for my sister. I thought again about Cai's offer to buy my contract. Charon seemed to almost sense what I was thinking. He reached out and tapped a finger on the iron ring I still wore around my neck.

"When I put this on you, Fallon, I never meant for it to be permanent."

The slave master stood and nodded a bow to me. Then he turned and left me sitting there in Sorcha's garden, wondering about the invisible armor—and shackles—that love could bind around a heart.

When I returned to my cell after the evening meal, I noticed that someone had been in my room. It would have been hard *not* to notice. The familiar shadows dancing on the bare stone walls looked wrong. They were thick and tinged with crimson. I squinted through the gloom and sucked in a sharp breath when I saw my oath lamp. In my absence, the brightly colored panes had turned black, reducing the flame within to a muted, reddish gleam. For a moment, I wondered if the Huntress Moon had transformed the delicate glass meadow bird into one of the Morrigan's battle ravens. It perched there at my window, waiting for me, belly full of the wandering fires of dead souls—

Stop it. The Morrigan is your ally, not your enemy.

I strode across the room, lifting the guttering lamp down. This was no magical transformation. Someone had rubbed the thing with a coating of the sticky black pine tar we used on the chariot horses' hooves—I could smell the pungent tang of it as soon as I picked up the lamp. Another prank.

Or a threat. Or a warning . . .

As I turned with the lamp in my hand, the lurid glow it cast revealed that the wall above my bed was covered in dripping black scrawls—words and pictures—calling me a Roman lover. At least, that's what I politely interpreted as their meaning. I couldn't read the words, but the images were plain enough. The threat was clear—someone at the ludus knew about me and Cai. I had to be more careful. If Sorcha found out there was actually something between us, she might very well bar me from the arena. That, in itself, was worrying enough.

But then I saw the bird. Arching above the vile pictures was a crudely rendered raven. With wide black wings and a huge, sharp beak frozen open in a silent shriek.

Definitely a warning.

I lit the wick of an old tallow candle and blew out the flame in the defiled lamp. Turning my back on the wall, I sat down on the edge of my bed and began, painstakingly, to clean away the soot-black stains from the oath lamp with a strip of linen. As I worked, I whispered a prayer of thanks to the Morrigan that I'd had the foresight to take the box of Charon's armor directly to the quartermaster to be stowed along with my swords in one of the caravan wagons. I hated to imagine what might have happened had I left it in my room. I would need my gear in pristine condition.

Because now, more than ever, I was determined to make my mark on the circuit. They thought they could frighten me with pictures painted in tar upon my walls? The pictures I drew would be in the sands of the arena, rendered in my rivals' blood. And the letters I carved with my sword? They would spell out *Victory*.

XXIV

CHARON'S WELCOME GIFT of armor marked me as a contender and went a long way toward convincing the crowd I was worthy to be in that arena. But ultimately, my reputation—such as it was to become—was sealed with the outcome of my very first circuit bout. The bout that would forever brand me as the Fury Killer.

The Ludus Achillea's traveling train had set out early through the gates of the compound, and there was an almost festival atmosphere as the girls and our handlers set off down the road, heading northeast into the Umbrian countryside. Our first performance venue on the circuit was in the town of Perusia. As the sun set, we made camp outside the walls of the town. We would sleep that night in tents kept under guard by our escort, Decurion Caius Varro and a dozen or so of his men.

As the stars began to flicker to life in the darkening sky

above us, I spotted Cai near Sorcha's tent speaking to his men. He turned, suddenly, as if he'd sensed me watching him. I felt a wave of heat wash over me as he stared at me across the distance. Even though the veils of smoke and sparks from the campfires, I thought I saw a raw longing in his gaze. There must have been something like that in mine too, but then I remembered the ugly pictures and words scrawled over my room: *Roman lover.* I quickly tore my eyes away.

I heard Elka chuckling.

"Little fox," she said, "you escaped from a cage once already. And love, the old crones of my tribe would tell you, forges cage bars stronger than iron. Maybe don't push your luck, *ja?*"

Love? No. Oh no.

I tried to tell her she was being ridiculous. But when I opened my mouth, nothing came out. Elka shook her head and clapped me on the shoulder before retiring to our tent for the night. I should have followed. I was tired, and most of the other girls were already chasing sleep. I watched Elka go and turned back to where Cai still stood staring at me.

We hadn't spoken since the infirmary, since I'd cracked Cai's rib and—perhaps even more painful to him, if Charon was to be believed—rejected his offer to buy my contract for a second time. I thought of Mael and how I'd pushed him away so that I could chase glory in my father's war band. I didn't want to repeat that terrible mistake, not with Caius Varro.

In the distance, I could hear the muted whine and ring

of metal grinding on stone. Beyond the boundary of our camp, the ludus weapons masters had set up a tent and would be busy, deep into the night, cleaning and sharpening swords and spears in preparation for the next day. The sound was a lullaby for a gladiatrix, but I was wide awake. I stood and threaded my way between the glowing circles of the fire pits.

"Decurion," I said quietly when I reached him. "May I ask you to accompany me outside the camp?"

Cai stepped away from his fellow soldiers, his gaze questioning. But he nodded. "Of course, gladiatrix."

We walked silently, side by side, to the camp entrance, where a ludus guard straightened at our approach and nodded respectfully first to Cai, then to me.

"I need to pay a visit to the weapons tent," I said to him. "I'll be brief."

He glanced at Cai and then moved aside. The dew-wet grass brushed my bare calves as I walked the short distance to the entrance of the tent. The canvas walls glowed golden from the fire within, and I could smell the tang of metal and wood wafting on the night breeze.

"Oro," I greeted the master smith. "I beg a favor."

He straightened up from the freshly sharpened spear blade he was attaching to a wooden shaft and grunted a query at me. A genius with metal, he hoarded his words like gold. I lifted a hand to the iron slave collar that circled my neck.

"Please," I said, an unexpected knot in my throat. "Take this off."

Oro's eyes gleamed in the firelight, and he muttered something behind his singed beard that might have been "About bloody time."

He went to fetch his tools, and Cai stepped up behind me, gently gathering my hair off my shoulders and lifting it out of the smith's way as he worked. I held my breath, and it was over in an instant. The bolt holding the ring together fell away, and Oro pried the ends of the iron open, sliding it from around my neck.

I let my breath out in a gasp and took the collar when he offered it to me.

"Thank you," I said.

He waved us away, turning back to the spear he'd been working on. I pushed the tent flap aside, and Cai and I stepped back out into the darkness. The stars overhead seemed brighter somehow.

"Take it," I said, holding the collar out to Cai.

He wrapped his long fingers around the broken iron circle and looked at me, uncertainty in his eyes.

"Consider it a promise," I said, wrapping my hand around his. "I understand now why you wanted to buy my contract."

He shook his head. "I never wanted to own you, Fallon. Only free you—"

"I know," I interrupted. I needed to explain how I felt in a way that I'd never truly been able to with Mael. "But don't you see? That's not real freedom—not for a Cantii warrior. There will come a day, Caius Varro—I *promise* you—when I will be able to buy my own contract. On that day, if you'll wait for me, I'll come to you, and we can be together as equals."

I smiled up at him and saw in his eyes that he finally understood.

"I'll wait for you, Fallon," he said, slipping my iron ring into the leather scrip hanging from his belt. "Forever, if I have to. Although I'd rather not wait *quite* that long, if it's all right with you."

I laughed and was astonished at how good it felt to do that without iron around my throat. I lifted a hand to my neck and felt the circle of calluses left behind, like a phantom collar. Cai reached up and ran his fingertips along my skin, and I shivered at his touch.

"The marks will fade," he whispered.

I nodded as his hand shifted to slide into my hair, and he brought his face down to mine and kissed me. The kiss thrilled through me all the way to my toes. I wanted to draw him down into the long grass and wrap his arms around me, but I didn't dare. We were so close to the camp, and even kissing him in that moment was a risk I couldn't afford to take.

With a reluctant sigh, I pulled away. At the same time, Cai seemed to remember himself and stepped back as well, but I could hear his breathing over the clang of Oro's hammer, and his eyes were large and dark in his face.

As he walked me back to the camp, I saw a familiar figure standing at the entry. My sister, her arms crossed and her brow knitted in an angry frown.

"Decurion," she said.

"Lady." Cai lifted his chin, and for a moment I almost thought he was going to salute. "This gladiatrix needed her equipment tended."

I choked, and Sorcha's left eyebrow arched sharply.

"What I meant was—"

Sorcha put up a hand. "Thank you, Decurion. I'll take it from here."

Cai nodded and strode off toward the legionnaires' tent, leaving me to my sister's mercy. As soon as he was gone, Sorcha rounded on me. I steeled myself for a tongue-lashing, but she paused when she saw my newly bare neck.

"It was Charon's suggestion," I said. "He seemed to think my armor would fit me better without it."

"I see." Her expression softened into a smile. "Well, Charon is nothing if not insightful. Go. Get some rest, Fallon. You'll need it."

If I thought she would have let me, I might have hugged her in that moment. But I contented myself with a shared smile and went to find my tent. For the first time since that collar had been hammered around my neck, I slept through the night without dreaming of escape.

When morning came, the crowds of the sleepy little town of Perusia were out in full force, filling the stands of the arena and spilling out into the marketplace beyond. The smell of roasting meat wafted on the breeze, and children raced through the crowds like bounding rabbits.

In the early part of the day, there were musicians and the bawdy antics of comic actors to entertain the crowds. That

was followed by displays of "exotic" animals. Unlike the
larger venues closer to Rome, the smaller arenas avoided
using rare and expensive beasts in favor of what amounted
to wrestling matches between handlers and trained bears
with trimmed claws and wildcats that weren't particularly
wild. Still, the crowd loved the theatrics.

Next up after the *bestiari* were the male gladiatorial
contests. The combatants were from two regional ludi and
were clearly well-known, judging by the cheers and cat-
calls that filled the air. Most of the matches were draws
or, in the cases where there was a clear winner, nonle-
thal. Gladiatorial bouts rarely ended in death. Only if one
combatant performed exceptionally poorly—or one performed exceptionally *well*—did a match end in anything
other than a win, loss, or draw in which both fighters left
the field alive.

I saw only one lethal fight that day.

One gladiator's trident had gone straight through the
guts of his opponent. Two of the tines stuck out obscenely
from his back, dripping red. I watched, my heart in my
throat, as the wounded gladiator sank to his knees in the
sand. He clawed his helmet from his head, face rigid with
pain, and gestured for the mercy blow. The crowd held its
breath as his opponent saluted him solemnly, then picked
up his sword where it lay in the sand and thrust the point
down through the other man's neck.

There was a moment of respectful silence. Then the
gladiator's body was dragged from the arena by hook-
wielding men dressed in outlandish headdresses meant to

resemble long-eared desert dogs. I had heard from Kronos that the men were playing the ritual part of an Aegyptian god of the dead called Anubis, whom the Greeks and Romans had adopted as a kind of guide for lost souls to their underworld. I shuddered as the jackal-men trudged past, dragging their burden behind them, leaving a trail of blood.

They will never take me out of the arena like that, I vowed. *Never.*

The men's fights concluded, and there was a midday break.

We were up next.

I swallowed nervously to ease the tension in my throat, glancing around to see if I could gauge how the others were feeling. I wasn't surprised to find Nyx and her crew positively champing at the bit to get out and do some damage.

Nyx had already proved herself a consummate performer. The leather straps of her armored kilt were just a little shorter than those of the other girls, and they were oiled, supple, and spaced so that when she moved, there were flashes of sun-browned thigh. Her helmet lacked a visor to fully cover her face, and I noticed she had carefully painted her eyes with dark kohl and stained her lips a deep red. Even the curves of her breastplate were more exaggerated.

I had to admire the way she played to the crowds. Flirting and fierce, confident, arrogant. When we'd first been led across the arena sands to the gladiator trenches, she'd paused to blow a kiss to a little boy sitting with his father in the first row of seats. Both of them had blown kisses back, and the crowd had cheered in delight.

Just before the first bout, I noticed Sorcha standing near the judges' bench, arguing vehemently with the games master. It surprised me. During the games, the master's word was law in the arena, and any dissention, even from the lanistas, could result in heavy fines or disqualification. I couldn't hear what they were saying, but I saw my sister throw her hands up in disgust and walk briskly toward me.

"Be careful," she said, reaching out to squeeze my shoulder hard. "And remember this: The most dangerous adversary is the one who already thinks they've nothing left to lose."

She left me standing there, and I turned to look at the girls from the opposing ludus, the Ludus Amazona. I could tell just from their equipment that they were well-funded. Two or three of their girls wore heavier gear and would likely be matched with our retiarius fighters, like Meriel. Most of the others were kitted out *thraex* style—with shield and sword—and I would probably be paired with one of them. None of them looked as though they fought dimachaerus-style.

The Morrigan willing, that would give me an edge.

As usual, Elka knew more about what was happening than I did. She trotted over and threw herself down beside me, her armor shimmering in the sun. Ajani had loaned her a tunic of scale mail that fit her reasonably well but made her look a bit like some kind of sea nymph, albeit one with a wickedly accurate throwing arm. Elka begged the roster of fights from the games master's assistant and was kind— or maybe cruel—enough to point out my match to me.

"She's from your part of the world." She pointed to a gladiatrix standing at the far end of the other trench. "Well, near enough, anyway. Eire-land."

"Really?" I squinted in the direction she pointed.

"Calls herself Uathach," Elka continued.

I groaned and gazed skyward. "Wonderful."

"What?"

"That's not her name," I said. "Unless she had a particularly hateful upbringing. It's a title. It means 'Terrible One.'"

"Huh," Elka grunted. "Everyone else calls her the Fury. She's a local favorite. Probably because she's a complete lunatic. At least, that's what I heard."

Looking at her, I didn't find that at all hard to believe.

The gladiatrix was short and skinny and terrifying to behold. She stood with her helmet resting against a cocked hip, all wiry limbs and leather armor, wearing a tarnished chain-mail tunic trimmed with bunches of long black feathers. Her head was shaved, exposing a pale scar that puckered her scalp in a long seam above her left eyebrow. Her nose had been broken at least once, and she was missing an ear. And there were whip marks—both fresh and faded—on her shoulders and upper arms and on the backs of her legs.

"That's an impressive collection of scar tissue," I murmured.

"I heard she got most of those souvenirs from the ludus guards," Elka said. "Not from other fighters. She's tried to escape over a dozen times, and the last attempt was right in the middle of a bout!"

I blinked at her. "You're joking."

She shook her head. "Leaped right over the wall and into the crowd. Tried to hack her way through the plebs to freedom. Each time they've flogged her to within an inch of her life, and *that* time they did it right in the middle of the arena in front of the cheering mob. She laughed and laughed through it all. Like I told you, they say she's mad."

"And she's my very first opponent." A shaky sigh escaped my lips. "The Morrigan hates me."

Elka frowned at me. "You shouldn't say such a thing," she admonished. "Your goddess has brought you this far. Maybe this is her way of telling you she thinks you're worth the effort."

I grinned wanly at her. "If that's the case, I wish she was just a bit less sure."

The shrill bray of the horns brought the crowd to its feet, and then it was our turn. The first of the gladiatrix events wasn't a combat but a competition: target shooting from the female archers of the competing schools. This was Ajani's domain, and I was on my feet with the rest of them, cheering her on as she sent arrow after arrow arcing with almost inhuman accuracy into the heads and hearts of the straw targets that had been set up at one end of the arena.

The archery contests were followed by a heart-pumping two-horse chariot race between three female drivers. Nyx drove for the Ludus Achillea, and she was both terrifying and exhilarating to watch as she took a turn on one wheel and cut off her opponents with a daring final burst of speed to win the race. Watching it made me long for my own days of riding behind Mael as we raced along the floor of the Forgotten Vale. It also bolstered my grudging respect for Nyx.

After the race, it was time for the bouts. The games master stepped to the center of the arena. The first name he called from the Ludus Achillea was Elka's.

"Go!" I gave her a slap on the shoulder. "Keep your big feet moving, and don't do anything stupid."

She grinned and thumped the butt of her spear on the ground, then slammed down the visor on her helmet. Pale blue eyes glittering fiercely behind the metal grill, she turned and loped out into the middle of the sand floor of the arena. Her opponent was a retiarius—fighting with trident and net—and she was good. Elka was better, but she still wound up on her back when the net took her legs out from under her. I jammed my fist against my mouth to keep from shouting curses as Elka rolled frantically from side to side, trying to avoid getting impaled on the trident's tines. After a near miss, the retiarius had to wrench hard to free the weapon from where it stuck in the ground, and Elka brought her spear up in a great sweeping arc. The butt of the spear shaft caught the other girl on the side of her head and, even helmeted as she was, sent her sprawling. The trident flew from her grip to land just out of her reach. Elka sprang up and kicked away the net. In a single long leap, she stood looming over her opponent, spear raised high for a killing blow.

With a sharp blast from the *cornua*—and a shout from the referee—the bout was over. Elka's arm muscles, tensed and ready to deliver the blow, twitched once, and then she lowered her spear to the applause and cheers of the crowd. She lifted the visor on her helmet and held out a hand to help her downed opponent to her feet. The girl grasped her wrist and stood with a nod of acknowledgment. Elka turned to the crowd and thrust her spear into the air in triumph, then stalked back to the Achillea bench, head high.

She threw herself down on the bench beside me, grinning smugly.

I shook my head and raised an eyebrow at her. "What did I tell you about your big clumsy feet? She almost had you there, you know."

"That was strategy!" she protested.

"Really. I didn't know 'clumsy' qualified as an actual tactic."

"Wait until *you* get out there," she snorted. "It's different with a crowd watching."

The matches continued one after the other, some good, some bad, none of them fatal. Then it was my turn. The Fury—Uathach, or whatever she was called—strode into the middle of the ring, her gait low and loose like a hunting cat's. I took a deep breath, adjusted the two swords in their scabbards on my hips, and squared my shoulders.

Elka saluted me with a fist to her heart. "Luck."

I saluted her back. "And two good sharp swords."

I stepped onto the sand, feeling the heat through the soles of my sandals.

I could feel Cai's gaze on me, just as hot.

Mine was the last match of the day. The crowd was both restless and seething with anticipation. What would the Fury do this time, they wondered?

And *who* was the hapless gladiatrix they'd sent to fight her?

I felt like bait on a fishhook, and it made me angry. I reached for my swords and drew them with a fast, showy flourish. The crowd wanted spectacle? I would give it to them. I threw my arms skyward, clashing the swords above my head, gazing defiantly. The crowd threw up a smattering of encouraging cheers, nearly drowned out by heckling laughter.

The Fury drew back her lips in a feral snarl and waited. She wasn't armed like any of the other gladiatrices; she bore no shield, no sword, no spear or trident or net, just a pair of axes held tightly in her scarred fists. I frowned, wondering what she would do with them—and then leaped madly out of the way when she threw one at my head! I barely had time to realize that my bout was already under way as the Fury sprinted past me to retrieve her thrown axe. Without breaking stride, she plucked it up from where it had stuck, haft pointing up, in the sand. Then she turned and charged straight at me, axes whirling as she swung them side to side.

I distantly heard Sorcha and Elka shouting commands at me.

It took me a few desperate moments of frenzied blocking and ducking to realize that Uathach's way of fighting
wasn't very different from mine. Different weapons, to be
sure, and the curved blades of the axes gave her a greater
chance to hook my swords away, but the movements—
the side-to-side slashing and the wide dual swings—followed a similar flow. The axe blades caught the sunlight at
the edges of my vision, and my own blades flashed up to
meet them. Sparks flew, pale in the bright air, as we chased
each other back and forth across the sand. We were nearly
evenly matched, and I didn't think it was the kind of fight
the Fury usually encountered. At first, I wondered if she
would grow frustrated, but I only saw in her eyes the slow-
dawning light of pure joy.

Oh, this one truly is mad, I thought.

And yet, there was a secret part of me that understood
that joy. *This* was the kind of warfare I'd dreamed about as
a little girl. The strength, the speed, the skill . . . *this* was the
dance I'd longed for—

Maybe without the kick to the stomach.

I was down on all fours in an instant, sucking sand-
gritty air through my teeth. The crowd roared, sensing
yet another victory for the Fury. I reared back and slashed
wildly at the space in front of me with both swords to ward
her off, but she wasn't there. Uathach had spun away,
retreating to a far-off distance. I could barely hear the hoots
of the crowd over my own wheezing gasps. But when my
adversary threw back her head and howled a bone-chilling
battle cry . . . *that* I heard.

I lifted my head and, in that moment, saw what she truly was.

Shoulders hunched, head jutting forward, arms stretched out like wings with iron feathers, shrieking and wide-eyed, she was Death. The Terrible One. She was Vengeance. She came at me. Legs pumping, arms raised and ready to bury those axe blades in my head and heart, she ran. There was nothing else for me to do—I couldn't block, I couldn't slash . . . I was on my knees and out of breath. In the very last instant before her attack, I slammed the hilts of my twin swords together and thrust them out before me.

The Fury never even broke stride.

She impaled herself on my blades.

Right through her heart.

That's the thing about good sharp swords. Given the right conditions, they will cut through almost anything— even armor, always flesh. Mine had found the weakness between the links of the Fury's ragged chain-mail tunic and then the space between her ribs. Her forward momentum did the rest.

I flinched, and then her body slammed into me, throwing me back down to the ground. For a horrible moment, I lay pinned to the sand by the weight of her, and I felt panic rise in my throat. I thrashed and struggled and heaved her off me. She rolled limply away, and I saw that there was still that strange, joyous light in her eyes. But it was fading fast.

"No," I murmured, crouching to hold her face between

my hands as blood bubbled up and spilled out the sides of her mouth, staining my fingers.

"Yes," she whispered back. She lifted a weak hand and pressed it to my heart. "It's yours now. Thank you . . ."

Her face relaxed into a peaceful smile. And then she was gone.

The crowd was shocked into silence at the sudden demise of their favorite whipping post. But they shook themselves free of that spell as I clambered to my feet, painted in the Fury's blood. The arena echoed with demands for my blood too.

I reached for my swords, still buried in Uathach's chest—they slid free with far less effort than I thought it would take—and I staggered in the direction of the Ludus Achillea bench. Catcalls and insults rained down as I tore the suffocating helmet from my head with one hand, dropping it in the sand behind me. I was almost back at the dugout when the two attendants with their grotesque jackal masks and their corpse hooks strode past me to drag the body from the arena. At the sight of them, I thought my heart would burst into flame. I turned and ran back to where the Fury lay sprawled, still and small.

"No!" I shoved aside the jackal-man. "You will not touch her!"

The crowd grew suddenly still again.

"She deserves a better honor than your kind," I snarled. "*Get away!*"

The attendants backed off, looking to the games master for direction. I slammed my still-bloody blades into the sheaths hanging on my hips and bent down. As gently as I could, I slid my arms under her lifeless legs and shoulders. Even though she was smaller than me, I'd expected her to be heavy and hard to lift because of her powerful strength. But emptied of all her fire and fight, the Fury's body was almost feather-light.

I cradled her to my chest and walked across the sand toward the yawning maw of the archway that led to the infirmary—and the arena morgue. Enraged as I was, it took me a moment to notice that the angry silence of the mob had melted into a swelling wave of applause and shouts of approval.

"*Victrix!*" they cried. "Victory!"

Just like that, I had gone from villain to hero at the whim of the mob.

They knew nothing. I knew what I *really* was.

I was an instrument of the Morrigan's will.

Once I'd laid the body out on a low stone bench in the dark vault of the morgue, I knelt beside her on the dirt floor. I vomited until there was nothing left, but still my body rebelled against me—against the thing I'd suddenly become—dry-heaving until it felt as though my ribs would crack.

"It's not as if she gave you a choice," Elka said quietly from behind me. I hadn't even heard her come in, but she was sitting on a stool beside the door. "You'll forget this in time."

"And what of you?" I leaned back against the cold stone bench support, wiping my mouth with the back of my hand. "What about the man you killed that first day, on the stage in the Forum? Do you still think of him?"

"Think?" She shook her head. "No. I don't have to think of him. His shade visits me almost nightly in my sleep. We're so familiar with each other now, he's almost a friend."

She said it half as a joke, but I could see the distant horror of the act in her gaze. After a moment, she shook herself from her reverie and stood. Then she held out a hand, helping me to my feet.

"If Uathach was so desperate to escape her life as a slave," I said, "if she saw that much more freedom even in death, then why didn't she just let one of her opponents kill her in any one of her bouts before me? Why fight so hard? Why even fight at all?"

I looked at Elka, searching her pale eyes for answers I didn't have. Then I remembered what Sorcha had said to me earlier about the danger of those who had nothing to lose, and I realized she'd been *almost* right. The woman who'd called herself Uathach, whom everyone else had labeled the Fury, did have one last thing to lose: her honor.

By beating her—*ending* her—in a good, fair fight, I'd let her keep it. She had died by the sword, and that was the way she'd wanted it. To lose myself in mourning Uathach's death would be to dishonor how she had lived her life. But to live my life the way she had—in restless fury, always seeking freedom over the next horizon—would be to cage myself inside a fate that was not of my own making.

Why even fight at all?

I thought back to the night of my oath swearing. I had come a long way since uttering those words in the darkness. I hadn't really understood them at the time—not fully. And I had not thought to find my kindred spirits—my tribe—so far away from home, but I had. Elka, Ajani, Sorcha. Even Nyx. I had found friendships . . . rivalries . . .

Family.

Family I wanted to keep safe the way Sorcha had wanted to keep her gladiators safe, by transforming the Ludus Achillea into a safe haven . . . in the days before she'd had to abandon that dream for my sake. *That* was why I would fight. That was why I would win. I was Victrix. Victory. At least, I *would* be. I said a silent prayer for the Fury and thanked her for giving me the fight that would send me hurtling toward my destiny.

I spoke the oath, Elka's voice joining with mine: *"Uri, vinciri, verberari, ferroque necari . . ."*

Simple words, simple promises. The very same oath the men swore in *their* rings of sand and swords. We were no different—except we were. And no one was more surprised by that than I. We were castoffs and slaves, orphans and unwanteds and used-to-be princesses. We were *infamia* . . .

But we were a sisterhood.

"Uri, vinciri, verberari, ferroque necari."

And we were mighty.

XXV

FROM THEN ON, the games in the towns that followed were easier. I fought, and I fought well, but I never again fought like I had against the Fury. I didn't have to. The circuit ended in a small arena on the outskirts of Rome, and by the time it was finished, all the girls of the Ludus Achillea were seasoned fighters.

And I was a tiny, growing legend. The Fury Killer. Victrix. Victory.

Whether or not I would be chosen as Caesar's Victory remained to be seen.

After the last fight, Sorcha had announced that Caesar's scouts had reported back to him and that the competition for the role had come down to just two of us: me and Nyx. We were to present ourselves to him in two days' time at his villa across the River Tiber so that he could interview us in person and decide for himself to which gladiatrix he would bestow the honor of the Victory role. The announcement generated a great deal of chattering and whispering in the hallways of the domus where we lodged in the capital. But it didn't account for the shouting and commotion I heard as I walked back toward my quarters.

I pushed my way through to see what the matter was and was brought up short by Ajani, whose expression was grim.

"Don't" was all she said.

"Don't what? Let me by, Ajani."

I shouldered her out of the way and saw a knot of girls gathered in the hall in front of the door to my room. Elka was there, storm clouds in her blue eyes. When she saw me she shook her head and strode toward me.

"What's going on?" I asked.

"Nothing. Someone's idea of a sick joke."

I looked past her, and my heart turned over. The door to my room was closed—and streaked with the blood of the dead bird nailed to it. Not just any bird. A crow. I swore and scanned the faces of the other girls who stood there gaping. I snarled when I spotted Nyx, her eyes fixed on the grisly sight.

"Nyx—"

I lunged for her, but Elka caught me by the arm.

"Wasn't her," she said. "It wasn't there an hour ago, and Nyx was in the dining hall the whole time. So were Meriel and Gratia. Lydia found the thing and was so hysterical when she saw it, it couldn't have been her."

That ruled out all of Nyx's most ardent minions. Unless there was another gladiatrix in the ranks trying to curry favor with her. For her part, Nyx had barely even seemed to notice that I was there. Her gaze was riveted to the door.

"It's a curse," she murmured. "An ill-luck omen."

"It's a *bird*." I pulled my knife from my belt so that I could pry out the nails that held the poor dead thing there, crucified like a slave.

Only, it wasn't dead.

As I reached for it, the crow—a juvenile, by the look of it—lifted its head and cawed weakly at me. One of the girls behind me screamed, and the bird struggled to flap its wings.

"You should break its neck," Elka said. "End its suffering."

I frowned. I wasn't sure how the Morrigan would take that. And I wasn't going to kill an innocent creature if I didn't have to, just because somebody thought it would be fun to try to frighten me. I glanced back at the other girls and saw that Neferet was standing in the crowd. I called her over, and she came, her steps only a little hesitant. Ever since she'd started taking care of Antonia, she'd been studying under Heron and learning medicine.

"Can you help me try to save it?" I asked.

She nodded and supported the weight of the bird as I worked the two nails out of its wings. Whoever had done this must have fed the bird something to drug it into a stupor first. Once we freed it from the nails that pierced its wings just below the mid-joint, it was plain that there wasn't anything else wrong with it. Neferet cooed gently to the bird, and it tucked itself in close to her chest.

"I'll keep it warm and clean the wounds," she said quietly to me. "It will probably never fly again . . . but perhaps it will live."

I nodded. "Thank you, Neferet."

"Who would do such a thing?"

"Someone who has no idea how angry they've just made my goddess," I said. "And me."

I spun on my heel and strode down the hall in the other direction, in search of a bucket and rag.

Sorcha found me just as I was cleaning the last of the blood from my door. It was plain she had learned about the crow. Her face was flushed, showing the whiteness of her scar in stark contrast, and angry sparks seemed to dance in the darkness of her damaged eye.

"It's nothing," I said to try and forestall what I knew was coming.

"It's *not* nothing." She glared back and forth from me to the door. "I'm pulling you from consideration for the Triumphs."

"You can't do that!" I felt a flare of panic.

"I can. I will." She thrust out her arm, pointing at the last of the rusty stain on the wood. "This is more than a warning, Fallon! It's a promise. It's a death mark, and I'm not going to let you go out there and—"

"Sorcha, please." Something in the sound of my voice stopped her cold. "We don't even know if Caesar will choose me. But if he does, I have to fight. Not just for me.

For you. For the honor of the Ludus Achillea and the House Cantii. You have to let me."

"No. My decision is final."

Just like when we were young. My sister could be the most bullheaded creature the gods ever let walk the earth. I felt like I was nine years old again, and I wanted to scream. "It didn't worry you to send me into the arena against the Fury," I spat. "How is this any different?"

"You weren't supposed to fight that madwoman," she said. "None of my girls were. She shouldn't have even been on the roster! I argued with the games masters until I was blue and out of breath, but they threatened to censure the whole ludus unless your match went forth. Caesar would have had my head."

"When are you going to stop protecting me, Sorcha? You say you can't treat me any differently than the other girls? Then don't!"

"This isn't a game anymore." She gripped my shoulders, her face close to mine. "For some, it never was. And now they've set their sights on you. I won't let that happen. You're going home to the ludus in the morning."

"Sorcha—no!"

"Pack your things."

Without another word, she turned on her heel and left me standing there, blood staining my hands and tears of frustration welling in my eyes. Suddenly, I realized I wasn't alone. I turned to see Thalestris standing at the opposite end of the hall from where Sorcha had stormed off. I turned

back to the door and angrily scrubbed at the last traces of
blood. The Amazon fight mistress came toward me, silent
as a hunter stalking prey, and stopped to lean on the wall
beside my doorway.

"It's natural for older sisters to worry," she said.

My hand holding the rag froze.

"You know?" I glanced up and down the hall to see if
we were alone, more than a little surprised. After Sorcha
made me swear not to tell our secret, I hadn't even told
Elka. I hadn't told Cai.

"Of course," Thalestris said. "I've always known. I am
the Lanista's Primus Pilus. We have no secrets, she and I."

I thought back to the night on Cleopatra's barge when
Sorcha had said the only people who knew I was her sister
were the three of us and Charon. She'd seemed adamant
to keep it that way, but I supposed she must have made an
exception for Thalestris.

"She's very proud of you," she said, interrupting my
thoughts.

I snorted. "I doubt that."

She grinned. "The Romans have a saying: *In vino
veritas.*"

In wine, truth. Romans and their wine, I thought. Back
home in Prydain the chiefs and freemen drank good dark
beer and spiced mead if they wanted to get to the truth of
things.

"There was a banquet one night," Thalestris continued.
"Only a month or so before the chariot wreck that ended
Achillea's career as a gladiatrix, back in the days when

she was the absolute darling of the city. That's when I first learned of your existence. One of Achillea's admirers was bemoaning the fact that there was only one of her. I'd never heard Achillea speak of her past before, but the wine had been flowing all night, and she was in a melancholy mood. She told the man that, in fact, she'd left behind a younger sister—a sister who showed great promise as a warrior, greater even than Achillea herself—and that she was filled with regret that she hadn't been able to see her grow to fulfill that promise. She boasted that you would have made a fierce gladiatrix. A champion."

"She said that?"

"She did. And now you are here." She shrugged. "Perhaps the goddess you both pray to has designed it that way."

"Or maybe she just has a twisted sense of humor," I said bitterly. "I'm here, I can fight—better than anyone—and now she won't let me!"

"As I said, that was before her accident," Thalestris said.

"I don't understand what that has to do with me. I'm not even a charioteer—"

"Afterward, we learned that the axle of her chariot had been tampered with."

I stared at the fight master.

"In the days before the race"—her eyes flicked to the damp planks of my door—"Achillea had ignored certain . . . portents. Warnings. Over the years, the games have become very dangerous, both inside the arena and out. The rivalries between the ludi are heated."

"She lied to me," I said. "She told me it was just an accident, not that someone had tried to *kill* her. Why would she do that?"

"She didn't want to frighten you," Thalestris said. "The very worst thing you can enter into the arena with is fear."

"She also told me she wouldn't treat me differently than the other girls."

"Perhaps her perspective has altered." Thalestris put a fingertip on the damp wood of the door, tracing the faint remains of the stain. "Or perhaps she would take the same course of action with any one of her charges."

"And do you agree with her?" I challenged. "About sending me back to the ludus?"

"The decision is hers to make, not mine," she said. "But no. I would send you back into the arena. You can't win the fight—whatever fight you face—by running from it. But think on this: It would break the Lanista's heart if she were to lose her beloved sister." She gazed at me steadily with her dark, unblinking eyes. "Believe me. I know."

With that, she nodded at me and glided off down the hall. I stood there for a long time after she'd gone, staring at the wet pink rag in my hands and wondering what to do next.

I skipped the evening meal, preferring to brood alone in my room. Of course, Elka wasn't having any of it, and she insisted on keeping me company while I fumed and paced. When there was a knock on my door I opened it, surprised to see Nyx standing there.

"What do you want?" I asked.

She glanced over her shoulder and then stepped inside, closing the door behind her. "I wanted to see if you were all right."

"Oh. Of course you did," I snapped. "And I deeply appreciate your obviously genuine concern. Now get out."

"Wait." Nyx shook her head. "That business with the crow? It wasn't me."

To my surprise, I could tell from her expression that she was actually telling the truth. Suddenly, I felt exhaustion wash over me. The animosity just became too much effort. I sighed and sat down on the bed.

"I know it wasn't you," I said, raking a hand through my hair. "Elka already vouched for you."

Nyx glanced at Elka, who shrugged.

"I just wonder who it was and what they think they're trying to prove."

"If I knew, I'd tell you."

At that, Elka snorted.

"I *would*." Nyx crossed her arms. "Look, I know I'm not *nice*. But I don't resort to dirty tricks, and I don't respect anyone who does. I fight hard and I fight well, and sometimes it's hard for me to admit when somebody else does too." She looked at me through narrowed eyes. "The Fury? I don't know that I could've beaten her."

"I'm not sure I did."

"You did. It was a good fight. An honorable fight." Nyx took another step into the room, her expression turning rueful. "I mean it. And for the first time since I've been at the ludus, I have someone pushing me to be a better fighter. Even if it kills me to admit it . . . I've needed that." She held out her hand. "We can still be rivals, but I want us to be friends too."

I hesitated. How would Nyx react if I told her that she no longer had to compete against me—that Sorcha was withdrawing me from the Victory challenge? I decided, considering everything she'd just said, that it might not be the right moment to enlighten her.

I stood and clasped Nyx's wrist.

She smiled and said, "Good. Listen, I have a patron here in Rome, a wealthy equestrian lady. She sent me word of revels taking place tonight."

"Revels?"

"A party. A big one. Very lavish, very exclusive, full of other rich patricians looking to spend money on pretty young fighters."

"I already have a patron," I said, careful not to name Charon.

"I noticed." Nyx pointed at Elka. "But you don't. And you could do better than Ajani's castoffs."

Elka lifted a shoulder. "I'm not fussy."

Nyx turned to me. "Come on, Fallon. We're all on edge after today. We deserve a bit of fun!"

I raised an eyebrow at her. "Did the Lanista gave you permission to go?"

She grinned. Wickedly.

I felt an answering grin spread across my face.

The domus we were lodged in was similar to the ludus

compound in that we weren't locked into our sleeping cells at night. But neither were we exactly free to wander the streets of Rome at will, and getting caught doing so would, I was sure, bear consequences. Nyx didn't seem to think it would be a problem.

"It'll be fun," she said.

"I'll go if Elka does," I said.

Elka blinked at me, but Nyx just grinned.

"Fine by me," she said. "I invited Lydia too. She could use some new kit, and she knows how to behave around men. But you have to be quick and change. Put on something nice. Fancy. Meet me down by the laundry scullery as soon as you can. Don't get caught. And *don't* tell any of the other girls!"

And then she was gone.

I plucked at the hem of my plain tunic. "Something nice?"

"Fancy?" Elka was dressed the same way as I was.

Reluctantly, I flipped open the lid of my trunk. In one corner, beneath the heavy cloak Ajani had given me on my first night at the ludus, there was a small folded pile of shimmery fabric: the costume Charon's women had dressed me in for the slave auction. As I gazed at the thing, the memory of that day—it seemed like a thousand more had passed since—came rushing back, washing over me like an incoming tide.

"You kept yours too?" Elka said wryly.

I laughed at her expression. "Is this a very bad idea?"

"You know we're slaves, *ja*?" she said plainly. "If

anyone catches us out, they'll think we're running. We'll be flogged."

"This *is* a very bad idea."

And yet neither of us was about to back out. Sorcha could try and keep me safe from death, but she couldn't keep me from living my life. And if I wasn't competing for Victory, it wasn't as if I had anything to lose. A reckless thrill surged in my heart at the thought of disobeying her, and it must have shown in the expression on my face.

Elka sighed. "I'll go get dressed."

I undid my braid and combed out the waves of my hair so it hung loosely over my shoulders. Then I slipped into my auction dress and fastened the shoulder brooches, belting the ensemble with a pretty fringed scarf someone had thrown me from the stands after one of my winning bouts on the circuit.

Elka and I met Nyx down by the scullery, and Lydia was with her. Nyx was dressed in an elegant pale yellow stola that fastened with silver brooches at her shoulders and left her toned arms bare. Her long black hair was dressed off her face with silver combs. Lydia wore blue, a necklace of amber beads, and an abundance of eye paint. We were all cloaked and hooded, and I was trembling with apprehension and excitement.

Nyx inserted a key into the big iron lock on the wooden door that led out to a back alley. I didn't ask where she got it, but it wasn't hard to guess. I'd noticed a handsome young kitchen slave making eyes at her when we'd first arrived, and Nyx was nothing if not resourceful. Again, that much was evident by the skin of wine she produced from beneath the folds of her cloak. Threading the narrow streets, we headed toward the Caelian Hill, where Rome's wealthy patrician families had built many lavish residences that looked far more like palaces than houses.

"You can't be all uptight on a night like this," Nyx said, passing the wineskin to Elka, who expertly tilted her head back and shot a stream of red liquid down her throat. "Ha! That's it. You drink like an Amazon!"

"Fight like one too." Elka wiped the back of her hand across her mouth.

"Better not let Thalestris hear you say that." Nyx grinned as Elka handed her back the wine. "She's touchy on the subject, seeing as how her mighty Amazon sister embarrassed the whole bloody tribe, distinguishing herself as the first ever gladiatrix to get killed. And by our own Lanista, no less!"

She offered the wine to me, and rolled her eyes when I hesitated. I stifled a sigh and reached for the skin. The wine was unwatered, rich and sweet. *Nyx must have pilfered the expensive stuff*, I thought. I took another long swallow and handed it back.

"Where are we going?" I asked, looking around at the unfamiliar buildings that loomed above the dark streets. We'd barely passed a soul, and most of the windows were shuttered tight. If not for the almost full moon above, it would have been like walking through ink-black fog.

"We're going to the Domus Corvinus, up on the Caelian Hill," Nyx explained. "It's owned by a very rich nobleman

who has far more money than he knows what to do with
and doesn't want to leave any of it to his greedy relatives.
So he spends it all on these extravagant spreads and invites
all of his friends, and everyone goes a little mad. His cooks
make all sorts of outlandish dishes like monkey tongues and
stewed starfish. And the entertainment is extraordinary!"

I wondered what constituted extraordinary entertainment at a Roman feast. I thought back to the gatherings
my father used to host where the young men of the tribes
would compete to see who could leap over the tallest bon-
fire flames and the bards dueled each other in song, shaping words and music beautiful enough to break hearts.
Where the women would dance barefoot across a floor of
naked swords . . .

My steps faltered as a wave of homesickness swept
over me, and I stopped in the middle of the street. I was
outside the ludus, unguarded, at night . . . what was there
to stop me from running away?

But even as the thought crossed my mind, I wondered
if I could bear to lose my sister again. Thalestris said Sorcha
would go mad with grief if she thought something had happened to me.

After everything she's put me through? I thought. *It would
serve her right.*

Even in the darkness, I could probably manage to
head in the general direction of the Capitoline Hill. And I
could smell the river. But if I got lost and wound up in the
Aventine district, then I was in trouble. The Aventine—so
we'd been warned—wasn't a part of the city to get lost in.

"Come *on*, Fallon!" Nyx exclaimed suddenly, reaching for my hand. "Don't be such a tortoise! We're in *Rome*. This is the most amazing city in the world, and we'll never get another chance to experience it like this. It'll be fun—you'll see!"

She handed the wineskin to me again.

I took another swallow, and my urge to run faded as the liquid heat from the wine coursed through my limbs. There was a faint buzzing in my skull like a swarm of lazy bees. Nyx was right. Escape, after all, would be awfully hard work. And I could certainly use a little less work and a little more fun in my life.

A little more sisterhood and a little less sister.

It's said that if you look hard enough, you could find any kind of indulgence in Rome. And that, in most cases, you didn't even have to look very hard. There was no admittance to the Domus Corvinus that night unless you were wearing a mask. Those who hadn't brought their own—and who, exactly, *had* brought their own? Elka wondered aloud—were obliged to choose one from a basket held by one of the pretty girls standing at the gated entrance of the estate grounds.

"I don't understand why everyone has to wear one of these," I said.

One of the girls holding a basket leaned in close to my ear.

"Because stuffy old men wrapped in purple-striped togas in the senate don't approve of such gatherings," she whispered. "They outlawed the Bacchanales decades ago, and Domus Corvinus parties are the closest thing you'll find to those!" Then she kissed my cheek, her perfume making my head spin. "Isn't that deliciously wicked?"

Some masks were made of linen strips wrapped over wire frames and stiffened with paste, and others were made of leather, molded into grotesque or fanciful shapes. They were all painted and decorated with jewels and beads or peacock feathers. Some were gilded or finished with silver, and some were even attached to elaborate wigs dyed in bright hues.

Nyx chose one adorned with a fan of peacock plumes. Lydia protested that she'd been about to choose that one, but she had to settle for one designed to look like a mosaic. I wasn't about to tell her that it made her look rather reptilian. Elka slipped on a mask festooned with downy feathers that made her look like an owl.

I'd only ever seen masks like that worn by the actors who performed between matches at the games. Something about normal folk donning them to disguise themselves in a crowd made me uneasy. The anonymity the masks granted the revelers felt almost dangerous.

"Oh, stop dawdling!" Nyx complained. "Just pick one. We're going to miss all the fun!"

I shook off the moment of apprehension and plunged my hand into the basket, snatching up the first mask my fingertips brushed—a pretty thing with layers of delicate green and gold leaves fanning outward like a sunburst. I settled it on my face, and the girl tied the ribbons behind my head.

"That suits you, little fox!" Elka said, her mouth turned up in a crooked grin beneath the cloud of feathers she wore. "You look like one of the *alfr*—a woodland sprite come from the sacred groves to dance!" Then she giggled.

I'd never heard Elka giggle before.

I turned to Nyx. "What was in that wine?" I demanded.

"Just a bit of mandragora," she said, shrugging.

The minute she said it, I felt my own head start to spin like the wheels on an upended chariot. *Mandrake?* That was something the druiddyn used back home—a powerful intoxicant to help them fall into divining trances. And how casually Nyx had just brushed it aside. At the look on my face, she sighed impatiently.

"Everyone takes it at a party like this," she said, a sharp edge creeping into her voice. "Or poppy wine. Sometimes both. Don't be so provincial!"

The insult stung, but I wasn't about to let Nyx know it. And so, like an idiot, I snatched the wineskin from her and poured a stream of the liquid down my throat. When I handed the skin back, I tried to ignore the fact that my lips were tingling.

We climbed the path, and by the time we got to the house, Elka and I were both giggling. Arms wrapped around each other's shoulders, we tripped through the wide front doors of the palatial house and into a vast vaulted entry hall. And I suddenly understood why it was called Domus Corvinus.

Raven House.

It hadn't even occurred to me when Nyx had first said the name. But then I saw the enormous black-marble statue of a bird perched, wings spread wide, atop a pedestal in the middle of the atrium. I stared at it in astonishment. The sculpture was so lifelike that I half expected to hear the rustling of its wings. For a moment, my mind reeled back to the crow that had been nailed to my door, and I felt a rush of dread. I shook my head, hard.

The raven was sacred to the Morrigan, I told myself. If anything, this was a sign that she wanted me at this place. I ran my fingertips across the carved marble ridges of the raven's talons as I passed. Suddenly I realized I was alone in the crowd, and I glanced around for Elka, fumbling at the brooch holding my mantle closed with numb, clumsy fingers so I could pass it off to the waiting attendant who stood barring my way.

I made my way into the main part of the house and through to the enormous dining hall furnished with scattered arrangements of reclining couches and long tables groaning beneath the weight of the food and drink laid out on them. The sheer abundance was staggering. The sheer abandon with which the party guests indulged was even more so.

I marveled at it all. So this was what it was like to live a life of wealth and luxury. Noise and color and heady perfumes overwhelmed my senses, and I stood there gazing around at the glittering, torchlit spectacle. Lydia and Nyx had drifted far ahead of me—I could just see them, heads together and whispering before they were swallowed up by the crowd—and Elka was headed toward the nearest banquet table. I watched her weaving unsteadily through the press of bodies and thought to myself that I should catch up to her. That I should keep her in my sight. But by the time I'd fully formed that thought, she was gone.

Someone pressed a goblet into my hand, and I drank deeply.

Lithe-bodied, mostly naked dancers, boys and girls both, whirled past me trailing gossamer. Musicians on flutes and drums and harp-like lyres sat on raised daises in the corners of the room, the strains of their competing songs tangling in the air over the heads of revelers too busy gossiping or groping or shrieking with drunken laughter to even notice.

But then suddenly it was time for the main event of the evening.

That everyone noticed. It was what they'd come for.

A single cornua—just like the horns they used in the arenas—sounded a shrill, commanding note that echoed loudly off the elegant marble columns, and the room fell to utter silence. Even in my hazy state, I could feel the tension crackling like lightning as a figure in a tall gilded mask stepped forward. Raising an ornately decorated staff, he announced the combat that was about to take place between two rising stars of the gladiatorial world.

Gladiators, I thought, *at a party?*

The revelers cheered, some for Ajax and some for Mandobracius.

Mandobracius? Where had I heard that name before?

I couldn't remember. And the fog in my head wasn't helping. I stood, swaying, as two young girls clad in

short, filmy tunics drew aside curtains and the gladiators
stepped into the room. Torches flared, the light from the
flames catching on the edges of their armor and blades.
The men cheered rowdily, and the women leaned forward
in anticipation.

Both men wore visored helmets but less armor than
they would have in the arena—only broad leather belts and
battle kilts, shin greaves, and wrist bracers. The one named
Ajax was heavily muscled, oiled and gleaming, his skin a
deeply tanned olive. Mandobracius was paler, leaner, and
bore the swirling blue tattoos of a Celt on his chest and
back. His long dark hair spilled over his shoulders from
under the brim of a helmet crested with a plume of glossy
black feathers.

I shivered at the sight. Here was a warrior the Morrigan
could be proud of. He was worshipped by the crowd of revelers, who screamed his name out like he was a god. In that
moment, as the two men squared off and the crowd froze
in anticipation, I could think of nothing I wanted more. To
fight like that, to be adored like that . . . to win such glory
with nothing but my blades. I thought of the Victory role in
Caesar's Triumphs slipping through my fingers, and for a
brief, irrational moment, I wanted to gnash my teeth furiously right there in the middle of the revelry.

But then the two men stepped forward and saluted
each other, and I found myself leaning in with the rest of
the crowd. It looked as though both gladiators would fight
dimachaerus-style—just like I did—and I heard myself
cheering wildly at the prospect. The cornua sounded again,

ringing in my ears and drowning out my shouts, and the fight began.

Ajax went on the attack, and the smaller, more agile Mandobracius was forced into a hasty retreat, swords whirling like wheels as he blocked blow after blow. Ajax followed relentlessly, and the two combatants barreled through the crowd, heedless of causing injury to the spectators. Partygoers dove for cover, laughing as they picked themselves up off the floor after the frenzy had swept past.

The near brush with death was a heady elixir to the watching crowd. In those moments, the gladiators were like heroes and villains out of legend. The women shrieked giddily and the men drunkenly shouted encouragement while flashing blades came within inches of hacking off their patrician limbs.

I cheered as loudly as anyone in the room.

Ajax chased Mandobracius the length of the dining room and out into the courtyard, and the crowd spilled out after them, carrying me along in their wake. A gust of wind spiraled down through the roofless courtyard, and two of the stands of torch sconces guttered and extinguished, plunging a corner of the impromptu arena into darkness. I caught a glimpse of Mandobracius as he spun on his heel and disappeared into the throng.

The house slaves scrambled amid cries of outrage to relight the torches. When they flared to life again, Ajax stood in the middle of a small clearing in the courtyard, turning in wary circles. His opponent was nowhere to be seen.

Then suddenly, I saw a black-feathered helmet crest

bobbing up above the heads of the crowd. Ajax saw it too and lunged forward, thrusting his swords before him. The revelers shrieked—in real terror—and dove frantically out of the way as one of the beefy gladiator's swords plunged into the naked chest of the man in the feathered helmet. Ajax's prey staggered forward, into the open space beyond the crowd.

It was *not* Mandobracius.

The man's torso was far too skinny and lacked the swirling tattoos. His helmet wasn't even real. It was only a costume piece—one of the more elaborate masks at the party, designed to mimic Mandobracius's armor. The man wearing it had probably been an ardent admirer.

Ajax realized his mistake a moment too late.

He let out a soft gasp and looked down to see two blades protruding outward from his chest, the points red with his own blood. Ajax's spine arched, and he clawed weakly at the blades, sinking to his knees not more than a spear's length in front of me. As he collapsed face-first on the marble floor, the crowd went mad with bloodlust, howling and cheering and shouting the victor's name. I looked up from the dead man to see Mandobracius standing there, his tattooed chest heaving, the swords clenched in his fists painted dark with blood. Carried away in the moment, drunk on excitement as much as mandrake wine, I felt a savage elation. But when the bloodied gladiator raised his head and met my gaze, I felt my heart tear in two.

The gray eyes that looked out from behind the visor grate were as familiar to me as my own soul. The room

began to spin, and suddenly I felt as though I was suffocating. I reached up and clawed the mask from my face,
and the gladiator's mouth soundlessly made the shape of
a name. My name.

"Fallon?" He blinked rapidly. The bloodied blades
wavered in his hands.

Mael?

"Is that really you? Fallon—it's me." He reached up
and lifted the helmet off his head. There were raven feathers tied throughout his long dark hair. "It's Aeddan!"

Aeddan . . .

No. That wasn't possible. The last time I'd seen Aeddan,
he'd killed his brother. It was the wine, the mandrake. I was
hallucinating. As the apparition of Mael's brother reached
out for me, I turned and bolted from the room, fighting my
way through the crowd as if the Raven of Nightmares herself had come to claim me.

"Fallon!" the apparition called after me. *"Fallon!"*

My name echoed through the marble halls behind me
as I ran.

Domus Corvinus, I soon discovered, was like a laby-
rinth. Corridors turned into rooms that turned into atriums
that turned into yet more corridors. The crowds thinned
the farther away from the dining hall I got, until I was
thankfully, mercifully alone. I stumbled through a breezeway out onto a terrace. I leaned heavily against a marble
plinth topped with a sundial, trying to steady myself, but
it did little to quell the sensation that I was back on the
ship sailing across the Mare Nostrum. The ground seemed

to swell and heave, and the clouds in the sky above my head—I could have sworn—were breathing.

It wasn't Mael. Mael's dead. And it wasn't Aeddan.

No. It couldn't be. Aeddan had run home after murdering his own brother.

I stared down at the Roman numerals carved into the weathered face of the sundial, trying to remember what they were.

One . . . two . . . three . . .

What was the next one called? I could never remember the names of the numbers, and Elka and I had laughed about it every time she'd asked me to call out a number on her target wheel.

Thirteen!

Someone at the ludus had once told me thirteen was unlucky.

The sky, dressed in garish hues, reeled above me, and the ground beneath me heaved like a wave. I thought I heard a raven cry out in the distance. And then a pair of grasping hands, like talons, reached out from the darkness behind me, and a voice said, "Fallon."

I screamed.

And spun, flailing, wrenching violently out of the grip of whoever had me by the shoulders. A backward kick rewarded me with a grunt of pain, and suddenly I was free.

"*Grab* the bitch!" a female voice barked in the darkness.

A hand closed over my face, and I bit down hard. Another muffled cry of pain and I was free again, spitting blood as I lurched forward into a stumbling run. I bolted for the deep shadows beneath a stand of cypress trees, where I hoped to hide before sprinting for the nearest path leading back up into the house. But even though I could hear distant raucous merriment, I couldn't find any stairs back up to where the party still carried on. In the state I was in, I didn't even know which way was up, and when I did finally find a stone staircase—half-hidden by an over-grown thornbush—it didn't take me toward the revelry.

I could hear angry shouts behind me, so I pushed past the grasping branches and crept down the stairwell as quietly as I could. I didn't understand much in that moment, but one thing seemed abundantly clear: I had suddenly become hunted quarry. At the bottom of the stairs there was an iron gate secured with a chain, but it gaped enough for me to squeeze through. Without a moment to spare, I stumbled deeper into the shadows of what seemed to be a tunnel leading beneath the house.

"I did *my* part!" The female voice drifted down the stairwell. "I got her here. How did you manage to let her get away? He'll kill you if she manages to escape your grasp again. He'll probably kill me too—"

"Shut up!" That was Aeddan's voice. He sounded near frantic.

I held my breath and stayed as still as I could.

"She's a weak little gladiolus, and she's wasted with mandragora."

Nyx, I realized with a dread chill crawling down my spine. It was Nyx's voice.

"You're *useless,* Mandobracius."

Their voices grew faint as they argued.

They clearly hadn't seen me duck down the stairs, and that was my only advantage. I was certainly in no shape to fight. I was panting like a cornered animal, and I could barely even run. I had no idea where Elka was, and I desperately wished Caius were there in that moment. I was in dire need.

Dire need. All of a sudden, I remembered the scroll Charon had given me—the one that guaranteed my safety—and I fumbled at my waist. But of course I hadn't worn my leather belt pouch that evening. It had spoiled the look of the delicate stola I'd worn, and so I'd left it behind. The little vellum scroll was tucked away in my pouch, back in the traveling trunk in my room—in spite of Cai's and Sorcha's warnings and Charon's admonitions.

I was a fool.

The shadows of the cypress trees loomed menacingly on the walls of the stairwell where I hid, and I began to imagine them reaching for me. I had to get away from that place. My only option was to run, and the only direction I could go was down. As silently as I could, trying not to stumble against the walls in my addled state, I descended into a catacomb that ran beneath the Domus Corvinus and felt my way along, brushing fingertips against the rough-hewn stone. I heard water dripping and then, after what seemed a long while, what sounded like muffled voices.

A faint glow of torchlight at the end of the tunnel beckoned, and I crept toward it, hoping to find a servants' entrance up into the house. I found an archway instead.

It opened out into a vaulted chamber, and I peered cautiously around the wall. In the flickering torchlight, I had to look and look again before my bleary eyes fully understood what they saw. I listened hard to make sense of the sounds above the weird, low chanting. But then my eyes and ears put their senses together, and my stomach climbed into my throat.

The body of Ajax—the slain gladiator from earlier that night—lay naked on a polished black-marble slab. His olive skin was pale and slack and painted with blood. His face was turned toward me, and his eyes were open, vacant and staring into the afterlife from which his spirit would never return. A circle of robed and hooded figures wearing black-feathered masks hovered over him. Through the gaps of their huddled forms, I could see that they had split Ajax's torso open like the roasting carcass of a wild boar. I glimpsed the white gleam of his rib cage grasping like rigid fingers at the shadows, and I could hear the wet, gluttonous sounds of feasting.

Morrigan protect me—they're eating his heart!

The bile rose in my throat, bitter and searing, and I felt my own heart thud heavily in my chest. I clapped a hand over my mouth to keep from screaming. What manner of monsters had I stumbled upon? Did the revelers in the palace above have any idea what was going on in the catacombs beneath their feet? *Did Nyx?*

My head throbbed with the beat of my pulse, and the smell of smoke and incense and blood was overwhelming. Beneath their grotesque, black-feathered masks, the mouths and chins of the men gathered around the slab were stained crimson. One of them stood behind a set of golden scales, and I saw that in one dish lay a finely wrought feather made of gleaming silver. In the other . . . a raw, red lump of flesh quivered as the scales dipped and settled to rest on the marble slab with a thump.

The glamour of a celebrated gladiator's life suddenly shattered like glass in my mind, exploding outward in jagged pieces, the picture reshaping itself into a grotesque mosaic of blood and dishonor. Monstrous. I spun dizzily on the heels of my sandals and ran as swiftly as I could, stumbling blindly back through the black stone tunnel and out into the cool, fragrant air, praying to the Morrigan that the monsters in their lair hadn't seen me there. I scrambled clumsily up the stairwell and fell sprawling on the lawn. The grass whispered secrets and lies into my ears, and the earth beneath my shoulder blades was warm and breathing, expanding and contracting like the chest of the dead gladiator had before they'd torn out his heart.

I'd almost forgotten why I'd gone down into that tunnel in the first place.

Until Aeddan appeared out of the darkness.

I opened my mouth to scream but didn't make a sound. At least I don't think I did. I wasn't really sure of anything at that point. Aeddan sank down onto his knees in front of me and held his hands out, reaching for me.

"Fallon!" he said in a low, urgent voice. "I'm not going to hurt you! You have to listen to me. If they find you, they'll take you. I'm so sorry—this is all my fault."

"Who?" I managed to gasp. "What are you saying?"

He looked so much like Mael in that moment that I wanted to cry.

"I used to think it was all for the money," he continued, breathless, "but it's more than that. They worship death. There is a man they call the Collector—"

"Pontius Aquila?" I shook my head, trying to clear my mind enough to make sense of what Aeddan was saying. "The Tribune? What does he have to do with any of this?"

"These are his revels. Not every gladiator in his collection is destined for the arena sands. Some of them wind up here instead. Fighting in the *munera*—private bouts—for men who call themselves the Sons of Dis. They think they draw mystical power from the death of strong fighters."

"I saw them," I said. "Men. In the catacombs—"

"If you were close enough to see them, then you should thank the Morrigan you got away from them."

"It was horrible."

"Their practices are outlawed. They only meet in secret, and they're depraved. Cruel. The games aren't just *games* to these men, Fallon. It's a kind of madness."

"The gladiator . . . Ajax . . ." I looked up into his pale face. "Tonight is the second time I've watched you kill a man."

He squeezed his eyes shut. "Don't. Please. He was a friend to me at the ludus. I know his fate, and I weep for it. I had no choice. The munera aren't just entertainment. They're ritual. And they're always to the death—an offering to their underworld gods." The pain in his voice was real. "Ajax would have killed me just the same if he'd had the chance. Once we were pulled from the ludus to fight in the munera, we both knew that only one of us was walking away from that bout."

I gaped at him in disbelief. "What—why are *you* even fighting for a ludus?" I shook my head to try to clear the fog of confusion that wrapped around my brain. "You're no gladiator, Aeddan. You're a *king!*"

"I'm an exile, Fallon," he said quietly. "Again. Because of what I did to Maelgwyn. The Trinovante decreed me a kin killer and banished me from the tribe."

Right. Aeddan may have been a king, but he was also a murderer. In spite of the peril of my current situation, I felt a certain grim satisfaction that he hadn't escaped his punishment. It might have been the mandragora, but I imagined I could see the shade of Mael hovering darkly over Aeddan, haunting him.

"How did you end up back here?" I asked.

"When my uncle and I were first forced to flee to Rome, it was Pontius Aquila who offered to take us in. And when I found myself once more an exile in Rome, I wound up fighting for him as a gladiator in order to pay off all the debts my uncle had incurred."

I remembered Aeddan's uncle, as treacherous a fool as his traitor father.

"Depending upon Aquila's patronage was the only way I could survive here. And then I discovered that somehow, somewhere along the way, Aquila had found out about you."

"*Me?*"

"The great Lady Achillea's little warrior sister back home in Prydain. Better, stronger, and younger than the best gladiatrix they'd ever seen."

My head spun at the notion. I remembered what Thalestris had said to me about the time Sorcha had drunkenly bragged about the fierceness of the women of the Cantii and how her little sister had been the fiercest of the lot. So much for keeping me a secret. My own sister had betrayed me without even knowing it. And Aeddan had betrayed me too.

"Why didn't you tell me she was alive?" I demanded. "You knew Sorcha was in Rome, and you didn't tell me."

"Because I knew how much it would hurt you. I planned on telling you once we were married, on our journey here. I didn't think—"

"You didn't think about anything!" I raged. "Only your own selfish desires. You and Sorcha both. And now I'm the one in danger."

"It's not her fault," Aeddan said. "The blame is mine alone."

"What do you mean?"

"Sorcha couldn't have known that Aquila would become obsessed with you, Fallon—with the *idea* of you— but I did. And when he convinced me I should bring you here, I turned a blind eye to that obsession." Aeddan's face was full of misery. "He promised he'd make you a shining star of the arena if I did—hailed as a queen, adored by the masses. I didn't know. I didn't understand, but he convinced me to bring you to him. And then Mael was dead, and you were gone, and I . . . I was lost."

I could only stare at him.

The Morrigan's ravens had led me to this place—had led us both.

Unwittingly, I'd escaped from Aeddan's machinations only to wind up in the very place he'd meant to bring me all along. In dodging one fate, I'd fallen victim to its twin. In the distance, I heard voices calling. Aeddan heard them too. He grabbed me by the shoulders and lifted me up off the ground, half carrying, half dragging me across the lawn toward a garden wall.

"Run, Fallon!" he urged. *"Run!"*

Blind, animal terror drove me as I leaped for the top of the wall. It was only as high as my shoulder, but my bleary clumsiness had me scrabbling and clawing to climb over, scraping the skin of my hands and knees. Once on the other side, I bolted down a road that led back into the shadow-bound streets of the city.

In my mind, there were black-feathered monsters chasing me as I ran.

XXVI

THE LIGHT ON MY FACE WAS WARM, and the blanket covering me, soft. Somewhere nearby, a fountain trickled water with a sound like bells chiming, and birds sang sweet melodies to each other. The room smelled faintly of lilacs.

And I felt like Death herself.

I struggled to roll over on my side as my stomach churned and my head swam dizzily. I gritted my teeth hard against the rising tide of bile creeping up the back of my throat, and when the feeling finally subsided, I forced my eyes open and squinted in the pale morning sunshine. The open, glass-paned window above my head was draped with a gauzy curtain that billowed in a gentle breeze. There was a vase of lilacs on the sill, and the walls of the room were washed in a pale green that was almost white. The effect was cool and soothing.

And utterly unfamiliar.

For a terrified few moments, I thought I might still

be at Domus Corvinus, and the overwhelming urge to flee pushed the sensations of sickness far into the background. I clutched at the soft woven blanket covering me and almost flung it aside. But then I realized I was entirely naked beneath it. And I was not alone in the room.

"You're safe," Cai said quietly.

His voice had a quality to it that sounded like disappointment.

I squinted at where he sat on a low chair in a corner of the room. I was having trouble focusing, but he looked weary—as if he hadn't slept well, or maybe not at all—and I wondered what he was doing here . . . wherever "here" was.

I struggled to sit up without letting the blanket fall away. My head was pounding like a blacksmith's hammer on a sword blade. Cai stood and moved to a table beside the chair where he'd been sitting. It held a cup and a pitcher, and he poured me water, which I gulped at thirstily. Then he handed me a new, clean stola. It was plain but finely woven, with simple fastening brooches and a belt.

"Here," he said. "Put this on."

I glanced at the clothing and then at him. And then down at the blanket that covered me. Cai rolled his eyes and turned his back.

"I won't look," he said. "But I'm also not leaving. I'd like to get you out of here and back to Achillea's town house without anyone noticing."

I slipped out from under the covers and into the simple linen shift as quickly as my muddled state allowed. The room tilted perilously with every move I made. As I was fastening the second shoulder brooch, my fingers fumbled, and it fell to the floor. Cai stooped to pick it up. He stood and brushed my hair from my shoulder, fastening the brooch for me. Then he fetched my sandals—the only things I'd worn the night before that seemed to have survived the adventure—and knelt before me, slipping my feet into the straps. As he did so, I heard the sound of gentle female laughter coming from outside the room.

"Where are we?" I asked. "What *is* this place?"

Cai stood up, an expression that I could only describe as embarrassment crossing his face. "This is, um, well—"

"We call it a House of Venus."

I turned at the sound of the familiar voice and saw Kassandra, the girl from my days in Charon's slave caravan—the one who'd given me her shoes—standing in the doorway. With the door to the hallway open, the subtle perfume of the lilacs on the windowsill was displaced by a heavier, cloying haze of incense. "Thank you," I mumbled.

"For what?" she asked.

"For the shoes," I said, struggling in my foggy state to find the right Latin words. "Back when we were in Gaul."

Cai snorted. "You have more than shoes to thank her for."

I looked at him blankly.

He nodded at my former cage-mate. "She's the one who found you and brought you here."

"I didn't have much choice," Kassandra said. "You were in no condition to travel on your own. As it was, we were barely able to carry you this far."

I looked back and forth between them, hopelessly

muddled. "Where am I? The House of Venus? What is that?"

"Most people call it a house of whores," Kassandra said with a dry smile. "That is why Caius Varro hurries to spirit you away from this place. Before your bright rising star is tarnished by association."

The two of them might as well have been speaking in Greek. "I don't understand," I said.

"You attended a party last night at a house on the Caelian Hill, didn't you?" Kassandra asked.

I nodded and put a hand to my forehead, which throbbed mercilessly.

"I was there too." When I looked at her, she shrugged. "They hired some of the girls from this house to serve as hostesses for the revels. We left with our escort when things began to get out of hand—as they often do at those sorts of affairs—and that's when we found you, lying on the side of the road at the bottom of the hill. You were insensible. Babbling." She offered a sympathetic smile. "But I recognized you, and we brought you here. I sent word to Caius so that he might come and take you back to the place where you belong."

I wasn't sure where that was anymore. I wasn't sure of anything.

"How do you two even know each other?" I asked.

"Kass has been a friend to me since she was sold to this place," Cai said.

Oh, I thought. *Of course.* A friend. I felt my cheeks redden.

She laughed, shaking her head. "What he means is that this place entertains its fair share of politicians and patricians. So I occasionally find myself in possession of information that could prove useful to a certain consul of the Republic. I'm really Caesar's friend, if you want to think of it that way." She put a hand on my arm. "But I trust the Decurion. And you should too."

Cai reached out and took my other arm. "We should go now. We have to get you back to the Achillea town house."

"Why?" I asked. "So they can flog the skin from my bones? I didn't have leave to go to those revels. None of us did. Sorch—I mean, the Lanista—is going to be furious," I said. "I'll be very surprised if she doesn't just send me packing back to the ludus to muck out horse stalls until I'm too old to throw a spear."

"Us?" Cai asked.

"I went with a few of the other girls. It was Nyx's idea." Thinking back on the beginning of the evening—which was substantially clearer in my memory than the rest—I realized I hadn't actually seen Nyx drink from the wineskin. Or Lydia, for that matter. Only Elka and me. "She's the one who put mandrake in my wine."

"What?" He backed off a step, frowning. "She drugged you? Tell me what happened."

I did—at least I tried to—in halting, disjointed phrases, piecing together the events of the night leading up to the brutal entertainment and the death of the gladiator. Then I drifted into silence, drawing a hazy blank on what had happened next.

"Why would one of your sisters from the ludus do such a thing?" Kassandra asked.

"Because Nyx wants Fallon off her game." Cai looked at me. "You're her only direct competition for Caesar's Victory in the Triumphs."

I barked a laugh. "Then she's gone to a lot of trouble for nothing. Achillea told me yesterday that she's withdrawing me from consideration."

"What?" Cai was dubious. "Why would she do that? You're the best she has."

"She's overreacting," I said. "Someone's been trying to frighten me. Nothing more than harmless pranks, but Achillea thinks they're real threats."

"What kind of pranks?"

"Trashing my room and ruining my things, leaving bloody feathers on my pillow. Yesterday there was a raven—"

Suddenly the brain-numbing fog vanished, as if blown away on a stiff breeze. The protection it had offered me from the horrific memories of that night vanished with it. The image of the raven statue in the foyer of the Domus Corvinus bloomed like a black flower in my mind, its wings spread wide, its cruel beak open in a frozen shriek. I remembered the silver feather in the dish of the scale. The dead gladiator on the altar in the catacombs . . .

"Fallon!" Cai reached out as I swayed on my feet.

"What is it?" Kassandra asked. "What's wrong?"

The words came rushing out, breathless and frantic, as I told them about Aeddan and his fight with the gladiator

Ajax. How he told me he'd been trying to find me ever since that night back home. I told them about running, hiding . . . and finding the vaulted underground chamber. My voice grated as I described the robed men in the masks with the scales.

His heart . . .

I closed my eyes and came to a gasping halt. I could almost hear the sounds of them eating his heart, and the bile rose in my throat.

Cai and Kassandra exchanged a glance, and Cai looked as if he thought I was still dosed.

"Did you see anything like that?" he asked Kassandra. "A gladiator fight or . . . or the rest?"

She shook her head. "My hostess sisters and I were restricted to one of the courtyard salons while we were there. And they never keep us long at these parties—we cost too much—just until everyone is drunk enough not to notice our departure."

"And are you absolutely *sure* of what you saw in that chamber, Fallon?" Cai asked. "It was dark, and you weren't in your right mind."

"You don't believe me. Neither of you."

Kassandra shook her head. "No! No . . . it's just—"

"Ridiculous? Outlandish?" My voice climbed hysterically upward. "The idea that there were a bunch of madmen eating a dead man's flesh? Is that so much more of a stretch to believe when the evening's entertainment was watching two men fight to the death? Is this what kind of city Rome is? The so-called beating heart of the civilized world? Ajax's heart *wasn't* beating anymore, I assure you!" I took a deep breath and tried to calm down.

"I understand." Cai put up his hands and shared another glance with Kassandra. "Do you know whose house it was?"

Again Kassandra shook her head. "They never told me."

"It was called Corvinus," I said. "Domus Corvinus."

Cai winced and squeezed his eyes shut. "Pontius Aquila."

I nodded, even as I felt the blood drain from my face. Aeddan hadn't lied, and Sorcha had been right. I was being hunted by the Collector.

Cai didn't seem convinced. "Aquila is a hard man," he said. "Even cruel at times, if his reputation is to be believed. But he's also the Tribune of the Plebs. A respected citizen. He's not a . . . a barbarian."

"Are you going to tell Caesar?" Kassandra asked quietly.

"Tell him what?" Cai rounded on her. "That a runaway gladiatrix—a runaway from *his* ludus—out of her head on mandrake-spiked wine was witness to a munera? At what, from the sound of it, might as well have been a Bacchanale?"

My heart sank with the truth of his words,.

"Those kinds of revels—not to mention the ritual Fallon speaks of—have been outlawed in Rome for decades," he continued. "I'm sorry. No one would believe you, Fallon."

"I believe her," Kassandra said quietly.

I looked at her. "You do?"

"I believe a lot of things most people don't," she said. "Because I hear the secrets most people keep hidden. When people have so much money that they can do anything, buy anything, *be* anything, then they start to look around for the things money can't buy. Strength, courage, nobility . . . they see it in others. And they want it."

Cai nodded in reluctant agreement. "The men"—he looked at me—"and women who fight . . . they become like gods. Like Hercules or Aneas or the Amazon warrior queens of legend. They're worshipped and coveted—and, eventually, destroyed. The mob will build you up only to tear you down. But the ones like Aquila who see themselves as masters of the arena? They will ultimately seek to devour you."

"I wish you didn't mean that quite so literally," I said in a choked whisper.

Cai put a hand on my shoulder. "I'm not going to let that happen."

For the first time, I truly believed him. Kassandra went to fetch me a cloak to stave off the early morning chill so that Cai could take me back to the Achillea town house. As we left, she gave me one last warning.

"Please, Fallon," she said. "Be careful. Your world, I think, could prove far more dangerous outside of the arena than within it."

Out in the street, Cai paced silently at my side.

"I grew up with him," I said.

Cai stopped and looked at me.

"Aeddan. The gladiator—Mandobracius—the one I spoke of. He was the brother of a boy I loved back home." My voice was quiet, muted by the stone walls of the houses that lined the narrow street. "His name was Mael, and I was going to marry him. Aeddan and Mael fought over me and . . . and Mael died. Aeddan killed him."

Cai's arms were around me suddenly, and I felt my tears soaking into the fabric of his tunic. I hadn't realized I was crying.

"I tried to stop him. . . ." I took a breath to steady my voice. "I ran after Aeddan, and that was how the slavers found me."

"Fallon, I'm sorry."

"I meant to tell you . . . I did." I looked up at Cai. "But I never thought I'd see him again. Only he's here now, in Rome, and I—"

"Fallon." Cai smiled down at me, tightening his grasp. "You're the Fury Killer. He can't hurt you now. No one can."

I tried to smile back, but I knew that it wasn't Aeddan I was afraid of hurting me. When the time came, I would face him again and I would fight.

No. I was afraid of Cai hurting me . . . of him walking away.

But he didn't. For a long time, we stood in the laneway with Cai's arms around me. He didn't question me; he didn't judge me. He didn't leave me. He just brushed the tears away until they stopped running down my cheeks.

XXVII

I RETURNED TO THE DOMUS ACHILLEA with my head and heart bruised from the horrors of my night at the Domus Corvinus only to find that Elka had been flogged.

Caius had distracted Kronos at the gate while I slipped into the town house courtyard. Once inside, I made my way up to the room I shared with Elka, passing through corridors that were deserted and silent. I found Elka lying facedown on her cot, the bare skin of her shoulders and back crisscrossed with lash marks still seeping blood. Ajani was with her, carefully applying salve to the wounds.

I was horrified. And furious. "She had no right!"

"She had *every* right." Elka's voice was muffled by the thin pillow she lay on. "She owns us. We broke the rules."

"I broke the rules!" I almost shouted. "I made you go with me—and where's Nyx? I'll kill her!"

"Nyx is down in the laundry this morning," Ajani said in a flat voice, "serving out her own punishment."

"In the laundry?"

She raised an eyebrow at me. "For pilfering food from the kitchens last night, of course. Her only crime, it seems."

When the girls of the Ludus Achillea had been roused from their beds, Ajani explained, my absence did not go unnoticed. Neither did the fact that Elka—who didn't even remember how she'd gotten home—was still intoxicated from Nyx's evil brew. The domus staff were rounded up and questioned, the ludus guards were turned out into the city to hunt for the fugitive—me—and the gladiatrices were banished to their rooms and, in Elka's case, punished.

She had told Sorcha the truth about what we'd all done— as far as she could remember it—but then Nyx had argued, protesting that the only place *she* was guilty of sneaking off to that night was down to the larder to pilfer a late snack. The kitchen boy confirmed having seen Nyx raiding the pantry. He'd received ten lashes for not reporting the theft. I wondered what Nyx had traded in return for that little lie. The only other person who could confirm or deny what had actually happened was Nyx's lapdog Lydia.

"Lydia crawled trembling to the Lanista and told her how she'd heard you and Elka planning to escape," Ajani said, her lip curling in disgust as she covered Elka's shoulders with a square of linen bandage. "And how she'd been too afraid to do anything about it—because *you*, of course, had threatened to cut out her tongue if she did."

I didn't even know how one would go about cutting out a tongue, but I vowed, upon hearing Ajani's story, that I would learn.

I'd been willing to believe that Nyx had truly had a change of heart. That we were sisters, like she'd said. Like we'd oathed. I ran a shaking hand over my face. My skin felt too tight, stretched across the bones of my skull, and the inside of my head was full of sheep's wool and hobnails. Mandragora was *truly* awful stuff.

Ajani stood, wrapping up the leftover bandage. She left it and the pot of salve on the little table. With all the other girls confined to their rooms, she was taking a risk even being there, but I was grateful. "That's my own magic," she said, pointing at it. "My own herbs. Better than anything Heron has, but don't tell him I said so. Keep the cuts clean and lightly wrapped. Tell her she *cannot* fight before they're fully healed."

"I'm fighting in the Triumphs," came the muffled protest.

"You'll scar."

"Don't care."

Ajani rolled her eyes and made an emphatic gesture in Elka's direction. I thanked her, and she hugged me before wishing me good luck with the Lanista and ducking out the door. I closed it behind her and leaned on it heavily. I felt like I'd been trampled by a team of oxen, and I could only imagine how Elka felt, with the mandragora aftereffects on top of what must have been scorching pain from Thalestris's whip.

"What happened to you last night?" she asked.

I shook my head, not even sure where to begin. "It's a tale long in the telling. Rest, and I'll tell you the whole story later." I reached over to gently smooth a wrinkle from her bandages. "I'm so sorry, Elka."

"Don't be. It wasn't your fault."

"No. You're right," I said. "It was Nyx's. And I'm going to kill her."

I found Nyx alone in the laundry, shrouded in steam and the astringent stink of lye soap. She was hanging on to the pole that spanned across the tops of the huge wooden tubs, her tunic tucked up in her belt and her legs boiled-lobster red as she stamped her feet up and down in a soup of hot gray water full of dirty linens.

She didn't notice me walk through the door. I skipped a formal greeting and went straight for trying to drown her in the tub.

I used my shoulder to hit her from behind square in the middle of her back, and she fell face-first into the water. I tumbled in after, reaching for her neck so I could hold her head under, but she thrashed and flailed, slipping out of my grasp. I grabbed a length of sodden linen and slapped it hard across her torso, knocking her over. She fell back, cursing and sputtering. I saw her eyes go wide behind the curtain of her dark, dripping hair as she realized who it was that had attacked her.

"You deranged bitch!" she screamed at me. "What in Hades are you trying to prove?"

"That if you want to get rid of me so badly," I shouted, "you'll have to do it yourself!"

She retched out laundry water and clambered to her feet. "What are you talking about, you lunatic?"

"I know now why you convinced me to go to that house

last night," I said. "Did you also nail that poor bird to my door just so we could have something to bond over?"

"I told you I had nothing to do with that."

"I know all about Pontius Aquila—"

"You don't know anything," she sneered. "Aquila is deluded if he thinks you worthy of his collection. You're nothing but a naive little barbarian who got lucky in a fight. You don't deserve to call yourself a gladiatrix. You never will."

"Why do you hate me so much?"

"You don't belong with us!" she screeched.

Her eyes were red and streaming, and I didn't know whether it was from tears or the acrid wash water, but the raw agony in her voice brought me up short. I stepped back, sloshing through drifts of clinging laundry, to steady myself on the edge of the tub. My burst of rage was spent, and all that was left was the ghost of mandrake wine and a deep weariness.

"She's *not* your sister," she said, her voice ragged. "Not anymore. She's mine!"

I grew still. "What are you talking about?"

"Achillea." She scrubbed a hand over her eyes. "Before you came, I was her favorite. I've always been her favorite, because I've always been the best. Now it doesn't matter how well I fight. Now she barely even looks at me when I'm in the arena. Because of you. Victrix. The Fury Killer. Everyone thinks you're so perfect. At least Pontius Aquila respects my skills."

"Really. Is that why he's using you to get to me?" I asked.

She glared at me, murder in her eyes.

I shook my head. "How did you even know I was Achillea's sister? Did Aquila tell you? Is he your real master, Nyx?"

"Shut up," she snarled. "My loyalty lies with the Ludus Achillea and it always has. More than yours."

"How did you know?"

"I heard the Lanista talking to Thalestris about it." She pushed the dark hair back from her face and wrung the wash water from it. "About you. And how desperate she was to protect her poor baby sister from all the big, bad monsters in Rome."

"Like the monsters I saw at Domus Corvinus last night?" I said. "Do you know what they do down there in the catacombs? Do you know what happened to the gladiator Ajax?"

"I know he lost." Her expression was cold and pitiless.

"They butchered him—"

"I don't care!" she shouted, covering her ears. I think she knew, or at least suspected, Aquila's true nature—she just didn't want to admit it. "One day it will be me fighting in those houses on the hill, living in luxury and treated like a goddess. Just as well as that ungrateful fool Mandobracius."

I was sickened by Nyx's idea of what we were and sick at heart to think that the night before I'd clamored for a man's death for the sake of entertainment. That wasn't what being a gladiator—or a gladiatrix—was supposed to be about. No matter what the mob thought, we were better than that.

I was better than that.

All of the righteous fury drained from me as I stood and climbed out of the laundry tub. I no longer wanted to make Nyx suffer. I figured she was suffering enough without my help, even if she didn't know it. I left her there with her rage and hatred and her deluded lust for glory.

"I'm not your enemy, Nyx," I said over my shoulder. "I won't be."

"From the sound of it, *you* have more enemies than you can handle, gladiolus," she called after me. "I don't even think I have to fight you anymore. I can just sit back and watch as others tear you to pieces."

I went back to tell Elka everything that had happened, but Sorcha flung open the door to our room before I could get a word out. I braced myself for the beating she would give me, but then she was across the room crushing me to her chest in a fierce hug.

"Thank the Morrigan," she whispered into my hair. "I thought they'd taken you from me."

After a moment, Heron entered, carrying his leather satchel full of medical supplies.

"Ajani took care of her already," I said as he strode over to Elka's cot.

"I'll be the judge of that," Heron grumbled, peeling back the layers of linen bandages with a brisk efficiency that somehow didn't even draw a flinch from Elka, who actually managed to roll an eye at me. Heron muttered to himself and unstoppered the little clay pot and sniffed at the salve. Then he stood without opening the satchel. "Whatever Ajani salved the wounds with, I want her to make me up a batch." He glanced back at Elka. "I'd say she'll sustain no lasting damage that would keep her from the arena. Alternatively"—he shot Sorcha with a disapproving stare—"you could simply refrain from flogging the academy's assets."

Then he was out the door and gone.

Sorcha stared after him, unfazed by the rebuke.

"Told you I'd be fine," Elka mumbled, turning her face back into the pillow. Within a few moments, she was gently snoring.

I shook my head and turned back to Sorcha.

"Why are you soaking wet?" she asked.

I ignored the question and glared at her silently.

"What's that face for?"

"You had Elka *beaten*."

"Yes." She nodded. "I did."

"But not Nyx? Did you really believe her story about a midnight kitchen raid?"

"Of course not," Sorcha said. "But it gave me an excuse not to whip her out of commission. As of this morning, I thought she was my only contender for the Victory role in the Triumphs."

"Sorcha—"

"Don't."

"Don't what?"

"Plead for me to reinstate you as a contender."

I bit my lip in anguish.

"Because I already have." She sighed. "I discussed it with Thalestris, and she convinced me I was overreacting. Of course, I *should* have both you and Nyx thrown in irons and hung from the rafters for the stunt you pulled last night, but I really don't relish informing Caesar of the appalling lack of discipline at his ludus. Now that you've returned unscathed, I'll send you both to his villa so he can make his choice between the two of you—Minerva help the poor man!—and call it a day."

I could barely contain the excitement I felt. But I was still angry—with Sorcha, but mostly with Nyx—over Elka's punishment.

"I'll win the Victory role," I said. "But I still want Nyx to pay for what she did. She took me to that place on purpose so I'd wind up in trouble."

"Leave Nyx be," Sorcha said and put a hand on my shoulder. "Vengeance is never the right path to take, Fallon, no matter where you think it might lead. If I were you, I'd let Nyx think she's gotten away with something. She hasn't. And though it saddens me to say it, because she's been dear to my heart these many years, she will get what's coming to her. The Morrigan watches over you and will see to it, as she sees to all things."

I fleetingly considered telling Sorcha about what had really happened in the house on the Caelian Hill and just how much trouble I'd *actually* encountered at the Domus

Corvinus. About Aeddan and Pontius Aquila and the so-called Sons of Dis who worshipped death itself in the cata-combs. It was the prudent thing to do—especially if Aquila had really turned his sick, covetous gaze my way. But Sorcha had only just reinstated me in the Victory competi-tion, and if she thought I truly was in peril, she would defy Caesar himself and send me packing back to the ludus, no matter what, to keep me safe. After it was all over I would tell her, I promised silently.

But would the Morrigan protect me? I wondered. I was beginning to think that perhaps my goddess just watched. Watched and waited to see what kind of trouble I could get myself into next.

XXVIII

I CAN TRUTHFULLY SAY THAT, in private, Gaius Julius Caesar was nothing like what I'd expected. I attended Caesar the next day at his private estate on the west bank of the River Tiber, escorted there on horseback by Decurion Caius Varro and a handful of his men, along with my rival for the Triumph, Nyx. It was a near-silent ride. She stonily refused even to make eye contact and Cai kept a respectful distance from us both. But in the few, brief moments when I caught his eye, I could see the warmth of encouragement in his gaze.

I also couldn't help but notice the great care Nyx had taken with her appearance. As Caesar's gladiatrices, we were both in full fighting kit, weapons and armor polished to shining, but Nyx was also wearing smoky circles of kohl around her eyes and a crimson stain on her lips. And the tunic beneath her armored skirt was a handsbreadth shorter than mine. If she hoped to seduce Caesar—*actually* seduce him, rather than in the way Arviragus had counseled me—then I suppose she was to be commended for the effort.

When we reached Caesar's sprawling villa, Cai turned us over to his praetorian guard. Nyx was the first to take her audience, and I was left to wander the gardens under the watchful eye of the guard. The air was fragrant with the sweet smells of cedar trees and flowers. And my hands were sweat-slick on the hilts of my swords.

I paced back and forth, arguing with myself over my chosen course of action. Then, when it was finally my turn, I took a deep breath, fighting against the terror that swept me head to foot. I was about to meet Gaius Julius Caesar: conqueror, commander, master strategist . . .

A man.

He's just a man. Not a god.

He breathes and bruises and bleeds just like any other man.

And at that moment, he was sitting in a beam of sunlight, reading a vellum scroll. Caesar was slender, tall but not towering, with fine hair combed forward to flatter a high forehead and a mild blue gaze. He was handsome in a sharp-featured kind of way, and strong. His lean physique did nothing to conceal the corded muscles of his forearms and the breadth of his shoulders—but he did not look like a man who had conquered the world and slaughtered hundreds of thousands. There was no dried blood beneath his manicured nails, and his teeth, straight and white, did not drip blood. There were no Gaulish chieftains' heads hanging from the pillars of his audience chamber. Instead the

room was pleasant—breezy, full of sunlight, sparsely decorated, and smelling faintly of juniper.

I was almost disappointed. Arviragus's prison was
more mythic than this.

There was, of course, one mythic aspect to the room:
Cleopatra. Just as I remembered her from our first meeting
with Sorcha, she commanded respect and admiration—
and even a certain breathless kind of awe—on sight. She
reclined elegantly on a couch next to Caesar's chair and
gave no indication that she and I had ever met. And I suspected, just from the way Caesar's gaze lingered on her
face when he occasionally glanced up from reading, that
he was hopelessly in love with her—which was something
else I hadn't expected from him: a human heart. But *that*,
I hoped, was exactly what drove the man more than anything else. And I planned to use that to my best advantage.

Before my interview, Sorcha had once again cautioned
me against revealing my identity as her sister. Caesar
had been good to her, she said, but that did *not* mean he
wouldn't use a familial connection against her if he ever
found it necessary. Family, she'd said, was the greatest
strength—and the greatest weakness—one could have. I
aimed to prove Sorcha's theory right.

To that end, I did something that I never thought I'd do.

I willingly bent my knee and bowed my head before
Julius Caesar.

The silence stretched out in the room, broken only by
the creak of armor from the praetorian guard who stood

near the back wall. He was far enough away that, for a fleeting instant, I imagined I could cross the distance and have my blades in Caesar's chest before they could cut me down. Retribution for the assault on my land, the humiliation of my father and Arviragus . . . I would die the instant afterward on the point of the guard's blade, but it would be a noble, useful, good death. Instead of spilling my blood out in some silly game played before mobs and madmen. Wasn't that worth it? Wasn't that the truest kind of freedom?

And what of Sorcha? What of your sisters at the ludus?

What of their freedom?

I stayed where I was, stone-still and staring at the floor. It seemed like I would stay like that forever, until finally I heard the vellum scroll snap shut and Caesar seemed to notice that he had a visitor.

"Please," he said mildly. "Do get up."

I rose and stood, uncertain of what to do. Sorcha had assured me that Caesar would set the protocol for the interview as it happened. She had said there was no use preparing for what was to come because whatever it was would be unexpected. So far she was right.

"Ah, Fallon," he said, his gaze placid and appraising all at once. "My Lanista, the Lady Achillea, tells me that you grew up in Britain."

"*Prydain*, my lord," I said.

He raised an eyebrow, and I winced internally. Had I just corrected Gaius Julius Caesar?

"Your pardon, great Caesar—"

"Not at all." He waved away my apology. "Perhaps I am the one who should apologize for my inability to make my tongue obey the shape of your native language."

I saw Cleopatra hide a smile behind her hand.

"You're very gracious, my lord," I said and lowered my gaze to the tiled floor in an attempt to appear docile.

"I can be." Caesar gestured to an attending slave. "Get the girl a chair and a cup of wine."

The slave produced the amenities as if by sleight of hand, hovering until I'd sat and sipped, and then retiring silently to his place by the door.

"Now," Caesar continued, "my question, Fallon, is this: Do you remember the days when Rome came to the shores of your home?"

I nodded. "I remember well, my lord."

"And what are your memories of those days?" he asked.

"I remember running through the fields with my friends, racing to the tops of the cliffs so we could look down on the soldiers as they marched," I said. "I remember the sun shining brightly on their armor. They dazzled me, like the gods themselves had come to our land."

Caesar leaned forward. "You must have been very young," he said. "Were you frightened?"

Frightened? I thought. *No. Angered. Spitting mad and wanting to fetch my wooden sword so that I could take on the whole lot of you filthy invaders single-handed.*

Caesar must have read my thoughts in the expression on my face. Cleopatra's grin spread into a full, white-toothed smile.

"No!" Caesar chuckled. "No, she was not! Look at that, my queen . . ." He got up to pour me more wine himself, even though I'd barely touched what was in the delicate goblet I held in white-knuckled fingers. "I can see that you were the furthest thing from frightened. Probably ran back home and got your own toy sword."

"So please you, lord, that's exactly what I did," I said, taking another sip of wine. "You still won."

At that, he laughed again. Heartily.

"Indeed I did, Fallon," he said. "It's what I do." He leaned one elbow on the carved arm of his chair and rubbed his chin, regarding me.

"Barring that long-ago occasion, my lord"—I lifted my gaze to meet his directly—"I also win."

Cleopatra went still, watching Caesar as he watched me.

After a long moment that tested the breaking point of my nerves, he smoothed a fold of his purple-striped toga and said, "Would you win for me?"

"I already have, Caesar," I said and took another sip to prepare for the sheer audacity of what I was about to do. "The Ludus Achillea is yours. I am yours. My victories, also yours."

He nodded, as if that was the right answer. I suppose it was.

"This pleases me. The Britannia Spectacle is neither the largest nor the grandest spectacle of the Triumphs," he said. "But it is the one that means the most to me, the one nearest to my heart. When I was on campaign in—forgive me—*Britain*, I lost someone very, very dear to me."

My pulse hammered in my ears. This was my chance, my opening.

"And so did I, mighty Caesar." I put the goblet down on a little table and stood. "And it was your fault."

Caesar went completely still. I held my breath . . . and then drew my swords. The reaction was instantaneous. The praetorian guard was across the room in the blink of an eye, blade drawn and ready to defend Caesar. And there was another blade pressed to my throat, held by the slave stationed by the door. It seemed he was more than just a simple houseboy.

I lifted my arms slowly and held my swords out away from my body, dangling them harmlessly from my fingertips, but my eyes never wavered from Caesar's face. Neither he nor Cleopatra had moved.

"I am the second daughter of Virico Lugotorix, king of the Cantii tribe of the Island of the Mighty," I said, knife at my throat biting against my windpipe with each word. "My sister was Sorcha ferch Virico, warrior of the Cantii. You took her away from me and gave her the name of Lady Achillea."

Caesar's eyes narrowed slightly—his only reaction.

"These swords were a gift from her. You watched her bestow them on the night of my oath taking. One of them, she carried with her when you took her from my home. The other, I carried myself, on the night the slaver Charon took me."

Caesar murmured something to the guard and motioned the slave back toward the door. The cold pressure of the blade eased away from my throat, and I gulped at the air. The praetorian guard moved off to one side but kept his gladius unsheathed. The realization that I would never have succeeded in assassinating Caesar washed over me. It almost felt like relief.

The one thing I'd thought I wanted all my life was suddenly so unimportant in the face of the thing I was about to ask for. "I want my sister back. Will you help me?"

"What would you have me do?" Caesar asked slowly.

"Grant me the role of Victory and let me fight for you."

He shook his head in amusement. "I was going to do that anyway. I thought you Celts were better bargainers than that—"

"I'm not finished," I interrupted. It earned me a frown of displeasure, but I raced on regardless. "I will win the crowd and bring you glory. I will make them love me more than any other gladiatrix who ever set foot upon the arena sand. I have heard of the kinds of matches in which those who fight can win their freedom if they win the crowd—"

"Those instances are rare."

"And so am I." I flipped my swords over in my hands and, crossing them at the hilts, set them on the floor and stepped back. "I lay my swords at your feet and my fate in your hands, mighty Caesar. If you judge my performance worthy, if I can make the people of Rome love me like you loved your daughter, Julia, then I ask one favor."

"Your freedom."

"No," I said. "What I want is my purchase price."

"I heard it was rather substantial. At the time, I didn't

understand why Achillea would do such a thing." Caesar's lip curled up at one corner. "Now I do."

"She used that money to buy my life when she could have used it to purchase the title to the ludus, as you'd agreed."

"That title will cost more than just your slave price."

"Sorcha—Achillea—can pay the difference," I pressed. "And if it's still not enough, I have this."

I fished in the leather pouch at my waist and found the little rolled scroll Charon had given me, along with my armor. I handed it over to the praetorian guard, who gave it to Caesar. I silently begged the slave master to hold true to his word—my need *was* dire—and it was for my sister, whom he loved. Caesar glanced at the black wax seal, and I could tell from his face that he recognized the insignia. He broke the seal with his thumbnail and unrolled the vellum. His eyebrow arched.

"And if it's *still* not enough," I said, "my sister can turn my contract over to you, and I will continue to fight in your name until I can win enough to someday buy it back myself and—"

"Fallon."

"My lord?"

"A good bargainer knows when to stop pleading their deal."

I bit my lip and fell silent.

After a moment, Caesar sighed. "My daughter, Julia, was not so very much older than you are now when she left this world. She died in childbirth while I was off

campaigning in your lands." As he spoke, I was shocked to
see the sheen of unshed tears that rimmed his lashes. "She
was such a light, like a clear, shining flame . . . I see her light
in you. It is *you*, my dear Fallon, whom I would choose to
honor Julia's memory by fighting in the guise of Victory in
the reenactment of my conquering of Brittania."

I held my breath.

Caesar leaned forward in his chair, his gaze sharpening
like an eagle spying prey. "And if—*if*—you win the crowd,
then you will have your deal." Then he shook his head,
chuckling. "I think Julia's spirit has guided you to this
moment. But from this moment on, you're on your own.
Don't disappoint me, gladiatrix."

I could sense that our conversation was over, but there
was one thing I needed to know before I left. "May I ask a
question, my lord?" I said.

"Would it be in my power to stop you?" He smiled.

"Why?" I asked. "Why the games? Where I come from,
there is no such thing, not really."

Cleopatra answered for him. "Rome was built by a
nation of warriors, dear girl," she said, her dark eyes twin-
kling. "And now that they've conquered most of the world,
there's no one else to kill! So they're obliged to satisfy the
Republic's bloodlust here at home with their games."

Caesar smiled at her teasing. "The Daughter of the
Lotus—no stranger to bloodying her *own* blade on occasion, I might add—is right, to a degree," he said. "The
people crave the games—the excitement, the thrill, the violence. We are a nation born of blood. If we do not at least

attempt to satisfy those cravings, then we will turn inward and fall to corruption."

He dismissed me with a wave of his hand. I turned to leave, almost giddy with relief that I had successfully argued my case with Caesar.

That relief was short-lived.

"One more thing," Caesar said, raising his voice just enough so that I would stop in my tracks and turn back. "Not that you seem to need any added incentive, but you should know that I've made a wager on the outcome of your competition. If you lose, I will be obliged to sell you to the Ludus Amazona, as I have already done with your rival, Nyx. She'll be performing opposite you, playing the role of that goddess of yours. You know the one I mean— the Morrigan."

Nothing, it seemed, was ever an easy win with Caesar.

Cai had been instructed to escort me, after my audience, not to the town house in the capital but back to the Ludus Achillea. Sorcha and the other girls had already set out for home, and we would meet them there. Nyx, Cai told me, had been sent directly to the Ludus Amazona after her meeting with Caesar. I shuddered to think what her reaction to his decision had been—and just how venomously she was plotting to take me down when we met in the Triumphs. I put it out of my mind, determined instead to enjoy the fact that I'd just emerged from a battle of wits with one of the most brilliant strategists alive relatively, if not wholly, unscathed.

I had changed into a simple tunic and trousers so that I could ride, and we traveled at a pleasantly languid pace, just Cai and me. I couldn't help smiling. At midday, halfway to Lake Sabatinus and the academy, Cai led us off the road to a shaded hollow carved out of a hillside by a little tumbling waterfall. We dismounted and sat upon the grass, and Cai unpacked a lunch of cheese, pickled eggs, bread, and wine. I sat with my arms wrapped around my knees and watched him spread our meal out on a square of white linen.

I sipped from the cup Cai passed me. "He wasn't anything like I expected," I said, my mind still reeling from my sparring match that afternoon. "Caesar, I mean. And yet..."

"Yet he was?"

I frowned and nodded. "I guess I just didn't expect that I would *like* him."

Cai paused in lifting his cup to his lips. Sunlight and green shadow dappled his face, and I wanted to run my fingers through his tousled hair.

"He's very likable," Cai said eventually, leaning back on one elbow in the grass. "Unless you're at war with him. A lot of people are."

"I know that well enough," I said.

"I don't just mean tribes and nations. I mean right here in Rome. And after the Triumphs, you'll be seen as Caesar's creature, you know."

I laughed. "Assuming I survive long enough!"

I'd meant it as a joke. Cai didn't take it for one. He put

his cup down on the grass and rolled back up to kneel in front of me, his expression deadly serious. For a moment I thought he was angry with me.

"You still don't want me in the arena," I said. "Do you?"

"No." He shook his head. "I was wrong about that—about you. I should have given you more credit, Fallon. I've watched you in every single fight in the circuit. After your first one with that madwoman—"

"She wasn't a madwoman."

"Well, she fought like one." Cai smiled before growing serious again. "But that's not my point. Or maybe it is. The thing that the Fury was . . . was *the Fury*. And I didn't think you could be like her. I didn't think you *should* be."

I looked away. "Maybe you were right."

"No." He shook his head emphatically, and there was a strange, feverish intensity burning in his eyes. "I wasn't. Fallon, I have watched you get yourself in and out of scraps for months now. I've watched you fall down, get pushed down, and even throw yourself at the ground at times! And every time—every single time—you've hauled yourself back up to your feet, and you've stood straighter, stronger, and as more of the thing that you are. And that is a gladiatrix. A fighter. A warrior. And a damned good one."

He reached for me, his long fingers closing gently on my bare shoulders and sending a shiver through me.

"If I'd taken you away from that," he said, "if you'd *let* me take you away from that, I don't know what you would have become. But this is what you are—who you are. Who I love."

His mouth was nectar-sweet as he kissed me, and we fell back together into the soft, cool grass beside the stream. Even though Cai had just told me he loved me for the gladiatrix I'd become, I thought to myself in that moment that it was a very near thing. Caesar could have easily chosen Nyx to carry his honor into the Circus Maximus for his Triumph. He could have cast me in disgrace from his marble halls that day as unworthy. He could have ordered me sold or turned out into the streets. He hadn't. Instead, I had bargained successfully with Julius Caesar. He'd bestowed the highest honor ever to grace a gladiatrix upon me.

And that hadn't even been the best part of my day.

Cai loved me.

My journey from Durovernum to Rome had seen me plummet to the depths of despair. But then I'd found my sister. I'd found Cai. I had become a part of a family that I truly cared about. And I knew what I had to do to keep all of those bright, beautiful things from vanishing like smoke on a breeze. I had to win the Triumph, woo the crowd, and send Nyx crashing down in defeat.

XXIX

"IF YOU'RE NOT *a worthy adversary, Fallon, you're target practice.*"

My sister's words echoed in my mind as I stood swaying, drenched in sweat, soaking in the sounds of braying war horns and the howling crowd. Bloodlust, thick and tangible, rolled like a heat wave over the arena sands.

Target practice.

The words she'd said to me so long ago Sorcha had repeated that morning as I'd readied myself for the arena. "Remember," she'd said, "keep moving. You're either a weapon or a target. Don't be someone else's target practice. Make them yours."

I had grinned and told her that she was going to have to come up with a few new sayings. That I'd known that one by heart for many years. I'd half expected her to tell me not to be such a brat, but she just hugged me and helped me with my weapons.

And then she'd said, "Win the crowd, little sister."

"I will."

I hated the fact that Caesar had decreed I should wear special armor that he'd had made for the occasion. I would have much rather worn the armor Charon and Cai had commissioned for me—it fit far better. This new armor was too loose, made evident by the fact that the point of a sword had already found its way between the side buckles under my arm. The wound wasn't deep, but I could feel the blood running down my rib cage, past my hip. But Caesar's shining armor was all part of the show. I was no ordinary gladiatrix on that day. I was Victory.

And Victory, in the eyes of Romans, had to look like Rome, like her legions.

Only fancier and showing more leg.

The whole spectacle was like that. The Roman side was entirely too shiny and, in my opinion, rather too pretty—with the notable exception of Damya, with her dragon-scale armor and fearsome, bulging muscles—and I'd never seen an actual Celt dressed as outlandishly as the tattered, feather-bedecked fighters from the Ludus Amazona we were up against. The games masters had decorated the arena with massive gilded eagles and billowing cloth to mimic ship sails at one end. On the other end, they'd erected towering, fearsome wicker statues made to look like the horned and demonically deformed wicked "gods" of the backwater barbarians. I would have been offended, but I barely noticed the trappings the moment after I entered the arena and the fight began.

It wasn't really the battle for Prydain, and I wasn't really Fallon.

I was Victory.

Which means I have to win this fight, I thought grimly.

The Ludus Achillea gladiatrices had already fought their way through the front ranks of the Amazona "Celts" when a peal of war horns sounded in the air. I sent my sparring opponent sprawling into the dust with a backhand swipe from the flat of my blade and turned to face the new threat. There was a rush of fresh warriors through the archway at the end of the Circus Maximus—along with chariots and fresh archers—but still no sight of Nyx.

I scanned the fighters and saw she wasn't there. Even in a helmet or one of the outlandish costumes, I would have known her. It seemed the games masters were holding off on the appearance of the Briton war goddess, the fearsome Morrigan. But I did recognize another familiar figure in the crowd among the ranks of the Briton princes they sent at us. Mandobracius, the notoriously savage gladiator with his raven-feathered helmet and woad tattoos, led the charge.

"Aeddan," I whispered through clenched teeth.

I ran straight for him, dodging other engagements as I pelted across the sands. In the back of my mind, I could hear his brother's voice, distorted by fog and echo, from that horrible night. Aeddan saw me coming and raced to engage me. The visor on my crested helmet covered my face from the brim to beneath my cheekbones. He wouldn't know who I was—to him, I was just another warrior, just another life to cut short, like Mael or Ajax.

The fact that I was female wouldn't spare me, I knew.

I was Cantii. He was Trinovante. Our women had always fought and died alongside our men.

The twin swords Aeddan wielded flashed, throwing sunlight into my eyes, dazzling me. I'd almost forgotten that he'd fought dimachaeri style that night at the Domus Corvinus. I'd never realized that it was a skill that ran in the family. Aeddan was good—almost as good as Mael had been—forcing me to block a frenzy of blows with the kind of genius born of sheer desperation. My luck held, but it wouldn't hold long. He knew how to fight me. He might even have known how to beat me.

But not today, I thought. *Today, I am Victory.*

When his next attack came, I feinted to one side and spun low to come at him with an upward dual thrust of my swords. He twisted like a viper to evade, whirling away in the instant before my blades hit home. It gave me a moment to breathe—but only a moment. All around us, the other combatants fought in knots of twos and threes. From all sides, ranks of archers fired volleys of arrows when the ferocity of individual duels waned, just to keep things lively.

When Aeddan came at me again, I backed away and stumbled. I fell onto my back, cursing. That should have been the end of me. But my tumble caused him to over-shoot his mark, and his blades sank harmlessly into the sand next to me. Rocking onto my shoulders, I launched myself forward in an arc, landing in a crouch. Driven by the energy of the crowd, I ran recklessly toward him, chasing him backward with hewing strokes and howling like a Fury for his blood.

I ducked under his double slashes, which sheared a chunk of bristles off the horsehair crest on my helmet, and dodged around his left flank. I landed a blow with my sword on his shoulder as I swept past. It was enough to gouge a scar in his thick leather armor and shift him off balance. It also gave me time to catch my breath, or so I thought—

"Fallon, MOVE!" I heard Elka scream.

"Lugh's teeth!" I swore and dove wildly out of the way as a spear pierced the ground right where I'd been standing only a moment before.

"Pay attention, you fool!" I muttered through a clenched jaw and dragged my focus back to the fight—just in time to see Aeddan charging toward me in a dead run, his two swords flashing. I slammed my own blades back into their sheaths and plucked Aeddan's spear out of the ground. Wielding it like a staff, I swept it overhead and blocked the blows he rained down on me. Suddenly, a volley of flaming arrows arced overhead, trailing dark crimson smoke. We fought dead center in the arena, right in the thick of it, and Aeddan flinched as one of the arrows punched into the ground beside him.

I took advantage of the moment, ducked low, and rammed the butt of my spear into his side. The breath left his lungs in a *whoof* as he stumbled sideways, and I followed up with a series of swift, vicious jabs. One of them bit into the large, hard muscle of his thigh, below the edge of the armored skirt he wore. Not deep, but painful. Aeddan's leg went sideways, out from under him, and he fell heavily to his knees.

The crowd cheered madly.

I raised my blades high up over my head, muscles tensed for the killing blow. Aeddan stared up at me through the grill of his helmet visor, but all he could see was the gilded Victory mask that hid my face. He had no idea whom he was fighting, but I didn't have that luxury. I stared down into his gray eyes and lowered my swords. Confusion mingled with the pain in his gaze as I reached up and snapped open the buckle on my leather chinstrap, lifting the helmet and visor off my head. My hair fell down around my cheeks, damp and sticky with sweat, and the air was cool on my face.

Aeddan let out a choked gasp as he realized who he had been fighting.

The world seemed to spiral out and away from us.

Time stood still . . .

The world crashed back down on me, and the walls of the Circus Maximus closed in. I was losing the crowd—I could feel their mood souring against me—and I felt a swell of panic. It didn't matter anymore if the spectacle had been intended as pure pageantry. The mob smelled blood, and would have it. I raised my swords again, and Aeddan went stone-still, staring up at me. The hurt in his eyes washed away, and a calm acceptance took its place, almost as if he had been waiting for this moment.

And I couldn't do it.

High up in the stands, I saw Caesar stand beneath the crimson canopy and take a step forward. He lifted his arm high, fist clenched. His brow was creased in an angry frown beneath the laurel crown he wore, and my stomach clenched in an icy knot.

The crowd fell silent and held their breath.

This was not the way the spectacle was supposed to end.

And then the war horns sounded a third time, louder and harsher, a strident battle call. Aeddan and I both looked over to see the iron grate at the mouth of a cavernous archway grinding upward. Through it rode a nightmare.

The Morrigan made her entrance onto the field of the battle of Britannia in a chariot black as despair.

Standing on the deck of the chariot behind her driver, Nyx was impressive and terrifying to behold, costumed in black armor with a long cloak tiered and tattered to resemble wings flowing from her shoulders. Her face and limbs were painted with garish blue designs, and her eyes were ringed in thick black kohl. And they were fixed on me.

Her teeth bared in an animal grimace, she suddenly lunged forward and yanked her chariot driver up by the shoulders. She flung the driver from the chariot, seizing the reins herself. With a howl, she drew a whip from her belt and lashed the black horses madly, steering the war cart straight at me and Aeddan, who still lay sprawled on the ground at my feet.

"Daughter . . ." The voice of the goddess shuddered

through my mind like thunder—and suddenly I found myself grinning savagely. The Morrigan had not forsaken me. She wasn't against me.

The true Morrigan had shown herself to lead me to victory.

"Get up!" I snapped at Aeddan, sheathing my swords and thrusting out a hand to help him stand.

"Fallon, what—"

"You're going to prove to me that I didn't make a mistake by not killing you just now." I hauled him to his feet, ignoring the sting from the flesh wound under my armor. "You're going to help me show these people what it means to be a warrior from the Island of the Mighty!"

Not fifteen feet away from Aeddan and me, one of the swift, light chariots stood bereft of its driver, hitched to a pair of ghost-gray horses. I grabbed for Aeddan's wrist and ran, dragging him with me. Nyx's own chariot was almost on top of us.

"Come on!" I shouted. "Move!"

I heard cries of outrage as the crowd realized that we weren't waiting for Caesar to render judgment. I certainly wasn't. The mood of the mob was balanced on the edge of a knife—and I knew in that moment that was just where I wanted them. With Aeddan's help, I would take their outrage and turn it into wild exultation.

"You'd better pray to all the gods that you're even half the chariot driver Mael was," I said, grabbing the reins. I leaped up onto the chariot deck and tossed them to Aeddan and snarled, "Now drive for all you're worth!"

There was an answering gleam in his eyes, and he wrapped the reins around his hands, braced his feet, and shouted, "*Hyah!*" to the sleek ponies. They bolted into a gallop as he slapped the reins on their rumps.

The crowd roared at the sheer recklessness. Aeddan steered so that we would pass within arm's length of Nyx's chariot on our right. I shifted over and braced myself, drawing a sword with one hand and gripping the chariot rail with the other for balance.

Nyx's whip cracked, and I ducked instinctively. I wasn't quite fast enough, but neither was she. The wasp-kiss of the whip left a crimson welt on my upper arm. At the same time, I struck at Nyx's shoulder with my blade and drew blood. Our chariots were so close that the wheel hubs screeched as they scraped against each other. Then we were past, thundering toward a group of fighters who scattered out of our careening path. I glanced back to see that Nyx was already driving into a hard pivot. Her mouth was open wide, and she was screaming curses. She was the best charioteer the Ludus Achillea had, the best I'd ever seen.

And she was on us again in a flash.

Thrashing her horses mercilessly, Nyx caught up with us and rammed her chariot against ours, almost knocking me off the deck. With only one hand on the reins, she slashed at me with a gladius drawn from a sheath at her belt, and I slashed back. There was no finesse to our mad duel, no technique. It was all down to whoever landed the first lucky blow.

The crowd gasped and shrieked in salacious horror.

The chariot wheel hubs sparked, grating against each other. The horses screamed and fought the traces. In the distance, near the end of the arena, where the chariot track curved and doubled back, I saw Elka's familiar blonde braids—and the sunlight glinting off the head of her oath-gift spear.

"Aeddan!" I shouted. "Drive straight! *Straight!*"

"There's a *wall* straight ahead!" he shouted back. He tried to haul the horses to the left but Nyx headed us off. She was hemming us in with her chariot, trying to drive us in the direction of the wall—exactly where I'd just told him to go. Because, yes, there was a wall, and if we hit it, we'd crash and very likely die. But between us and the wall, there was Elka—and her spear.

"Do it!" I shouted again. "Hold . . . hold . . . now! Veer sharp!"

Aeddan fought with the reins, sawing the bits into the horses' mouths as we hurtled toward the arena wall. I heard Aeddan cursing loudly with the effort. And then, suddenly, the beasts gave in, leaning into the turn so sharply that our chariot went up on one wheel and almost flipped onto its side.

For a moment, we were free and clear of Nyx's wheel hub.

"*Elka!*" I shouted at the top of my lungs. "Pick a number!"

She grinned madly and shouted back, "Thirteen!"

Then she drew her spear back, sighted, and threw . . .

The gleaming slender missile shot toward us and passed through the spokes of Nyx's chariot wheel just as if Elka were in the ludus yard with her rotating practice target. The spear spun up against the chariot undercarriage, jamming the wheel. The chariot shot upward, arcing through air like it had been unleashed from a legion catapult.

I owe Elka a new spear, I thought.

Nyx screamed, arms and legs flailing frantically as she sailed up and over her horses' heads. Her chariot burst into kindling, needle-sharp splinters of wood flying everywhere, and the horses, suddenly free of their traces, bolted wildly in opposite directions. I ducked my head as Nyx landed with bone-crunching impact on her shoulder in the sand and collapsed like a child's cloth doll.

Aeddan eased the horses away from the swiftly nearing wall, back onto the straightaway portion of the track. We swept past the ranks of the Achillea gladiatrices, where Elka stood watching us with her mouth agape and Ajani stood behind a picket line of flaming arrows ready to be nocked. Aeddan pulled back on the reins, but I slapped his shoulder.

I wasn't finished yet.

"No!" I shouted. "Make them run faster!"

He shot me a look but let the reins slide out through his hands.

"Ajani!" I shouted, waving my arm in the direction of where the grotesque, wicker effigies—the supposed dark, barbaric gods of Britannia—stood leering at the far end of the arena. "Pick me a target!" I shouted. "Light it up and show us the way!"

With a wild grin, Ajani plucked one of the flaming

missiles from the burning pitch trench in front of her. She drew, sighted, and loosed. And again. And again.

In rapid succession, flaming arrows arced over the heads of our galloping chariot horses, illuminating a path like a trail of shooting stars toward the center effigy.

"Faster!" I called.

Aeddan gave the horses their head, and they were running full-out, necks stretched long and ears flat. Before Aeddan realized what I was doing and could reach out to stop me, I'd slipped past him and swung my legs over the low front barrier of the chariot car. Then I climbed out onto the draft pole that ran between the two horses and attached to their yolks. A fleeting image of Sorcha, balanced and flying, arms outstretched, danced across my mind. I banished it before I could imagine her falling. Before the wheels of the chariot ran right over her—

"*Fallon!*" Aeddan screamed at me. "What are you *doing?*"

"The Morrigan's Flight!" I answered, reaching back to grab the two spears that rested in hooks hanging off the chariot's sidewall.

"You're mad! It can't be done—"

"Shut up and drive!"

I held the spears out in front of me for balance and, without letting myself overthink what I was about to do, stepped out along the pole, one foot in front of the other. I concentrated on Ajani's path of arrows. The chariot flew over the flaming markers, and I saw them pass beneath my feet. Then Ajani fired her last shot, and it stuck not in the ground but in the leering wicker god. The effigy roiled with flame, and the arrow was followed close behind by my hard-flung spears—one through the heart, and one to a supporting leg. The whole construct buckled to one side and sank slowly to the ground, wreathed in fire, as if I'd just brought the god of the Britons to his knees. The crowd roared approval. I shifted my weight forward and flung my arms out to the sides as Aeddan eased into the turn . . .

And like the Morrigan herself, I flew.

The entire audience was on its feet cheering ecstatically as we did a victory lap and Aeddan guided the lathered horses to a halt near Caesar's canopied box. I slid to the ground, wobbly legged and dizzy, and spun in a mad, careening circle, thrusting my clenched fists skyward and shouting hoarsely. Aeddan leaped from the deck of the chariot and, caught up in the mad thrill of our win, whooped with joy and threw his arms around me.

And for a moment, it wasn't Aeddan. It was Mael.

The same gray eyes, the same build, his hair even smelled the same. I melted into the embrace, and his arms tightened around me. But he whispered my name, and it wasn't Mael's voice. I thrust Aeddan away from me with every drop of strength I still possessed. Then I cocked my armored fist back and plowed it into his face. He dropped to the arena sands, senseless, at my feet.

And the crowd went absolutely rabid with delight.

Victory was mine. Victory was *me*.

I'd shown the mob just how Rome had conquered the wild warriors of Brittania—through fighting, allegiances, betrayals, romancing, and rebuke—and they loved me for it. The breath heaved in and out of my chest. I threw my arms wide again and turned in a slow circle, and the roar of the crowd thundered over me.

And then, when a handsome young decurion in full ceremonial armor suddenly ran down the steps of the spectator stands, leaping the barrier into the arena to sweep me into a passionate embrace, I thought the cheers would bring the stones of the Circus Maximus tumbling down. When Cai set me back on my feet, I cocked my fist again—in jest this time—and when I didn't punch him but kissed him, long and slow on his glorious mouth . . .

Well.

I'd thought that my tribe back home—that the Celts in general—were the most hopeless of all romantics. But the way to the heart of the Roman mob, it seemed, wasn't just violence and mayhem. It was equal parts blood and roses.

The spectators howled, "Victrix! Victrix!" at the top of their lungs. They hugged and kissed each other and rained flowers down upon us. Cai spun me around until I was so dizzy I almost toppled over. When I turned to salute Gaius Julius Caesar, he beckoned me with a languid wave of his hand. I stepped forward and bowed deeply, fist over the place where my heart would have been—if it hadn't already been in my throat. His expression was inscrutable. The games certainly hadn't gone the way he'd meant for them to. Not that it was my fault—not *exactly*—but I didn't know how he would see it.

Was my improvisation clever in his eyes?

Or wildly impertinent?

Off to one side, I saw Cleopatra grinning with sly amusement, and I could have sworn I saw her wink at me. Not far from the Aegyptian queen, I saw my sister sitting with the other lanistas and ludus owners, and her eyes shone fiercely. She didn't even seem to mind that I'd very passionately—and very publicly—just kissed Caius Varro. After all, it had helped me win the crowd.

I squeezed Cai's hand, and he smiled down at me.

Not just the plebs but all of the spectators beneath the awnings—the men dressed in purple-striped togas, the women in butterfly-brilliant stolas, glittering with jewels— were on their feet. The crowd was giddy with anticipation, waiting to see what judgment the mighty Caesar would render on the performance. Even Caesar's wife, Calpurnia, bore a tiny smile.

None of that loosened the knot in my guts.

Caesar's opinion was the only one that mattered now.

"Gladiatrix Victrix!" Caesar called out, and the arena went silent as a tomb. "Come forth."

I held my breath and paced slowly forward until I was standing almost right below him. Caesar raised the hand that had been hidden in the folds of his toga . . . and I saw that he held the rudis—a ceremonial wooden sword—in his fist. The symbol of freedom for every gladiator and gladiatrix. In his other hand, he held a scroll, a declaration of the monies I'd just won.

Elka whooped for joy and pounded me on the back so hard I staggered forward a pace. And Cai was grinning ear to ear, even though—I saw it in his eyes—he thought he might be about to lose me to my home.

But he didn't have to worry about that. I *was* home.

"Most mighty Caesar"—I bowed deeply, still playing to the crowd—"I humbly beseech you to gift my winnings to my noble Lanista of the Ludus Achillea. My honor is her honor—hers and my sister warriors."

Caesar's eyes glittered with delight. I knew my part in our bargain, and I had my script well-learned. In the stands, I saw that my sister was on her feet, her mouth open in a silent cry of surprise. There were tears of joy streaming down her face, and it made my heart swell.

The look on Pontius Aquila's face, though, made my stomach clench.

His black eyes were fixed over my shoulder, on the wreckage of Nyx's chariot, and there was murder in his gaze. I glanced over to see Nyx climbing unsteadily to her feet, bruised, bleeding, her left arm hanging awkwardly from her shoulder socket. Aquila would rain down wrath on my former ludus-mate for her failure, I knew.

I thought of Sorcha's tampered-with chariot. Of the roster-fixing that had paired me with the Fury. There were a thousand ways that a man like Aquila could arrange for a spectacular arena death for his disgraced gladiatrix—or worse. An image flashed in my mind of Nyx on a marble altar in an underground vault. As much as she hated me, I wasn't about to let that happen.

I turned back to Caesar.

"For myself," I continued, before he could make any further pronouncement, "I beseech you to let me stay a gladiatrix. *Your* gladiatrix. To fight another day on your behalf and to continue to earn the love that the good people of Rome have shown me. I would ask instead that you grant the rudis and the freedom that goes with it to my noble rival, the gladiatrix Nyx."

Again, the crowd went wild with cheering.

Aquila's face flushed purple with rage.

The glittering in Caesar's gaze warmed to a gleam, and an approving smile lit his face from within. Not only had I bested *my* nemesis, but with that gesture, I'd bested his. He made a show of considering my request. Then he called forth Nyx, and she limped stiffly forward. Caesar presented her with the rudis, and she took it, her dark hair sweeping forward to obscure her face.

Granted release from her contract by Caesar's own hand, it would be unthinkable for her ever to enter into gladiatorial combat again—it would be an affront to his generosity. I fervently hoped his favor would protect her from the munera too. But when Nyx turned around, I saw just what I had done to her. She looked gutted. Hollowed out and horrified at the prospect of life beyond the walls of a ludus.

My very first opponent, Uathach—the Fury—had thirsted for that life so desperately that she'd been willing to die for it. But I'd come to realize that freedom—*real* freedom—was something that could be found in the most unexpected places, even on the sands of the arena. Nyx would have to find hers elsewhere. At least she might survive long enough to look, even if she wasn't about to thank me for that chance. Our eyes locked, and I knew in that moment that I had made an enemy out of an adversary, and I would most likely live to regret it.

But not today.

I looked at Elka and Ajani and all the rest of the Achillea girls.

Today, I am Victory.

Together, we threw back our heads and uttered the Cantii war cry.

Today, we are Valiant.

And I finally understood what it meant to be truly free.

Cowards die many times before their deaths;
The valiant never taste of death but once.
—JULIUS CAESAR, *William Shakespeare*

Dear Reader,

I have always been fascinated with past civilizations, and with ancient Rome in particular. It's a world of wonder—cultured, sumptuous, and brutal all at once—a place of mythic stature on par with Camelot or Atlantis.

Historians and archaeologists have revealed many tantalizing glimpses of what life was like in ancient Rome—but there is still so much *more* we don't know. *The Valiant* takes place in the Rome of my imagination, in the realm of "what-if" where fantasy meets history, a place where a young barbarian princess fighting for her life could conceivably come face to face with Julius Caesar. Or Cleopatra. If she can survive long enough.

Over the past few decades, the existence of female gladiators in ancient Rome has been the subject of much debate among historians. While there is ample evidence of male gladiators, ancient texts and artifacts portraying *female* fighters in the arenas are sparse. Lost to history, the lives of these exceptional girls and women are shrouded in mystery.

Were female gladiators a gimmick? A fad? Had they really even existed at all? In 2001, archaeologists unearthed an ancient Roman-era gravesite containing the 1,900-year-old remains of a woman that proved, virtually beyond a doubt, that female gladiators were real. And that they'd most likely led lives just as dangerous and dynamic as—and perhaps even more controversial than—that of their male counterparts. The lavish contents of the burial mound hinted at the wealth of the occupant, but the grave itself was placed beyond the boundaries of the main cemetery, marking the woman as a likely outcast from society.

Was this the lot of the gladiatrix? To live her life as both revered and reviled by the very people she fought so hard to entertain? These are the questions that inspired me to write about Fallon and her gladiator sisters—and their rivals—and the thrilling, perilous, extraordinary world in which they lived.

Uri, vinciri, verberari, ferroque necari!

—LESLEY LIVINGSTON